I0847139

FROM THE PCT WITH LOVE

PAMELA DEAN

PAM BOYER

Copyright © 2025 by Pamela Dean

All rights reserved.

This is a work of fiction. No part of this book may be reproduced in any form or by any electronic or mechanical means, including information storage and retrieval systems, without written permission from the author, except for the use of brief quotations in a book review.

ISBN: 979-8-9913924-4-0 (paperback)

ISBN: 979-8-9913924-5-7 (digital)

Cover art by: Sabrina Watts

Edited by: Kathryn Underwood

Proofread by: MLM

❀ Created with Vellum

Adventure brings you closer to who you are, not just who you want to be.

ONE
STEPHANIE

mile 707.4

I SNEAK ALONG THE GROUND, keeping my belly low. My knees scrape across the dirt and more than once I bang into a rock and mumble a curse. I must reach my goal, and I know it's now or never. He always sleeps outside. I don't even know if he brought a tent. He is such a weirdo.

I hear a slight snore in the distance and I know I'm close. I can't use a flashlight as much as I want to. I can't be discovered. Tonight's full moon makes this easier, but he always chooses to sleep among the trees, so he can become "one with the earth that birthed him" or some bullshit like that. God, I hate him.

I have tried everything the past few weeks. I have added a day to my trip, resting in one campground for two nights, I have hiked extra fast, pushing myself beyond what I thought was possible, yet every night we end up at the same spot. I think the little fucker is doing this on purpose. Well, except I have camped with some of the same people since I started, so it might be a coincidence. An annoying coincidence. It's like karma, or is it dogma? Fuck, I don't know. I squint into the darkness when I hear the snort and gentle snore again.

There he is.

I inch along until I'm right next to him. Holding my breath, I pull my small scissors from my belt and wait for my eyes to adjust. Because there is a God in heaven, his head is tilted to the side, exposing my prize. His neck is thick and covered in hair and dirt. I mean, we're all kind of dirty out here, but for some reason it irritates me that he is a mess.

With the moon shining down on his face, I pause, wondering what he looks like when he isn't out here. He could be handsome. He does have amazing eyes, I'll give him that. I have never seen anyone with eyes as green as his. I am letting myself get sidetracked. I gently run my hand along his beard where I think his jaw is, testing to see if he is really asleep. He doesn't move at all, his snoring steady and even.

I reach up with my scissors and quickly make one snip just above the top rubber band, wincing when the hair catches. I have to open and close my hand more than once before I get what I want. I clutch the stupid braid in my hand and inch back across the ground to my tent.

It's 1987 for fuck's sake, who still wears a rattail? I had to belly crawl all the way back to my tent so no one else from camp would see me. Pretty sure there was some rustling over by the campfire. I reach my tent and climb back in. I wait a few minutes, listening for any indication that he woke up. When all remains quiet, I zip my tent flap closed, sealing me in with my prize. I turn on my lamp for long enough to see I got the whole thing.

Good God.

A smile crosses my face and I know, even if he follows me all the way to Canada, at least I won't have to see that stupid, nasty braid ever again.

. . .

I SLEEP LIKE THE DEAD. Most nights on the trail I sleep pretty well, but last night? I was dead. Not asleep, unconscious is a better word. It was delightful. Maybe it was removing the rattail, maybe it was the fact that we are almost to a town and I know I can replenish my supplies. I don't know and I don't really care. I wake up feeling like a whole new woman. I stretch and yawn, rolling to face the door of my tent.

"Fuck!" I hear him yell from a distance.

Well, I guess Mr. Round and Round is awake. He must have reached back to fondle his stupid braid and discovered he is now no longer the owner of a "bitchin' rattail." I smirk in victory.

I started calling him Mr. Round and Round, or R and R for short, in my head the first time I met him on the trail. Ratt was always one of my least favorite bands and his stupid hairstyle made me think of them. I also couldn't get that song out of my head since the day I met Corey, and that is another reason I hate him. That song and the lame song about wearing sunglasses at night have been on repeat in my head for the last two weeks. Really, anyone in my position would have done the same thing. He brought this on himself, he has to know that on some level.

"Seriously? That took me like five years to grow!" the man-baby says loud enough for the whole camp to hear. If anyone was still asleep, they aren't now.

I glance over at the snipped braid on the floor of my tent and shove it to the bottom of my sleeping bag. I shudder as it slides past my leg. Why is it silky soft?

I unzip my tent and poke my head out, trying to look alarmed instead of amused. I spot him sitting on a rock with his head in his hands.

Shit. Is he crying?

Now I feel kind of bad. Like, did I just Delilah him? Was his strength in that stupid braid? Just as I am about to emerge from my tent to check on him, Trail Terry (lame nickname but whatever) walks over and sits down on the rock next to him, slinging an arm over his shoulder.

"Listen, Corey. I know you don't want to hear this right now, you're mourning and I get it, I do. But you gotta know that thing was disgusting. I think maybe a possum crawled over you during the night and gnawed it off. She returned it to where it belongs man. The earth." Terry pats Corey on the back and says, with emotion thick in his voice, "Mother Earth."

Terry gives him a weird seated side hug that almost knocks them both off the rock, then stands, walking straight toward me. He winks at me before veering off to where his tent was set up.

Oh God. He knows. Was I that obvious? Like if that thing goes missing I am the number one suspect kind of obvious? I say a silent prayer and thank you that Trail Terry is going the opposite way. He started the PCT in Canada and is on his way to Mexico. I won't have to worry about him spilling the beans.

I climb the rest of the way out of my tent and stretch before bending to slip on my sandals. I try and give my feet breaks from the hiking boots whenever I can. I have been on the trail for over two months, so the blisters and sore spots I had in the beginning are almost gone.

I walk cautiously to Corey bending at the waist like I am approaching a terrified dog. "Hey, everything okay there, Mr. R and R?"

"I lost my tail," Corey says into his hands. He hasn't lifted his head yet.

"That skinny little braid thing that hung down your neck?" I ask as casually as I can.

He finally lifts his head and levels his gaze at me. He squints like he's trying to decide if I can be trusted.

"Yeah. I had long hair in high school and even longer in college. I cut it all off when I started my career, but I left that one little piece as a reminder of who I was before the man took charge. Now it's gone."

He puts his head back in his hands and I feel less joy than I thought I would in this moment.

"Well, I am sure you can just grow your hair long again then have the barber cut all but a tiny scrap so you can braid it into a thin, weak ..." I stop talking, swallowing hard. I can't even pretend to be sympathetic to his loss. God, I am so screwed.

"I can't grow it back." He lets out a defeated sigh. "I was going to cut it off at the end of my hike. I guess Terry is right. Losing it on the trail is kind of fitting."

"See? That's the spirit!" I say, straightening out. "Well, Mr. R and R, I am going to start packing up. We're about a day's hike from Tahoe and I'm looking forward to a motel, a shower, and real food. See you around."

I head back to my tent and climb in. As soon as I sit on my sleeping bag, I think about the silky strand of hair that now lives at the bottom.

I shudder.

When I know he's not going to sneak up on me somewhere on the trail, I'll give the braid a proper burial. Until then, I'll lay low. I pull out a granola bar and peanut butter and eat my breakfast before I pack up.

An hour later I am on my way. I managed to avoid Terry when he said his goodbyes to the group. Corey hadn't started packing up when I left, so even if he stops in Tahoe I have a pretty good lead on him. I mean, no way we're staying at the same motel, right?

Ugh. He's probably at my motel. The universe hates me.

I check into the Pine Cone Motel around five. The key is attached to a large blue shape that I assume is a representation of the lake. I can't fit it in my pocket, it's so big, so I am forced to walk to my room carrying it like a platter. All I am missing is some cheese and crackers for this damn thing. When I open my room and step inside, I am immediately hit with a smell that while not unfamiliar, I'm unable to place.

What is that? Pepperoni? Sweat? Onion? I sniff around the room, picking up the pillows and holding them to my nose. Nothing really stands out as the source, so I shrug and start stripping out of my trail clothes. I swear these shorts can stand on their own now. I pull them off and drop them on the floor tugging off my shirt next. My body is not the same color that it used to be. I am tan of course, deep lines in various places. My legs show a steady line across the thigh, and since some days I had my socks pulled up to ward off scratches I only really have a consistent tan from my knees to about mid-thigh. I also have gone from T-shirt to tank top off and on since I left San Diego, creating a varied pattern of tan, white and sadly red when I forgot to put sunblock on. My entire body looks a little like Neapolitan ice cream.

I step into the shower and turn the dial, dodging the initial cold blast. Glancing down at my legs, I wonder if I should bother shaving. I don't have a ton of hair, but it's still noticeable and I plan on staying here for two days at least.

I lather my calf and slide the razor across the front, amazed at how wonderful it feels. I shave the whole lower half of both legs then lift my arm, wincing at the hair I find.

Good Lord. It's like a bird's nest. I hack my way through the jungle and finally wash and condition my long blonde hair. God. This is the most amazing shower I have ever taken. The shampoo smells like wildflowers, my hair feels thick and lovely. It's a shame my only plan is to call home, then curl up and go to sleep in an actual bed.

I dry off and wrap myself in a towel before venturing out to the room. I flop on the bed without bothering to get dressed. Naked feels good. My smooth clean skin on the bedspread feels, ew. What is that? There is a rough firm patch on the blanket. Gross. I pull the top cover off and try again, lying on the crisp white sheets.

Oh yeah, that's the stuff. I close my eyes and could almost fall asleep, but the phone call home is hanging over me. Mom will be expecting my call today. She has my whole plan written down and if

I don't check in within a day, she has the local law enforcement out looking for me.

Found that out the hard way near Yosemite. I got distracted by Mr. R and R and his stupid rattail and I forgot to call her. The next day a sheriff on horseback came through the trail asking if anyone was Stephanie Hartford.

Damn, for a hippie florist, my mom is strict.

I dial her number and laugh when she picks up on the first ring.

"Baby girl? Is that you?" she says. It sounds like she knocked something over when she picked up.

"It's me. Did you kick the dog's water bowl or something? What is that noise?" I ask. I am currently sprawled out like a person who fell out of a very tall building. I want all of my body to appreciate these clean sheets.

"Yes, stupid dog. I don't know why the bowl was there. He must be carrying it around again. I swear he has a problem. I am going to see if Oprah has any suggestions," my mom says.

"Oprah? Mom, what are you talking about?" I laugh.

"Oh! I didn't tell you? Our new vet! Her name is Oprah! Like the TV star! It is so fun. I just love telling people my dog is friends with Oprah."

"That's pretty awesome, Mom. How's the flower shop?" I ask trying to stall and not ask what I need to ask.

"It's busy as ever. Wedding season is in full bloom, you know."

"Right." I blow out a breath and say, "So any calls or letters for me?"

There it is, the reason I call. I mean I like to let Mom know I am alive, but I need to know if I have a job. I applied to over thirty different places and have heard back from about twenty.

"Well, there was a call on the machine today, I believe it was Sacramento. They said they were impressed with your academic achievements and hope you apply again when you have some—"

I cut her off, filling in the rest of that sentence. "More life experience."

"Yeah, I'm sorry honey," she says. I hear her cover the phone and cough a few times. Her allergies are always so bad this time of year. No point in asking her about it though, she always brushes off things about her health. She thinks because she drinks that wheatgrass crap, she's invincible.

"It's okay. I mean I am not sure why I rushed through college to graduate at twenty-one so that I could get turned down for every single job because I'm too young," I say, and I hear my mom sigh. This is not the first time I have complained about this since graduating last June.

"I should have gone to Canada with Becky," I say. I roll to my side, pulling my knees up into my chest.

"Well, that would have been fun, dear, but we talked about it and you know you would have been miserable. You did what your heart told you to do. Now you are doing that again. Gaining all kinds of experience on the PKT!"

"PCT, Mom. It stands for Pacific Crest Trail," I explain, for the millionth time.

"Oh right. You told me that, sorry, dear," she says. I feel bad that I didn't just let it go. I am just grumpy about the job prospects. I thought I had a chance with that school in Sacramento.

"You also got two letters. One from Napa and one from a place I have never heard of, want me to open them?" she asks.

"Sure." I try and sound hopeful but there are only about eight more noes that I can get on the West Coast, then I will have to start looking at other states.

"Okay, Napa says, 'thank you for your interest in the position of history teacher at our high school. We are currently interviewing for the position.'"

I feel hope rise in my chest.

"But since your age is too close to some of our students, we feel it would not be the best fit for our program. Please reach out in a few years, after...' She stops reading and says, "Well, you get the gist."

"Yeah, okay where is the other one from?" I ask.

"A place called Beaver Valley, Oregon," she says.

"I don't even remember applying there. Good grief. Okay, give me the bad news," I huff out.

"Dear Miss Hartford, thank you for applying to our little school district. We are currently in the process of opening a new high school and are in need of a history teacher." My mom's voice starts to rise in pitch.

"We would love to meet you in person to see if you would be a fit for our program. Can you be in Beaver Valley on August 3rd?" She practically screams the last line and I have to hold the phone away from my ear.

"They have a number on the bottom of the letter, get a pen! Stephanie, get a pen!!!" she squeals.

I scramble out of bed and look around the room like a lunatic. I dive for the nightstand and yank it open, finding a Bible, and because Jesus wants me to have a job, a pen and paper.

"Got it! Okay, what's the number?" I say breathlessly.

Mom reads it off and I write it down, reading it back to her a few times before we both agree I have it correct.

"Thank you so much, oh my God. This could be it. Mom, this could be the place where I have my first job! What's the name of the school?" I ask still clutching the paper to my chest.

"Furie High School," she says.

"What? That's a weird name for a school," I say. I must have heard her wrong.

"The letterhead has a man in a hat like Daniel Boone on the top, like maybe that is their mascot? Wait..." I hear Mom shuffling the papers. Then she giggles.

"It's a beaver. Not Daniel Boone. I guess they are the Furie Beavers," she says, fighting off more giggles.

"Okay. Are you messing with me?" I ask.

"Honey, I am not. If it helps its spelled F-u-r-i-e, maybe it's pronounced differently," she says, then I hear muffled laughter because my mother is about as mature as a ten-year-old boy.

"Thanks, Mom. Hey, I'm going to let you go. I need to go buy a beer or something to celebrate. This is the best news I have had in months."

We say our goodbyes and I hang up then flop back on the bed for a minute to let the possibilities dance around my mind and heart. I am a forever optimist, so these past few months of rejection have done a number on me. Now maybe things will turn around.

TWO
COREY

Mile 882.8

I CAN'T PROVE IT, but I am pretty sure that Stephanie chick cut my rattail off while I slept. I can't for the life of me figure out what would possess her to do such a thing. I thought we were trail buddies, well no, I didn't think that.

I kind of hate her, if I'm totally honest with myself. She's too short and her hair is too blonde. She also has this really annoying smile and big bright blue eyes.

I am in the middle of my "broody nature phase" and her cheery ass is really making that difficult. She has to be only like eighteen. That's probably why she's so happy, just about to start college, not a care in the world. Ugh. I wish I was at that point in my life again.

EVER SINCE CODEY WENT AWAY, I've felt pissed off and grumpy. I was snapping at everyone back home and they may have insisted I go on this stupid long hike so they didn't have to deal with me.

Whatever.

I am starting to realize that I am lost. I mean, not physically. I'm at the motel I was supposed to be at, on the day I said I would be. I called my family to check in and of course got the answering machine.

"Hey, it's me, I am in Tahoe. Still making my way to Oregon. Nothing has changed. I'll call again when I can." I hang up and flop on the bed. This bedspread looks a bit questionable. I mean, I know I've been sleeping on the ground for a month, but I do have some standards.

I close my eyes and picture my braid draped over my shoulder, thin but majestic. Damn, I didn't even have the heart to tell them about my loss.

Dad and Mom will probably be happy, but I know my sisters will be sad. Dee Dee taught me how to braid it, for God's sake. Linda showed me how to use just an extra dab of conditioner on that piece to keep it soft and tangle free.

I sigh and grab my ukulele, not my instrument of choice, but I couldn't carry my guitar on this hike even if I really wanted to try. Mostly because my jackass brother stole it.

Sitting on the edge of the bed I pluck away trying to find the chords for the words that have been dancing through my mind since this morning. If Codey was here, he would know just how to spin it. He would have a fucking rad song in no time. How can I miss and hate him all at once?

"Lost on the trail, my tail," I croon out the first line, the notes feeling right.

"My tail, the trail, yeah my tail. Trail is like tail but with an r, and the r is gone, yeah the r is gone." My voice cracks on that line and I set the ukulele down.

I can't write. I am too angry. I stand, strip out of my dusty trail clothes, and head for the shower. At least I can wash my hair and maybe try and get the stickers out of my beard. I have a patch of dirt on my knee that might actually be a new mole. I am curious to see if it washes off and if it doesn't I should probably see a doctor.

I WAS in the shower for a half an hour and only thought about that short blonde for a little bit. I may have imagined her in various posi-tions—bent over a boulder, or leaning against a tree. Nobody needs to know about that, I was just relieving a little stress, that's all.

I also worked on my beard, but after ten minutes of scraping my fingers through the damn thing, I am sure I still have stickers. I refuse to cut the stupid beard off. Not until I get to Beaver Valley. I am sticking to my plan, I'll shave it off, put it in a paper bag and bury it in front of the high school to symbolize the end of an era. I might even light a candle or some shit like that.

It's time I face the truth. I am an adult now even if I don't want to be. Codey on the other hand, is wandering around Europe with "the band" or whatever. The band I got kicked out of.

Fuck him.

What kind of shitty twin brother doesn't want to spend eternity together? That was my plan, until we got Yoko'd by that blonde chick. Fucking blondes. They ruin everything. That is my new theory at least.

Janet is a great singer, and hell, that girl can write a song, but when her mum needed her she ran back to London with my lovesick brother in tow. Last time I called home, Mom let me know how happy Codey is "across the pond." Apparently, he is applying for a work visa so he can stay there even longer. Good. I never want to see him again.

That's not true. I miss him so damn much it hurts. This raging dichotomy in my heart can't be good for me. My tombstone will read, "Killed by the whiplash of an angry broken heart."

I flop back on the bed and stand back up quickly pulling the crusty comforter off and tossing it on the floor in the corner. I need to sleep. Maybe I will feel better in the morning. I am so damn tired I don't even want to go find dinner. I close my eyes and I must fall asleep immediately because the next thing I know, a sliver of sun is shining right in my eyes.

I groan and roll over, blinking a few times to adjust to the room lighting. My stomach rumbles, so I grab my last granola bar and make the gross motel coffee. I have a lot to do today, but the most important thing is laundry.

I dig around in my pack until I can find something that is sort of clean. These shorts only have a few sap stains and that shirt didn't try and crawl away, so this is what I am wearing to go do laundry. I wish I could just stand there naked so I could wash everything. I lean against the desk and ponder doing just that.

I snap my fingers when I realize I have a bathing suit that is clean. Well, it's clean because I haven't actually been brave enough to wear it the few times I came across a lake or stream.

My dad got it for me and I am sure he thought it was funny, but you know what doesn't take up a lot of room in a backpack? A Speedo.

I pull the shiny red scrap of fabric out of the bottom of my bag and shudder as the fabric slips across my fingers. I straighten my shoulders and clear my throat. I can do this. I'll just buy a newspaper and sit and read while my clothes wash.

I PULL on the Speedo and spend more than a few minutes trying to adjust myself into the tiny thing. Jesus, is this man-sized? My ass isn't very covered, but more importantly my junk is on full display. Good thing I relieved some stress earlier, so hopefully there will be no tenting. Or escaping. That would be worse and the top of my dick is dangerously close to the waistband. I try and bend it down and to the left and the crown pokes out the side. That won't do. I glance down and try moving it to the other side. Nope, not there either. I wonder how men wore these in the seventies? I adjust myself back to the up position and notice the hair near my balls is peeking out. Did they shave or something back then? It looks like a tarantula is trying to crawl out both sides. Charming.

God, I hope no one is at the laundromat.

Lake Tahoe, California is a lovely little sleeper community in the summer. Mostly known for its ski resorts, it does get some visitors during the off season because of the beautiful blue lake that is full of snowmelt. How anyone thinks about swimming in it is beyond me since it is one degree above freezing all summer long. Well, not really, but once when I walked out into the water my feet felt like they were going to snap off. I didn't go in past my knees because I was afraid my balls would retreat back inside my body.

That was during the last family vacation that we took before Codey and I went off to college. Dee Dee and Linda were freshmen in high school and the six of us had the best time. We stayed in a cabin right on the lake, played board games, barbecued burgers and stayed up late into the night talking and laughing. Mom and Dad got drunk and told funny stories about life with two sets of twins. Most I had heard before, but I will never turn down a good story, especially one told by my drunk Mom. She fell out of her chair more than once and my poor father was laughing so hard he couldn't help her up. Those were good times.

I knew about this motel and the laundromat next door because of that trip, and as I stand in front of Tahoe Blue Suds, I let my eyes dance over at the vacation rental that holds so many good memories. It's two doors down and looks like it is currently being rented by a bachelorette party. I have seen no less than six very attractive drunk women stumbling in and out of the little log cabin. Impressive at ten in the morning.

I buy a copy of the local paper and go into the laundromat. Thankfully all the machines are available, so I pull out each item from my bag and give it a shake before dropping it in the washer. When the bag is empty, I glance over my shoulder at the door. I am alone in here, so I pull off my shirt, then slip off my shorts too. I really want to wash my socks as well, so I take those off, then pull my boots back on. I dump in the tiny box of soap I bought from the vending machine and push in my quarters.

The satisfying sound of water filling the machine hits my ears, so I walk over to the blue plastic chairs and take a seat. Oh shit, that's cold! I jump a little when I settle in. The plastic is like ice on my barely covered ass. I should have checked the size on this damn Speedo before I shoved it in my bag. This has to be a small.

The wash cycle is about thirty minutes and should be about that long to dry. I regret not stopping for a beer or something before coming here. I could use some liquid courage even if it is mid-morning. All I can do is pray no one else comes in. Sighing, I unfold the paper and start reading.

The main page of the *Tahoe Tribune* had a riveting story about the ever-changing problems of bears and tourists, so I don't hear the door to the laundromat open. I don't notice anyone until I hear what could only be described as a snicker.

I fold the paper down enough to see over the top, expecting to see a local taking advantage of the weekday availability. Instead I see an ass I have stared at for the past month. The same ass I may have pictured not too long ago while I was "relieving stress."

Damn.

I see her loading her clothes into the washing machine next to mine and her shoulders are shaking. Every now and then I hear a little squeak or maybe a snort echo through the washing machine tub.

Do I ignore her? Probably should.

I fold the paper back up and snap it in place. I've seen people do that in movies, and it's oddly satisfying. I start to read again trying to ignore the ridiculously cute laughter I hear.

I sigh and fold down the paper only to find her bent over the machine. She is on her tiptoes and seems to be reaching into the very deep washer. She probably dropped something in there and can't reach it because she is the size of a Barbie doll.

"Do you need help?" I ask.

"Nope," she says into the machine, then I hear echoes of laughter.

She finally pulls herself up and brushes her long blond hair out of her eyes. Tears are streaming down her cheeks and she's fighting off a major fit of laughter.

I narrow my eyes at her and ask, "Is there something you find funny?"

"Nope," she says again like that is the only word she knows, and covers her mouth to hide a little burp.

"Sorry, I met some very nice drunk girls two doors down, and they gave me a wine cooler. Haven't had a drink for a while, so I think it went straight to my head." She puts her fingers over her mouth.

"They shouldn't be giving minors alcohol," I say, because I am a grumpy motherfucker and I want to drive that home. I could shout, "get off my lawn" but that doesn't apply here.

"Minor? That's funny. How old do you think I am?" she says with a cute little tip of her head.

"There is no way you're much older than eighteen, I would actually guess seventeen but I don't think you could have gotten a trail pass unless you were traveling with a parent. So I'm going with eighteen," I say with all the confidence in the world.

"I am twenty-two, you moron," she says and hiccups. With her hands on her hips, I am sure she thinks she looks intimidating or something, but she really just looks like an angry Tinker Bell.

"Oh well, you look really young. I bet you hear that all the time," I say, and she grows even angrier.

"I do, it's not like I can help the way I look! Do you want to see my ID? I turned twenty-two last week." She huffs out then turns and slams the lid of the washer. I hear her push the coin slot in and her washer starts just like mine had with a satisfying swish of water.

Her shoulders start to shake again and she turns around and levels her gaze to me. "I'm sorry, I am trying to be a grownup here, but are you naked?"

"Me?" I ask.

"Do you see anyone else in here?" she asks, waving her hands around.

"No, and no. I have on a bathing suit." I puff out my chest trying to show confidence. I am feeling anything but confident. I feel like a complete idiot, but will I let this four-foot-eight pixie see me sweat? No.

"Lower the paper, Mr. R and R. I need to see this," she says, hands on her tiny hips, brow furrowed. Damn it, she's cute.

I take my time folding the paper like I'm in a diner in the 1940s and I just finished my cup of Joe. I set the neatly folded paper aside and stand up to my full height of six foot two. I watch her eyes as they start at my face and slowly move down, pausing on my chest, and abs. I may have tried to flex a little. I am trying to not think about how close the tip of my cock is to the top of this stupid Speedo. I'm too afraid to look down. What if it's peeking out? I mean, really, what would I do? If I tug the Speedo up, I risk a ball falling out. A very hairy ball.

I continue to watch her eyes stall out on my groin and to my horror my soldier twitches. In this scrap of fabric I know it's visible, obvious. Damn it. It waved hello. I mean a beautiful girl is checking him out, so I can't really blame him, but damn.

"Okay. Got it. Wow, I did not take you for the Speedo type, Mr. R and R. I thought you were more of a surfer boy, you know, long board shorts or something." She is still staring at my crotch and I feel things starting to swell so I grab the paper and sit back down, like I am going to read again.

"Well, this fit in my pack," I snap. I don't want to talk to her anymore. Especially since my cock seems to think talking to her might lead to something exciting. I try not to look at her either, but she has spun around and pulled off her T-shirt, so now she is just wearing some ridiculously short running shorts and a jogging bra. She dumps her shirt in the washer, then comes to sit next to me on the blue plastic chairs. I don't know what to do. Do I talk to her? Pretend she isn't here? Crap.

"Why do you call me Mr. R and R?" I ask because ignoring her isn't an option apparently.

"I don't want to talk about it," she says. She is leaning back in the chair with her short legs sticking out. She has her flip-flops on and I marvel at her tiny feet. It looks like she painted her toenails recently. My sisters do that, they say it makes them feel pretty. Wonder who this tiny thing is trying to be pretty for?

"Okay. So I can come up with a nickname for you and not tell you why?" I ask.

"Sure, not like we will probably see each other after this. Knock yourself out," she says.

"Okay, Thumbelina, consider it done," I quip.

"Is that a short reference?" she says, and I nod.

"Creative. I have been called Tinker Bell, and Steph-a-fairy, you know instead of Stephanie, so lame, but never Thumbelina."

"Well, my first thought was Yoda, but I don't know if you are wise yet. We might have to work up to that," I say as I flick open my paper again.

"Yoda? That little green dude on Star Trek?" she asks, with a little smirk.

"Star Trek?! You're kidding, right?" I fold my paper back down more aggressively than I meant to.

"Yeah, with Captain Stubing?" she asks.

"That's the Love Boat. Now you *are* kidding. Right? You have to be kidding," I huff out. I pinch the bridge of my nose to ward off the headache that is surely coming.

She just blinks at me, confusion crossing her face. "I don't watch a lot of television. Never have." She shrugs like she just said she doesn't breathe air.

I turn to face her, my ass cheeks squeaking across the plastic chair. "What are you even talking about? You don't watch television? Like ever?" I ask.

"Not really. I mean, I didn't have a lot of time when I was in high school and I went through college pretty fast. I didn't really have a lot of free time," she explains.

"You graduated college already?" I ask. I am shocked.

"Well yeah, I graduated last June." She levels her blue eyes at me like she is challenging me to argue with her.

I rub my hand over my face. Damn it. Now I find her interesting *and* attractive.

"I wonder if the girls at the bachelorette party over there would slip some dollars in your Speedo if you wandered over?" She jumps up and turns to face me. "Let's find out. The washing machine won't be done for another twenty minutes." When I don't immediately respond she turns and starts to walk toward the door then looks back at me with a devastating smile.

"Are you serious?" I ask.

"Sure, what else are we going to do?" she says with a one-shoulder shrug I find way too cute.

My mind immediately thinks of all the things I would like to do to her, but I push those thoughts away quickly since I have no way to hide what I am feeling.

"Sure, why not, Yoda. Sounds fun." I stand and drop the paper on the chair, catching up to her in two steps.

THREE
STEPHANIE

mile 982.80

OKAY, he totally called my bluff. I did not think he was going to stand up in that tiny little Speedo again, especially since I am pretty sure the I can see the tip of his dick poking out of the top.

Mr. R and R is packing. I don't know if I want to take him over to a bunch of drunk girls. They will maul him. I stop just short of the door, and because I am not equipped with brake lights, the dude runs right into the back of me. He stumbles a bit and grabs at me to steady himself. His large hands rest on my hips and I am not ashamed to say I feel things. I mean emotionally, not just the huge pole he presses into my back.

"Wait, maybe we shouldn't go. What if someone steals our stuff? You can't finish the hike in that thing," I say to the door, because I'm afraid to turn around. His hands are still on my hips and I feel his breath catch and his finger curl in slightly before he lets me go.

"Well, that's true. Plus, I think I'd run the risk of getting arrested for indecent exposure if I leave here." He steps closer instead of giving me room, so I turn and crane my neck up to look at him. God, he's tall, and those eyes. So green. I think of moss when the sun hits it, how it almost glows. I can see little flecks of brown and gold too. I could get lost in those eyes, I wonder what that would be like.

I swallow hard and lower my gaze so I'm staring at his chest. His very defined chest with just a light dusting of hair. Golden brown and calling to me. I could bury my face in there and not be found for weeks. I let my eyes wander a bit. I have never thought man nipples were attractive, but damn. His are.

I lick my lips suddenly feeling how dry my throat is. His gaze catches my tongue as it rolls across my bottom lip and I see his chest rise suddenly. I look back up at him and we lock eyes. I can feel my breathing change as his gaze travels over my face and down to my chest. His eyes flick back up to mine, like he didn't mean to look, and I suddenly don't know what to do with my hands. They are just hanging at the side of my body. Is that what hands are supposed to do? Do I look weird? Is he thinking, "Why are her hands just limp like that at the ends of her arms?" My fingers twitch a little and his breathing increases.

How long have we been standing here? Why is he so close to me? Why isn't he touching me? Oh God. I want Mr. Rattail to touch me. What is happening? This time he licks his lower lip, and I swear he leans down a little. My breathing just stops. Soon, my heart will follow suit, I can tell. This is where they find my body. Hiker found dead in laundromat. Man in Speedo questioned.

He reaches up and tucks some hair behind my ear, letting his finger trail down my neck. My whole body erupts in goose bumps and he notices. I see a slight smile cross his lips and he leans in a little further.

"Are you going to do something or just keep me pinned against this glass door?" I breathe out.

"What do you want me to do, Yoda?" he asks, his eyes locked on my lips.

"I don't know." I swallow hard and he watches my throat and I swear he groans. I feel like my heart is about to beat out of my chest. He has to see it, or at least the sweat that is forming on my chest.

"Do you want me to go sit down, Yoda?" he asks as he lets his right hand slowly move up my arm. With the lightest touch of his fingers he sends shivers up my spine. I can't speak—hell, I don't think I am even breathing.

I shake my head no, and he moves even closer. That wicked smile peeking out from his beard. How did we get here? One minute ago he was giving me a hard time for being short and now I am hoping he rips my clothes off? My head is spinning, my breathing shallow and ragged. His fingers finally reach my shoulder and they start the journey to my neck. I realize I have never been this turned on in my life. His big rough hand cups my chin and he tips my face toward him as he lowers his lips to mine. Just before his lips touch mine, he breathes in, like he wants to consume me. And I want that. More than anything else.

He finally lets his lips settle on mine, gently at first, then he moves his hand to the back of my head and pulls me closer. I moan. I don't mean to, I am not a moaner, I am quiet, polite, sweet some would say. Not now, now my body is on fire and moaning is like a pressure release valve.

His fingers dig into my hair and he swipes his tongue across my lips, which I immediately part for him. No, you don't have to take me on a date or buy me dinner. Apparently, you just stuff your very large penis in a Speedo and pin me against a laundromat door. I hear another moan and I am not even sure who it belongs to as our kissing becomes more frantic.

Apparently my hands figured out what to do because my fingers are currently dancing through that glorious chest hair. I slide them across his pecs and down a little to his stomach, careful not to go too low. His breathing catches and he tugs me closer so I wrap my hands around to his back and let my nails drag down to just above his ass.

His whole body is pressed against me and now I know if I were to look down there would be a huge dick poking out of a very tiny red Speedo.

As if he can read my mind, he pulls back from the kiss and straightens out. My eyes are at the level of his nipples so this isn't any better than when we were kissing. His dick is still poking me in the stomach. I think it moved, throbbed even. Good Lord. That thing is going to be the death of me. I look up at him and his bright green eyes have gone dark. He's breathing hard as he lets his hands trace up and down my back.

"I may have gotten carried away there, Yoda."

"Me too," I squeak out.

"I don't regret the kiss, I just um," he pauses and I pull away slightly and look down.

Oh. My. God.

"If you turn around I can just walk over and get that newspaper. I don't know if I am ready to introduce you to my dick just yet. I mean, he's ready and willing to say hello, but..." he trails off.

I should say something. I should speak words. Say, sure yeah, get that paper and cover your very large penis. I don't instead I lick my lips and fight the urge to lower my head and pull that magnificent thing into my mouth. I slide my hand up between us and grab him before he can back away. I gently squeeze him, enjoying how very hard he feels in my hand.

"I say, we finish our laundry, then you come back to my motel room, where me and your friend can be introduced properly." The words come out of my mouth, but it's like I am hearing someone else speak them. I apparently have no control over my body, let alone my words.

"That sounds fucking awesome," he says and dips to kiss me again. I hear a knocking sound and I think it must be the washer, gone lopsided, you know? But then it happens again followed by a little, "Excuse me. I need to get in there. My clothes are in the dryer."

The muffled voice snaps me out of my lust induced stupor and I step aside, unfortunately exposing Corey to the woman at the door.

"Never mind! I'll come back later!" she yells and scurries off.

I burst out laughing as Corey places his very big hands over his very small Speedo. He inches back to the blue chairs and sits gingerly.

"Okay there, champ?" I ask.

"Perfect. I love scaring little old ladies with my dick. She is probably calling the cops," he says and I look at him.

He is sitting there in nothing but hiking boots and what is essentially underwear. Tiny underwear. He might be right. She might be calling the police.

BY THE TIME his washing machine is finished he's able to stand with some minimal adjustments and transfer his clothes to the dryer. A few minutes later I do the same. I sit and wonder how to make small talk when I basically just told this man I barely know that I want to meet his penis.

"So, Corey, right? I can't call you Mr. R and R anymore?" I say and he laughs.

"Why not? I mean sure, you can call me Corey, but I kind of like Mr. R and R. Even if I don't know what it means."

"Okay I'll stick with that. Unless I am screaming your name, then it will be Corey."

"As in, oh God Corey, right there, harder Corey," he says with a smirk.

I gulp, because I can totally picture saying that. Seriously what has come over me? It's barely noon on a Wednesday and I am horny as hell. I blame the wine cooler. Well, and the fact that I got an interview. When I called the school this morning a very sweet lady scheduled me for August third at three in the afternoon. If I can get into Beaver Valley a few days early I will have time to find some nice clothes and maybe get a haircut or something.

"Sure, 'yeah Corey give it to me' sounds easier to say than 'Oh, Mr. R and R shove that big dick in all the way,'" I say.

"Big, huh?" He reaches down and adjusts himself then adds, "I didn't really expect you to be a dirty talker, Yoda. It's kind of doing things to me." He nods down and my eyes follow, unable to help myself, I smile.

"It's nice to know I have that effect on you," I say.

I didn't know I was a dirty talker either. To be honest none of this is like me. It must be the PCT. I have changed over the last few months, and this is what I have become. A dirty-talking horny hussy who attacks men in laundromats.

When his dryer dings, he rushes to pull out a pair of shorts and his shoulders visibly relax as he slides them on. He folds and rolls all his clothes and stuffs them in his bag while I wait for my dryer to finish. I notice there are no tighty-whities in his laundry. Does he not wear underwear?

Just as this question dances through my mind he holds up a pair of black briefs. He expertly rolls them and adds them to the bag, repeating the process until all that he has left are some socks. I realize I'm staring at him as he folds his laundry. Not just staring, but ogling. Has he always been this hot? He glances over his shoulder and winks at me like he can read my mind.

Thankfully my dryer is finished and I make quick work of repacking. Corey stands off to the side reading the message board by the door.

"Think I should leave an apology card for that old lady?" he asks.

"Couldn't hurt," I say with a shrug.

He grabs a scrap of paper and uses the pen attached to the counter by a thin chain.

"Dear old lady," he says, and I laugh.

"Don't say that! She probably doesn't consider herself old."

"Okay how about, 'Dear lady?'"

"Sure, that's better."

"Dear lady, I am sorry you saw the tip of my very erect penis. The Speedo I was wearing was not built for a man of my size." He glances over at me for approval and I nod.

"Perfect. It's accurate and heartfelt," I say.

"I got felt up, probably wouldn't have been as erect if I hadn't been groped," he says.

I HAVE NO REGRETS. I give him a little wink and say, "I am not sorry about that."

"Let's get out of here before she comes back. Do you want to come to my motel or go to yours? I am right here at the Pine Cone." He reaches down into his bag and fishes out the giant lake-shaped key chain. Of course.

"Um, that is where I'm staying too, room 116. Where are you?"

"Room 115." He laughs and so do I. Of course we're neighbors.

"I'll set this down, and maybe go grab pizza and some beer?" He has one eyebrow raised like he's wondering if I've changed my mind.

I have not.

"Sure, or we could go eat after," I suggest.

"I like the way you think." He reaches over and gives my ass a little squeeze and I feel my face flush red. My stomach does a little flip and I amaze myself by reaching out to him. I tangle our fingers and press my palm into his giant hand.

Where this brave girl came from is a mystery. I kind of like her. It seems like Corey kinda likes her too, so that is nice. The last guy I was with was so boring. It was my last semester at UC San Diego and I felt like I needed to have a fling. This guy in my credential program had flirted with me off and on all year, so I asked him out for drinks. While we were out at the bar, the chemistry was palpable, but once we went back to his place, he became a weird fumbling mess. Maybe he didn't think I would agree when he offered? I don't know. I just know I left his place a half hour later, sexually frustrated and regretting my choice.

Thankfully he didn't seem to notice my disappointment, and I was able to blow him off the next week in class since the program was winding down. I didn't want to hurt him. I just wasn't feeling it. He kissed like he was looking for something in my mouth and he did not know what to do with his hands, or his dick really. In and out and all done.

Corey gave my hand a little squeeze as we got to our doors. Since he had his key out, we went in there. As soon as we stepped in I realized how lucky it was that we chose his room. I think his severed braid is on my nightstand. I am betting that would kill the mood for him.

"Do you want to put your bag in your room?" he asks, and I shake my head no, worried he might follow me over there.

"Okay, should I put on some music or something?" he asks.

The enormity of what I am about to do smacks me in the face and I turn to him with what must look like panic on my face.

"Hey, Yoda. You can change your mind. I won't be mad. I don't want to pressure you into doing something you aren't comfortable with. I know we both got carried away back there. Let's just go get a pizza."

"Maybe we could sit and talk a bit?" I squeak out. I haven't changed my mind, not at all, but I *am* nervous. I don't do things like this.

"Sure." He drops his bag and goes to sit on the bed. Before his ass makes contact however, he stands back up and yanks the bedspread off.

"They must never wash those things. I felt a few very weird stiff patches that I don't want to think about," he says as he tosses it in the corner. He sits and pulls off his hiking boots, so I sit too and slide out of my flip-flops. I set my bag next to the foot of the bed and scoot back to lean against the headboard.

"Comfortable?" he asks.

"Yeah, my room is just like this, gross bedspread and everything. I pulled mine off too. As soon as I got out of the shower last night I lay sprawled out on the sheets like a starfish. It was amazing."

"Naked?" he growls out and scoots a little closer to me on the bed. I smile like an idiot, then narrow my eyes at him in an attempt to be serious.

"I tend to shower naked, yes." I deadpan while fighting a giggle.

He makes another sound in his throat and he reaches to adjust himself. "I should throw this stupid Speedo away. It's so tight it doesn't take much for me to outgrow it."

"Growing already?" I raise an eyebrow at him.

"You are very hot, I can't help it." His right shoulder raises in a shrug. God, he is cute.

We sit in silence, me desperately trying to think of something to say, or ask him. Thankfully, he doesn't seem as uncomfortable. He reaches out to touch my thigh and I feel sparks of electricity as he moves his fingers up and down my leg. Chills chase his fingers as they blaze a path closer to my stomach. He repeats this pattern gently over and over until I begin to relax. He must see it because he says softly, "Feeling a little more comfortable now?"

"Yeah, I am. That feels good," I respond, and my voice sounds different, kind of breathy. I am not the breathy type.

He moves closer to me on the bed, grabbing at my hand. He brings our joined hands to his lips and kisses softly along my hand, then moves to my fingers. I watch, mesmerized, as he kisses where our hands are joined, his lips grazing me and him, and I find it very erotic. His beard tickles and his full lips are making me wish they were on my mouth again. They were soft and supple and I need them more than I need air.

I turn to face him more, sliding my leg up a little for balance as I reach for his face and pull him up to me. As soon as our mouths connect, I moan again. I arch toward him, unable to keep my body away from his. His breathing grows more rapid and he snakes his hands up into my hair, angling my face to where he wants it. He is too far away so I scoot a little then let out a frustrated noise. His body is all the way over there and while I am loving the contact of our lips and tongues, my knee touching his hip isn't really cutting it. In one quick move, I straddle him, pinning him to the bed as best as I can.

His hands move from my hair to my hips in a flash. This time he groans and moves his hands down to my ass, holding me in place as he thrusts against me. My little nylon running shorts provide very little in the way of coverage and I swear I can feel him hardening with each thrust.

"I've never wanted to fuck someone as bad as I want to fuck you. Please tell me you're on the pill, because I only have one condom and there is no way once will be enough," he says into my ear.

My vision goes hazy as he grinds into me and I start to pant. I know he asked me a question but I can't even think. My body is moving on its own and I can feel my release barreling down on me.

"Oh God, Corey, I am going to—" I say, but he swallows my words, covering my mouth with his in what can only be described as the most passionate kiss I have ever experienced. Passionate doesn't describe the heat and need as he devours me, but it's the only word that comes to mind. Maybe later I will have a better word. My core tightens and I feel like if he were to stop what he is doing I would die. This friction, the buildup to my release is incredible, addictive and heavenly.

I feel it hit me. My whole body tenses and I whimper as he continues to thrust himself against me. My orgasm continues on and on like my body can't get enough. Eventually I shudder and collapse onto him, letting a breath escape my lungs in a moan. He gives me no time to relax before he is flipping me over onto my back. He yanks my shorts aside and slides a finger gently through my wet folds.

"Oh God, you're so wet. Fuck, that was sexy. Can I take these off?" He leans forward, kissing me before I can answer.

I pull away from his mouth long enough to say yes, then dive back in for more. His lips are perfection and he knows how to use them. He starts to slide his tongue across mine, then sucks on my bottom lip just enough to earn another whimper from me. Just as I am getting into the kiss he pulls away and tugs at my shirt. I help him remove it and my jogging bra and he pulls his T-shirt off as well. I dive for him, pushing him onto his back. I have never been this bold or felt this kind of out-of-control lust. I run my fingers along his chest, kissing and licking at his nipples. I follow that trail of hair right down to the top of his shorts. I pop the button and tug on the zipper.

"These shorts need to go, and let's finally get you out of that Speedo," I say.

He smiles and puts his hands behind his head. "Have your way with me, Yoda." He lifts his ass as I tug on his shorts and once I free his legs I move back up to get that Speedo. The head of his cock is fully exposed and one ball is threatening to escape.

"How are you even wearing this?" I ask as my eyes take in the feat of strength the Lycra is currently performing.

"It's getting painful. I'd appreciate it if you could hurry," he rasps out.

He lifts his ass again and I tug the tiny thing free of his hips. I slide it down his legs and move my hands back up his thick thighs, pausing when I reach the massive thing he was trying to hide in the Speedo.

"Good God," I say reverently. My fingers trail across it as I marvel at how hard he is. I never thought the male body was that exciting, and I certainly never thought a guy's equipment to be sexy, but holy crap. This is perfection right here in my hand. He's rock hard, but the skin is soft, silky almost. I slide my hand up and down his length a few times because I can't help myself. The tip is leaking precum, so I bend down and lick it off. He fists the sheets and his eyes squeeze shut. "Holy fuck, that feels good," he grunts, and thrusts up into me.

"You like that?" I ask softly moving my lips across the swollen crown of his cock.

"Baby, I like everything you do," he says and I realize if anyone else had said that to me, I would have laughed. Corey says these things and I just want to climb him like a tree.

FOUR
COREY

mile 882.8

HER PLUMP, full lips just wrapped around the head of my cock and I swear I about blew right then and there. I groan as she slides down further pulling me into the hot wet heaven of her mouth. She is sucking and licking like she is starving and I am all she needs. She reaches her hand up and gently cups my balls, lightly rolling them, squeezing.

Without meaning to I thrust up into her open mouth. My hips know what my dick needs and thankfully she doesn't object, she just sucks harder, swallowing as I hit the back of her throat. Her small hand is still working my balls while the other is pumping me slowly, like she has all day. I wish I did, this is not going to last much longer. I'd be embarrassed about how quickly she has brought me to the edge, but I am hoping she takes it as the compliment it is. She is my undoing, in every way. I prop myself up on my elbows so I can watch as she takes me into her mouth as far as she can. God, what a sight. Her beautiful full lips sliding up and down my shaft, and her breasts swaying with each movement. It's quite possibly the most beautiful thing I have ever seen.

My balls tighten and I warn her, "I'm going to come." I grunt, trying to hold off if she wants to move out of the way, but she doesn't move. She sucks harder and moves her hand faster until I explode, thrusting my hips as I unload into her mouth. She swallows it all, gulping it down. She doesn't take her mouth away, just moves her tongue lazily along my shaft. Her hands are still busy and I try and control my breathing. I slowly lower to the bed and she pulls her mouth off me then kisses my stomach and moves up my body stopping to kiss each nipple. I have never had a girl do that before, and her wet mouth grazing over my chest feels like heaven. I fucking love it. It's like a jolt straight to my dick when she nibbles at one then drags her hand through my chest hair with the other.

"Jesus, woman. You are magical," I say, grabbing her tiny body and pulling her up to me. She lies on top of me and starts to caress my beard, then runs her hands up to my hair. It feels so good, like she is trying to feel every inch of my body, like she is trying to learn me. I feel overwhelmed, but in the best way. I let my fingers tickle her back and slip under the waistband of her shorts.

"These can come off, you know?" I whisper in her ear and she lifts her head up and kisses me once slowly then pulls away and looks into my eyes.

"Well then, take them off. I believe you wanted to earlier and I distracted you with my lips on your cock." She looks down at me with those big blue eyes and I am lost in her immediately. I pull her into another kiss, unable to keep my lips off her. I kiss her again and again, letting my hands dance around her face and down her neck and chest. I need to touch all of her, feel her breasts, her nipples. My mind is racing to what I want to do next and I feel like my heart is going to jump out of my chest.

What is this? I have never felt this kind of pull towards a woman. I had my share of fun in high school and college but never like this. I need to touch every part of her, start at her toes and work all the way to these luscious lips then make my way back down. I want years to worship this woman.

I reluctantly pull away long enough to flip us over so she's on her back, then I slide her shorts off, pausing to appreciate her beautiful body. I climb back onto her, straddling her thighs and let my eyes feast on her, the dip of her stomach, and the slight swell of her hips, then up to her small but perfect breasts. I trace a thumb under the swell of each and smile when she arches up into my touch. "Look at you. God, you are so beautiful, Stephanie," I say.

"Thank you." She pulls me down onto her, and I go willingly, covering her whole body with mine. I love the feeling of having her pinned beneath me, safe. It seems she likes it too, as she is currently tracing delicate patterns on my back. It's intimate, tender, like you would do with the one you love, not a quick fuck, not a fling. Because that is what this is, right? I look down into her eyes and I see what I'm feeling reflected back. At least that's what my heart wants to believe.

I lean in and let my lips linger softly over hers, kissing with more passion than I thought I had in me. She responds and slides her hands through my hair arching her hips toward me. She parts her legs, and I rest the tip of my cock at her entrance. I am almost completely hard again, I feel a throb of need rushing through me, as I gently move, pushing in slightly. I can feel how wet she is, how ready she is for me. I wait, poised at her entrance and focus on kissing her. I could kiss this woman forever and instead of that thought scaring me, it turns me on. The thought of her like this, under me, open and ready, is intoxicating. I want to ask her if she feels it too, but I don't. I can't take it if she says no. If this is a one-time, one day of mind-blowing sex that I'll remember on my deathbed, then I need to be okay with that.

I push the thought out of my mind, and pull my lips off hers, moving to her neck and down to her perfect breasts. I kiss and suck on her nipples before making my way down her stomach. I slide my hands under her hips and kiss her on each hip bone, earning a giggle.

"Stop, that tickles," she says, but she is squirming and opening her legs like she wants me to continue my journey.

I dive in, moving my lips and tongue over her, into her. She is so wet, but she is also tiny and I worry about hurting her. I gently slide one finger in and groan at how tight she is.

"You are so perfect," I say moving my finger out and through her folds. I circle her clit and dive back in this time using two fingers and she moans and arches up off the bed.

"What are you waiting for, Corey? Just put that giant dick inside me."

"I don't want to hurt you," I say with a chuckle, because damn, this woman is everything.

"You won't, just go slow, but please I need you," she says as she reaches for me, grappling at my shoulders, encouraging me to climb up on to her beautiful body. I slide back up, kissing her with more force this time, nibbling harder on each nipple. I can feel my cock hanging heavy between us and I inch closer. I position myself between her legs and she widens to give me better access. I reach down and guide my tip to her entrance and push in just a little. She gasps and tilts her hips causing me to slip in further, and we both groan. I drop my forehead to hers.

"You okay?" I pant out. My whole body erupts in sweat.

"Fuck yeah, give it to me, Corey, God, you feel so good. So damn good." She grabs my ass and pulls me into her, crying out in pleasure as I push all the way in.

"More, come on, move, you aren't going to hurt me. I want you to fuck me," she says and I look down into that sweet face that has gone dark. She rolls her teeth over her lower lip and I smile.

"Okay, hold on baby," I say and I pull out and then slam back into her. She moans the sexiest moan I have ever heard so I do it again and again. I roll my hips and she adjusts her legs so her feet are resting on my ass pushing me in, matching my thrusts. I can't help myself, I look down into those eyes and feel my heart expand.

Shit.

This girl. What is she doing to me?

"Oh God, yes, right there Corey. That is so good. I'm so close, please don't stop."

I would do anything for this woman, so I continue to pump into her until she screams my name. I watch her face to see her fall apart because of me, I did that. I made her feel that good, and the knowledge of that pushes me over the edge. My balls tighten and I feel every ounce that I give her. My body is shaking and my breathing ragged as my thrusts become frantic and jerky.

"Stephanie, oh God," I say and collapse on top of her.

We lay like that, me a 200-pound pancake, smashing her tiny pixie body until our breathing regains a normal rhythm.

"Um, wow. That was, um..." she pants out.

"Yeah. Wow," I say, lifting myself off of her enough to see her face. As soon as I look into those eyes my lips are on hers like there is a magnetic pull. Fuck. What is she doing to me? I kiss her softly, slowly, like I just discovered the missing piece of me. Like the mysteries of the universe are here within our lips tangling together.

Someone's stomach rumbles and we both laugh.

"I guess we should eat or something," she says. She is tracing tiny circles over my back and it tickles. I don't want her to stop, not now, not in an hour. I want this always.

"Yeah. We need food. Can I ask you a question first?" I say, trying to remain calm.

"Sure, hit me," she says.

"Can we do that again or was that a one-time thing?" I hold my breath waiting for the answer, praying she is as into me as I am into her.

"Oh, we are totally doing that again. Your giant dick is my new favorite thing." She kisses me deeply and I feel a twitch down below. Damn it.

"Okay, cool, yeah, I would really like that. Let's go get pizza. I need pizza." I roll off her and reach for my shorts and T-shirt. I have to dig through my bag and get a pair of underwear. No way I'd risk going commando with this girl around. I'd be tenting my shorts in no time.

"I am just going to duck next door and um, drop my bag. Maybe change my shorts." She says as she tugs back on the tiny running shorts.

"Cool, okay," I say, but I'm thinking, *Don't leave! I'll go with you, what if you don't come back!?*

I am so screwed.

She ducks out, taking her bag of clothes, so I sit on the bed and finish getting dressed. I rub my hands down my face and marvel at what just happened. I can hear her muffled voice and I wonder who she is talking to. I hope she hurries back. I am hungry and apparently crazy because I miss her already.

FIVE

STEPHANIE

mile 982.8

"OH MY GOD, oh my God, oh my God!" I say as soon as I shut my door. "What the hell was that? How is he so awesome? Why does he have a magical dick? Seriously, I can't believe I want to go back over there and climb on top of him again, but I do! Holy shit. I am in so much trouble." I grab the severed braid and shove it back into the bottom of my sleeping bag. I splash water on my face and change into some different shorts. No underwear, because what's the point?

I wish I had something cute to wear, but then I guess it doesn't matter to Mr. R and R, Corey, Sex God. I pull on a different T-shirt and slide my feet into my sandals. I glance around the room and grab the enormous key and step outside finding Corey waiting. He has his hands shoved in his pockets as he leans against the railing.

I can't help but smile. God, he is so cute. How did I not see it before? I mean, I guess I did see past the stupid rattail a little. I knew he was attractive, but now? Now that I know what he can do?

I am in so much trouble. I feel like I have thought that before, but wow. My head is spinning. I know what that means now. Oh my GOD. It's like that song. He spins me right round, baby, right round.

"Hungry?" he asks, stepping toward me.

"Starving." I take a step toward him and he reaches his hands out to link with mine. He lowers his head and bends down to kiss me and as soon as his lips touch mine, I moan.

He drops my hands and pulls me closer, cradling my body gently as his lips dance over mine. We are never going to make it to a restaurant at this rate, so I pull back and look up into his beautiful green eyes.

"Burgers or pizza?" I ask and I notice my chest rising and falling like I've just run a marathon.

"Burgers, they take less time to cook," he says and I laugh.

"Sounds great."

We walk down the street to the local burger joint hand in hand. I think I am floating beside him. We order at the window before sitting at one of the picnic tables by the water. We both ask for a beer and the server doesn't blink at him, but of course I get carded. I know someday I will be grateful for my youthful face, but now it's just annoying.

"So Corey, are you going all the way to Canada? I don't think we ever talked about it," I say, taking a long drink of my beer.

"Nah, I'm stopping in Bend. My sisters are going to the junior college there, then will transfer to Oregon State University. I am meeting up with them to help them get settled," he says.

"Oh. So, like after that you aren't going on? Wait, didn't you start the hike in LA?" I assume he will be flying back from Bend.

"Yeah, I dropped in near Los Angles. I start a new job at the end of August, so my hiking days are over once I get to Bend. How about you? Going all the way?" he asks.

"That's the plan. I have one stop kind of near Bend, but then I will be going on. My mom has talked about flying up to Canada to meet me, then we'd see some of the area together before we fly home," I say. I suddenly have a twisting pain in my stomach.

"Home is San Diego?" he asks. I notice he's looking into his beer instead of at me.

"Yep. Born and raised. Went to college there," I say.

"What was your major?" he asks.

"History, with an emphasis on American history," I say, starting to feel nervous with the questions.

"Oh, that's cool, what do you do with a history degree?" he says, not looking at me.

"Um, I haven't decided yet," I lie. I don't really want to explain that my all-time goal is to be a history teacher at a high school because I had the best teacher ever and it sparked something in me, and now no one will hire me because I look like I'm twelve years old.

"What about you? What did you study in college? I mean I assume you went? Oh God. Did you go?" I ask.

He just laughs, "Yeah, I went to UCLA. Graduated two years ago. I majored in math with a minor in music."

"Interesting. I think I have seen you play that tiny guitar. Do you play, like, in a band?" I ask, and he stiffens.

"I used to, but they went a different direction. Hey, I'm going to go see if our food is ready. I'll be right back." He stands and walks away before I can say anything else. Shit, did I make him mad?

This is awful. I like him so much and I seem to have lost the ability to carry on a normal conversation, maybe because everything else we talk about takes us away from the trail, and makes me realize how little time we have left. I don't want to think about Bend, Oregon Corey. I want PCT Corey, or better yet, Mr. R and R.

By the time he returns to our table carrying two little red plastic baskets with our burgers and fries, it occurs to me that we don't have to tell each other everything. This, whatever it is, has an expiration date. We should just enjoy what time we have left, part ways in Bend and have amazing memories.

"Here you go. God, these look so good. I almost ate both of them on the way over here," he says and I laugh.

"I would have killed you. Thanks for going to get them," I say, and before I can lose my nerve I say, "Hey, Corey?"

"Hmmm?" He looks at me over his burger which now has an enormous bite missing.

"Well, um, I don't know how you're feeling about what happened back at the Pine Cone, but I'm going to go out on a limb here and tell you that was the best sex of my life."

A huge smile spreads across his face and he sets the burger down.

"I agree. It was the best sex of your life." He pauses, then says, "But it was the same for me."

I roll my eyes and continue. "Anyway, as I was saying, we only have a few weeks, maybe a month left together. I mean, that is, if you want to keep hiking together? Oh God. You can totally go on ahead or I can go first and try and stay out of—"

He grabs my hand and smiles at me until I stop talking. "Stephanie, I have never had so much fun with someone. I would really like to continue whatever this is, for as long as we can."

My stomach flips a thousand times and I grin, unable to stop myself. I am sure I am blushing. "Okay so we just keep on, keeping on, until Bend?" I ask.

"Yes," he says, and I see a flicker of something cross his face that I can't place.

We continue to eat until there is nothing left in the red baskets but greasy checkered paper. I had finished my beer long before my burger, so I sit and wait for him.

"So, I realize it's too late to really have this conversation, but you're on the pill, right?" he asks. He is running his finger across the condensation on his beer bottle, not looking at me.

"Oh God, did I not answer you?" I say, my eyes wide.

"No, but I was distracted too." He waggles his eyebrows at me.

"Yes, I'm on the pill, I'm sorry I didn't answer. I was so overwhelmed." The words come out of my mouth before I can think about how they sound. Corey reaches for my hand again and looks at me with those moss-green eyes. Rubbing his thumb across the top of my hand, he doesn't speak, but his eyes say he is feeling the same thing. I watch him swallow, then he leans forward.

I feel such a pull to him. I lean in as well and our lips touch. Softly at first, then when I scoot closer the kisses become more frantic. Desperate. That's the word for how I feel, desperate to be near him, have him.

I pull away and say, "Yeah, overwhelmed is a good description."

"Yep, that sums it up. How long did you calculate for the trip from here to Bend?" he asks, his lips barely touching my lips again.

"Bend? Um, I'd have to look at my journal." I press my mouth to his again. My air is there, I need it. I need him. "Want to go back to your room?" I ask.

"Fuck yeah," he says. He stands and pulls me up too and we hurry to toss our trash and stack the baskets.

SIX

COREY

mile 882.8

I CAN SEE the sun peeking through the cheap polyester curtains. There is a very sexy thigh draped across my body and blond hair in my face. I didn't dream it. Holy fuck, this girl is something else. It was like we couldn't get enough of each other last night. I feel like a Goddamn king. I start to stroke her arm and back, tickling her lightly until she squirms against me.

"Good morning, Yoda."

"Good morning, Mr. R, I am officially making it shorter, just so you know," she says into my chest.

"No objections here." She obviously doesn't know my last name, and I won't tell her. I think back in Yosemite a ranger came through looking for her when she forgot to check in with her mom, and I have been trying to remember her last name ever since. Hannigan? Henry? I can't ask for hers without giving mine away, and I think we have decided to just ride out the month together and part ways at Bend.

I am trying to be okay with that. I have time. Maybe she will start to annoy the heck out of me by then. Right now I can't imagine that, but who knows.

"Are you hungry? I need food. You are an animal." I kiss the top of her head and roll out from under her and grab my shorts off the floor. No telling where my T-shirt is.

"Yes, I mean I'm always starving these days. I need breakfast and I really need to replenish my supplies. I only booked two nights. How long are you staying?" she asks. I can tell she is still unsure if I want her around. I wish I could tell her how gone I am for her without freaking her out.

I laugh, then say, "I only booked two nights. We're pretty in sync with our schedules, aren't we?"

"I've noticed that. I mean I thought for a while you were following me." She sits up on the bed and looks around for her clothes. Her perfect tits just stare at me, calling to me. I shake my head to regain some control. I see her shirt but not her shorts. Man, we must have ripped each other's clothes off.

I duck down and find her shorts and my T-shirt under the bed along with someone else's used condom. Gross. I won't tell Stephanie about that. In my real life, away from the trail, I would never take a girl like her to a place like this.

I have noticed that a lot lately. I am changing. I don't know if it's because I'm doing this crazy long hike or if it's because Codey isn't with me. It's the first time in my twenty-five years that I haven't had him by my side. I am starting to feel like I'm my own person for the first time in my life. I don't know how I feel about that.

"Here. I think these are yours." I hand her the white jean cutoff shorts.

"Eeew. No, these are mine," she says, holding up a pair of blue denim shorts.

"Oh God." I drop the mystery shorts and shudder. "We need to check out as soon as possible, then maybe stop by the health clinic."

"I feel like we will be okay since we managed to stay in the bed. If we had gotten crazy and tried to do it on the floor, I'd be checking into the hospital for some IV antibiotics." she says with a laugh.

"Sounds like you have given that some thought," I say, and she nods rapidly. God, she's cute. I wonder if she knows that, or if she's one of those girls who doesn't know what she has to offer. Hopefully I find out she is a conceited bitch somewhere between here and Bend.

"So do you want to grab breakfast, then go get our supplies, or shop first?" I ask.

"Shop first. I'd rather be all ready to go when we eat. I mean that is just what I have always done." She is tucking her long hair up into a rubber band thing that seemed to appear out of nowhere.

"Cool, okay. Did you want to shop together? I mean we can meet up after or ...?" Now it's me sounding like an insecure ass. Did she need a break from me? Damn, I wish Codey was here so I could ask his advice. I have never had a relationship with a girl without the help of my twin on the simple things. I am not what you would call a ladies' man. Codey, on the other hand, could talk the pants off a nun, or whatever that dress thing they wear is called. It's not called pants, I know that much. Dress? That doesn't sound right, either.

"You look like you're trying to solve world hunger. What's going on in that handsome head of yours?" she asks, walking to me like she and I have done this a million times. She wraps her arms around me and buries her head against my chest, fitting perfectly against me.

"You don't want to know. It involved nuns." I squeeze her a little and she snuggles in further. God, she feels so good in my arms. Her light tiny laughter makes my heart do a little flip.

"Okay well, I am going next door to shower and get my stuff together. I'll see you out front in a half hour?" she asks.

"Sounds good. If you shower here we'll never leave," I say, stepping back.

"I thought the same thing," she says, looking up at me. I bend to kiss her softly, pulling away again before things go too far. Hell, they have already gone too far if you ask my stupid heart.

As soon as she leaves, I strip again and head for the shower and enjoy the warm water as I wash off. So far I haven't minded just rinsing off in creeks and lakes. I thought it would bother me but having shorter hair has helped. I still miss my tail. Maybe I should let my hair grow long again. I wonder what the high school in Beaver Valley would think of a long-haired math teacher?

I spent some time repacking my backpack, getting everything in just where I like it, then filling all my water bottles. This next trek should be cooler through the pines so I won't be sucking down the water as much. I wonder if Stephanie is ready yet. I glance around the room and decide to kick the white shorts back under the bed for someone else to find, then head out to the office to turn in my key.

I step into the small lobby, set my pack by the door, and look up to see a freshly showered Stephanie talking to the manager. She is telling him about the trail and how long she has been hiking so I just listen, enjoying the sound of her voice. He makes a few inappropriate comments to her, but she holds her own. She's a pretty tough cookie, and I don't know if I like that or not. I am trying to find things to dislike about her and so far, it's not going well.

"You okay?" I ask. I am waiting for her to adjust the straps on her pack.

"Yeah, why?" She looks at me with those big blue eyes.

"That guy was gross, I just thought maybe it bothered you," I say, glancing back at the hotel door wishing I could go put my fist in that guy's face.

"Him? Nah, I get comments all the time from dirtballs like him. Sometimes they avoid saying anything because I look so young. But that guy knew how old I was because I had to show him my ID to rent the room." She adjusts the weight of her pack then asks, "Ready?"

"Why did you have to show your ID? I didn't have to do that," I say, following her out onto the quiet street.

"Well, you are a tall man who looks like an adult. I am a short girl with a baby face." She shrugs. "Before Yosemite I stayed at a place and the front desk girl slid me a paper saying if I needed help to blink twice. I think she thought I was a runaway or something." She looks over her shoulder at me and I smile.

"I could see why she would worry. I really thought you were a minor when I first saw you on the trail. I thought you were with those two gals, you know who I mean?"

"Barbara and Grace? The gal with the short brown hair and her blonde 'friend' who argued about song lyrics?" She makes little air quotes with her fingers when she says the word "friend."

"Yes! Them. I thought you were one of their daughters or something." I say falling in behind her.

"That's funny, no, I have been on the trail with them since San Diego though. They started at the beginning of the trail so they have been on longer than me. They watched my mom drop me off at my start point and assured her that I would be safe," she explains.

"Was your mom worried about you?" I ask, as we wind our way through the mostly deserted town to the store.

"Rose? Worried? That is funny. No, she was more stressed about getting back to work than about me. She went on a two-month-long road trip by herself after she finished college, so to her it was just a normal thing," Steph says.

"Wow. Really? That's kind of cool, you're exploring just like your mom then," I say. We reach the store and I hold the door while she grabs a cart.

"Maybe a little. I mean I thought I'd get a job right after college and that hasn't happened, so I am doing this until I find something."

I walk alongside her as we put stuff in, grabbing mostly the same things. "I get that." I have so many questions, but hold back. I know that if I get to know her more, leaving her will be even more difficult.

"Oh score!" she yells, and she grabs two boxes of the Nature Valley granola bars off the shelf. The peanut butter ones. The best ones. Thankfully there are two more boxes that I grab and toss in the cart. I would have had to fight her if there wasn't. Those things are fucking amazing.

Once we have all our food, we make our way outside to pack

everything into our backpacks. I admire how organized she is, then realize her pack is almost as heavy as she is.

"Did you weigh your pack before you left?" I ask.

"No. I didn't want to know. I'm guessing it's over sixty-five pounds. How about you?" she says.

"Yeah, I did. I like math, remember? Numbers matter to me. My pack is exactly sixty-seven pounds with all my food and water. But I am six foot two and weigh two hundred pounds. You are what, four foot eight?"

"I am five foot two, I'll have you know!" She stands as tall as she can and I fight a laugh.

"What do you weigh? Do you even register on the scale?" I ask with a smirk.

"Sometimes I have to jump a few times to wake it up, but last time I checked I was a hundred and eight pounds."

"How are you carrying more than half your body weight on this trail?" I stop and grab her arm, forcing her to turn to me.

"Strong legs. I was a cross-country runner in school." She shrugs like it's no big deal.

"Well, if you need me to carry something," I start, and she cuts me off.

"Don't do that," she says as she narrows her eyes at me.

"Do what?" I ask.

"Start trying to take care of me. I have been fine up until now, and I will continue to be fine. Just because you shoved your magical dick in me repeatedly yesterday doesn't mean I am suddenly unable to handle my own shit," she says angrily.

"Magical, huh? Okay. I like how that sounds. How about my new nickname is MD? Oh! Like I'm a doctor. You could call me Doc and we would be the only ones that know why!" Hope fills my chest, but she just blinks at me.

"No. You will continue to be Mr. R. I might add the other R back in if you piss me off, but I am not calling you Doc," she says, a small smile returning to her beautiful face.

I laugh and shake my head as she walks off in front of me. We stop at a little breakfast place before hitting the trail, each of us loading up on carbs and protein. After a bit we are on our way again.

We have to wind our way through the rest of the town before the trail picks up and veers off away from civilization. It's always my favorite part, when the town noise dies off and the trail takes over. I clear my head and listen to the sound of my hiking boots pounding out the miles.

This time, though, it feels different. Like I am on a team, instead of the solo trek I have been on for the last two months. I feel like I did before Codey left. I feel connected to someone, no that isn't right. I feel whole.

Damn it.

Maybe instead of hoping I grow sick of her, I should find a way to make her stay in Oregon.

"What has been your favorite part of the trail so far, Mr. R?" she asks as the trail gently slopes away from Tahoe.

"Meeting you," I say as easily as I take a breath.

She stops and I run right into her. She turns and looks up at me with those big beautiful blue eyes. Eyes that look like Lake Tahoe in color.

"Seriously?" she says in almost a whisper and I nod, bending to kiss her.

Her lips meet mine, just as hungry and I fight with all my strength to pull back. "What has been your favorite part?" I ask while trying to discreetly adjust myself in my shorts.

"That," she says, pointing to my hand on my crotch.

"My magical dick?" I ask but she shakes her head no.

"I like knowing I can do that to you without really trying. I don't think I have ever had that effect on a man before," she says, and stands on her toes to kiss me again.

"I don't believe that for a second," I say.

"It's true, Mr. R. Guys mostly think of me as a friend or like a little sister." She shrugs and turns back to the trail.

SEVEN
STEPHANIE

mile 1040.6

I NEED to get my head out of the clouds. This guy is killing me, with his amazing conversational skills, his dry sense of humor and of course his magical dick. I look at every break in the trees as a potential place to drag him off and lick him like a popsicle.

I guess it wasn't the wine cooler. It's me. Or it's him. I have never felt like this before. I never cared that I didn't have a boyfriend or even regular dates. I've never been one of those girls who needed a man in my life. My mom is the same way—all she needs is her business and her best friend Ivy. My best friend Becky and I always managed to have fun without stupid boys. Becky and I against the world. Girls rule and boys drool, all that stuff. But now? I can't stop thinking about him and last night.

"You want to stop for a break?" he asks like he can read my mind.

"Sure," I say, trying to sound casual.

He steps off the trail and into a small clearing. He slips his backpack off and sits on a rock, reaching down to untie his shoes. I smile, we're thinking the same thing! I drop my pack and pull my shirt off. As soon as I drop my T-shirt I see him pulling his sock up and twisting it a little before sliding his foot back into his boot. He looks up to find me shirtless, staring at him.

"Oh! Wow, okay, I was just fixing my sock. The elastic must be giving out, and it was sliding down in my boot. Why am I telling you this? Fuck, you're so pretty," he says, standing up and grabbing my waist to pull me into him.

"I don't think there is enough tree cover here for me to do what I want, mind if we head into that grove a little more?" he asks, running his thumb along my cheek.

"Okay. Sure, yeah. I mean if you want to, I thought you were," I say, but he stops my rambling with a passionate kiss.

"I want to," he says. He grabs both our packs and ducks into the trees on the other side of the clearing. I follow him behind a big rock and before he even sets our packs down he says, "I pictured doing this, with you. Out here with nothing but the mountain air between us. There's a boulder like the kind I pictured bending you over." He motions to a mostly flat rock that is about thigh-high to me. "Drop your shorts and put your hands down." His voice is rough and commanding and I like it. Who knew Mr. R could be so bossy.

I immediately do as he asks because I am a trail ho now. I look over my shoulder at him as he moves in behind me, his shorts pulled just low enough to let his dick out. He drags it up and down my center and I spread my legs farther to allow him more access. I arch my back and moan as the tip slips in.

"God, you're so wet, what were you thinking about back there on the trail, Stephanie?" he says as he reaches his hand around to play with my nipple. Thank God this is a thin bra.

"This," I say squirming with pleasure.

"Fuck, why are you so perfect for me?" I hear him mutter and I choose to ignore it. Instead I push my ass back into him, encouraging him to move. We both sigh when he's seated all the way in.

"Jesus, you feel so good," he growls.

"I can't get enough of your huge dick, Corey," I say as he moves faster positioning his hips. I feel his balls slapping me faster and I think neither of us will last long. I thought in the bright daylight, I wouldn't be as brave with the dirty talk but, I just say things like this now. The words tumble out like we have always done this. My moans and comments seem to spur him on. He's hitting that perfect spot and he starts to move faster making us both desperate for release. I feel him try and slow as his breathing grows faster.

"No, don't stop. Fuck me, Corey, I'm so close, please don't stop," I say and that's all it takes for him to unleash on me. He slams into me and I gasp as the orgasm hits me, then him, almost at the same time. I reach back and grapple for him, hoping to keep him as close as possible. My legs are shaking, my chest heaving, gasping for air. He pulls out and spins me, pulling my face to his. He kisses me softly, slowly, passionately and I feel my heart expand as a satisfied moan escapes my lips.

"You are incredible," he says, kissing down my neck. His beard tickles so I giggle then rub the spot.

"You are pretty incredible yourself," I say, looking around for my shirt. I pull my shorts back up. I have never had sex with half my clothes on. Hell, I have had sex with Corey more in the last two days than I have my whole life. It just keeps getting better too. It has to be the mountain air.

We put ourselves back together and pop back out onto the trail. I hear voices behind us and so does Corey. I hear him chuckle and he says quietly, "Guess we finished just in time."

"No shit," I way with a laugh. The voices grow louder.

"It is not 'excuse me, as I kiss this guy' I don't care what you say," a woman's voice says. It's followed by another almost yelling, "Well, what the hell is he saying then?"

I stop and turn to smile at Corey. "It's Barbara and Grace," I whisper. "Last chance to hide and let them pass us."

"Nah, maybe we will make better time if I can't pull you off the trail and slam my giant dick into you again." He waggles his eyebrows at me and I shove him. Of course he is solid muscle and doesn't budge. He just leans down and kisses me sweetly.

"I knew it! Pay up!" I hear over Corey's shoulder

"You said by Mount Shasta. I don't owe you shit." Barbara chuckles.

"That's not fair, I still called it! I get the last chocolate bar. A bet is a bet!" Grace says and they both stop on the trail and smile at us.

"Hello" I wave feeling a little bit like I was caught doing something I shouldn't.

"What's up, ladies?" Corey says with an easy smile.

"You, from the looks of things. Don't you have any decency?" Barbara points to Corey's pants and we both bend to look, causing both women to roar with laughter.

"Nothing much, hiking and arguing like we do, what's up with you two? You look guilty." Grace peers at us, her eyes shifting back and forth.

"Us too, I mean we're hiking, we aren't arguing or anything. Just left Tahoe a while ago and now we are moving on, up the trail. Hiking. You know?" I say wiping my hands down my legs.

Barbara makes a noise in her throat like she knows what we just did behind that rock and Corey thankfully changes the subject.

"What song are we arguing about today?" he asks.

"I think it's by Aeroplane."

"AEROSMITH. Jesus, Grace. It's actually by Jimi Hendrix. I can't believe you didn't know that." Barbara shakes her head and starts off again, squeezing past us on the trail.

"Oh! I know that song!" I say, pleased that I have this one. All the other songs they have argued about, I was unfamiliar with. "I think they are saying 'excuse me while I kiss the sky' but we can see if Mr. R and R thinks I am right?"

"Yep, that's it. We sang a cover of that when I was still in the band," he says, and I notice the slight drop in his shoulders.

"Now see, that makes more sense. I didn't think radio stations would play a song about two dudes macking," Grace says.

"But they will play songs about reaching down between my legs to ease the skirt back," Barbara says, making Grace yell. "That is not how the song goes and you know it."

"That's how I sing it," she says with a wink.

I laugh even though I have no idea what song they are talking about. I really need to increase my music library. Being away from my mom might be good for me. I grew up listening to her stuff and even in high school didn't find bands I liked as much as the music she would play around the house. Saturdays were for cleaning and CCR.

CREEDENCE CLEARWATER REVIVAL was her all-time favorite. The music that came on the radio in the car always caused her to sigh and change the channel. I like Def Leppard and a few other rock bands but can really only say I know the lyrics to a handful of the newer songs.

"What's your favorite song, ladies?" I shout out as we all continue down the trail.

"Rocket Man!" they both yell and I have to admit, I am surprised.

"What about you, Corey?" I ask, and he reaches up to scratch his beard. The trail is wide enough here to walk side by side and I am enjoying the occasional brush of his hand against mine.

"All-time favorite song? Probably CCR's 'Have You Ever Seen the Rain?' What about you?" He looks down at me like he didn't just say my favorite song.

"Um, you won't believe me if I say. How about my second favorite?" I ask.

"Tell me. Is it that song they were fighting about?" he asks, nudging me with his elbow.

I bring my hands to my face and rub. "Same as you. I am not just saying that either, I grew up with CCR on in the background like constantly, like they were the soundtrack to my childhood. My mom loves them."

"Damn. Okay, How do you feel about the Eagles?" he asks.

"Love them. All the songs. I used to listen to the Hotel California Album when I was studying for tests. Then when I was stuck I would just sing the songs in my head and the answers would just come to me." I shrug, like this is how everyone's brain works.

"Did you get good grades in school?" he asks, and I contemplate lying.

"Sure, you know I was kind of a nerd though, didn't have much else going on," I say, thinking that sounds better than telling him I'm obsessed with learning new things and got straight As in high school and college. I also got a perfect score on both the CSET and CBEST, the tests required to teach in California, not that it matters. Apparently they don't hire teachers based on that, just on if they look older than their students.

"How about you? Was school your thing, or were you busy rocking out with the band you were in?" I ask and notice a slight shift in his gait.

"I did alright in school, I mean mostly As. I am not going to tell you the class I got a C in, you won't like me anymore," Corey says.

"Corey! Did you struggle with history?" I ask, not hiding the delight in my voice.

"All those dates got me confused. I couldn't remember which thing happened first!" He throws his hands up in the air. "When we studied one part, I would do great, you know? But then at midterms or the end of the year, there were always questions like 'What happened first, the War of 1812 or the Spanish-American War?'"

"War of 1812, the Spanish American War was like 1898," I say without having to think.

"So it was at least in the 1800s? See? That's why I got confused. I mean who can remember that many dates?" He throws his hands in the air and just about knocks me off the trail.

"Easy there, big guy. I am kind of top heavy here with all my water still full." I laugh as I scramble to stay on my feet.

"Shit, sorry, Yoda. When they find you at the bottom of the ravine should I blame the War of 1812 or the Spanish-American War?"

"How about just say that I died on the Old Oregon Trail. That is more my speed," I say finally gaining my stride again.

"Oh my God, did you play that game?" He asks. He has to let me go in front because the trail has narrowed again.

"Yeah, well at school. We don't have a computer at home. My mom is kind of anti-technology. But in the computer lab in high school and even a little in college I played. I died of dysentery almost every time," I say.

"Same here! I wiped out an entire family and lost an ox in the river. My brother had convinced me it was tied to real life somehow, so I felt like I had murdered people. I wasn't the sharpest kid I guess." He laughs and so do I.

"Are you and your brother close?" I ask and when I hear nothing behind me I stop and turn around.

"Corey, are you and your brother close?" I say again because he must have not heard me the first time.

"We used to be, I lost him," he chokes out.

"Oh, my God. I am so sorry! When?" I ask as I reach for his hands.

"Earlier this year," he says into the dirt.

"Is that why you are on this hike? Is it in his memory or something? Like something you thought you would do together before he died?" I say and his head snaps up to me.

"He didn't die! Jesus, Stephanie." He shakes his head like *I* am being dramatic.

"You said you lost him, what else was I supposed to think!" I screech.

"Oh, right, sorry. No, I lost him to a girl. He went to Europe. Jolly old England to be exact," he says. His eyes narrow and his lip twitches up in a snarl of sorts.

"Well." I pause, not sure why this is such a big deal. Of course I don't have siblings so maybe it is a big deal. "That must be difficult. Is he older or younger?" I ask, turning back around to continue down the trail. He is kind of a drama queen. Maybe that is why I will hate him. It's a good reason. No one likes a drama queen.

"Younger, but only by about five minutes. We're identical twins," he explains.

"Oh, no wonder you are feeling like you lost him! Is this the longest you've been apart?" I ask, kind of relieved there's more to the story.

"Yeah, I thought we would always just be together, but then he met her, and she was all that mattered. I guess I was hoping this hike would help me find myself without him, you know?"

"I think we are all looking for a part of ourselves out here," I agree, and we fall silent. We hike on for a while like that, neither of us feeling like we have to fill the silence. It's nice.

I haven't been paying attention to how long we have been walking since we've been talking so much, and when I glance at my watch, I am surprised to see it's just past one.

"Hey, want to stop and eat? It's after one," I say.

"No shit? Wow, you really make time fly, Yoda," he says with a chuckle.

"Well, we weren't hiking the whole time. I don't know how long that trail break was earlier," I say, wanting to remind him of our passionate boulder experience.

He laughs and says, "That couldn't have taken too much time. Thank God I have a magical dick because I can't last long with you."

"Could you two discuss your sex life a little more quietly? I am trying to enjoy my sandwich," Grace says poking her head up from behind a rock.

"And I am taking a nap!" Barbara yells.

"Shit, sorry," Corey says and I blush.

"You owe me that chocolate bar," Grace says and Barbara laughs.

"It's not Mount Shasta! You were right, but your timing was shit. How about half?" Barbara asks.

"Deal," Grace says, and I hear a kiss. We walk past the boulder and find the two snuggled into each other.

"What were you betting on?" Corey asks as he sits across from them and digs into his bag for some food.

"When you two would get together," Barbara says.

"What?" I spit out.

Barbara shrugs and Grace says, "Sure, I mean even Trail Terry saw the sparks flying. He thought you were already together, but we set him straight."

I flinch at the memory of Trail Terry and his knowing wink. God, I am glad that long-haired hippie is on his way to Mexico with my secret.

mile 940.6

"DAMN. I thought I was pretty stealthy with my attraction. You mean everyone at that camp below Tahoe knew?" I laugh as Grace and Barbara both nod. "I wasn't even sure back then, why in the hell did you think we would get together?" I press for more information as I pull my one and only deli sandwich from my pack. I notice Stephanie spreading peanut butter and jelly on a piece of bread and it makes me smile.

"That." Barbara points at me.

"What?" I ask, looking around. I notice Stephanie's lip between her teeth as she tries to hold the piece of bread while putting away her jar of peanut butter and jelly. She has a dab of jelly on her cheek and I want to stand up, walk over and lick it off her face.

"The way you watch her. She's making a sandwich for Chrissake, not stripping!" Grace says with a chuckle.

Stephanie looks up at the three of us and with a full mouth says, "What?"

"Mr. R and R looks at you like he wants to gobble you up, he always has," Barbara says with a laugh. "First day he came up behind you, I thought he was going to fall off that ledge. That's when we made the bet."

"You two need to get a new hobby," I tell them.

"Listen, arguing about song lyrics and predicting other people's love lives are all we have. Don't take that away from us," Grace says. She stands up and Barbara watches her stretch.

I guess that is what I look like when I am looking at Stephanie. Love in my eyes, or at the very least lust. She has something over me, I haven't quite figured it out yet, but damn, she is incredible.

"How long have you two been together?" Stephanie asks.

"Ten years," they say at the same time.

"Met in college. She and I were assigned the same dorm room because we were both on sports teams. I played softball and Grace here ran track. I guess they knew what they were doing because it didn't take more than two nights before we pushed our beds together." Barbara winks at me and I look over at Grace who is rolling her eyes.

"It was longer than two nights! You make me sound easy! It was after I went and watched you pitch. That was at least a month into our semester. Don't be making shit up," Grace says.

"I like to keep things real, you wanted me the minute you walked into our tiny little dorm room!" Barbara says.

"She was unpacking and had a variety of vibrators that she laid out on the bed. I was curious." Grace shrugs.

Barbara laughs and points at Grace. "I offered to show you, and you said no. If I remember correctly."

"That is correct. I did say no. To be honest I had never seen a dick or a vibrator and I walk into my new dorm room, barely out of my parents' home, feeling like I could finally spread my wings and here is this girl." She gestures to Barbara and smiles. "She's just confident and proud and like, look at all the dicks I have."

Stephanie laughs and covers her mouth. Damn she is cute.

"Well, it wasn't your dick collection that got me," Grace says, holding out her hand to help Barbara up off the ground. "It was your vast knowledge of all things music." She pulls her into a kiss and I can't help but stare.

"Damn, you two are so fucking cute," I say.

"Thanks, we think so. If we make it to Canada without killing each other, we're going to get married," Barbara says.

"Married? Can you do that?" I ask and Stephanie shoots me a look.

"What? I mean is it legal?" I clarify.

"It's a fair question. No, it's not legal, but we're going to have a ceremony and make it official to each other. I mean, that's all that matters to me. I know Grace wants more than that, but..." Barbara shrugs, stopping before she finishes the thought.

"I just want everyone to know I am yours," Grace says, wrapping her arms around Barbara.

"Honey, they know." She pulls back and kisses Grace.

"We are going to head out. See you on the trail, I'm sure." Barbara says with a wave. We watch as they help each other into their packs and head off on the trail. I move closer to Stephanie. She has finished her sandwich, but she still has jelly on her cheek. I weigh my options and throw caution to the wind. I lean in and kiss her then grab her face gently and run my tongue up her cheek like a mother cat cleaning her young.

She screams and tries to pull away. "Oh my God! What are you doing? What is wrong with you? Don't lick me!" She is laughing and almost falls off her little rock as she tries to get away from me.

"Seriously, what is wrong with you?" she says again, and I can't help but laugh.

"You had jelly on your face. What else was I going to do, Yoda?"

"Tell me? Point to it like a normal person?" She rubs her fingers over the spot.

"It looked delicious," I say, and it comes out like a growl. She turns her big beautiful eyes to me and a slow smile spreads across her face.

"You are insatiable," she says, then stands and steps in between my knees. "But so am I." She tugs off her shirt and drops it on the pine-needle-covered forest floor.

I reach up and cup her breasts wondering how we will make it to Oregon on time.

RETURNING to the trail after a delicious lunch and an even better dessert, I watch her walk on ahead and feel like the luckiest bastard on the planet.

We decided to camp just before Truckee, because we didn't want to share a campsite with anyone else. By we, I mostly mean me. I don't want to share this woman with anyone for the next month. It's almost July, so that means I have four weeks to get to know her and try to find a reason to hate her so I can let her go, or find a way to convince her to stay with me.

I sit on a rock and watch her expertly set up her tiny little tent. I have one, I just prefer to sleep under the stars most of the time. I did set up my tent once or twice in the first hundred miles, because I wanted to get away from the bugs, but now I don't even notice them.

"Want to share my tent? It said on the box it was a two-person, but we are like a person and a half." She shrugs and smiles.

"I would love to share your tent, Yoda." *For the rest of my life* floats through my head and I rub my face. Jesus. This is going to be rough.

She opens the flap and ducks in, carrying her bag with her. I can see her moving around in there with the sun behind her illuminating her tiny frame. It's like an old-fashioned peep show and I am into it. I can see her lift off her shirt then shimmy out of her shorts. I hear her grunt, then the very sexy shadow topples over.

"Shit, forgot to take off my boots."

I laugh louder than I mean to and walk over to the tent. "Need any help?" I ask.

"No, you and your giant body need to wait out there till I get situated, then you can come in."

"Giant body? I am offended. I'm a regular-sized human, you're just freakishly short," I say.

"While that may be true, we will fit in here together if we are lying down, and that is it." I hear from inside the tent.

"Okay, I'll just go back to my rock and sit. Take your time," I tell her.

I dig into my pack and pull out a snack. We will need to eat dinner before we turn in for the night, but I am not sure what she wants to eat. I bought quite a few shareable items because even if she doesn't want me to worry, I have no idea how she is carrying that heavy pack on her tiny frame.

I pull out two packages of my favorite Mountain House stew and my crackers, setting them next to me. I gather rocks and make a fire pit to cook the soup and almost have it finished when Stephanie pops her head out of the tent holding the same pouch.

"Want to share my stew? I was thinking how good that sounded, but I only have one pouch." She looks down at my fire and my stew pouches next to it and smiles.

"Great minds think alike, I guess," I say with a wink.

"It is kind of making me nervous, you know?" she says. When she doesn't elaborate, I raise an eyebrow. She tosses her stew back in the tent and steps out throwing her hands in the air. "You know, we just get along so well and have this amazing chemistry. I just don't get it."

"I know. I'm trying to ignore all the signs since the universe seems to think we're only allowed to be together for a month," I say. There is no point in pretending I am not totally into this girl. I am sure she knows.

"I hate the universe," she says and plops down on the ground next to me.

"Me too, but we have more time. Let's get to know each other more. I am sure you have qualities I will grow to hate," I joke, and she gives me a half smile.

"Okay, but childhood stuff. I don't really want to get to know awesome adult Corey. Tell me things about how you picked your nose a lot as a kid, or that you were one of those audio-visual kids that would push the film projector around to each class." She snaps her fingers then adds, "No! I know, you played football in high school and college!"

"You hate football?" I ask, totally confused.

"With a passion, so if you played, that will really help me to hate you a little bit." She pinches her fingers together in the universal symbol for small.

"Damn, I played baseball and ran track. I am not built for football," I say.

She lets out a big sigh and leans back on her hands. "I fucking love baseball. Please don't tell me you were a pitcher. Say you were shortstop or rode the bench." She is watching me as I open the cans and dump them into the cast-iron skillet.

"I was totally not a pitcher. I definitely didn't get a scholarship to UCLA and play for a year, not pitching. I wasn't rated best in the league in high school with most strikeouts." I stir slowly, glancing at her to see her reaction.

"Damn, that's too bad. Fuck, why are you so perfect?" she says, blowing out a puff of air.

"Okay I was totally messing with you. I did play ball, but like right field, and no scholarships. I had a pretty terrible time at bat. I think we are safe in me not being the sports God of your dreams. I played guitar in my band, well my brother's band. So that was really my focus."

"You say that like if you had applied yourself, you would have been a better baseball player. Is that true? Can I be disappointed that you are not good at applying yourself?" Her eyes are narrowed as she gives me the once-over.

"Nah, I tried. I busted my ass my whole junior year and I still sucked at hitting. Codey got all the athleticism. Pretty sure he stole some of mine in the womb."

She tosses a small pine cone at me and laughs. "That is not how it works," she says.

"Okay whatever you say, but I disagree. Hey, grab your bowl and pull mine out of the pack there, if you don't mind." I motion to my pack.

She gets up and goes back into her tent for her tin bowl and spork, then pulls mine from my bag. She holds each while I fill them then waits for me to sprinkle the crushed crackers over each one. We settle into a peaceful silence as we eat.

I can hear voices coming up the trail and I curse my bad luck. We are kind of tucked in off the trail, and maybe they are determined to get into Truckee for the night. Hopefully they will keep going.

"Hey! This looks like a great place to stop for the night!" the tall thin man says. His friend thankfully disagrees.

"No, I told you we stop in Truckee and you're getting that wound looked at. If I have to see that nasty cut for even one more day, I am just going to push you off the nearest cliff."

"You're a pussy. It's not that bad," Tall Dude says.

"How would you know? It's on the back of your leg. Trust me, the thing looks infected," Angry Friend yells out.

"Chill dude, okay we will go on into Truckee." Their voices trail off as they get further away and I hear Stephanie let out a breath.

"Thank God. I don't want to see whatever they were talking about," she says. She is scraping the bottom of her bowl savoring the last bite.

"Do you want more?" I ask and she shakes her head.

"Nah, I'm full. You can finish it off," she says and she stands to rinse out her bowl.

"Why don't you tell me something awful about yourself while I eat?" I say.

She raises an eyebrow at me and says, "Well there are so many things, I am not sure where to begin."

"What do your parents do? That seems like a safe first date kind of question," I say.

"Oh, first date huh? Okay. I would say we are about at our fourth date, but whatever." She tosses another pine cone at me and I catch that one. It's tiny and perfect and reminds me of her, so I tuck it in my bag when she looks away.

"My mom owns a flower shop near San Diego. She and my father never married, so I um, don't really know him. Not sure what he does with his life, or if he is even alive. I don't think she ever told him about me." The way she says that makes me think she has said it a lot.

"Oh, wow. Do you want to find him?" I ask.

"I used to, when I was younger. We did a family tree project in sixth grade and I had a pretty sad tree, it was more of a limb. Think Charlie Brown's Christmas tree, anyway, that made me want to know more, but my mom was pretty vague about him. I know his name, but that is it."

"Do you have his last name?" I ask, and she shakes her head.

"Nope, my mom's name. Don't worry, I won't tell you. Wouldn't want you tracking me down in a year when you can't forget how awesome I am," she says, and I try to laugh. "My father's name is Brian Tuck. My mom met him on her solo road trip. She said they spent a wild night together and then she moved on. She didn't know she had gotten pregnant with me until she was back home."

"Oh man, that's nuts," I say, unsure what else I can say about that. It sounds eerily similar to what is happening here. I bet that Brian dude would have loved to know he had a kid. Especially an awesome kid like Stephanie.

"Hey, why do you look so sad?" she asks, taking my empty bowl from me. She tips a small amount of water in and swishes it around before using her little scrub pad to clean the soup out.

"I just feel kind of bad for him. He never got to know you, or even know he had a kid. What if you were the only kid he ever had?" I say.

"Yeah, I thought of that too, but what can I do? I mean I could look in phone books when I am near where she traveled on that trip, but that's a hell of a cold call. Excuse me, are you the Brian that had sex with a woman named Rose twenty-some-odd years ago? You are? Guess what, Dad?" She laughs and so do I.

"Yeah, that would be a hell of a phone call to get," I agree.

"My mom is a free spirit, she didn't ever marry or even really date. Her one true love is her flower shop. I think if she hadn't accidentally gotten pregnant, she would have been happy being just a shop owner." She pauses and looks at me. "You know what's really weird?"

"What?" I ask.

"Her favorite time of year is spring and summer when all the weddings happen. Like she loves weddings so much. I never understood that."

"Well, maybe she just sees the possibilities, maybe it wasn't for her, but she loves to see the happy couples," I offer.

"Maybe, anyway, that's my big reveal. What about you, what do your parents do?" she asks.

"They're both teachers. My mom teaches kindergarten, and my dad is a special education teacher at a high school. Made for pretty great summers as a kid," I say and I see her put her face in her hands.

"Damn it, Corey. I was hoping they were like investment bankers or sold insurance or something. I love teachers. Teachers are the best people in the world. You are not helping me out here."

I laugh and adjust my pack so I can lean back on it against the boulder. It's a lot cooler up here than before we got into Tahoe and I glance up into the fading night sky. Clouds are forming.

"We might get some rain tonight. Good thing you set your tent up," I say.

"Yeah, I was thinking that too. You're lucky I offered to share!"

"I am lucky," I say, and we lock eyes. Damn, those blue eyes are going to haunt me. Her lips part and I know she is about to say some-thing, but she stops. Instead she stands and walks over to me and straddles my lap. I wrap my arms around her waist and get lost in her eyes. She is studying my face letting her gaze travel over my beard, my eyes, and nose. She reaches up and tucks some hair behind my ear then trails her finger down my neck.

We don't talk, I just make small circles with my thumbs under the hem of her T-shirt as she strokes my face. She scrapes her fingers through my beard and I feel like I should purr. I want to tell her how good it feels but I can't speak. I just lean back and let her touch me.

Her hands move up into my hair and around the back along my neck. She touches where my bitchin' rattail used to be, and I think I see a cloud cross her eyes. I still think she is responsible for my loss, but to be honest I don't even care anymore.

She gently massages my scalp and I feel my eyes grow heavy. There is something about having my hair played with that has always made me sleepy. I let my eyes fall shut and she continues to rub my scalp and then my shoulders. She has tiny hands, but man, she has some strength in those fingers. I moan and I feel her shift closer on my lap.

"If you keep making noises like that I won't be able to finish this massage," she whispers in my ear and my whole body erupts in chills.

I grab her hips a little more firmly and slide her toward me. One little whisper in my ear and I am uncomfortably hard. I want her to feel what she does to me and when she makes contact, her hips start to move. She tosses her head back and rotates her hips over me, making small deliberate circles.

I am one second away from ripping her clothes off when we hear a loud crack and the whole sky lights up. The boom that followed was way too soon after the flash. She scrambles off me and dives toward her tent. I grab my bag and follow her, not worrying about the small cook fire.

Just after she zips the flap the downpour hits. The rain is pelting the tent like golf balls bouncing on the fairway.

"Holy shit, that was close!" I laugh.

"That was! Do you remember that storm that caught us just after Yosemite? I thought for sure my tent was going to just lift up and blow away with me inside!"

"Fuck yeah, that was a bad one, but it was over quick. I was really grateful that ranger had told me it was going to rain. I think that was only the third time I used my tent."

"Why don't you use your tent?" she asks.

"I don't know, it's nice to see the stars. I am also a lazy motherfucker and usually when I have got to a camp spot, I am just too tired to care."

"Well, there you go. That's something I can hate about you! Thanks Corey. I was really starting to think you were perfect."

I scoot my backpack over against hers and pull off my sleeping bag. Mine is a big thick two-person bag, another reason I have been okay outside. I see she has the mummy style and I swear it must be a child's.

"Nice sleeping bag. Does Barbie mind that you're borrowing it?" I ask.

"Ha ha. I was hoping to share yours tonight. If we used mine I think you'd only get a leg in—" She stops talking mid-sentence and her eyes fly open wide. Her mouth makes this cute little O and I swear she squeaks.

"What? Are you okay?" I ask.

"I'm good, great actually. Just tired." She stretches her arms in an exaggerated yawn and I cock an eyebrow at her.

NINE
STEPHANIE

mile 1040.6

CRAP. I totally forgot that stupid rattail is in the bottom of my sleeping bag. I almost offered to unzip it and lay the darn thing flat as extra padding.

He's looking at me funny. Oh God. He knows.

I tried stretching and I don't think he bought it. I look around desperate for a distraction. He asks again, "Are you okay?"

I whip off my shirt and unhook my bra faster than the time I fell into an ants' nest.

I put my hands on my hips and try to be seductive. I smile and bat my eyelashes at him. Problem is it's pretty dark in here. Thankfully another flash of lightening hits and he sees me. Before it goes dark again I see him pull off his shirt. I feel him crawl toward me.

"Wait, let's get your sleeping bag laid out first." I kick my bag out of the way and try and dissolve the braid with my thoughts.

"Okay yeah, good idea." Corey grabs his bag and unrolls it. My eyes are adjusting after the flash, and I can see his broad muscular back. His muscles are flexing and moving as he adjusts in the small space with his bag. The rain is really coming down and I wonder about the guy with the infected cut. I hope they were able to get under shelter. I feel momentarily guilty then wonder why I am thinking about that while this very sexy man is in my tent.

I scoot out of the way so he can get the bag down, sitting in the corner to take off my boots. He sighs and lays back, putting his arms behind his head.

"Come here you tiny, beautiful thing," I hear from the darkness.

I slide my shorts off and crawl over to him, my seductive ways lost to the pitch black night. At least he can't see that I am still sweating. All I can think of is that thin, soft braid coiled in the bottom of my bag like a sad little snake waiting to strike.

I shudder.

"Oh baby, come here, are you cold?" he says in a deep sexy voice.

"Yes, I am chilly. So cold. Yes," I say weirdly. Fuck, I am so glad it's dark.

"Look, I don't know why you are being weird all of a sudden, but get over it so I can ravage you," he says close to my ear.

My breath catches and my worries dissolve. "Okay, right."

I slide into the bag next to him and he pulls the flap over both of us. He runs his hands up and down my body, warming me. The silky snake braid starts to fade from my mind and thoughts of ecstasy flood my senses. God, his hands are amazing. I feel prickly, like electricity is dancing over my skin everywhere he touches me. I wonder if he feels it too. This connection between us, it's something.

I wish for the millionth time that I could continue whatever this is. My heart aches and before I can stop it a tear slides out of my eye. Then to my horror I sniffle, followed by another tear. Damn it.

"Are you crying?" Corey says in my ear. His voice is soft and sweet, like velvet caressing my cheek.

"Maybe," I whisper.

"Why, baby? What's wrong?" he whispers back and if he wasn't so close to my ear I wouldn't have heard him over the rain.

"I don't want to say," I mumble.

"Are you thinking it's not fair that we can't continue this? Because I am. I've never felt this way before," Corey says, and I stop breathing.

I roll up onto him and strain my eyes to see his beautiful face. "Me either," I say against his mouth. I kiss his lips, loving the way his beard tickles me. He responds and wraps his arms around me, pulling me even tighter against him. I want to melt into him. I want to be a part of his body, dive in and get lost. I don't want this to end, not tonight, not ever.

He reaches down and squirms to get out of his shorts and I try and move off him so he can, but he stops me. He holds me in place and growls in my ear. "No, you're not going anywhere. I need you on top of me. I need to feel your weight on me, pressing into me. I am going to make love to you, slowly and thoroughly. Stephanie, God what are you doing to me?"

I combust, melt, dissolve, fight the urge to tell him I think I am in love with him. I wiggle out of my underwear then settle on him enjoying the feel of his skin on mine. I spread my legs a little, reaching back to guide him into me. He has his large hands on my hips pushing me down and my nipples drag against his chest in the most delicious way. I roll my hips, encouraging him in further, and he starts to move me up and down his length in a more deliberate way. I move up a little and kiss him as he holds my hips and lifts into me over and over. It's slow, calculated, and delicious. My mind goes blank and my body takes over, moving in time with his. I feel his hands move up and he cups my face, kissing me so passionately I lose my breath. Lightning flashes and I see him. His eyes are open and staring into mine. I suck in a breath, overwhelmed with the way he's looking at me. This isn't like what we did in the hotel, or behind that boulder. This is different. Intense. Meaningful. I think about him, how he feels against me, inside me and I stare down into his eyes.

Even if it's dark I know he is looking back. We kiss as our movements become more urgent and I feel my orgasm hit just as Corey grips me and shudders.

"Fuck Stephanie, oh God, Christ." He pulls me into him, wrapping his arms around me as I continue to quake. I can't pull away, I can't look at him. Instead I press my chest to his, feeling his heart hammering out *don't leave, don't leave, don't leave.* Maybe that's my heart, maybe it's his. I don't know.

I don't even realize I have fallen asleep until I hear the silence that comes after a downpour. The early morning sun is making shadows dance across the tent and I roll, sliding to Corey's side. He tightens his grip on me and moans a protest.

"Where do you think you're going, Yoda?" he asks in a gravelly morning voice.

"Just giving you some space. I think I slept on top of you all night."

"Did you hear me complaining? You weigh like a pound and I liked feeling your heartbeat," he says as he rolls toward me.

I turn to my side and snuggle into him as he wraps his arms around me again. This is nice. I can't think about when this ends. I am just going to enjoy it while I can. All of the ifs run through my head as I let my fingers dance through his chest hair. If I knew I had that job, I could tell him where I'd be. If he wasn't stopping in Bend we would have more time. If I knew what my life held I could try and hold on to this wonderful man. If. If. If.

"I can hear your brain working, Yoda. Relax and enjoy. We have a whole month together. We will figure this out," he says, and I nod.

Once the sun is a little higher in the sky, we crawl out of our warm cocoon and I unzip the tent. The earth smells clean and fresh and there are chipmunks and birds scurrying around. The moss on the trees looks extra green and I wish I could capture a piece to remind me of him.

· · ·

WHEN HE IS out of the tent I go back in and roll up my sleeping bag. I think about handing him the severed braid, but since we will be parting ways soon, I decide to just keep it. I glance around my tent before setting my bag outside. This little space has been my home for the past three months. I can't believe how little I need out here.

In college my dorm felt oppressively small. This tent is only a little bigger than Corey. That is all I need. Frustration rips through me again and I fight off the tears. When I step out of the tent I don't see Corey. His backpack is leaning against a nearby tree but he isn't around.

I bend and start to dismantle my tent pulling the poles out one by one and folding them up. I lift and shake the whole thing trying to rid the last bits of water from the top. I wonder when we are heading out. I'd like to give this some more time to dry out. I put my hands on my hips and look around for a place to string a line to drape the tent over. I should have waited to take it down, let it dry a little more.

"Why do you look like an angry Tinker Bell?" I hear from over my shoulder.

"My tent is still a little wet and I already pulled the poles. I was going to drape it over a line but I'm not sure where to set that up."

Corey drops an armload of sticks into his fire ring from last night.

"You work on getting that to light and I will hang the tent. I have some clips in my bag that will hold it up." He starts over to his back-pack and digs around until he comes out with a small bag with a clothesline and some heavy-duty clips. I watch as he strings the line the clips my tent to hang. With it hanging flat, the water runs right off.

"This wind will help dry it out in no time. How's that fire coming along?" he says and turns to see me warming my hands on the already growing fire.

"Damn, woman. You are good," he says and chuckles.

"Thanks!" I smile at him like a damn fool while he pulls out his cooking things. I reach in my bag and get out what I want to eat for breakfast, thinking since there is a fire going I will have something warm instead of my dried apples and granola bar with peanut butter. I opt for another of my Mountain House meals. By the time we finish eating, the tent is dry, so I fold it up and get it back into the tent bag. That and my sleeping bag are finally in place on top of my backpack, and I duck out to use the bathroom.

When I return, Corey is standing on the trail ready to go. He smiles at me and my stomach flips over.

"Ready, Yoda?"

"Ready, Mr. R."

We walk and chat about nothing and everything. Occasionally, when the trail is wide and we can walk side by side, we hold hands. I don't even notice the passing of time, let alone the miles we have gone until we make it to a paved road. Corey stops and stretches his arms above his head.

"Want to cross, then take a break?" he asks.

"Sure. I could use some water. All that talking has me more thirsty than normal," I say. Corey grabs my hand and squeezes and as we cross, we notice a person in a car parked by the trailhead. We watch as she climbs out. She puts her hand on her forehead to shield her eyes as we walk toward her.

I squint back at her, I know her. Shit. What is she doing here?

"Stephanie! Oh my God I found you! It is you!" Ivy runs toward me and tries to hug me but only manages to press herself into my front, unable to get her arms around me and my pack.

"Ivy? What are you doing here?" I ask, panic filling my lungs instead of air.

"It's your mom, honey. I need you to come with me," she says grabbing at my hands.

"No, tell me what's wrong first!" I yell. I feel sick, the pine trees waving in the wind throwing off my center of gravity.

Ivy wrings her hands and looks at me, then Corey. "She had a fall, she, um, broke her hip. But Stephanie, honey I just—" She pauses and looks at the ground then up at me. She swallows hard and I see tears in her eyes. "There is more, but I—" She looks at her watch and says, "I can tell you on the way. We have to get to Reno so we can catch the next flight. We don't have any time."

"Go, Stephanie. It's okay. Go," Corey says in a small voice.

"Okay, yeah, I mean I guess I have to. God, Corey, I am so sorry."

"Don't apologize, Just go. Be careful. I lo—" he starts to say, but I put my lips on his before he can finish. I can't hear that. Not now. Not as I am about to lose him.

"Be safe Corey. Mr. R, Doc. Thanks for everything. I will never forget you," I whisper against his lips.

"I'll never forget you Stephanie, Yoda, Thumbelina," he says.

I turn and see Ivy with the trunk open waiting for me and my backpack. I pull it off and shove it in the small rental car trunk slamming the lid. I feel lighter without the weight of my pack, yet I can barely make it to the open passenger door. Corey walks over and leans in to kiss me, letting his lips linger for only a second before he closes the door and slaps the roof of the car. Ivy pulls away and just like that my heart is ripped out of my chest. I feel it tumble on the asphalt behind the car.

"What happened?" I say, turning to my mom's longtime best friend. This must be bad if she came all this way to find me. I mean, right? She wouldn't pull me off the trail and away from what could be the love of my life for a broken bone.

"Honey. Your mom has bone cancer. That's what the doctors say, I mean the tests all show that." She stops and takes a breath, gripping the steering wheel like it had done her wrong. I wait because none of this is making any sense, and I hope she will tell me it's all a mistake. "She fell off a step stool, at the flower shop, you know the one she painted with all the roses?" Ivy says like any of that matters.

"Bone cancer? What? How? She wasn't sick, she isn't sick. I just talked to her!" I shriek. There is no other way to describe how my voice sounds. Shrill, terrified.

"Honey, I know. She didn't know. She's been complaining of aches and pains, you know, but nothing severe. Her back has been hurting for the last six months. The doctor said it's riddled with tumors." Ivy's voice catches at that and I look at her. Her eyes are puffy and red-rimmed. A tear slips out and slides down her cheek. She doesn't bother to wipe it away and soon another tear is racing down her cheek. I watch as they fall on her leg. I have never in my life seen Ivy cry. I've seen my mom cry, not a lot but a few times. Ivy is the rock. She's who took me for stitches when I fell off my bike. She's the one who would pull the splinters from my hand or put the bandages on my scuffed knees. Seeing her cry makes something inside me start to unfurl.

"I am so glad I found you. I met some women at the trailhead that said you were behind them, but I had no idea if they were right. God, honey." She shakes her head and grips the steering wheel even tighter. Her knuckles are white now. White knuckles and tear-stained cheeks that make my stomach lurch.

"Barbara and Grace," I say softly. I will never see them again, or Corey. My head is starting to hurt, and my chest feels tight. I squeeze my eyes shut and ask, "Ivy, is she going to die?"

She glances at me then back at the road staring straight ahead. She squares her shoulders and shakes her head a little, like she is steeling herself. "I think so, honey. It's really bad. I am so sorry." Her voice is low and tight.

We ride the rest of the way in silence, Ivy fighting a steady stream of tears and traffic, and me lost in my own pain and regret. Why did I leave her? Why did I think this stupid hike was a good idea? I lost three months with her. Three months I will never get back, three months that only brought me someone who I'll never see again. Someone I didn't even get to really say goodbye to. I close my eyes as we enter the airport parking lot. Ivy winds the car through the maze of a parking lot to the rental car return and pulls into an open slot. I get out and walk to the trunk to grab my pack. Thoughts race through my mind, bouncing around like a pinball machine, minus the fun flashing lights. I adjust the pack and wonder do I check this? Take it on board with me? Do I have enough room on my credit card for a ticket?

Ivy is talking to a man in a bright yellow shirt. She hands him the keys and he gives her a hug. She has that effect on everyone. She could meet someone and know their life story in two seconds. That rental car guy will probably send her a Christmas card every year from now on.

She looks back at me and gives me a weak smile. "Ready honey?"

"Yep," I say, noting how far away my voice sounds.

We walk into the airport and Ivy leads us to the Delta ticket counter.

"Two tickets to San Diego. Next available flight, please."

"We have one leaving in twenty minutes, or the next one is not until six tonight," the lady says and Ivy lets her shoulders relax a bit. "We will take the first one."

"Okay, I have seats left on that flight," the woman at the counter says.

I stop listening and reach into my pack to pull out my wallet. I hand Ivy my credit card but she waves me away. Instead she hands me a tag for my backpack and I loop it through the top, then watch as an attendant grabs it and places it on a conveyor belt. Dirt clumps fall from the pack and crumble on the smooth black belt. I watch it, mesmerized as it travels further and further away from me. It passes through a flap and I finally blink.

Memories of the last few months flood my vision and I fight tears and nausea. Guilt for wishing I hadn't been found, guilt for missing the last three months with my mom, hit me like a slap to my face and I lean my head back to catch my breath. I notice Ivy has started to walk away from the counter, so I follow her. We make it to the gate and walk right on and take our seats.

Ivy buckles in, then reaches for my hand. I hold her hand and notice her soft clean skin. My hand is tan and calloused and dirty. I am dirty, something I never noticed while hiking. Sitting here in this clean airplane next to Ivy I feel sweaty and gross.

"Are we going straight to the hospital?" I ask.

"No honey, we will go by your house first. I know you probably want to take a shower and change into some clean clothes. After-noons have been kind of rough on your mom so we will wait until after dinner to go," Ivy says then takes a deep breath. "She doesn't know I went to get you. She's going to be really mad at me."

"You did the right thing. I am not mad. Thank you, Ivy," I say wishing that was all true.

She squeezes my hand and I lean against the window, suddenly unable to keep my eyes open against the pain in my heart.

I don't wake when the wheels hit the runway or when the people around me start to stand. Ivy nudges me and for a moment I think I am back in my tent with Corey's strong arms wrapped around me.

My eyes fly open and I look around, disoriented and miserable.

"We're here, honey. Let's go." Ivy and I are two of the last people on the plane. She is standing patiently waiting, her face still showing signs of her crying.

I wipe my hand down my face and say, "Sorry. I didn't mean to fall asleep."

She gives me a small smile and holds out her hand to me. We walk out and make our way to the luggage carousel to wait for my pack. It drops and winds toward me and I feel like I got a piece of myself back. I grab it and lift it off, slipping it back where it belongs, on me.

"Did you go for a hike?" An older gentleman in a suit says a little too close to my ear.

"What the fuck do you think?" I snap, and he rears back.

"Easy there, just asking!" He throws his hands in the air and I feel bad for a moment. That moment doesn't last long as I turn and follow Ivy out to the parking lot.

Midday traffic isn't terrible, and Ivy pulls into our driveway in no time at all. How long have I been off the trail? Where is Corey now? As soon as Ivy drives off and I am alone I burst into tears. She gives me an hour to shower, then she is coming to get me to take me to see my mom. Uncontrollable sobs rack my body and I drop to the floor, unable to take one more step away from him.

TEN
COREY

mile 960.6

MY FEET ARE MOVING, so I know I'm getting farther away from her. God, I can't breathe. What happened? How did I let her slip away? Why didn't I go with her? Yeah, that fucking brilliant idea popped into my head about ten seconds after her taillights dropped over the hill. I yelled and waved my arms and thought about hitchhiking to the airport, but defeat overwhelmed me. Instead I sank down against a tree trunk and cried like a baby for about a half hour. I am pretty sure my wailing called a bear because I heard a lot of brush crashing and crunching. I got up and dragged my sorry ass down the trail, grateful no one passed me. Now as I walk all I can think is how her airplane is probably already over LA. About another hour passes before I make it to a clearing and hear familiar voices.

"Barbara, you can't seriously think it's parsley, sage, rosemary and lime. That doesn't even make sense," I hear Grace say.

. . .

"IT'S LIME. Not time. That makes even less sense. At least a lime is a food like the rest. You can't eat time!" Barbara argues, but I hear the sarcasm in her voice.

"Thyme is a seasoning. It's even spelled differently!" Grace says and she's about to continue when she sees me. "Oh, Corey! Did that lady find Stephanie?"

"Yeah. Her mom is hurt. I guess she's probably on the plane home by now." I drop my backpack and flop on the ground beside them.

"Damn, I am so sorry. Did you at least exchange numbers?" Barbara asks, and I want to scream.

"No, we didn't. I am only going to Bend, and she was going all the way to Canada, so we knew it was a short-term thing. What's the point?" I know how pathetic I sound, but I don't care.

"Oh man, that sucks. You two seemed so good together. Did her mom's girlfriend say what was wrong?" Grace asks.

"Girlfriend?" I ask.

"Well, yeah. She said her partner's daughter was on the trail. I mean, I guess she could have meant something else. I just assumed," Grace says with a shrug.

I think back to what Stephanie had said, about her mom never dating or having a man in her life. Huh. If Rose was gay, that could explain why she didn't try to find Stephanie's father.

"So you're giving up in Bend? Why?" Barbara asks.

"My little sisters are starting at the junior college there with the plan to transfer to OSU as juniors. My parents are retiring and moving to Bend but they aren't sure when they can make the trip up. I promised them I would help the girls get settled before I start my new job," I say. I pull some food from my bag, opting for a peanut butter and jelly sandwich instead of bothering with cooking anything.

"What's your job? Is it in Bend?" Grace asks.

"I'm a math teacher. I got hired at a new high school in a small town just north of Bend. It's called Beaver Valley."

Both women fight off laughter, but Grace is the one who says, "We should totally come check it out. I like beavers a lot."

"Well, I am sure you'd love the high school even more then, damn thing is called Furie High School. Their mascot is a beaver," I say. I take a big bite of my sandwich and feel a dab of jelly leak out on to my cheek. Damn. Everything reminds me of her.

"There is no way that's true!" Barbara howls with laughter.

"Well, no it's spelled different than furry and it's pronounced 'foo-ree' but still, the kids are going to be awful about it I am sure," I say.

"Oh, without a doubt. I mean maybe you could get away with that at an elementary school, but junior high or high school? Fuck no," Grace says.

"I agree," I say before taking another bite. Maybe I'll choke on the peanut butter and die.

"So you're a math teacher huh? I wouldn't have guessed that in a million years," Grace says.

"Yeah, well I taught at a pretty laid-back charter school in the LA area, mostly rich movie star kids, so I was allowed to keep my awesome long hair. They didn't care that I looked like a surfer rocker dude," I explain.

"Yeah, I could see that," Barbara says.

"What do you ladies do?" I ask, wanting to talk about something other than my depressing life.

"I am an orthopedic surgeon and Grace is the head chef at a small winery outside of Napa," Barbara says, and my mouth drops open.

"Holy shit, are you serious?" I sputter.

"What's throwing you? The surgeon part or the chef part?" Barbara says with a smirk.

"Both, I guess." I run my hand through my hair.

"Why? Because we're women?" Grace asks not unkindly.

"No, because you can't be that much older than me! Good Lord, I feel inferior," I shake my head in dismay.

"No, you're just a baby, what are you, twenty-four?" Barbara asks.

"I'm twenty-five, I thought you were like twenty-eight tops," I say.

"I'm thirty-five and Grace is thirty-four. She is only four months older than me but likes to pretend she's a lot older," Barbara says.

"That isn't making me feel better. You have grown-up jobs," I say, and they both laugh.

"Being a teacher is a grown-up job. We need teachers, don't sell yourself short," Grace says with a smile.

"I know, I just don't know if I will stay a teacher. I did what my brother wanted to do. He got his credential, so I did too. I thought that meant we would have summers off together to travel and play in our band. Didn't really work out that way, and now I wonder if I would have chosen teaching if it hadn't been for him," I explain.

"Where is your brother? You must be very close if you planned your life around him," Grace says.

"He's my identical twin, and he's currently in London with a girl he met in Los Angeles a year ago." I try not to sound mad, but I fail.

Both women give a knowing nod. I finish my sandwich and lean back farther wondering if I should push on or just camp here with them.

"Stay here tonight, Corey. We have beer," Barbara, who is apparently a mind reader, says.

"Beer? Seriously?" I ask with my eyebrows raised all the way to my hairline.

"It's not super cold but yeah, down in the creek is a six-pack. Why don't you go grab us each one. Let the rest stay in the water. Maybe our second one will be colder." Grace waves her hand down the trail a bit, pointing to where the creek must be.

I go and retrieve three relatively cold beers and hand each of them out, sitting again by my pack. I crack open the can and take a satisfying sip from the can. It's not ice-cold, but pretty close. The amber liquid slides down my throat and starts to coat my frazzled nerves.

"Thank you for this. I am glad I caught up with you two. I was really struggling out there today," I say.

"Because of Stephanie leaving?" Barbara asks.

"Yeah, and other things, you know? I came out here to figure things out and she was a really nice distraction. Now that she's gone, I am back to trying to figure out my life. I hate it." I finish the rest of my beer in two gulps and smash the can on the rock next to me. I let out a long deep burb and blink. "Sorry."

"Don't apologize, dude. Go get yourself another beer or two. You can have mine. I'm betting a little booze-induced sleep would do you good tonight," Grace says.

I stand and say thank you, then walk to the creek and pull the rest of the cans out. I open one and chug the whole thing before walking back over to the ladies.

"Thanks." I hiccup and they both nod.

"Are you sleeping out under the stars or setting up your tent?" Barbara asks as she stands.

"Outside," I say.

"Okay you and Grace can visit, while I set our tent up. I am not a fan of bugs crawling up my nose in my sleep," Barbara says.

Grace and I talk about her job and how she and Barbara managed while Barbara was in medical school. All of it makes me feel like shit for not going with Stephanie. I could have flown back to Bend to help my sisters. I could have driven the moving truck with my crap back, instead of my parents doing that. The options of how it could have worked dance around and taunt me. The beer is only helping me feel a little less shitty.

When Barbara returns to the campfire I am swaying on my ass and decide to call it a night. I grab my sleeping bag and head for the trees. As soon as I climb in, I breathe deeply, capturing her smell. I can almost feel her sweet tiny body pressed against me. I roll to my side and bury my face in the warm flannel, hoping I can at least dream of her.

ELEVEN

STEPHANIE

"mile 0"

THE FIRST TIME I saw my mom in her hospital bed, I felt my heart break into a million pieces. It was like a water balloon hitting the ground, fragments of latex and water shooting out in every direction. My heart wasn't just broken, it was shattered. The second time and third were no better. Ivy went with me at first, but now she goes on her own. She says it's better to spread out the visits. I met with my mom's oncologist and heard all kinds of things no child should ever hear. My head was spinning and my heart that was bruised and battered threatened to stop more than once. I wondered if the doctors knew how fragile I was as they droned on and on about the outcome and prognosis like my mother was just a case they happened upon.

"You have to go to your interview, Stephanie," Mom says in a tiny voice that sounds like it's being piped in from another room. I squeeze her hand gently and say for the tenth time, "I am not leaving you, Mom."

"Honey, you have to be a Beaver. It's the best. Beavers are amazing," her little voice says from the bed.

I roll my eyes and try not to laugh. We've had the same conversation every day. They have her pretty medicated, which is managing her pain, so I am grateful, but it makes it hard to have serious conversations with her.

The oncologist explained that there was no way to fix her fractured hip since the bone was so diseased. He doesn't expect her to live much longer and said really helpful things like if we had caught it sooner, maybe they would have been able to give her more time. I almost kicked him right in his dick when he said that, but thankfully Ivy was sitting with me and her gentle hand on my shoulder reminded me that I wasn't that kind of a person.

"Mom, no job is more important than spending time with you," I say, and she shakes her head.

"Steph. You have to go. What's the date?" she asks.

"It's July tenth, Mom," I say and take a sharp breath in, caught off guard by my traitorous mind wondering where Corey is. I could probably figure it out. I mean, I know we were making it anywhere from ten to fifteen miles a day. Sometimes we pushed it more, before we were together. I think the most I went in one day was twenty miles. That was the day I tried to ditch him and his stupid hair. I still haven't unpacked my backpack. It's just resting against the hallway closet door, where I dropped it ten days ago.

"Good, you have time. You don't have to be there until August third. Stephanie, my will is in the safe in the back bedroom," she says.

"I know, Mom. I met with your attorney yesterday. Thank you for telling me where it was." It was so hard to have the same conversations over and over. Sometimes she lets a new nugget slip out so I want to listen, but the repeating is so hard. My beautiful, intelligent mother is trapped by medication and pain and cancer.

"Under my mattress is an envelope for you. Don't look at it until I am gone. Oh, and don't look in my nightstand. Maybe have Ivy clean that out," she says before closing her eyes.

"Already done, Mom. You told her to take care of that yesterday," I say softly.

"Oh thank God. No daughter should have to see her mother's vibrator," she says without opening her eyes.

"Jesus, Mom." I start to laugh, my shoulders shaking, and she glances over at me and smiles.

"I love you so much, baby girl," she says.

"I love you too, Mom," I say and watch as her eyes flutter shut again.

I hear a little tapping on the door and squeeze Mom's hand gently again before standing. I turn to find Ivy in the doorway and she motions me out to the hall.

"Hi, I thought you were coming later?" I ask.

"I know I said that, but I was hoping to catch you. I um, wondered what you wanted to do about the flower shop? You met with the attorney, right?" I notice she isn't looking at me, instead she is dragging her foot across the ugly hospital linoleum.

"What do you mean?" I ask, even though I don't want to talk about this. It's the last thing I want to do, actually, talk about my mom's belongings that no longer matter.

"Like, are you interested in taking your mom's spot, working with me?" She blows out a breath and I reach out and pull her into a hug.

"No, Ivy, I am no florist. You should keep the shop. You are co-owner, right? I don't want anything from it."

"No honey, I can't just take her half. I will pay you for it. I just wasn't sure, since you haven't found a teaching job." Her voice trails off and I laugh for the second time in days.

"Thanks Ivy, but florist was never my backup plan." I turn and flatten my back against the wall, hoping if I don't have to look her in the eyes I can manage my own pain better. I lean on the wall and she joins me.

"Your mom really wants you to go to that interview up in Oregon," she says.

"I know. I'm not leaving her," I say, wondering why I even have to explain this.

"Have you called them to cancel?" Ivy asks and my stomach twists.

"No. I haven't managed to do anything but come here and go talk to her attorney. I feel like I have fallen into an alternate universe. I don't even know what I'm doing half the time," I say.

"I feel the same way. I have to keep all the weddings we had scheduled and talk to the brides like everything is normal." She leans over and whispers dramatically, "It's not normal, Stephanie."

I laugh again. "I know what you mean. I ran into the store to get milk and eggs the other day and the clerk asked how my day was going. I burst into tears and left without my groceries."

"Oh honey, I'll ask Paul to go shopping for you. He can drop off essentials after he's done with the daily deliveries. It's hard to manage all of this." She puts her arm around my shoulder and pulls me in resting her head on mine. I am so grateful for Ivy. She has been a part of my life ever since I was born. She and my mom are inseparable, best friends, and business partners.

Rose and Ivy Florist is one of San Diego's premier florists and usually booked out two years for weddings. My mom and Ivy both have amazing artistic vision when it comes to flower arrangements and brides seek them out for their original ideas. I saw them use wine-glasses in a bride's bouquet once and thought they had lost their mind. But the bride loved it, and the next year other florists were copying the design.

I try not to think about how Ivy is going to do on her own. I have enough on my plate, without worrying about someone else's grief.

"Thanks for coming to get me, Ivy," I say, and she nods. When I turn to her I see for the first time how much she has aged. She has worn her hair pulled back in a tight braid as long as I've known her, but since I've been back she hasn't bothered. Her long dark hair has streaks of grey that frame her face nicely and her brown eyes look darker. I can only assume the grief has dulled them.

"I am going to head home and give you some time with her. Thanks for always being there for my momma." I pull her into a hug.

"Of course. She has my heart. She always has," Ivy says into my hair.

THE NEXT MORNING my eyes fall to my backpack leaning against the door. I know I have to unpack it. I just haven't had the heart. Maybe part of me hoped I could go back. Drop back in where I left off and finish the trip. Maybe find Corey. I know that isn't going to happen now. I have been trying to let him go, trying to tell my heart that it's over. I can't process that and losing my mom at the same time. I am ashamed to admit I have pictured ways of finding him including stalking all the freshman girls at the junior college in Bend to see if they have a big brother named Corey.

I pull the backpack over to the living room and plop on the couch. I undo the straps holding my sleeping bag first and let it flop onto the carpet. I stare at it, knowing what lies on the bottom. Sighing, I pick it up and undo the cords that hold it rolled up, then flip it out. Pine needles and dirt fly through the air and the smell of the trail hits me. I reach in and fish around until I feel the silky strand between my fingers.

When I pull it free of my bag, I sink down onto the couch and clutch the stupid thing to my chest. I let the tears fall. No one is here to stop them, no one here to comfort me. The pain and grief swallow me and I allow it. I let my mind go blank and the pain in my chest cracks open until I can feel it in every inch of my body. There is nothing else to do but curl into a ball and cry.

The oncologist said there are stages of grief and explained what they were and how everyone has a different timeline. I nodded along, like I understood. I didn't, not until now.

I must be at despair. I don't know if that is even one of them but that is all I feel. Maybe this is the depression portion? I feel it in all my cells. I know he said there was denial, I never had that luxury.

There was not a moment to feel the "this can't be real" because it has all happened so fast. Anger will come later I know, at least the anger that relates to losing my mother. I am saving that for later. I can't let that hot coal start a fire that I can't extinguish. He mentioned bargaining, which made me laugh. Like if I could have my mother back I would give up everything? I already did that and she is still dying. That just circles me back to anger. My life is shit: I lost an amazing guy, I am about to lose the only family I have ever had, and to top it off I have no job.

The attorney assured me my mother's life insurance policy would take care of my needs for a long time, but that is almost worse. What am I supposed to do with my time when she is gone? I can't just sit here in this house where I grew up, without her. I start to feel like I can't breathe so I sit up and rub my eyes. I set Corey's braid on the table and get back to work unpacking my bag. Once I have carried all my clothes to the laundry and started a load, I walk back out to find Ivy in the living room holding a picture of her and my mom to her chest.

She stares at me for a moment before saying quietly, "She's gone, baby girl."

"What? What do you mean she's gone?" I say, afraid to step closer to her. That will make it real.

"I went by this morning and when I left the room for coffee she went into cardiac arrest." She pulls the picture back and trails her finger over what I can only assume is my mother. Then she sets it face down on the end table. I stare at the back of the frame where a scrap of paper says, "Coronado Beach 1961" with a little heart around the words. I am finally able to walk to Ivy and I pull her into my arms. We speak at the same time, offering words of comfort and love but I feel like I am tethered to earth by a fragile strand. No words of comfort can mend this agony or strengthen my hold on my sanity.

The next few days are blurred into an ugly stained glass. The funeral home, the cemetery, the random people bringing food to the house, the phone calls and the flowers delivered. All the Goddamn flowers. They're everywhere, without my permission. Flowers meant to soothe? But they're not hers, not Ivy's, and it's like a slap in the face reminder that she's gone. That she will never bundle daisies together and wrap them with ribbon and lace again. She wouldn't, but other people are out there sticking flowers in vases, tying ribbons and placing notes of sympathy, and the anger I've avoided starts to bubble just a bit farther up.

I hate them. I've seen Ivy glare at the flowers as well, so it isn't just me. She's been by my side through all of it, holding me, making me laugh at memories that weren't mine, but things she and my mother shared over the years.

I, all at once, am grateful that my mom had a friendship like theirs, and jealous of the closeness they shared. Ivy has been caring for my mother's dog since she fell and asks if she can keep him. I agree it's for the best and feel guilty that I haven't worried even once about the little dude. I guess part of me just knew Ivy had it handled.

"Barkley never really liked me, so I guess I should be thankful you are willing to take him," I tell her.

"Well, you were in your first year of college when your mom got him, so he just didn't know you, honey. It's okay. Barkley and my cat Ginger get along really well. It would be a shame to separate them now," Ivy says.

"I agree." I am leaning on the counter in the kitchen. Ivy has been helping me go through Mom's paperwork for the last two hours.

The phone rings and I roll my eyes. I have answered this thing more in the past week than all my time as a teenager.

"Hello?" I say.

"Hello, may I speak with Rose, please?" a woman says. Her high-pitched voice sounds familiar, but I can't place it.

"I'm sorry, Rose has passed away. This is her daughter Stephanie. Can I help you with something?" I say in a practiced tone that I've perfected recently.

"Oh! Stephanie, you are who I was trying to reach, but when I last heard you were on the PCT heading our way," the woman says.

"Who is this?" I ask. I furrow my brows and cock my head, alerting Ivy that this phone call is different than the hundreds of others I have taken.

"This is Miss Gee. I was just calling to confirm and to remind you of your interview time. Are you still planning on coming? You must be dealing with so much right now."

"Oh, the school in Beaver Valley, right? Um," I glance over at Ivy and she is nodding ferociously, mouthing the words *yes* and *go*, over and over. She even gives me an exaggerated thumbs-up.

"Um, August third, right?" I ask to clarify and buy myself some more time. When Miss Gee says yes, I glance at Ivy who has stood up from her chair and is holding her hand to her chest, perhaps trying to calm herself.

"I think I can be there. I would really like to interview for the position, I just might be a little frazzled. My mom passed after a very short fight with cancer and I didn't even know she was sick," I explain.

"Oh dear, that is just awful. I am sure everyone will understand and I can tell you, we don't have any other history teachers to interview, so it's really just a formality. I wouldn't string you along and have you come all the way up here under your circumstance and not give you the job. You know?" she says. I have to fight the urge to pull the phone away. Her voice is like Minnie Mouse. She is saying very kind and good things but it's hard to listen to without laughing.

"Yes. I will be there then. I um, I'll just fly into Bend and rent a car then? Is that the best way to get to you?" I ask.

"Yes, dear. We can arrange all of that now that you aren't hiking to us. I'll have one of our secretaries send you a letter with the details of the flight and rental car. We look forward to meeting you on the third."

I thank her and hang up. I'm shocked that this school district is doing so much to have me come for an interview. Should I be worried? Before I can give it more thought, Ivy dives toward me and hugs me.

"I am so proud of you! Your mom wanted this so badly for you," she says, and I smile.

"She did this," I say, the realization hitting me like a punch to the gut. "She knew I wouldn't leave to go to that interview while she was still with us. She let go on purpose." I wipe my eyes with the tips of my fingers, hoping to stave off another onslaught of tears. I can't believe there are any left after the past few weeks.

"I thought the same thing. She talked about it every day, asking me what the date was, and if you would have time," Ivy says.

"Well, I better like the school then since she worked so hard to get me there," I choke out.

"You damn well better love it my dear." Ivy pulls me back into a hug.

THE LETTER with my flight and rental car information arrives via certified letter two days later. It looks like I fly into Bend on August first and have a room at a hotel through the weekend. I see she has moved my interview time up to eleven on the third. I notice there is not a return ticket and I smile. Looks like I have a job. Thanks, Mom.

I spend the next two weeks packing and going through things at Mom's place. Ivy helps when she can and sends the shop's delivery drivers to help me when she's busy. Donation centers come and pick up all the things I wasn't planning on keeping, and I give her neighbors all a little something to remember my mother by. I book a moving company to come and pack the house into a truck and they will meet me in Oregon once I have a place to call home.

I sit on the couch and lean my head back. It has only been three weeks since I left the trail, so much has happened. I still think about Corey, constantly wondering where he is. He might already be in Bend if he decided to push himself. Should I try to look for him? I know he said he wasn't staying there, that he had a job near there. Damnit, why was I so afraid to ask questions? I bet if I had made it all the way to Bend with him, we would have learned more about each other. There is no way I wouldn't have asked more questions.

I guess it just wasn't meant to be. I try and tell myself that, but I know it isn't true, and it breaks my heart.

mile 1481.7
July 10th, 1987

OREGON. Fucking finally. I have a hundred and ninety miles to go, or about twelve more days. I would have quit a long time ago if it wasn't for Barbara and Grace. They've hiked with me every day, taken me under their wings and may have decided to adopt me. We discussed the legality of it and I don't think they really can, plus it would hurt my parents.

Part of me wanted to do this on my own, and I tried. After the night I chugged three beers in less than a half hour I marched out on my own, dragging my hungover ass up the hill and into the next valley. I might have cried again. If you cry among the pines and no one is around to hear it, did it actually happen? It did if two stubborn women are less than a mile behind you arguing about movie lines. Apparently their song fights had run their course, and they have moved on.

"Corey we're stopping at Callahan's! My treat," Barbara shouts at me from the trail.

"I heard you the first time!" I yell back.

"She's just really excited about the hot tub and wine. It's been months since she has had her nightly soak and sip," Grace says as she hikes past me, somehow unharnessing energy I didn't know she had.

"You seem pretty excited to get there too!" I yell as she continues to power walk down the trail.

"They have a beef stroganoff that is talked about all over the place. She is jealous and wants to taste it to see if she can figure out their secret," Barbara says, catching up to me.

"I see, so you both are crazy," I say, and she laughs.

"Sweetie, if you are just now figuring that out, we've done a good job." Barbara says to me over her shoulder.

As the hotel comes into view, I immediately think of Stephanie. If she was still on the trail with me, we could have stayed here together. I could have treated her to a nice meal, ravaged her perfect tiny body in a king-size bed that probably doesn't have crusty patches. Why the hell didn't I get more information about her? I am such a fool. I let the best thing I ever had slip away.

Grace and Barbara walk to the front desk and I see two totally different women emerge as they speak to the hotel clerk.

"Dr. Barbara Miles checking in and I will require that second room."

"Yes, Dr. Miles, I have that information right here, I see you requested the Jacuzzi room and a standard room, is that correct?"

"Yes," she says in a tone I have never heard Barbara use.

"Okay, and you requested a bottle of our best red to be sent to the Jacuzzi room. Did you want a bottle sent to the standard room as well?" she asks, and Barbara looks over her shoulder at me.

I shake my head, but she turns back and says, "Yes, that will be fine. Please send a snack tray to both rooms. We will need something before dinner."

"Of course, Dr. Miles. Is there anything else I can get for you?" the clerk asks.

"No that will be all." Barbara turns and gives me a ridiculous thumbs-up and I laugh.

"You really don't have to treat me like this. I would be fine sleeping on the trail tonight," I say, like the sad sack I am.

"Nonsense. You belong to us now. Like a lost puppy, we are going to get you to Bend in one piece so you can help your sisters move into their apartment. Then, I am sure you will be the best math teacher the Furie Beavers have ever seen."

I can't help but smile. These women have saved me. They could have just hiked on, forgotten all about me and my sad life, but they didn't. Tonight, I'm going to take an hour-long shower, eat decadent snacks, and drink wine before dinner. I am excited about seeing my sisters and my parents. That is what I need to focus on, not Stephanie and where she might be, what she might be going through.

When I get to my room, I call home to check in and my mom answers.

"Hey Mom! I am about twelve days out from Bend. How's the packing going?" I ask.

"Oh, honey! It's so good to hear your voice. We are so excited to see you! How are you? Have you shaved your beard yet? Is your hair long? How are your feet? Do you need new boots yet or will the ones you have last until you get to Bend?"

"Mom? Mom!" I shout into the phone.

"Yes, dear?" she says.

"LET me answer a question *before* you ask the next one!" I laugh and she apologizes.

"Sorry dear, I am just sick about missing your calls. The last two times you called we were out and, I just about died when I got your message. Can you talk, honey? I have so many questions."

I sink into the bed and let her soft sweet voice wrap around me and comfort me. If you looked up "momma's boy" in the dictionary right now, my picture would be there. I have never wanted to hear my mom's encouragement more than right now.

I tell her about the hike so far and about Barbara and Grace and Trail Terry and that one weird guy I met just past Mount Shasta. He was convinced there were people living under the mountain. He said they are called Lemurians. He had a lot to tell me, and I am sure that I developed an aneurysm while I listened.

I hesitate, but then I tell her about Stephanie. Not everything of course, but I tell her how she and I got along and how I screwed it up by not asking more questions or following her.

"Honey, I am so sorry. I think you need to look at it like you know what is possible for you now, you know? I mean, you can love someone if you find the right person. I know you didn't think that would happen for you when Codey met Janet. I know you felt left out," my very wise mother says.

Man, I can't pull anything over on Mom. I did feel left out, I still kind of do feel that way. "But Mom, what if she was it? What if that was my one shot and I blew it?" I ask.

"I refuse to believe that. Listen if that girl is supposed to be with you, the universe will find a way to get you back together. I know that deep in my heart, honey. Have faith and wait. That's what I have always said, isn't it?"

I laugh because my mom is a walking bumper sticker. She has so many sayings that I can't keep them straight. I just agree with her. "Sure, Mom, yeah you always have said that," I say, then to change the subject I ask about my sisters. "How are the girls? Are they ready to start their adventure?"

"Sure, you know Dee Dee is packed and ready to go, and Linda hasn't even started. I am convinced they switched one of them at the hospital. How can twins be so different?"

"Well, they aren't identical, so you know they are more like regular sisters who have the same birthday," I explain even though she knows this.

"Right, who both rudely forced their way out of my vagina on the same day. Why couldn't I have one baby after you two! Do you know I couldn't poop for a week without crying when I had you and your bother?" My mom practically yells.

"I've heard," I say, and rub my hand down my face. God, I've missed this woman.

"Your father and I have listed the house and I think our offer on the place in Bend will be accepted. I mean I wrote them a letter, Corey, who can refuse a letter from a kindergarten teacher?" I can hear the smile I know is plastered on her face.

"Retired kindergarten teacher Mom, you're retired," I say, knowing that will make her grumble.

"Don't remind me," she sighs.

"Hey, Mom, I need to let you go, I have to get in the shower before dinner. My trail friends I told you about are expecting me to join them," I say as I stand from the bed.

"Okay dear. We will see you soon! I am so excited I can barely stand it!" She shouts the last part.

I hold the phone away from my ear and laugh. "Me too, Mom. Hey if Codey calls, tell him I said hi."

"Oh, I will honey. I love you C," Mom says.

"Love you too Ma." I hang up and make my way to the shower. I strip out of my dusty trail clothes and step into the clean blissful space. The hot water hits me and I moan, grabbing the soap and lathering my entire body. I even sit on the shower bench and scrub my feet. I have never in my life been this dirty.

The shower pressure in this hotel is downright sinful. I swear two hundred gallons a minute are currently pounding down on me. I am so happy until I think of her. And then I'm immediately torn between grabbing my cock and enjoying the memories I have of her, or pounding my face into the wall. I opt for the less painful option, knowing if I showed up at dinner with a bruise on my forehead questions will be asked.

I try and dress for dinner, knowing the only thing I have that even remotely passes as nice is a button-up polyester Hawaiian shirt and a pair of moderately clean khaki shorts. I have flip-flops or dirty hiking boots, and I opt for the boots since my feet, even if they are clean, look like troll feet. There are callouses and blisters on top of my callouses and blisters.

When I get to the dining hall my friends are already seated and apparently packed clothes for this occasion.

"You both look lovely, are you sure you want to dine with me?" I ask and Grace stands to give me a quick peck on the cheek.

"Yes, sit. You look fine. We knew this was going to be a stop of ours, so we brought something nice, it's no big deal," Grace says as she sits back down.

"If you say so," I say. There is a table next to ours with three remarkably beautiful women and I can't even care.

The waiter comes and takes our order, and I defer to head chef Grace Walker, ordering the same thing that she does. Dr. Barbara Miles goes rogue and orders the fish.

"How can you come all this way and not get the beef stroganoff? You are impossible!" Grace says, but there is a twinkle in her eye.

"I will take a bite of yours, we both know that you will also steal half of my fish, so let's quit pretending, shall we?" Barbara looks over her wineglass at Grace and it makes my heart hurt. They are so in love. I want that. I thought I had that. For the first time in my whole life I met someone who felt like she was the other half of me. Damn it.

"Still thinking about Stephanie?" Grace asks, pushing a full glass of wine toward me.

I sigh for dramatic effect, but also because apparently sighing when you are really sad feels good. Who knew? Not me, because I have never been this sad. That kind of shocks me and I realize that I wasn't this torn up when Codey left. I thought I was, I thought it was the worst I have ever felt. Nope, good to know I can feel even worse. I drop my head onto the table and sigh again.

"Buck up. No crying at dinner," Barbara barks at me.

I sit up and force a smile. "Sorry. I know I am pathetic. Sorry."

"WE WILL ALLOW this shit for one more day," Barbara says, holding a finger up to drive her point home. "One more day. Then you are going to pull up your big-boy pants and strap a smile on that face." Barbara lets loose a tiny hiccup.

"Strap a smile on? Is that even a saying?" I ask.

"It should be. I mean I like a good strap on." Barbara wiggles her eyebrows.

"Jesus, Barb. Let's not make the young man uncomfortable at dinner," Grace says, laughing into her wine.

Barbara waves her hand and smiles, "You're right. Sorry, Mr. R and R. Hey, why did she call you that?"

"No idea. One of the many things I thought I would get to ask her." I shrug and take a big drink of my wine.

"Did you have a trail name for her?" Grace asks. She is leaning forward, resting her chin on her fist.

"Yoda," I say.

"Oh, because she was so small. Barbara and I had a day-long discussion about how she was carrying that pack. I think she was hauling like over half of her body weight. She must have freakishly strong thighs," Grace says.

"Yeah, I had the same questions. She was small, wasn't she?" I say wistfully.

"Ivy, her mom's partner, said that Rose was tiny just like her," Barbara says, swirling her wine in the glass. She pauses then looks at Grace. "We met Rose! Remember when Stephanie got on the trail? That must have been her mom we talked to!"

Grace nods and squints like she's trying to remember Rose but eventually shakes her head and takes a drink of her wine.

"You spoke with Ivy, I mean more than telling her Stephanie was on the trail?" I ask, hope sneaking into my thoughts.

"Well, sure, she was pretty distraught. We stayed with her for about an hour. I knew you guys were behind us, but you must have gotten distracted because it took you longer than we had estimated." Barbara looks pointedly at me and I smile.

"Well, I did have a hard time keeping us on the trail. Damn, that girl was everything," I say.

"Ivy thought so too," Grace says, then adds, "She seemed pretty worried she wouldn't get to her in time."

"Jesus, what is going on with Rose?" I ask.

"Well, Ivy said she fell and broke her hip, but I am thinking there is some underlying pathology that she didn't want to talk about. Doesn't match up, a woman in her fifties breaking a hip from such a low fall," Barbara says with a shake of her head.

"Well, damn," I say.

Grace changes the subject once the food arrives. She takes small bites and discusses the possible ingredients. Barbara was right, in between bites of her stroganoff Grace sneaks bites of the fish, easily finishing half.

AFTER AN AMAZING MEAL and even better wine, I make my way back to my room. I strip and climb into the clean crisp sheets buck naked and sleep like the dead. When I wake up, I roll over and blink at the alarm clock. Nine. I haven't slept 'til nine in months. I rub my eyes a few times, running last night's conversations over in my head. Ivy, Stephanie's mom's friend and business partner. Stephanie said her mom owns a flower shop.

Huh.

What if she used her name in her store, like what if the store was Ivy Rose flower shop or something? San Diego is about as big as Los Angeles, but I could call information and start asking for a florist by that name, or some combination of that name, right? I mean, what would be the harm in that?

I feel the hope that flickered through my mind last night grows bigger. Peace washes over me, settling my heart into a normal rhythm. I have a plan, and that is a hell of a lot more than I had yesterday.

THIRTEEN
STEPHANIE

mile 0
July 20th, 1987

PACKING IS GOING WELL, my old room is already pretty empty from when I moved out to go to college, so I move to my mom's room, dragging empty boxes with me.

I sit on the edge of her bed and flop back. I wonder where Corey is, where he's sleeping. He should be in Oregon by now, at least or near the border. I have thought about changing my plane ticket to a few days earlier to wander around Bend, but that just seems sad and pathetic. If I didn't find him I would be even more depressed during my interview. God, I hope Miss Gee was telling the truth and this is just a formality. If I end up not getting the job, I will just fly back here and start looking again. That thought makes me feel like I ate rocks. I scoot back into Mom's bed further and roll into her pillow, breathing deep. My mom smelled like fresh-cut flowers all the time. I used to imagine little cartoon flowers following her around like a

Disney princess when I was little. I wonder how long her pillows will smell like her? How long does that sort of thing last?

I get up and walk to her closet. I took what I wanted and already had a charity come and pick up the rest, so all that is left in here are a few small boxes of papers and some photo albums. I pull all those down and put them in the box without opening them. I glance back at her bed and have a flash of a memory: Mom telling me there was an envelope under her mattress for me.

I walk over and lift the edge and slid my hand between the mattress and the box spring, immediately hitting a thick envelope. After pulling it out, I sit again on the bed. It feels so weird to be here, in her room, on her bed without her. I slept in here with her a lot when I was little. We would talk and giggle and she would rub my back until I fell asleep.

I turn the envelope over to see her beautiful handwriting.

"TO MY BABY GIRL"

TAKING A DEEP BREATH, I open the seal and pull out a thick pile of papers. At the top of the first one it's dated the day after I was born.

June 2, 1965

Dear baby girl,

You are sleeping and I wanted to take this time to write to you, to tell you just how perfect you are. You are all I have ever wanted and now that you are here, I feel complete.

I named you Stephanie Iverson after two women who mean the world to me. I hope that if you are reading this as an adult you know them, and feel their love.

Much love baby girl,

Your mom,

Rose

I flip through the stack and find a letter for every year until I turned eighteen. I stare at the first letter and rack my brain for a Stephanie that my mom would have known. I've always known my middle name was the same as Ivy's full name, but didn't know there was someone else. I lean across the bed and grab the phone then dial the flower shop.

"Rose and Ivy, this is Ivy, can I help you?" she says in her professional tone but it's flat, not the full-of-life lady I have always known.

"Hey, it's me," I say shifting on the bed to get more comfortable.

"Oh, hi honey, how are you doing? I was going to stop by with Barkley after work to see you. Do you need anything?" Ivy asks.

"Not really, I'd love to see you. Hey, Mom told me about this envelope under her mattress and I just pulled it out. It's letters to me, like from since I was born."

"Oh? Huh, you don't say. Letters? What, um..." She clears her throat. "What do they say?"

"Well, I have only read the first one. She said I was named after two women, obviously my middle name is for you, but who is Stephanie? Why didn't we ever talk about that?" I ask.

There is silence on the other line and I think maybe she has hung up, until I hear a shuffle of papers.

"Ivy?" I ask.

"Sorry, yes, I'm here." I can hear things being moved around.

"Okay, so in the letter Mom said she hoped I would know these women I was named after and I can't think who this Stephanie person is, do you know who she means?" I ask again, thinking Ivy must just be distracted by work.

"Yes, honey. She is no longer with us, I am afraid. She took her own life about a year after you were born."

"Oh God! Why?" I ask and take in a sharp breath.

"Well, it's complicated. Maybe your mom says something in one of the letters. I just don't feel comfortable talking about it over the phone. Maybe we can talk when I stop by later?" Ivy asks.

"Okay, sure, yeah I'm sorry, I know you are at work, and you must be so busy," I say.

"It's okay honey, I can always make time for you, but that story might take longer to tell." She breathes out and it sounds like she shifts her phone to her other ear.

"Of course. I have no other plans, so whenever you want to stop by is fine," I say.

"Sounds good," Ivy chirps and says goodbye quickly.

I look back at the stack of letters and wonder if I should wait for her to read the rest. I decide to take them to the kitchen and I pour myself a glass of wine before turning to the second letter.

"Dear Stephanie,

Oh, how fast this year has gone! You are such a smart little girl and walking around like a maniac. I can't keep you in one room for very long. You are going to be a reader, I can tell since books are your favorite thing to carry around. As I write this you have a copy of Flowers for Algernon by Daniel Keyes tucked under your pudgy arm.- Maybe someday you will read it.

I have sad news. Since I wrote last, my dear friend Stephanie has passed away. She lost her battle with her demons. When you are older I will explain more. She was a wonderful human and Ivy and I will miss her dearly.

Speaking of Ivy, we got a new space for our flower shop! Business is really starting to pick up and I am grateful that she helps so much with you. We are quite the team, her and me.

Oh dear. I just heard a thud, that is probably you pulling out more books. I love you, my baby girl.

Your mom,

Rose"

Well, that wasn't really helpful. I flip to the next year where she talks about how easy it was to potty-train me and how I really liked to play in the mud, she mentions the business doing well and that they are hiring an actual delivery driver.

The next few years are just about the same, but I am starting to remember the things she is talking about. The science fair project I did on how fast different flowers grow, the year I decided to have everyone call me Nellie Ross because I had read that she was the first woman to become a governor of a state. Sadly, I wasn't as young as I thought. Man, no wonder I didn't attract a lot of boyfriends. I was in the seventh grade when I did that! In my memory that was around the fourth grade. Damn.

Each letter is a nice recap of my year and I find myself laughing more than being sad. It is a wonderful gift to have this insight. The last letter is short and Mom's handwriting seems rushed.

"Dear baby girl,

I guess I can't really call you that anymore since you just turned eighteen. I am so proud of you finishing your first year of college on the Dean's list. You really are incredible. Now that you are an adult I want you to have some information."

My heart feels like it's going to stop, and I fold the paper over and take a long drink of wine before continuing.

"I know I have told you your biological father's name before, and I said I didn't know where he was. That part wasn't entirely true. I can't say that he is still there, but when I met Brian, he was in Bend, Oregon. He was taking classes at the junior college there and hoping to transfer to OSU to become a teacher. When you told me that you wanted to be a teacher it made me so proud. He doesn't know about you, and I can't be sure how he would react if you looked for him, but now that you are an adult, you have that right. I wish I had more infor-mation for you, sweet girl, but that is all I know. I better go, we are getting ready to go out to dinner with Ivy and a few of your friends to celebrate your birthday and the start of summer. I am so grateful to have had you in my life. I love you more than all the flowers on earth.

This time there is no signature. The letter just ends. I remember yelling to her to hurry up that night. Ivy was waiting in the living room and neither of us could figure out what was taking my mom so long. Ivy was complaining that she was hungry and I know I just wanted to get dinner over with so I could go hang out with my friends. Now I feel like shit. I wish I had known how short my time would be with her.

I fold the papers back and put them in the envelope. Wow. I wonder if Brian went on to become a teacher? Bend, Oregon seems to be a vortex for my life's unanswered questions. I feel like going up there for this interview (and hopefully this job) might be the start of something good. Even if I can't find Corey, I might find my father.

What does one say when meeting a man who doesn't know you existed? "Hey there, nice to meet you. I assume I have your eyes, since my mom's are brown and not nearly as wide. She also has brown hair and I have blonde hair. I mean she and I are exactly the same size, but that's about the only attribute I got from her." I pause and imagine a short stocky man with blonde hair. Maybe he is short too?

Good Lord, I am rambling to an imaginary person. What on earth would I say to his face? Thankfully a knock on the door pulls me away from the downward spiral of what I would say if I found him.

"Hi honey, I finished early," Ivy says, holding her purse and a leash. Barkley is sniffing the doorway like he isn't sure this is his old home.

"Come on in. I just finished reading the letters," I say, and I notice her reach up and grab the back of her neck. She drops the leash, but instead of running to explore what had been his home for more than five years, he just sits by Ivy's feet and looks up at her.

"Learn anything interesting?" she asks, and I catch a hint of nervousness.

"Not really, I mean she told me that when she met my father he was in junior college in Bend and he planned on going to OSU to be a teacher. I guess I got that from him. Did you know that?" I ask and she nods.

"Your mom was worried if you knew before you were eighteen and went looking for him it could turn out badly. She was trying to protect you," she says almost defensively.

I shrug. I don't really care, I mean if I had my way, I would never meet him. I wish my mom was still alive and she could die of old age, but since I am now essentially an orphan, the idea of meeting him is more appealing.

"She worried that he would think you were after money. Like support or something. We always, I mean *she* always did just fine supporting you, and we, I mean *she* didn't want him involved." Ivy looks down at Barkley, who has lain down, resting his chin on her foot.

"I know you and Mom were close. I always wished I could have a best friend like you, Ivy. I really appreciate that, I want you to know how much it means to me that she had you," I say, reaching for her hand.

"Thank you. She meant so much to me. I can't believe she's gone. I should have pressed her to go to the doctor last year when she started to complain about her back. I bet that was the first sign and we both ignored it. We blamed the work we do. I am sorry, Steph. I should have pushed her more." Her voice cracks a little and it breaks me.

"Please don't do that. I don't think if we knew a year ago it would have changed the outcome. Then we would have spent the whole year knowing we were going to lose her. I really don't think I could have taken that," I say while squeezing her hand.

"Yeah, I guess." She looks around the space that has been home to so much love and starts to cry. "I am sorry, it's just hard to be here without her."

"I know. I wish I had asked for an earlier flight into Bend. I wish I was going tomorrow. I hate being here too." I say then feel guilty for feeling that way. That is how it has been: I have a feeling that overtakes me, recognize that feeling, feel guilty for having that feeling. It is exhausting.

"Want a glass of wine?" I ask and she nods enthusiastically.

"God yes." She reaches up and wipes her eyes. Barkley gets up and thumps his tail on the ground.

We walk to the kitchen and I pull out another glass and just in case, a new bottle. Barkley never leaves her side, resting his face on her feet again as soon as she sits.

"He's pretty glued to you," I say.

"Yeah, I think he knew she was sick. I think he worries he will lose me too. He's very clingy. I have started bringing him to work with me because he's just a mess if I don't. Poor little guy. We both miss her." She bends down and pats him on the back.

I take a sip of wine and smile at her. I don't want to push, but I am curious about the friend I was named after. As if she can read my mind, Ivy sighs and says, "So did your mom explain about our Stephanie?"

"Not really, just that she lost the battle with her demons. I think that is what she said, it was pretty vague. Was this woman depressed?" I ask.

"Yes, and her family was terrible. Very strict and demanding. Stephanie was a free spirit and wanted to live her life her way. I think if she had a more supportive home life, she wouldn't have given in to her depression. The whole thing was so very sad, but not that uncommon for the time, I mean I think it still happens more than we hear about," Ivy says.

"There was a boy in my high school who died by suicide. I remember him as being really quiet and withdrawn. He didn't really have any friends, but he sat in front of me in like three of my classes. He and I were always tied for high scores on tests, anyway one Monday he just wasn't there and by Wednesday there were rumors, you know?" I say.

Ivy nods and takes a drink of her wine.

"By Friday the school counselor came into our class and let us know. I remember a kid behind me snickered. Actually laughed. I turned and glared at him so hard I thought I was going to lose an eyeball." I take a drink of wine, flooded with memories of that day.

"That's awful, but maybe he was a nervous laugher, you know? Your mom would laugh if I got hurt. Maybe that wasn't intentional," Ivy says quietly.

"Maybe. I hope that was it," I say.

"Suicide is an awful thing, and so many people who are suffering don't know how to escape their pain any other way. There is always a better way, Stephanie, always, but sadly we can't always know that is their plan so we can't step in and help. I was very angry with our Stephanie for a long time after that, because there were so many ways we could have helped her. I wish she would have given us the chance."

"I'm sorry," I say, unsure what else to add.

"It's okay, it was a long time ago. Did your mom say anything else in those letters?" she asks, looking at me over her wineglass. I watch as she takes a big gulp.

"Not really, just recapped what happened each year. It was fun to see what she thought was important," I say and Ivy snorts.

"Yeah, well, everything you did was important to her." Barkley looks up at her and whines a little. She reaches down and pats his head before taking another drink of her wine.

"Steph, I am going to be buying out your mom's half of the flower shop, I know you don't want me to do that, but I am. I met with the accountant and I think I can give you the full amount by the end of the month. I had to move some funds around," she says, and her voice sounds tight.

I cut her off. "Ivy, stop it. I don't want your money. The shop is yours."

"I can't do that, Steph, your mom wanted you to benefit from all her hard work, and I do too. I can't just walk away with what she built for you."

"I graduated from college without a penny of debt, I know you both worked your asses off so that could happen. No. Just no, Ivy. I won't take your money. This house is paid for and Mom left me with a life insurance policy. I'll be fine. Please. Please don't give me more money." I feel a knot form in my chest.

Ivy stares at me her eyes searching my face, then blinks slowly and nods. "Okay, I will respect your wishes. I thought she would say something in her will about what she wanted in regard to that, but since she didn't, I wanted to do the right thing, you know?"

"The right thing is that it is yours. You and mom have worked on that business for over twenty-five years. It's yours, Ivy," I say firmly.

"It has been a long time. We used to joke about it in high school, our names being so perfect. I didn't think it would happen, but she did. She knew, she always knew what she wanted." Ivy pauses and opens her mouth like she wants to say something, but doesn't. "Are you all ready for your interview?" she asks after a moment.

"I think so. I was wondering if I should get a haircut. I mean I've always just had long hair, maybe I could look older if I got a more modern haircut?" I ask.

"Sure, yeah that would be nice. Your hair is so pretty, but if you had bangs or something." She cocks her head to the side, examining me.

"OH! Bangs! That is what I need!" I slap the table.

"Penny would fit you in. Call her." Ivy reaches for my hand and squeezes it.

"Are you sure? I haven't seen her since Tim and I split up." I wince.

"Honey, her boy is ridiculous and she knows it, plus that was high school! Call her now, she would love to hear from you." Ivy smiles at me. I'm hit by how lucky I am to have this woman in my life.

I sigh and grab the cordless phone and call, making an appointment for Monday of next week. The week I leave. God, I hope it goes by quickly.

FOURTEEN
COREY

mile 1673.7
July 23, 1987

"COREY, GET YOUR ASS IN HERE!" Grace yells and I flinch. That woman can be terrifying. I imagine her bossing around people in her kitchen and my balls shrink to the size of grapes.

"Coming! Sorry, I had sap on my shoe." I walk into the real estate office and take off my backpack.

"Mr. Richie! It's so great to finally meet you in person," the agent says. She is about five feet tall and has hair like Dolly Parton. I hold out my hand and she grabs it with both of hers. She smells like pine trees, or maybe that is just me. I have lost the ability to smell anything but nature.

"Your parents wanted me to show you three properties in Beaver Valley and one here in Bend. The drive in the fall and summer is fine, but we do get snow here starting in about November. It can last all the way until the end of May sometimes.

Keep that in mind, okay?" Her voice is sweet but a little conde-scending.

Grace looks at me, then at the agent, and says with authority, "He doesn't need to see the one here in Bend. He will need to live in Beaver Valley. He told us he wants to immerse himself in all things Beaver. He can't do that if he's here in Bend, now can he?" Grace is using her scary chef voice with the agent and I imagine her balls shriveling too.

"Of course, well, that is just fine. Now will you be accompanying us to view these properties?" she asks nervously.

"Yes," Barbara and Grace say in unison and I just nod. Why these women have decided to come along on this part of my journey is beyond me, but I learned a few days ago that they get what they want. All the time. Even when it's over something stupid like where I live.

"Alright, well, let me see if George is back with the van." Millie stands.

"You do that. Chop-chop, Millie. Time is money," Grace shouts. She turns to me and gives me a smile. "I can't believe we're going to see Beaver Valley. I am so happy right now I can't even breathe," she says, and Barbara nods. "It's like the motherland. We should get married there on our way back."

"You are still going to make me hike all the way to Canada, aren't you?" Grace says, rolling her eyes.

"Hey, a deal is a deal. I will never have this long of a break from work again. I told you, you want to marry me, we hike the PCT without killing each other, then you will be Mrs. Dr. Barbara Miles."

"Why aren't you going to be Mrs. Grace Walker?" Grace puts her hands on her hips and I look at Barbara. I feel like I am watching a tennis match.

"That would never happen. Do you know the amount of paper-work I would have to fill out to change my name? No thank you."

They continue to argue while Millie emerges from the back holding a set of keys. "Excuse me, but if you're ready, I can take you to the van. The properties are about a twenty-minute drive from here, so if you feel the need to continue this argument we can do it on the road."

Oh, a surprise from Millie, turns out she is not a total pushover and she knows how to handle things. And by things, I mean bickering women. The drive over the hill is absolutely beautiful, mostly because it is happening without me moving my legs. I am so fucking tired. If I have more than a ten-minute walk anywhere for the rest of my life I will be upset. I am never hiking again, that's for damn sure.

"Over here on the right is the high school. I believe you said that's where you will be teaching?" Millie asks and I nod.

"Say the name, Millie." Barbara pokes her shoulder.

"The name?" she asks, feigning innocence.

"Yeah, the full name, if you don't mind." Barbara leans back in her seat and a smile spreads across her face.

"Um, it is spelled differently than it is pronounced. I know it can be confusing but Francis Furie discovered the valley when he was working his way across this great expanse. This valley was thick with beavers," Millie explains. I hear Grace snort from the back seat followed by a thud. Probably Barbara hitting her in the arm.

"Francis Furie was a great trapper and was able to snatch many of the beavers. There is a story about one beaver that was like his Moby Dick. He just couldn't snatch that one," Millie explains. She is staring straight ahead with a death grip on the wheel. I don't think she is enjoying this.

"His dick? You don't say. I have never heard a beaver compared to a dick in that way," I say, knowing the ladies behind me are probably in tears fighting the laughter. Who knew professional women could be so immature?

"Well, Moby Dick, you know, was the one whale that Captain Ahab couldn't catch, so that one beaver—" Millie tries to continue.

"That couldn't be snatched," Grace fills in, shouting from the back of the van.

"Right was nicknamed Dick, to be more exact Beaver Dick," Millie explains.

"Got it. So the school is?" Grace asks.

"It's the Furie Beaver High School," Millie says finally with a roar of laughter from the back of the van.

"I'm sorry, I found them on the trail and I haven't been able to ditch them," I whisper. It seems Millie doesn't know what to do. She wrings her hands on the steering wheel.

We drive a little further into town and she turns onto a street. I crane to see the street sign but miss it.

"Which one is this?" I ask, and she stops in front of a small home with a chain-link fence surrounding the worst patch of grass I have ever seen.

"This is 609 Bald Street."

"Oh, come on!" Grace yells, and she and Barbara fall into each other laughing.

"So my address would be Bald Street in Beaver Valley? No. Nope. Not even getting out of the van," I say, and Millie blinks at me.

"So should we skip the one on Whet Street?" she asks.

"I will buy the fucking house on Whet Street!" Barbara yells from the back seat and Grace starts howling.

"Yes, please, what is the last one?" I ask, crossing my fingers for a normal street name.

"It's on Main Street. Very close to the school. Actually my favorite one, but I wanted to be fair and show you all the ones I had told your parents about," Millie says. She sounds tired. I don't blame her.

"We would love to see that one. Thank you," I say, and I turn to glare at the ladies in the back of the van. Grace's face is buried in Barbara's shoulder and she is shaking so hard she's struggling to breathe. Jesus. I should have said no when they asked if they could come.

We pull back around to the school and I see a small white house trimmed with dark forest green. The front door is also dark green and there are small planter boxes filled with flowers under each window. It looks like something you'd see on a postcard.

"How many bedrooms?" I ask.

"It's a two-bedroom, two-bath. Recently remodeled. New kitchen and bath and the floors were redone after an unfortunate incident with some local wildlife," Millie explains.

"Say what now? Wildlife? Oh God, please tell me it was overrun with beavers," Barbara says, poking her head over my shoulder.

"I'd rather not say, but it did involve a few beavers and maybe a cougar. We really can't be sure." Millie parks in front of the small house and it feels like I just got home.

I wish I hadn't pictured Stephanie coming out through that front door, but I did. I blink it away and smile at the ladies, then say, "Okay, let's see this!"

WE CLIMB BACK in the van an hour later. Somehow I have agreed to make sure the second bedroom will be a guest room set up for Grace and Barbara to visit any time they want.

The kitchen is very nice and there's ample storage throughout the home. Compared to the prices in the Los Angeles area I feel like I'm stealing this place. I lived at home with my parents my whole first year of teaching, so I was able to save enough for a down payment. I try not to think about how I was planning on buying a house with my brother. He had been saving too, and we would talk about the awesome place we could afford together.

I refuse to dwell on that now. We all return to the agent's office and she fills out the paperwork to make the offer on 22 Main Street. I give Millie the number for the school and the hotel I am staying at until my parents arrive. They should be here in a day or so.

Millie assures me she'll be in touch and that the owners are really motivated to sell. She is sure the place is mine.

Barb, Grace, and I all walk back to our hotel and decide to get dinner. I really enjoy their company, even when they're acting like children. Well, especially when they are acting like that. We go into the pizza place next to our hotel and I order us a large pizza while Barb goes to get a pitcher of beer.

Grace waves at us from a booth and we make our way to her. Barb slides in and kisses her cheek, then pours her a beer before helping herself to one. She passes the pitcher and a glass to me.

"I really liked that place, Corey. I think it's a great starter home, and I hear the skiing is amazing around here, so now that we have a place to stay you can count on us for at least a few times a winter!" Grace says.

"For sure. I need to see Beaver Valley covered in snow," Barb says. She takes a long drink from her mug and leans back into the booth.

"So now that you're here, are you going to try and find her?" Grace asks.

I SIGH. "Yeah, I mean I guess, I realized I could call Information and ask for florists in San Diego with Ivy and Rose in the name. Now that I can give a contact number, I guess it can't hurt to try."

"Thank God. I can't live knowing your face looks like that. You will scare your students. Math is already a sucky subject, if you walk around like a grumpy bastard while you teach, you could turn kids away from higher education!" Barb says, pointing her finger at me.

"Thanks Barb," I say, raising my mug to her.

"Anytime, Corey."

WE ALL TURN when a group of people comes in the door, all wearing Furie Beaver High School shirts, and a few carrying binders with the school logo.

"I wonder if those are other teachers at your school?" Grace whispers.

"Probably. I am not going to go say hello while I still look like

Bigfoot. I have a plan to get a haircut and shave tomorrow before my parents get here, so let's just lay low, shall we?" I say.

"That's fair. You look like crap," Grace says, and Barbara agrees.

"Thanks, ladies."

The group comes and sits at the table near us and their excited chatter is nice. It seems like they all get along and when a tall man comes to the table with a full pitcher of beer and mugs for everyone, they let out a cheer.

"Mr. Brian, you are the best! Are you sure you can't stay and just be our principal?" a woman asks.

"No, trust me, you'll be fine with Garrett. He's a great guy and has tons of experience starting a new school. He and I taught together here in Bend when I finished my credential program. I know you will all like him and his leadership style. He's a lot like me." Mr. Brian smiles and it's contagious. Everyone seems relaxed and happy, something that my last principal wasn't capable of instilling.

Barb and Grace are talking quietly and leaning into each other so I keep myself busy eavesdropping. A woman who has a very high-pitched voice speaks next, and I know that must be the Miss Gee I talked to on the phone. She looks nothing like I pictured her. She is tall with short hair cut into an aggressive wedge. She is wearing a black button-up shirt that is snug against her neck. Her white blazer with shoulder pads makes her look like she could tackle everyone at the table. A pair of glasses hangs on a chain from her neck, and I am sure when she wears them they sit low on her nose.

"I just want to say, we have four more interviews next week. The music teacher is a no-show. He's not coming." Miss Gee raises her hand to stop the onslaught of questions. "I knew he was a bad choice, I am not going to say it again. We will make some calls and find a better fit. The history teacher is coming in on the third, and so is our Spanish teacher. Both are the only applicants so hopefully we like them. Oh! I should mention to everyone our history teacher candidate just lost her mother to cancer. She assures me she still wants to come but said she might be frazzled."

"Got it. Okay, I can't sit in on those interviews, but I am sure you and Garrett-Mr. Davies can handle it," Mr. Brian says. His voice sounds very familiar. I am pretty sure that's the guy I spoke with in my phone interview.

"Do we have a plan for the first day of school?" one of the other women asks and Mr. Brian nods. "Yeah, we will go over all of that at our first staff meeting. I expect everyone will be available on August tenth. Miss Gee, is that the start date for teachers?"

"Yes, Mr. Brian, that is correct," she answers.

I tune them out when the server carries our pizza over and sets it in front of us. My mouth waters and I wish it was all for me. I can see Barb and Grace looking at it and wonder if they're thinking the same thing.

FIFTEEN

STEPHANIE

mile 0
August 1st, 1987

I TAP my foot anxiously waiting for the taxi. Ivy offered to take me, but I feel like I need to do this all on my own. I check my watch and look out the front curtain for the tenth time.

I finally see the yellow sedan pull up and I am grabbing my bag and out the door before he can get out to come knock. He made it as far as the back of the car where he has popped the trunk. He is only a few minutes late, but I am so nervous. I just want to be at the airport.

"Hi!" I say as I hurry to the back of the cab. I toss my bag in the open trunk.

"Miss Hartford?" he asks.

"Yes, that's me. I am all ready to go," I say, sliding into the back seat and slamming my door. I grab the seat belt to pull across me. He looks down at me and shrugs, returning to his seat. He pushes the meter to turn it on and off we go. My stomach feels like I ate bricks for breakfast and I wonder if I can get a ginger ale on the plane.

I close my eyes and picture my mom waving to me from the porch. I let the tears slide down my cheeks. I have learned something in the last few weeks. Tears don't stop if you fight them, they just build up and spill out anyway. Better to cry and move on. After the taxi drops me off, I walk through the airport focused and determined. This is everything I have worked for and I owe it to my mom to try and enjoy the process.

My plane lands in Bend, Oregon, and I make my way to the front of the building to get another taxi to the hotel. Apparently you have to be twenty-five to get a rental car. So lame. Thank God for taxis. I have all weekend to explore and have made an appointment with a real estate agent named Millie. She offered to show me a few houses in Beaver Valley that are for sale, and a couple of places for rent.

If I don't get the job, if something goes wrong, maybe I'll stay here anyway. It is lovely. The tall trees and lush green lawns everywhere make me feel happy. I was able to get a cab quickly and as we drive to the hotel I see a sign for the Pacific Crest Trailhead out my window. My heart constricts and I suck in a breath. I am just about to look away when I catch sight of Barbara and Grace heading onto the trail. I turn in my seat, unable to speak and watch them disappear into the forest.

"Oh my God," I whisper. It's all I can muster, since I can barely breathe. My mind whirls with all the what ifs and my stomach starts to churn. Do I yell for the driver to stop? What would I even say to them? I can't do this. I can't worry about where Corey is right now. I have to get through this interview and then I can decide what to do.

I spend the weekend exploring Beaver Valley. Millie is a delight. She is a short woman that reminds me of Dolly Parton. She has a daughter about my age that she introduces me to, so at least I will have one friend in town. Kristen is getting her real estate license like her mom and has a lot to tell me about the new high school where I'll be working.

It must be my haircut, because no one seems to think I am too young to be a teacher. Penny not only gave me bangs, but also nice long layers and some darker blond streaks. I absolutely love it. I feel like Meg Ryan, except my hair is still long. I chickened out when Penny offered to chop it off short. It still hangs to my shoulders, but with all the layers I can't braid it if I tried. I like that. I can't fall back into my old habits.

I learn from Kristen that our principal is not going to be at school when we start, because he is moving down from Alaska. The woman I spoke to on the phone, Miss Gee, is famous in the valley for her cheesecake, not her Minnie Mouse voice. That wasn't mentioned at all. Weird.

The kids that will be going to Furie Beaver High have been bused into Bend for the last two years while the new school was built. I love the idea that I might actually get to teach the first class to graduate from this school. It feels important, and I close my eyes and blow out a breath, trying to calm my mind. I grab a book from my luggage and read until my eyes are heavy. Since my interview is at eleven, I need to get to sleep so I can wake up too early and get ready. It's likely I'll be awake at six or earlier. I close my eyes again and this time try and picture what I'll say to the interview panel. In the past twenty-some-odd interviews I attended there were three people, usually a teacher, a parent and the principal. I wonder who will be deciding my fate tomorrow.

MY EYES DRIFT OPEN and I blink a few times and stretch. I have never slept so well in my entire life. I roll lazily to my side and glance at the clock, my heart leaping out of my chest when I see the time. It's ten!

Holy fuck. I have less than a half hour to get ready and get to the lobby for a cab. What the hell happened? I never sleep this long. I throw the covers off and trip trying to get to the bathroom. I fall hard to my knees and scramble to the tile floor in front of me. I throw the shower curtain open and turn the water on while stripping out of my tank top and shorts.

"Shit, shit, shit," I yell into the shower stream. I was going to style my hair, take time to go over my potential answers to their interview questions and now I have to shove myself into my outfit and run to the lobby to call a cab.

"Shit!" I yell again, this time loud enough to warrant a knock on the wall from next door.

"Sorry!" I yell, washing my body quickly. I won't make it, I'll be late. I will be late for a job interview. The only shot I have at actually getting a job as a teacher. Fuck.

I get out of the shower and put gel in my hair, scrunching it like Penny showed me, then bolt out to my room and put on my black slacks and cream-colored blouse. It has a high neckline and pearl buttons. I thought it made me look sophisticated and older when I tried it on, but now as I fumble with the stupid buttons, I want to cry.

No crying, no crying, you can do this. I look at the clock on the nightstand and I still have ten minutes before I have to be in the lobby. I apply a bit of mascara and thankfully remember to brush my teeth at the last minute. I also use the hotel's hair dryer enough to at least not have dripping wet hair. Damn, I wish I could just put my hair in a French braid and be done. What was I thinking?

I check myself in the mirror and grab my purse before hurtling down the hall to the elevator. I push the button for down ten times and a very helpful man behind me explains how pushing the button a lot doesn't make it come faster. If I was positive he wasn't sitting on my interview board, I would kick him in the nuts.

I run to the front desk and ask the clerk to call a cab for me and she smiles. "There are three out there now! Take your pick!"

I WANT to leap across the counter and kiss her but I know that would take up precious time. Later, I will kiss her later. I run outside, wave at the cabs, and glance down at the door. I stop, frozen in place.

Rose Taxi Service is written in beautiful script on the door. There is a red rose under the lettering and I glance at the driver. He waves me over with the biggest smile and I climb in. Mom is taking me to my interview. My heart swells and I know in that moment everything is going to be okay. My shoulders relax and my lungs let go of all the anxiety-filled air I sucked in during my frantic race to get here.

I arrive at the school with about five minutes to spare and walk in the front door, my head held high. *This is my school. This is where I teach. This is my destiny.* I let those words run through my mind as I make my way to the office.

"Hello, my name is Stephanie Hartford and I'm here for an interview," I say, as I approach the counter.

"Miss Hartford. I am so glad you were able to make it. I'm Miss Gee." A tall thin woman with a high-pitched voice reaches her hand out to me.

"Oh, we spoke on the phone!" I say, meeting her hand with mine.

"Yes, we did dear, how are you doing?" she says with that little head tilt people do to show sympathy.

"Moving forward. It's all I can do," I say, and for the first time in a month I feel like I am not lying. People want to hear you say you're fine or that you are managing and none of that is true. I am not fine, and I am barely managing. I am moving forward though, so yay for me.

"Well, we are so happy you are here. They are just finishing with someone and I'm afraid we will have to wait. Our math teacher, Mr. Richie, who was sitting in on the interview in progress, got called away to help with a family matter, so our physical education teacher Mr. Wallace will be in for your interview. I appreciate your patience," Miss Gee says, and I nod. She motions to a row of blue plastic chairs and I smile. I swear these are the same chairs that were in the laundromat in South Lake Tahoe. I sit and lean back, remembering Corey in his ridiculous red Speedo, ass cheeks squeaking on the plastic.

I wait for about a half hour before Miss Gee tells me they're ready for me. I am led to a small conference room where I am intro-duced to Mr. Wallace who is not only the PE teacher but will also be teaching cooking and maybe doing yearbook. A parent of one of the sophomore students currently being bused to Bend for classes smiles at me like I am her long-lost friend, so that is a good sign. I hear scur-rying from down the hall, and Miss Gee says, "Coming! I'm coming. Sorry, dear."

She takes her seat next to the others and turns to me with a big smile. Her smile is almost as big as her shoulder pads, but not quite. Wow. Those things up this close are intimidating. I feel like I am sitting across from the Chicago Bears defensive lineman, The Fridge.

I fold my hands on the table in front of me and smile.

They smile back.

I blink.

They all blink at me.

I swallow hard and start to sweat.

Finally, Mr. Wallace realizes he's supposed to ask me a ques-tion, so he starts. "Miss Hartford, you have impeccable transcripts and your advisor from your year of student teaching has written you a very impressive letter of recommendation. What makes someone with your qualifications want to work in such a small town?"

Oh, I was not expecting that. I've never had a question like that before. He thinks I am too good to teach here? Is that what he's saying? My hands start to sweat and I move them off the table to rub them on my slacks.

"Well, I appreciate your small town and I have always wanted to move out of the San Diego area. I felt like it was a wonderful opportu-nity to see what Oregon has to offer," I say, wondering if that made any sense at all. I almost said that I have zero memory of applying to this school, but I manage to keep that quiet.

"I heard you were hiking on the PCT until recently, is that true?" the parent asks, her eyes wide like I had landed on the moon.

"Yes, I started near my home in San Diego and I made it to just past Truckee, California, when I was called home for an emergency," I say, trying to keep my voice calm.

"Well, you are the bravest person I have ever known. I haven't slept in a tent ever, not even once, and I am so afraid of snakes that I couldn't even look at Steven's art when they did their reptile unit. I don't know how you did it," she says and she literally puts her chin in her hands and stares at me like I am Madonna putting on a private concert for her.

Miss Shoulder Pads leans in and says, "I also think you're amazing. We have another teacher who has done some hiking. I think you might have some things to talk about. Mr. Richie, our math teacher, says he likes the outdoors and has hiked. Maybe you will have a friend in him!"

"Do you have any experience with beavers?" Mr. Wallace asks, startling me.

"Like real live ones? No, I am afraid I have never seen one in real life," I admit.

"They are tricky little buggers. I live by the creek and more than once they have diverted the water so it runs right into my garage. The valley is thick with them. Are you going to live here, or commute from Bend?" he asks.

"I think I will live here. I looked at a few places over the weekend, but wanted to see how today went before making any final decisions," I say. I feel my upper lip break out in a sweat and fight the urge to wipe it away.

"Oh, honey. You have the job, welcome to the Furie Beavers!" Miss Gee says.

"Yes, welcome!" The parent stands and reaches for me across the table. She seems to want a hug, but I can't manage with the conference table between us, so I just awkwardly pat her back.

"So that's it? I got the job?" I ask, looking at the three of them. They are all smiling at me. I might throw up.

"Yes, welcome to Beaver Valley, my dear. You are going to love it here!" Miss Gee says as she escorts me back to the office to fill out my paperwork.

I wasn't asked any questions about my teaching style or discipline techniques. I thought there would be at least a few questions like that. There have been at literally every other interview I have had, and let me tell you, there have been a lot of them. What kind of place is this?

SIXTEEN
COREY

August 3rd, 1987

"WHAT KIND OF PLACE IS THIS?" my mother yells from the front yard of my new home.

"It's a magical place, Dorothy!" Henry, my father says as he carries the last of my boxes up the driveway.

"It is, isn't it?" My mom opens her arms wide and spins in a circle like she is the lead in *The Sound of Music*. I rub my face, wondering if I will ever feel like my parents aren't weird.

"Thanks for all your help. I could have waited until tomorrow to do this. I was in the middle of interviews at the school. This isn't really a family emergency," I say.

I keep looking over my shoulder worried Miss Gee or someone from the school will drive by and catch me doing something I could have done tomorrow. My parents called Furie Beaver High and lied, saying we were having a small family crisis simply because they couldn't wait to see the inside of my house. Dad had driven the moving truck all the way from LA and parked it out front, then they stayed in a hotel last night. They refuse to stay with me tonight, claiming their hotel is the best they have ever seen. Their house in Bend will be ready next week. I really hope they aren't planning on staying at the hotel for the whole week—that would be ridiculous.

My mom pulls my father into the house and closes the door, leaving me standing in my yard alone. My neighbor to the left wanders out to check the mail and looks over at me squinting, so I walk over to introduce myself. He is a tall thin man who is more the shape of a croissant than a bread stick.

"Hello! I'm your new neighbor Corey, nice to meet you," I say, hand extended.

"No," he barks out.

"No? I don't understand," I say.

"No, it is not nice to meet you, and no, you are not my new neighbor. My kids are trying to sell the house and are making me move into a senior apartment closer to them." The old man slams the mailbox door shut, then opens it again and slams it one more time, breaking the hinge. That seems to please him, so he takes his slippered foot and gives the post a kick.

"Oh, well I am sorry to hear that," I say.

"Fuck off," he says, flipping me off as he walks away.

He is charming. I guess I'm glad he's moving. Walking through my front door, I catch my mom slapping my dad on the ass. He yells out, "Later Dorothy!" She laughs like a lunatic. How long have they been like this? Maybe I am glad they're staying at the hotel.

"I unpacked your kitchen already, dear, you can start on the bathroom stuff or your bedroom. I didn't know if you had embarrassing things you wouldn't want your mother to see," Mom sing-songs.

"Embarrassing things? Like my underwear?" I ask confused.

"No like lube or hemorrhoid cream," she says over her shoulder.

"Jesus, Mom, no! I have nothing like that." I wipe my hand down my face.

"Ignore her, she has been reading some very questionable literature now that she's retired. Puts all kinds of crazy ideas in her head," my father says as he pulls a level out of his pocket and checks a framed picture he just hung. I guess I don't get to decorate my own house. Okay.

I walk to my room and pull the box marked "clothes" and open it to find all my shirts. I can tell this is a box Mom packed because each shirt is folded perfectly. The next box I grab is one I did, a wad of T-shirts stuffed in with dirty shoes right on top. In my defense I packed when I was in a bad mood about my brother.

I set out on the PCT searching for myself, for a way to deal with feeling abandoned and I am surprised to say it worked. As much as it pains me to admit, if Stephanie hadn't left, I wouldn't be where I am now. Barb and Grace allowed me a few days of pouting and feeling sorry for myself, then they really made me do the work. Grace made me answer some tough questions I had been avoiding since Codey left for Europe.

She had taken some psychology classes when she first got to college, before the chef thing took hold. She helped me see that teaching may be something we were both interested in, but it's okay to do it without Codey. She said to give it a full year before I make any decisions that would change my career. I felt a big weight off my shoulders once I agreed to that. I can do a year.

I really did enjoy teaching at that charter school, and I guess I thought it was only because my brother was on the same campus. Grace said I can have that connection with other teachers, that I can make my own friends. I think that is what was the hardest about him leaving. We had friends, but they were *our* friends. It felt weird to hang out with them by myself. I kept expecting Codey to walk in or say some smart-ass thing. I felt like I was not as fun to the guys without him.

I pull out a box marked "bedroom decorations" and rip off the tape. I reach in and grab the picture of me and Codey at our high school graduation. Big stupid smiles stretch across both of our faces and it's hard for even me to tell who is who. I should call him tonight. I have been a dick.

My parents work until every last box is unpacked and broken down, then they load all the flat empty boxes into the back of the moving truck and drive back to Bend, leaving me alone in my new house. I stand and look around, unsure what to do. I guess I'll sit and watch television, although after going without it for so long, I can't really say I missed it. I grab my high school yearbook instead and flip through the pages, wondering what it will be like for the kids who will attend Furie Beaver High.

A knock at the door startles me out of the past and I close the book and set it on the coffee table. When I open the front door I am met with my new school's principal.

"Hello, Corey?" He sticks his hand out, so I grab it and shake, smiling at him.

"Mr. Brian! It's so nice to meet you in person. Come in, I um, am just getting settled."

Mr. Brian looks around my completely unpacked home.

"My parents came and helped me. My mom was a kindergarten teacher for thirty years, she can't help herself," I say with a wince.

Mr. Brian bursts out laughing. "I understand that completely, my wife is a first-grade teacher. The most organized person you will ever meet. Oh, and please, just Brian. You can drop the Mr.," he says flashing his blue eyes in my direction.

"I'm sorry, is Brian not your last name? I must have misheard on our phone call," I say.

"No, it's not, I taught special education before going into administration and I had the kids call me Mr. Brian because my last name sounded too much like a cuss word," he says with a chuckle. "I still introduce myself as Mr. Brian out of habit."

"What's your last name, Sheet?" I say, proud of my quick wit.

"No, it's Tuck. At school you'll know me as Mr. Tuck until Garrett Daniels comes down. He should be here in a few weeks." He continues to talk and I stand frozen. I look at his wide blue eyes and what must have been blonde hair at one point. Holy shit.

"You're Brian Tuck?" I say slowly.

"Yes, and you're Corey Richie, our new math teacher. I am glad we have that straight." He laughs and I catch a glimpse of Stephanie's humor.

The sarcasm, the eyes, holy shit those eyes. I don't know what to do. I am sure I'm sweating. I might throw up. God, I wish Grace and Barbara were here. "Come in, sit! Do you want a beer?" I ask, forcing myself to act normal.

"Sure, that sounds great. I hear your sisters are enrolled in the community college in Bend? Did you know that's where I started?"

I break out in a second layer of sweat. The first one not sufficient to cover what I am going through.

"You don't say, and what year would that have been?" I ask for no reason, quickly doing the math, Stephanie was born June first. She turned twenty-two on the trail so she was born in 1965. Her mom would have been in Bend around October or November of 1964.

"I started in January of 1965, but moved here early with a buddy. We bummed around, went to parties, met people, you know? Let's see, I moved to Bend in August of '64. I wasn't at the junior college for long, transferred over to OSU and met my wife. We have been married twenty years," Brian says.

"Do you..." I clear my throat. "Do you have any children?"

"Yes, two boys. David is going to be starting his freshman year at high school and his brother Trevor is starting eighth grade."

David, Trevor, and Stephanie, who are your children. How nice. I feel a bead of sweat run down my face. Fuck. What do I do?

"Beer!" I yell and dart toward the kitchen grabbing two bottles and returning too quickly. Damn, I should have hung out looking for glasses or something.

Brian is sitting on my couch now. Stephanie's *father* is sitting on my couch. A girl I met on the PCT and quite possibly love. A girl I don't know how to find. Damn it.

"Here you go." I hand the opened beer to Brian, and he takes it and leans back into the couch.

"Listen I really appreciate you stepping in with the interviews today, I heard you had a little family emergency so that is why I stopped by. I want you to know, we are here for you. Whatever you need."

"Oh God, no, it was nothing like that. My emergency was that my parents are nuts. They are recently retired and they drove the moving truck up here from LA. I am sorry to say my mother lied, not knowing I was doing interviews. I think she probably thought I was just setting up my classroom." I let out the truth because there is no way I can think up a lie in my current state.

"Oh! Well, that is good news. I was worried that there was something serious. Our history teacher recently lost her mother to cancer, so I guess I jumped to the worst conclusion."

"That's understandable, and I am sorry to hear that. What an awful thing to go through. I hope her family is able to help her with all of that," I say. I am grateful for something else to think about.

"I imagine so, I wasn't in on her interview. I had an appointment I couldn't reschedule. I hear she is great. We have a wonderful group of new and fresh young teachers. I think our oldest teacher is thirty, the youngest is twenty-two! I wish I was going to stay on as your principal in a way, this group is going to be dynamic." He tips his beer bottle at me and I clink with him and drink.

"I am really excited about the coming year. I think your model is one that should be copied nationwide," I say, not even lying.

"Theme teaching will be the future, I am sure of it. I love your ideas about incorporating math assignments that fit with the history lessons," Brian says.

"Math only makes sense if you can apply it," I say, and he nods at me.

He takes another drink and says, "I agree. I have to tell you, I hate math. I never understood it, I struggled with it, and I didn't develop a good relationship with numbers. That is part of why I am so excited about this school. Garrett has something similar up in Alaska, which is why I recommended him for this spot."

"Why can't you stay on? It seems like you really love the whole idea and the teachers who have been hired."

"I can't. I have another year in contract with the Bend Unified School District. I am 'on vacation' while we wait for Garrett," he says, making air quotes. "They know I'm here, and I'm doing them a favor really. The Beaver Valley kids have made our high schools a little crowded."

My brain is still in overdrive trying to understand what I am supposed to do with the information I have. He continues to make small talk until his beer is done then stands and shakes my hand.

"Corey, it was a pleasure to meet you. I am looking forward to getting to know you more."

"Thank you, Sir, Brian, Mr. Tuck, Brian," I say and he laughs.

"Brian."

"Right. Brian who was definitely in Bend, Oregon in the fall of 1964."

He cocks his head at me and I smile.

"See you next week!" he says and I walk him to the door, sweat pouring off me like a stream.

"Brian, wait," I say.

"Yeah?"

"Um, do you remember a girl named Rose, that you would have met in 1964?" I say before I can give it any more thought.

"Rose?" He scratches his chin and then his eyes go wide.

"Oh, Rose! About this tall?" He holds his hand up to about Stephanie's height, so I nod.

"Yeah, she was a nice girl, you know her?" He doesn't appear uncomfortable at all.

"Um, I met her daughter on the PCT," I squeak out.

"Her daughter, huh? Well, I guess she figured it out," Brian says with a small smile.

"What do you mean?" I ask.

He rubs his hand down his face and says, "Well, when I met Rose she was struggling. She wasn't sure what she wanted. The sixties were a confusing time for some, a lot of experimenting, you know? So when I met her, she was on a quest of sorts to find herself. I guess she figured it out. I am glad to hear she got married and had a daughter. I know she said she wanted children."

"Um, yeah. So you knew her well then?" I ask.

"We hung out, dated I guess you could say, for about a month. She was a lot of fun," Brian says.

Now what? Shit. Do I just tell him when I have no way of finding her?

"So how did you make that connection? Did Rose's daughter mention me?" he asks, and I blink.

"Yes. Well, no. She said her mom went on a road trip to Bend. And she met a nice guy named Brian Tuck. She told me that because I said that I was stopping in Bend. She was going to Canada, so she wasn't stopping here, in Bend," I say, and wonder if maybe I could have slipped one more 'Bend' in that sentence.

"Oh well, it is a small world, isn't it?" Brian says giving me a smile that reminds me of his daughter.

"It really is," I say.

"Have a good night, Corey. See you at school next week!"

I let him leave and watch him as he walks to his car. I continue to watch as he drives away. I rub my hands on my pants and think about throwing up in my bushes. Instead I go inside and dial 411.

"Information, can I help you?"

"Yes, I am looking for a florist in the San Diego area, can you help me with that?" I ask.

Once I have a few options, some very promising, I sit and make another call. One I should have made a long time ago.

"Hello?"

"Hey Codey, it's me," I say.

"Hey, it's about damn time. How are you, brother?"

I sink into the couch and lean my head back, closing my eyes.

God, I miss him. "I'm good. Just hanging out in my new house in Beaver Valley. You think you and Janet can come for a visit sometime?" I ask, afraid of the answer.

"Yeah, we're saving for our tickets already. I want to wait until Dad and Mom have their place in Bend so I can see everyone, you know?" he says.

"Sure, yeah, that makes sense. Cool. How's the music thing going?" I say, trying to hide the hurt in my voice.

"It's not, I've been working at a music store teaching guitar and bass. I have a full client list and it is keeping me super busy. I really like it, Corey. I don't know why I didn't think to study music in college and become a music teacher."

"You can still do that, we are only twenty-five." I laugh out loud.

"True, I like the stability of it, and Janet is still writing songs. She sold a few that you might actually hear on the radio someday. I can't say who the artist is yet, but when it hits I'll let you know."

I can hear the pride in his voice and it makes me feel like even more of an ass. Why wasn't I more supportive? I shouldn't even act like I don't know the answer to that, it's because I was jealous. I was afraid I would never meet someone like Codey had.

I take a deep breath and launch into the story about the PCT and meeting the most amazing woman of my life, then losing her, then meeting her birth father.

"Holy shit! Are you going to tell him?" Codey asks.

"You think I should?" I ask as I rub my hand over my face.

"Fuck yeah, I mean he has a right to know. Plus, maybe he will find her and bring you back together! Could be a win-win," he says.

"That's why I called, I needed your input. Thanks so much, dude. I am going to call him right now and tell him. I just couldn't do it in person. I didn't want to see his face if he was mad about it, you know?"

"Shit, I get that, but she's what twenty-four, twenty-five?" he asks.

"No, she's only twenty-two. She graduated high school at seventeen and rushed through college, then started the PCT down in San Diego."

"Fuck, that's hot," Codey says and I laugh.

"I thought so too. Dude, I need to find her. I can't believe I let her go."

"You will, call those places you told me about and let me know what you find out. Hey, now that you know how to use a telephone maybe we can talk more often? I really miss you," he says, with a softness in his voice.

"I miss you too, thanks, Codey."

"For what?"

"Not being mad at me. I was an ass," I say, with a sigh.

"You were, but you are my other half. Can't stay mad," he says, and instead of feeling guilty like I should, I just feel grateful.

SEVENTEEN

STEPHANIE

August 4th, 1987

"IVY? IS THAT YOU?" I ask.

"Yes, sorry honey, I am here. Did you have your interview?"

"I did! I got the job, and Ivy, I think I just bought a house!" I squeal into the phone.

"What? Well, that was fast! How exciting for you. What is the school like?" she asks.

"I don't really know, I only saw the office and the conference room. I get to go in later in the week and set up my classroom. I bought a car too, I feel like there are so many things happening I can't think straight." I sigh and lean against the headboard of my hotel bed.

"I understand that honey, your mom would be so proud of you. I'm so proud of you. I'm so glad you called me," she gushes.

"You are? I'm not bugging you?" I ask, and I hear her take a sharp breath in.

"Stephanie Iverson, you will never bother me, not ever, do you hear me?" Ivy says and I hear the sincerity in her voice.

I hug the phone to my ear wishing it was her wrapping her arms around me. This has been so hard to do on my own. On the trail I thought I was such a grown-up. I was on my own, blazing my way. Now I feel like a little kid pretending to be an adult.

"Okay, thank you, Ivy. How are things there? How are you?" I ask.

"I miss her so much some days I don't want to get out of bed, then I remember a bride wants her bouquet and Rose loved weddings more than anything. I can't let her down," Ivy says.

"Thank you," I tell her.

"For what, dear?"

"For sharing her passion. It's like a piece of her is still here in you. I don't know what I would do without you, Ivy," I say. I wish I had told her how I felt more often.

"Oh honey, I feel the same way about you," Ivy says.

We talk a while longer catching up on all the things. I explain about the houses I looked at and how the streets have very unfortunate names. Besides Whet Street, I saw a house on Bald Street and one on Deeper Ave. Then magically a house that hadn't even been listed on the MLS became available. It's on Main Street. Thank God. I tell her how the current resident is an older man who needs to move closer to his children. He isn't happy about it, but the house is in his kids' name, and they felt it was time. Their dad had fallen one too many times and they want him to move before the snow starts to fall.

They expect to move him next week sometime and we are doing a fast escrow since I have cash. I still can't believe I will just own a home, just like that. Thanks, Mom. All of this is because of her.

"Tell me more about Beaver Valley, dear, is it everything you imagined?" Ivy asks.

We speak for over an hour, laughing and crying and when I hang up I feel like I ran a marathon. I decide to walk to a local pizza place that I've heard is good.

The place is empty except me and an older woman sitting at a table alone reading the paper. I order a personal size pizza and a beer and sit to wait. I hear her fold her paper and am taken back to Corey in the laundromat wearing nothing but boots and a shiny red Speedo.

I have an idea wash over me thinking about that day. I could leave a note on the community board at the junior college saying I was looking for a guy who had twin sisters at the school. How many Coreys would fit that bill? Once I have a local phone number to include on the note, I'll do that. I can't help but wonder if he is still thinking about me? Did he wonder where I was, like I'm constantly doing with him?

After dinner I make my way back to the hotel and press the button for the elevator. Riding to my room, I decide that I will write a note explaining where Corey could find me. Maybe I should attach the rattail? That way his sisters would know the note was really for him.

Settled with my plan and a full belly, I fall asleep easily. I wake up to an unfamiliar phone ringing.

"Hello?" I mumble.

"Hello Stephanie, this is Miss Gee. I hope I didn't catch you at a bad time, I just wanted to let you know that the school will be open tomorrow for teachers instead of next week like we had discussed. Everyone is clamoring to get in and set up their rooms, so I want you to know you can come too, even if it's just to see the space."

"Oh, that's great, Miss Gee! Thank you so much. I have a few boxes of things arriving, but they won't be here until Wednesday of next week. I will come by though, I want to see my classroom. I'm very excited!" I sit up and brush my hair out of my face.

"We are too dear. You are in the math and science wing. Your room is 6A right next to math and Mr. Richie in 6B. He's the one I told you about who likes to hike."

"Oh perfect, thanks," I say.

"Anything else you need or are you getting settled here okay?" she asks.

"I am doing great, thanks. I had pizza from the place you recommended and it was delicious. I think I am going to like it here just fine," I tell her.

"That's wonderful, I will see you tomorrow. Stop by the office for your key," she says and I thank her and hang up.

Maybe today would be better spent calling the moving company and the real estate agent. I would like to see the place I bought. I left that little tidbit out when I told Ivy I had bought a place. I was so desperate to have a normal street name, I signed the papers sight unseen.

I climb out of bed and head to the shower ready to tackle my day.

MY DAY TACKLED ME. I am not prepared for this, doing all this alone, without my mom. I just can't. I drove past my new house and it's adorable, not as cute as the place next door that is white with green trim and freaking flower boxes, but it has charm. I will probably repaint the outside a happier color. Brown just isn't me. But like that decision, all the decisions are mine alone to make, without input from Mom. She won't know this part of my life. She won't ever come here to see me and the thought of that cripples me.

I called Millie at the real estate office and she told me the kids were coming to get their father and sign the papers tomorrow, and the moving company would have everything cleaned out by next week. They were okay with me renting the place from them while we wait for escrow to close. I pray to God all my stuff fits and that the inside doesn't smell like hot dog water.

My movers now know the date they can arrive, I have transferred my mail, contacted everyone I could think of to give them my new address, and called to set up my phone. I decided not to get cable. I never watched a lot of television growing up, so why start now? I could picture myself curled up on the couch with a cup of tea and a good book after a long day of teaching.

Maybe I could get a dog, or better yet, a cat. I could get a cat and name him Mr. R. That sounds like something that would make me feel a little less lonely.

EIGHTEEN
COREY

August 5th, 1987

DAMN, that conversation went about as well as one would expect. "Hey, so remember that girl I met on the PCT, turns out she's your daughter," I had said to him.

To his credit Brian wasn't a jerk about it. In fact, he seemed only a little rattled, but more than anything he seemed sad. He said he wished he had known so he could have been in her life. I told him what a wonderfully funny and intelligent woman she was. I told him all I knew was her first name was Stephanie. He of course asked if I knew where she was and I had to tell him no. That was the hardest part. I explained how Ivy had met us on the trail head near Truckee and in less than five minutes she was loaded in the rental car and gone. There wasn't time to do much else than wave goodbye. It was a scene that played over in my head a hundred times. Each time I tried to change the outcome, but until they invent a time machine, I guess I have to live with the fact that I made the worst choice possible when I told her to go.

"I'll go with you," I say out loud, because that is what I should have said that day. Miss Gee cocks her head at me.

"What, dear?" she asks in her very high-pitched voice.

"Oh sorry, nothing. I was thinking out loud," I explain.

"Okay. Here is the key to your room. Be sure to pop over and say hello to the new history teacher. Miss Hartford is right next door."

"Will do, thanks." I walk down the hallway toward my room and think about going in my room first, but I don't even have my stuff with me. I just came today to see the space and make plans.

I knock on the closed classroom door and hear a muffled "come in."

I open the door and step into the room where I see the nicest ass since I was on the PCT and following Stephanie. This ass is small too and whoever the owner is appears to be stuck in a cabinet.

"Are you okay?" I ask, laughing.

"Not really, I crawled in here to see if there was an outlet and my hair got stuck in the hinge. If you could maybe get the janitor or something, that would be great." Her voice sounds like she is about to cry so I move closer.

"Here, I can open this other door and crawl in too, I might be able to reach up and free your hair," I say, opening the cabinet next to her. I get on my knees and crawl in flipping to my side when I get in far enough.

Her head is turned away from me and I can see a lock of her blonde hair stuck in the hinge on the back of the cabinet.

"For some reason there is a long piano hinge running the length of the cabinet top, but it wouldn't open. They nailed it shut," she explains.

"I was just about to ask why you didn't just open the lid." I wiggle closer and tug once, freeing her hair.

"There you go. You are a free woman." I shimmy out of the cabinet and she does too, both of us on our knees as we back out. I stand and brush off my pants and my eyes travel up her small frame. I reach her face and the question I had about if there was a plug in the cabinet poofs out of my mind like a candle in the wind. Two feet from me I see the biggest, bluest eyes, perfect tiny nose, and rosebud lips that are currently making a very cute O shape. Her hair is different, shorter and she has bangs and little wisps of hair that frame her beautiful face. She has put back on some of the weight she lost on the trail too, her face is fuller.

My eyes fly open wide and I say, "Stephanie? Is that you?"

"Corey? Oh my God!" She screams, then throws herself at me, almost tackling me to the ground. I quickly regain my balance and grab her pulling her close to me, needing to feel her tiny body against mine. Before I can speak, her mouth crashes into mine, and her hands are holding my face. She is kissing me with a frantic hunger and I match her, moaning as she slides her tongue along mine. I open my mouth further and she dives in, taking what she wants, as she pants and moans and grinds against me. She lets her hands fall to my chest and she twists my T-shirt into her fists, pulling me down to her level.

My heart is beating out of my chest as I try and comprehend what is happening. How is she here? I am about to pull away and ask that, but her lips are making my brain mushy and my thoughts foggy. I'll figure the why and how out later. Right now her lips are on mine, she is in my arms and both of us seem to have forgotten that we're in her classroom. I grab the back of her head and hold her in place, not wanting her to take even one step away from me. I want to strip off her clothes, bend her over a desk and take her right here, right now.

"Oh! I see you have met. I was coming to introduce you two, but that hardly seems necessary," Miss Gee says from the open doorway. I am not sure if that was amusement or disgust in her voice.

"Oh my God!" Stephanie yells, pushing me away, which gives a very wrong impression.

Miss Gee steps closer and looks around for something to hit me with, I guess. I hold up my hands and say, "Miss Gee, it's okay. We know each other!" I step a little closer to Stephanie, who is shaking like a cold chihuahua. I reach and grab her hand, interlacing our fingers. I can't believe she's here.

"Stephanie, is this true? Do I need to call the police?" Miss Gee is narrowing her eyes at me.

"Oh God, no please don't. Yes, I know Corey, wait." She turns to me, mouth hanging open. "Are you Mr. Richie? Mr. R?"

I smile, so fucking happy that I get this moment with her. "Yes, that's why I wanted to know why you called me Mr. R and R." I laugh.

"Oh God. That is so funny! No that is not it, that is not why I called you that." She pauses and looks at me with those big, beautiful eyes. "Oh my God, Corey, I can't believe you're here. I can't tell you how scared I was that I would never see you again," she says and throws herself at me again, forgetting Miss Gee entirely.

I hold her tiny body against mine and struggle to remain professional. I wrap my arms around her tightly and turn us so I can see Miss Gee. "Stephanie and I met this summer on the PCT. We got separated, and ..." I start to explain but Miss Gee waves her hand dismissively.

"Just maybe save the kissing for later," she says and smiles, walking out the door. I notice her come back and open the door wider, as a gentle reminder that we are in fact in a public place.

Stephanie is still wrapped around me and I kiss the top of her head and squeeze her tighter. I feel like every prayer, every birthday wish that didn't come true was saved for this moment and I am okay with that. This is all I want. This is all I need.

"How's your mom?" I ask as I pull back a little. I see her face fall.

"She passed away. She had bone cancer. That's why she broke her hip. It was pretty quick after the fall, but at least I got to say good-bye," she says, tears welling up in her beautiful blue eyes.

"Oh, my God. They told me one of the new teachers had lost her mother recently, that was you. Wait, was the thing you had to do near Bend an interview for here?" I ask, everything falling into place.

She takes a step back and sits on one of the desks, so I do the same. Sitting across from her, I wish I could have her sit on my lap, but we already got carried away once.

"Yeah, I almost canceled it, but Mom was really set on me coming up here, and I think she let go so that I would. I had told her I wasn't leaving her to come up here for the interview and two days later, she was gone," Stephanie says.

"I am so sorry," I say, not knowing what else to say.

"Thanks. So did you get your sisters all settled?" she asks, and I nod.

"Yeah, my parents are over in Bend. They helped me get settled in my new place and I think their moving company is coming next week."

"Wait, your parents? But I thought they lived in LA?"

"They both retired and moved up here. My sisters will be at OSU soon, and both want to stay up here after they graduate, and I am up here. It made sense to them to come too," I explain.

"That's great, Corey. You have family here. That must be so nice," she says wistfully, and my eyes go wide again.

Oh. My. God. Brian. I told him. Shit.

"Uh, yeah family close by is nice." I start thinking how I can possibly find a way to tell her when there is a knock on the open door.

"Hi, I just was passing by and heard voices. Thought I would step in and introduce myself!" a deep booming voice calls out.

"Brian!" I yell, then cover my face with my hands. I wonder if I click my heels together and say "there's no place like home" a few times if I will be transported out of what is about to be the most awkward moment in the history of time?

Stephanie turns and holds out her hand. Everything moves in slow motion as I watch their hands connect.

"Hello, I'm the interim principal Brian Tuck, you must be Stephanie?" he says.

I look at Stephanie and watch the realization cross her face. Her eyes, her blue eyes, mirrored back at her in our principal's, are huge.

Shit.

"Yes, I'm Stephanie Hartford," she says, blinking a few times, then looking over at me. I think she is wondering if I remember her telling me the name of her biological father. I sure did. I also told her biological father about her.

Shit.

"I am sorry to hear about your mother. Thank you for agreeing to come up for the interview. I am sorry I wasn't able to attend. I hear you made a wonderful impression." Brian leans back on the desk. He's so calm, so relaxed. Almost like he doesn't know his whole world is about to change.

"Thank you, yes, my mom, um, my mother Rose." She says the name slowly, watching his expression. If I hadn't just told him, or maybe if I wasn't sitting here, sweat dripping from my face, he might not have put two and two together.

He knew his daughter was named Stephanie, and that she was twenty-two. He turns and looks at me with the same wide blue eyes and I nod.

"Mr. Tuck, allow me to introduce you to your daughter. Stephanie, this is your biological father. I am sure you have a lot to talk about so I will just leave you to it," I say, then scramble off the desk and run out of the classroom. Once I am in the hall, I sprint down the long hallway barreling out the door. I don't stop until I am at the front door of my house.

I can get my car later, or never. I probably should look for another job, a new house.

Holy shit.

NINETEEN

STEPHANIE

August 5th, 1987

CAN you get whiplash standing in a room? Is emotional whiplash a thing? I have opened my mouth to speak at least five times but no sound comes out. The man standing in front of me has my eyes. His hair is a mix of blonde and grey, with more of it grey, but it's thick like mine. A handsome man, he has wrinkles around his eyes like he has spent his life laughing and smiling. I wipe my hands on my jean shorts and stare at him.

"Stephanie, I think Corey is right, we have a lot to talk about." He looks around, his gaze landing on the open door.

"Do you like pizza?" he asks, and I nod, unable to do anything else. I am not even sure if I am breathing to be honest. I think my lungs have forgotten how to work.

"Let's get out of here. I'll buy you lunch and we can sort this out without anyone walking in." He motions toward the open door and I walk out. Stunned. Shocked. Those are the two words that enter my mind as I follow my father out to his car.

My father. Holy shit. I haven't even been able to process the fact that Corey is here, and I am hit with this? Did my mother know? Is that why she was so determined that I come here? Why not just tell me? My head is swimming, my chest hurts.

"Here we are," Brian says, pulling up to the pizza place I was at last night. Neither of us has said a word on the drive over.

"Oh, they have great pizza!" I say. It's my attempt to sound normal and I hope he buys it. I climb out of the car to follow him inside. I breathe deeply when I step up next to him and we both read the board. The garlic smell is making my mouth water and I glance over at Brian wondering if he also likes garlic. My mom hated it, said it tasted like armpits.

He asks what I want, then steps up to place the order allowing me a moment to duck into the bathroom. I splash water on my face and stare in the mirror as the water runs down my cheeks. I don't recognize myself. My heart is thumping and my stomach rolls a bit. Jesus, how do I go sit and have pizza?

Steeling myself, I head back out and find my father sitting where I sat last night. He has a pitcher of beer in front of him and two ice cold mugs. That simple thing makes me settle a bit. A smile tugs at the corners of my mouth. Maybe I can do this, maybe this will be okay. My mom also hated beer. I guess I know where that love of mine comes from.

"Thanks for this," I say, sliding in across from him.

"Of course. This is a lot." Brian takes a big gulp of his beer then says, "I just learned about you yesterday. Corey told me when I told him my last name. Most people call me Mr. Brian so when I told him I was actually Mr. Tuck, he figured it out."

"Oh! Yes, I think Miss Gee called you Mr. Brian too. I wouldn't have known. I didn't know." I look down at the table and trace my finger along the wood grain. "I almost didn't come for the interview because of my mom, but she really wanted me to come. She let go because I said I wouldn't leave her," I explain.

"You know, I didn't know about you, I want to get that out in the open right now. If I had known, I would have wanted to be a part of your life. I am working really hard not to be angry with your mother," Brian says in a rush of words.

"I know. She told me about you. I have always known your name, but not where you lived," I say.

"Did your stepfather not want me in the picture?" he asks.

"Oh, my mom never married. She and her friend—" I start, and he says, "Ivy, her friend Ivy."

"Yes! You know Ivy?" I ask.

"No, your mom talked about her, but I never met her," he says.

"Oh." My shoulders slump a little.

"I guess you wouldn't have, Mom said she had one wild night with you and continued on her road trip. She didn't know she was pregnant with me until she got back home. She always said she didn't know where you were, but I recently found some letters and she told me last time she saw you, you were in Bend," I explain.

"I see, well, some of that is true." He shifts uncomfortably in his seat and drinks another huge gulp of his beer.

I wait, trying to be patient, watching him. He and I both tug on our bottom lip when we are stressed. I also scrunch my nose up when I'm thinking. Who knew those were hereditary traits?

"Your mom was on a road trip, I mean that's what she told me. She stayed in Bend for a month though, it was not a one-night fling. I considered her, well, not my girlfriend, but someone I was seeing," he says. He looks down at his hands and I sense a shift in him.

"She told me that she was—" He stops and looks at me, seeming to be weighing something.

"Go ahead, it's okay," I say, trying to be encouraging and open to whatever he has to say. His shoulders relax.

"She was in the middle of exploring who she was. I assumed

when Corey told me that Rose had a baby that she had gotten married. I thought you were the product of that marriage until Corey told me the truth. I was going to look for you. As soon as I found out, I knew I wanted to find you."

"What do you mean? Exploring who she was?" I ask. I feel a knot forming in the pit of my stomach.

"When I met your mother at a party my friends were having, she was talking to a group of girls, they were passing a joint around and I joined them. Rose and I hit it off, or at least I thought we had. As the party wound down we were the only two left by the campfire. I leaned in to kiss her, and she stopped me." He glances up. "I'm sorry, is this too much?"

"No, it's fine. I mean I know you had sex," I say and wave at myself.

He chuckles. "Corey said you had a great sense of humor. Okay, well, she told me no. That she wasn't into guys."

My stomach bottoms out. I manage to squeak out, "What?"

"I thought she maybe wasn't interested in *me*, but we had such a connection, or so I thought. I asked more questions. We ended up staying up all night talking," he says.

I can't speak. The server comes and sets the pizza down and I glance at it, unable to picture putting food in my mouth.

"She said that she thought she was gay, that she had a friend, Ivy, who she thought she might be in love with. I had never known anyone like that, so I was curious. I asked her if she had ever been with a man and she said no," my father explains.

"Okay," I manage.

"We decided that maybe we should kiss and see what she thought of it." He looks at the table for a beat then grabs his beer and finishes it, then immediately pours another from the pitcher.

"So that, um, that worked out then," I say and pick up my beer. I down it in two gulps and set the mug on the table.

Brian raises his eyebrows at me but continues, "Yeah, well, like I said, she stayed in Bend for a month. We, um, we were together more than once and I thought she realized that maybe she did like men," he says.

"Right, because you had sex, lots of it apparently." My cheeks grow hot and the room feels like it is shrinking. Nothing like meeting your father and hearing about his sex life all in one day.

"I am sorry, this is a lot, but when I was talking to my wife about you last night ..." Brian shifts in his seat, clearly uncomfortable. Right there with ya, Dad.

"Your wife knows about me?" I squeak out.

"Yes. You have two brothers who are excited to meet you. I mean they think that's something that will happen eventually, since when I told them, I didn't know where you were," Brian explains.

"Right," I say, blinking at him.

"Anyway, my wife and I thought maybe Rose went home and found a nice man and got married. Well, then Corey called and told me the rest of the story. Cindy was right there when I got the news. We called the boys in and told them right away. No secrets in the Tuck home," he says, winking at me.

"Right. Well, that must be nice. The no-secret thing. What's that like?" I say, and Brian cocks his head at me.

"Come again?"

"I was just wondering what it is like to grow up in a house where people don't keep secrets, Brian. Because that is not how I grew up. My mom was in love with Ivy? Her best friend? Her business partner? My mom was GAY?" I shout the last part and Brian goes pale, the color literally draining from his face as I watch.

"I thought you knew," he says, and all I can do is shake my head.

"I have to go. It was nice to meet you. I am sure I will see you around or something." I climb out of the booth and run to the door panic rising in my chest. Thank God the hotel is close by. I sprint to the front entrance, pausing only to wait for someone pushing a luggage cart out the double doors.

I run to the elevators and jab the up button, hitting it again for good measure.

. . .

GAY.

My Mother?

Gay?

What the fuck?

"HELLO?" Ivy says.

I yell, "Were you and my mother a couple?"

"Stephanie?" she asks.

"Who else would it be? Unless you have other lovers who have daughters?" I am angry and she is going to get the full force of it.

"Okay, calm down, what are you talking about?" Ivy says in that measured voice I have heard her use with hysterical brides.

"Well, let me tell you about the day I had. I ran into the love of my life, the guy I told you about from the PCT? Yeah, so funny story, he works at my new school!" I say louder than one should say into the phone.

"What? Wow, that is really wonderful, Steph," she starts, but I cut her off.

"Yeah? Is it? Because apparently Brian Tuck is my principal. You know *the Brian Tuck*," I yell.

"Oh," Ivy says.

"Yeah, oh. So Brian said when he met my mom she was confused and apparently thought she was in love with her friend Ivy and thought she might be gay. Did you know that?" My voice was still louder than I wanted it. I probably should have calmed down before calling her.

"Steph, honey. Maybe I should come up there. This doesn't seem like a conversation for the phone," Ivy says, but I don't know if I can take seeing her.

"So you were together? Fuck. Why did you lie to me? Why did *she* lie to me?" I sob, the words coming out in halting breaths.

"Honey," she starts, but I cut her off.

"Don't 'honey' me! Why didn't you tell me?" I slide to the floor and lean against the bed. My head hurts and there is a vise gripping my heart. Everything I knew, my whole childhood was a lie.

A fucking lie.

TWENTY

COREY

August 7th, 1987

I HAVE COME every day to the school trying to find Stephanie, and I've missed her every time. Today I am camping in front of her fucking classroom until she comes in.

My class is all set up, the textbooks arrived yesterday and those are on the shelf ready to be distributed. I hung some posters and of course my mom came in and changed everything. I really don't know why I bothered.

So I have no reason to be at the school, except to see her. I went full on "Every Breath You Take" crazy. I looked in her class window and could see she had put up some things, like the Declaration of Independence and a picture of a woman I didn't know. Across the top of the poster it says First Female Governor Nellie Ross.

Huh.

You learn something new every day.

I hear footsteps and I look up to see her with her arms full of books, so I jump up and rush to help.

"Hi! Here, let me get that for you." I grab at her books and she clutches them tighter, twisting to get away from me.

"No thanks. I got it," she says.

Oh. She's mad.

"Okay, listen I was hoping we could talk," I say, wanting to add "And then go home and wrap our bodies around each other because I have missed you more than air," but now doesn't seem like the time.

"There is nothing to talk about, Corey."

"So, we're okay?" I ask, hopeful.

She doesn't answer, instead she just glares at me and pushes past me.

"Stephanie, wait," I say.

"Leave me alone, Corey," she says.

"No," I say, stepping in front of her.

"No?" she asks with a glare.

"No, I just found you, I am not going to just leave you alone. I found you! You are here! I missed you so—"

She walks past me, stopping what I was saying, as she pushes her door open.

"Yoda?" I say to her back. She sets the books down and turns slowly, lifting her gaze to mine.

"What, Corey? I have a lot to do. I don't have time to talk to you."

"I don't understand. I thought you were happy to see me, I know that things got weird with meeting Brian and all, but I was thinking we could go for a drink or something and talk about it?" I say, watching her face for something. Her expression is flat, her eyes cold.

"We won't be doing that. I need to focus on my job, Corey. I have a lot of work to do, and I'm dealing with a lot right now. I move into my new house tomorrow and I just don't have the energy to add *you* to that list."

"Oh. I see. Okay, well listen, I'm sorry I told Brian, I didn't think I'd ever see you again and I—"

"You what?" She steps forward and jabs me in the chest with her finger. I see fire flash in her eyes. "You thought you would tell my story? You would tell the man I wondered about my whole life that I was his daughter?"

"I didn't know what to do, Stephanie! I thought I had lost you, and I guess I thought if he knew, he would want to find you too and then—"

She cuts me off again. "You'd be a hero? Is that what you thought?" she yells.

"Well, no but I did think you would be happier than this," I say.

"You have no idea what you've done," she hisses out. She pushes past me into the hall. I want to follow her, I do, but apparently that is not my thing where she is concerned so I just watch her go.

Again.

I slump onto her desk and look around the room, unsure what to do next. I sit there for longer than I'd like to admit, hoping she'll come back, *worried* she'll come back. Not sure which one is more terrifying. I hop off the desk and make my way to the office.

"Miss Gee, is Mr. Tuck in?" Tuck in, I laugh to myself, wishing these were simpler times so I could tell him my joke.

"Yes, let me tell him you're here," she says and rings his office.

"He says to have a seat, he is with someone." She shrugs her shoulders, so I sit.

Stephanie stomps out past me without looking at me. I don't even think she saw me. Brian comes out rubbing his face. "Come on in, Corey." He motions to me so I stand and follow him.

He points to the chair across from his large wooden desk and I sit, immediately sinking a full inch below it.

He takes his place behind his desk, towering over me. "Sorry, we do that on purpose so when the students get called in here, they feel the fear. You can move over here." He pulls out a more normal-size chair next to him and I quickly move.

"Well, I can see that would work. I was scared and I didn't even get called in!" I say trying to lighten the mood.

"She tried to resign," he says.

"Shit. I mean—" I stutter but he waves his hand at me.

"Why? Did she say why?" I ask. I feel sick.

"Yeah, she said it was too much. I explained I'm only here for a few weeks. I have actually called Garrett and asked him to speed up his move and he is working on it. I don't want to make her uncomfortable, Corey." Brian looks as distressed as I feel.

"I understand, does she know that?" I ask, wondering what they talked about when I left. Maybe he was an ass. He seems like a nice guy, but maybe he led with *I can't give you money* or some bullshit like that.

"She does. I told her that we would take this at her pace. I think I overwhelmed her with information the day we met." Brian shakes his head.

"What do you mean? She knows you are her father. Wasn't that what you guys talked about?" I ask.

"Well, there is a lot more to the story with me and her mother. I don't feel like it is my place to tell you since apparently she didn't know," Brian says.

I lean back in my chair. "Her mom is gay. Ivy is her lover," I say, matter-of-factly.

"Yes! How did you know?" he asks.

"My trail friends Grace and Barbara. They were the ones that Ivy met first, when she was looking for Steph. They spent about an hour with her, knowing that we were on the trail behind them." I stop myself, realizing that I am speaking not only to my boss, but Stephanie's father.

"These women were hiking the PCT?" he asks.

"Yeah, they are great. They met in college and have been together ever since. They live near Napa. Barbara is an orthopedic surgeon and Grace is a chef at a winery in Napa. They um, are a couple," I say, unsure how Brian feels about that. Maybe that is why I am telling him random facts about my friends.

"Oh, I see. And they knew after talking to Ivy that she and Rose, were involved?"

"Yeah, well that is what they thought. Ivy never came out and said it, but they were pretty sure. Barb was also pretty sure that there was something going on, like cancer, with Rose. I guess she was right."

"About more than just the cancer," Brian says.

"So you knew?" I ask.

"Well, it was 1964 and there was a lot of experimenting. More down in California of course but I had heard things, even if I didn't personally know anyone who was gay. When I met Rose…" he stops and drums his fingertips on the wooden desktop. "God, she was beautiful. She was this tiny little thing with long brown hair, beautiful deep brown eyes and the sweetest smile."

"Sounds like Steph," I say.

"She has my eyes. I would have known, even if you hadn't told me. If she and I had talked and she said her mother's name was Rose, I would have known, I would have figured it out on my own," he says with compassion I don't feel I deserve.

"I feel terrible. She is very mad at me for telling you," I say.

"I know. She mentioned that. I guess I understand." He sighs.

"I wish I did," I say before I can think about it.

"Well, if I hadn't dropped the bombshell about Rose being in love with Ivy, we might both be in a better position." Brian leans back in his chair.

"Is she leaving?" I ask.

"No, she signed a contract. She is here for a year, whether she wants to be or not," Brian says.

"That sucks," I say, and he nods.

"Not an ideal way to meet a long-lost child." He looks at me intently and asks, "Do you think she hates me?"

"No. No, I think she just lost her mom, and now everything she thought was true just got flipped on its end," I say. I wish I could go to her, comfort her. I don't know how to do that. I don't know how to be the strong one.

TWENTY-ONE
STEPHANIE

September 2nd, 1987

"WELCOME TO US HISTORY, I'm your teacher, Miss Hartford. On your desk you will find the syllabus and the theme for this month. If you are heading to science next, you will be learning about the cooking process used during the time period we will discuss here. If math is your next class, then you'll be learning about the money system of this time period. Anyone have English next?" I ask, and three students raise their hands.

"Wonderful, you will be reading a novel about life aboard one of the many ships that were sailed from England in hope of a new exciting life. My job as your history teacher is to tie all that information together. We all work closely as a team here at Beaver Valley High School, and I not only encourage questions, but require them," I say to the sea of blank faces. I hear a few groans but continue on. "I have office hours at lunch and after school. I am available to help you, and I prefer a proactive approach rather than having you wait until the week before finals to discuss issues with your grade. Any questions?"

Five hands shoot up and I smile. "Yes?" I point to the girl in the second row.

"HOW OLD ARE YOU?" she asks and the other students nod in agreement. I guess I fooled the adults but no way was I going to pass one over on the students. They can see past bangs and a shag cut, even with dark blonde woven in.

"I'm twenty-two years old." More hands shoot up. "Are there any questions about the syllabus?" I ask and everyone lowers their hands. "Wonderful. Now if you can turn to page two in your textbooks, we will begin."

I JUMP RIGHT in since my least favorite thing about the first day of school was hearing the teacher tell us what they would *eventually* teach us.

The next period and the next are the same and my day ticks on until lunch. I prop open my door and walk back to my desk, then pull my lunch from the bottom drawer.

"Hey, you coming to the staff room?" Gloria asks. She teaches Spanish one and two and is a whole hall away, but has managed to worm her way into my heart nonetheless.

"Nah, I am eating here. I promised the kids I would be available if they needed me," I explain.

"Chica, come on. You need a break. I need to complain to someone roughly my age about these teenagers!" Gloria slumps in the doorway.

I laugh. "It's the first day, Gloria. How bad can they be?"

"Well, I had them pick their Spanish names, and the first two kids said 'Ganador.' That is the worst beer on the planet. I swear they sell it at gas stations for a nickel a six pack."

"That explains why they like it!" I say with a laugh.

I like Gloria. She's older than me like most people are, but she has a kind motherly way about her. She knows nothing other than I am new to the area and I am only twenty-two. She doesn't know any of the other drama that's plaguing my life, and I find solace in that.

"Promise me you'll start eating in the staff room soon? The English teacher scares me. Her eyes are on the side of her head." She holds her hands up to show me and I laugh again.

"I promise. I am doing this for the first week then I will adjust to what they actually need," I say with an easy smile.

"Okay mi amiga!" She taps the doorjamb and walks out into the hall.

"Any chance I could join you? That teacher scares me too," Corey asks as he leans on my open door. God, he's so handsome. Without his beard he looks younger, more devastating. He got a haircut too, very short on the sides and longer on the top. He gained weight like me since he isn't eating freeze-dried food and hiking ten-plus miles a day. He looks delicious. I want to run my hands all over him. Why did he have to go and ruin everything?

I wait too long to answer, so he walks in and pulls a student desk in front of mine.

"How's your first day going?" he asks as he unwraps a sandwich.

"Fine," I say. I want him to stay so badly, but I am also furious with him. My stomach hurts so bad I don't even know if I can eat.

"Yeah, me too. Thanks for asking. I have this one kid, maybe you had him too. He is in the A group so I bet you did have him. Man, that neon-green shirt he was wearing gave me a headache," Corey says, laying out the rest of his lunch on his desk. He has a bag of chips and a Pepsi.

I snort by accident and see a slight smile cross his face.

"Anyway, I think Beaver Valley is going to be pretty great. With the exception of the guy who lives next to my house, I have no complaints at all." He takes a big bite of his sandwich and chews like we have lunch together all the time.

I have to fight with all my might to not ask him what is wrong with his neighbor. I haven't been able to move into my place yet. The kids are having a difficult time extricating their father. He is apparently doing things to sabotage them at every opportunity and has unfortunately caused some damage to the place. They assured me that it was all being handled but I have no choice but to stay in my hotel. The movers put my stuff in storage so I will have to hire new people when I finally get in the place.

Corey ignores my silence and goes back to talking about his students and what a great idea the theme teaching is, and I find myself relaxing a little. Damn it.

A small knock on my door has me leaning around Corey to see girl I had in first period. Allison. "Miss Hartford? Are you busy?" she asks in a voice barely above a whisper.

"Not at all, come in, Allison. This is Mr. Richie and he was just leaving." I give him a small smile and he nods.

"Hello, Allison. I think you were in my second period this morning!" Corey says standing and motioning to the desk he was sitting in. "You can sit here. I was just leaving like Miss Hartford said."

Corey walks out and Allison slinks in and sits in the desk like it might bite her. I wrap my sandwich back up and fold my hands in front of me. She squirms in her chair and fixes her shirt then smooths her hair. She is looking everywhere but at me.

"Allison? Did you have a question about what we talked about in class?" I ask.

"No, you did a great job of explaining things," she says to her desk.

"Okay, are you having trouble with something else? I am here to help, but I do need to know what it is, so I can do that," I say gently.

"Do you remember the boy that sat in front of me?" she asks.

I close my eyes for half a second and picture first period. He was tall, with black hair slicked back with so much gel I worried he might leave an oil slick. "Jeremy?" I ask, and she nods.

She fidgets in her chair, then says, "Can I not sit by him? Or maybe I could just move to a whole different group? He is in like all of my classes."

"Yes, because he is in A group with you. We talked about that briefly, that some of you would have more than one class together. I am sure as the semester goes on you'll be so busy you won't even notice him," I say. Jeremy seemed like a nice enough kid and I don't remember him turning around and bothering her.

"Ugh. I knew it. I just—" she stops talking and looks around as if contemplating her next words. "I've had to deal with him since we were in the second grade. I just need a break, you know?" she says, sounding a little more confident.

"Well, I tend to move people around a lot. We will be working in groups and the desks will get moved. It's the first day, Allison. Maybe he has changed since you saw him last. Why not give him a chance?" I say.

"Fine." She stands and huffs out of the room, the shy girl act gone.

Oh yeah, I know her type and if I had my way I would make sure Jeremy was sitting next to her in every single class. That would be unfair to him though, I bet he isn't a fan of her either.

I make it through the rest of the day and the staff meeting without too much trouble. Brian is a very nice man and it is clear he has the respect of all the teachers and staff here. I was the only one who was relieved when he said Garrett would be here by Friday.

Apparently, he agreed to come early when he found out about me. That isn't something Brian announced, just something he told me in private. He has stepped way back and said I'm in charge of how we proceed. If the whole *by the way your mom is gay* thing hadn't been dropped I would be excited about getting to know him. I just can't shake the pain of learning that everything I knew growing up was a lie.

. . .

IVY and I had quite the fight, something that has never happened. I never fought with my mother either. I am not sure what to do now. The things I said hurt Ivy, I know, but she lied to me. They both did and since I can't yell at my mother, Ivy had to take it all.

I know I can't keep this up. This anger is eating me alive. I feel so alone and confused.

TWENTY-TWO
COREY

October 10th, 1987

GOOD LORD, what now? I peek my head out the front door and look toward my neighbor's house. He has gone on a full-scale war against his children. First, he boarded up the windows and then tried to dig a moat around the whole property. Thankfully he got tired of digging and gave up, but there was still a good-sized ditch across the front path.

I can hear the hum of a small motor and from my front porch I see a few tarps. I sigh and step out into the yard, then stop dead in my tracks. He has a paint sprayer and is currently spraying the house with the most God-awful color of purple I have ever seen. He's not even covering the area, more just spraying paint like some elderly graffiti artist. He's covered the door, handle and all, and is now moving to the driveway, to paint— well, the driveway.

Awesome.

I glance out to the road and wave at my neighbor across the street. She makes the sign of the cross and goes back inside her house.

I stand watching, not knowing what else to do. Millie, my real estate agent, drives by and slams on her brakes when she sees what's happening.

"Jesus! John! John, you can't do that! Turn that damn thing off!" she yells from the street. I don't blame her for not getting closer. John does not have a good grip on the sprayer and is sporting more than one bright purple stripe across his pants.

"Get away from me, Millie!" he yells. He turns to aim the spray gun at her, just as the thing sputters to a stop. Purple paint drips out of the end of his wand and I brave a few steps closer.

"That color is an interesting choice John," I yell.

"Fuck off!" he yells back. Well, at least he is consistent.

"John, the house has sold. Escrow is set to close on Tuesday, you're vandalizing someone else's home!" Millie sounds pissed, but she hasn't come any closer. I see Mrs. Wentworth across the street peeking out of her curtains.

"I'm not moving! Go back to Dollywood, you bleached blonde bimbo!" John yells and kicks at the sprayer unaware that it stopped because the paint can is empty. He will figure it out soon, I'm sure.

"I am getting the sheriff involved, John. You have gone too far!" Millie stomps back to her car and speeds off and I hear John chuckle. He walks over and picks up another paint can, transfers the feed hose into it, and starts the sprayer up again. It chugs and spurts a few times and the bright purple sprays out. John uses the wand like he is watering the lawn. I shake my head and walk back inside.

I feel bad for whoever bought that place. That dude has snapped. I walk into my kitchen and open the fridge, like I did three or four other times earlier. Amazingly, no magical fairy has gone grocery shopping for me. I sigh, close the door and grab my keys. I can't put this off any longer.

When I back out of the garage and pull past my house, I see John has changed paint color. Neon yellow is now dripping off the purple stripes and he waves jovially at me.

What a fucking nut job.

Beaver Valley Market is packed on this lovely fall Saturday and I run into more than one of my students with their parents. It takes me a very long time to get what I need and get to the register. As I'm putting my stuff on the belt I feel the air shift. I know she's behind me. I wonder if she knew it was me here? She avoids me pretty well at school and I am trying to give her space, but my heart is having a hard time with that plan.

"Hi, Corey," she says, so quiet I almost don't hear it.

"Hey, Yoda, how are you?" I ask, continuing with my task. Maybe if I don't make direct eye contact, she'll stay.

"I'm getting by. Moving into my new place this week, so that is good," she says.

I glance down at her basket. She has some fruit and a few boxes of granola bars and that's it. "Where have you been staying?" I ask, turning to look at her. I didn't know she was still waiting to move. I figured she was already in her new place. She sighs.

"At the hotel. It's not ideal, but my escrow doesn't close until Tuesday. I guess there was a problem with the current owner," she says.

I CLOSE my eyes and lean my head back. It all makes sense. "Steph, is your new house on Main Street?"

"Yes, how did you know?" she asks.

"Don't drive by there today, I don't think you will want to see what John has been up to," I say. I turn to the clerk to tell her I want paper bags. She starts to scan my items and Stephanie reaches out and touches my arm.

"How do you know the owner's name is John?" Her eyes are wide and I'm sure she knows. The universe has always done this to us, why would now be any different?

The clerk tells me my total and I write out the check before turning to Stephanie. I hold out my hand to her, "Nice to meet you, neighbor."

"No! Are you serious?" She says and I see her fighting a smile. She rolls her lips together and I see that beautiful twinkle in her eye.

"Dead. You know the little white house with the green trim?" I ask and she slaps her forehead.

"I love that house. Damn it, Corey," she says.

I step aside and let her get her groceries then we walk out together. We stop once we get to the parking lot. "Where are you parked?" I ask.

"I walked. I'm just up the hill at the hotel, so it seemed silly to drive." She shrugs.

"Yeah, so—" I start, but she cuts me off.

"I really like your hair, and I'm still not used to you without that beard," she says, making me smile.

"Yeah, that thing was itchy. It's buried in front of the school. Don't tell anyone that," I say. I look over my shoulder, worried someone might have heard me. I am afraid to move, I don't want her to leave. I want to keep talking to her, hold her again. Kiss her.

"Gross Corey, you buried it?" she says and laughs.

I shrug. "It was my plan, a signal to myself and the universe that I am a grown-up now."

"No more sleeping among the trees that birthed you, huh?" she says with a big smile this time, and I feel a part of my heart unwind.

"I forgot I said that to you. I would like to go on record that I didn't really believe that. I was just in a mood over my brother." I am hanging on to the shopping cart for dear life.

"I get it," she says.

"Hey, why don't you come over? I mean if you want to see what John has done to your house, I can drive you," I say, jumping in with both feet.

"You sure? I don't want to put you out. I can just take my car," she says, looking up the hill toward the hotel.

Before she can think about it more, I take her bag of groceries and put it in my basket, then walk us both to my car. I pop the trunk, load her bags in, and put mine down. Before I shut the lid I look at the bags, mine surrounding hers, and I like the way that looks, like they are protecting hers, not letting them fall over.

I open her door for her and close it gently. Then I rush around to open the driver's side door. I can't believe my luck. If I had been a few minutes later or earlier I would have missed her.

We drive in silence, but when I turn onto Main Street and her new house comes into view, she shrieks and covers her face. "Oh my God!" she says peeking through her fingers.

"He's been busy since I left for the store. I wonder how he got on the roof?" I ask. I have to admit the giant FU across the roof is a nice touch.

"What on earth is wrong with that man?" she asks.

"I don't know. He's pretty happy with himself though." I motion to the man currently lying naked in the yard with what appears to be a margarita.

"I hope he put on sunblock," she says, peeking through her fingers.

I look over at him and he is now flipping us the bird with two hands while resting his drink on his stomach.

"I wouldn't worry about him," I say as I pull into the garage behind my house. I get out and pop the trunk, then grab everything including her bag, and head to my back door. I hear the crunch of her shoes, so I know she's following me, but she is very quiet.

I open the door and wait for her, breathing her in as she passes. God, I want to grab her and kiss her and hold her and be happy that we found each other. But I have been talking with Grace, and Barb when she has the time. They told me I have to be patient and not rush her. I need to be the good thing, not add to her stress.

"So, John is nuts," she says, and I nod.

"It appears that way. He told me to fuck off the first day I met him. That was nice." I start unloading my groceries onto the small table in the kitchen.

"Can I put these in your fridge for now?" she asks.

"Of course." I bite my cheek to stop myself from asking her to just move in until the crazy situation next door is sorted out. My mind is squeezing inside my skull. It is taking all my strength to be cool like the ladies coached me. I can't let them down. Once the food is put away, I motion toward the living room and ask if she wants to sit and talk.

"Thanks, I would. You can't see my house from there, can you?" she asks.

"Not unless you step off the porch. Now that I know you own it though I am putting a wall of windows along that side of the house."

"Please do that," she says with a laugh. God, she is here. In my house. On my couch.

"I didn't think I would ever see you again," I say, turning my body so I can see her better. I pull my knee up and rest my arm across the back of the couch.

"I know. God, I am such a mess. I feel like someone put my life in a blender and hit pulse."

"I bet. I am sorry I contributed to that in any way," I say.

She turns to face me, mirroring my position on the couch. Our fingers less than an inch apart.

"I know. I was pretty mad," Stephanie says with a little scrunch of her nose.

"Was?" I ask hopefully.

She takes a deep breath and says, "I can't keep this up. I lost you, then my mom, then Ivy. I can't fix the last two, but I am hoping that I can fix this." She motions her hand between us.

"You want to give us a try?" I say, then clear my throat and try again without the prepubescent squeak. She laughs and those Tahoe blue eyes dance.

"I do. Do you?" she asks. She inches her finger toward mine and lets just the tip of her index finger brush against mine.

I swallow hard and clear my throat again. "Can you excuse me for a moment?" I ask, and her eyes widen, but she nods.

"Thanks." I stand and walk to the cordless phone on my desk and grab it, then head to my bedroom. I close the door and sit on my bed to dial the number to the hospital.

"Hello, may I speak to Dr. Barbara Miles? I understand, can you please tell her it's Corey? I really need to talk to her?"

The girl on the line sounds irritated but puts me on hold. Good Lord what is with her hold music? That is awful. Thankfully Barb picks up quickly.

"Corey? What's going on? Are you hurt?" Barb says, and she sounds out of breath.

"Oh, sorry Barb, no. Stephanie is here. She is in my living room and she just said she wants to give us a chance," I whisper-hiss into the phone.

There is silence on the other line, then a big sigh. "And you left her and went to call me?" she asks.

"Well, yes. I didn't know if I was supposed to still give her space or if I can wear her like a coat from now on," I say, a little louder this time.

Barb barks out a laugh, "Fuck, I've missed you. Go ahead and follow your heart now, kid. Just maybe let her be in charge still, okay?"

"Really? Okay, thanks, Barb. Sorry to pull you away from patients. Oh, and hey, your hold music sucks," I say.

"I don't have hold music. That shit I can hear now? That is not coming from my end, what's going on there?" she asks with a laugh.

"I will find out. Thanks Barb, I'll call soon!" I say and hang up. Crap what is that?

I walk out to the living room to find Stephanie still on the couch but making a face. "Are you playing mariachi music?" she asks.

"Is that what that is?" I say, scratching my head.

"Yeah, I mean it's not good, but I think it's a mariachi band."

I walk to the front door onto the steps. John is standing in his yard, still mostly naked and not one, but two mariachi bands are playing. Wildly different songs. Like a battle of sorts. John is smiling like he just won the lottery. He's also doing a little dance. I am grateful he has on his boxers. His boxers and one cowboy boot.

"Wow," Stephanie says, walking up behind me. "Should we call someone?"

"Who? Animal control? Mariachi maintenance?" I say and chuckle. Fuck, I am funny.

John has started to dance faster and hop around on one foot, which causes the lead guitar player in the band on the right side of him to start making loud encouraging noises. Left side band steps up their tempo and starts to dance along with him. This is seriously the craziest thing I have ever seen.

Just as I am about to say that, a limo pulls up and out climbs an Elvis impersonator and of course a clown. I blink and look over at Steph who just shrugs and motions me to come back inside.

"That was a lot," I say, rubbing my face. I can now hear "Blue Suede Shoes" being sung with a backup of two different unknown songs. I am sure if I looked out my window there would be juggling.

"Let's pretend it's not happening." Stephanie holds out her hand to me and I let her lead me back to the couch where we sit.

She turns and reaches up to touch my face so I scoot in a little closer. "Can I?" she asks.

"Yeah," I rasp out. I pray I don't melt into a puddle. She trails her dainty hand down my jaw and I take a deep breath, relishing her touch. My eyes close and I press into her hand.

"It's so different, Corey. I used to try and picture you without your beard. I wasn't at all correct," she says. That makes me open my eyes and look at her.

"Before or after we got separated?" I ask.

"Both. On the trail, but back in San Diego too. I'll have you know, I had a plan when I moved up here," she says, dropping her hand.

"A plan?" I ask. I am sad that she moved her hand away and wonder what to do to get it back.

"Yeah, for how I would find you," she says.

"Oh! I had one of those too. What was yours?" I ask.

"Well, I was going to wait until I had my phone hooked up, then go to the junior college and find their student message board and leave a note for your sisters."

I laugh and ask, "My sisters? Do you know their names?"

"No, I don't know if you ever told me, but I was going to say to the twins that have a brother named Corey who hiked the PCT," she says, and I laugh.

"That is good. I would pay money to see Dee Dee or Linda find that note," I say.

"But then I got stuck in a cabinet and there you were. Can we go back?" she asks, her blue eyes wide and hopeful.

"You want to crawl in that cabinet again?" I furrow my brow, confused by her request.

"No, but I want a do-over of our reunion," she says and she scoots closer.

"Okay, how do you wish it had been?" I ask.

"Well, we can keep the whole stuck in a cabinet thing, because that moment when I crawled out and saw you..." She shakes her head and her lips part into a smile that is so beautiful I lose my breath.

She looks into my eyes then down to my lips then back up to my eyes. "So what if after that, when I saw you and realized that it was you, we kissed."

"We did do that," I say, watching her mouth, wishing I could kiss those perfect lips.

"Yeah, but what if we hadn't been interrupted?" she whispers.

"Oh."

"Yeah, what if Miss Gee and Brian minded their own damn business that day?" she says, as she scoots a little closer.

"What if I had locked your door?" I say, reaching my hand out tentatively, touching her thigh.

She licks her lips and watches my hand trail along her thigh.

"I don't think I could have waited for you to lock the door. I needed you. You were all I could see."

"Yeah?" I rasp out. Fuck, I'm already hard. We aren't even really touching.

"Yeah, I just, my body just reacted. I knew I had to have my lips on you." She is moving closer to me on the couch and I'm torn between seeing where this goes, and pulling her on top of me. I hear Barb in my mind, telling me to let her be in charge, so I wait.

"I couldn't believe you were in front of me. Those beautiful big blue eyes," I say.

She swallows hard and moves so we are touching now. My skin on fire where we are connected. She traces her hand up my arm, pausing to tug on the sleeve a little.

"I really like you in a button-up. If we hadn't been interrupted, I would have probably enjoyed undoing these."

"Show me," I say, in more of a growl.

She climbs on my lap, and I lean onto the couch, afraid to move or close my eyes for fear this whole thing is a dream.

TWENTY-THREE
STEPHANIE

October 10th, 1987

I CAN'T BELIEVE I'm here. I waited outside that stupid grocery store all morning hoping he would be doing his shopping. I knew I had to make things better. I can't keep this up anymore. Seeing him every day, and not being able to touch him, hold him, was getting to be too much. Now I am currently straddling his lap showing him what would have happened that first day we saw each other if we hadn't been interrupted.

"I would have wanted to rip off your shirt, to get to that glorious chest, but I have some control," I say, trailing my fingers up and down his chest, stopping to play with the buttons.

"Do you, Yoda?" he says, his eyes hooded. Fuck, he is so sexy.

"Not really. Not when it comes to you," I admit.

"I like that," he says.

"You like that I have no control?" I ask.

"Yes, because that first kiss we shared, when I had you pressed against the door of the laundromat? I lost my control then and haven't found it since," he says, letting his tongue peek out and wet his lips.

"I remember that kiss, I think about it sometimes," I say.

"Sometimes?" he asks. His hands are resting gently on my hips and I know he wants to take control, but for some reason he's not. I like it. I need to be in control right now.

"Sometimes late at night, when I can't sleep, I think about how your lips felt on mine," I whisper close to his ear.

"Do you touch yourself when you think about that kiss?" he asks curling his fingers to grasp my hips more.

"Yes," I say, then nibble a little on his ear.

He groans and presses his fingers firmly into my hips, his thumbs digging into the soft flesh just below my hip bones.

"We are getting off topic. I believe I was showing you what it would have been like if we hadn't been interrupted," I say, leaning forward to nip at his ear again.

"Right, go on then, what would you have done?" he says, shifting on the couch a little.

"Well, I would have undone this button," I slide the button through the hole and push his shirt open a little, then trail my fingers down.

"I would have wondered if you shaved your chest hair, since your beard was gone," I say, slipping another button through its hole.

"What do you see?" he asks, watching me like I am his next meal. God, I want to be.

"I see the same awesome chest hair that I danced my fingers through back in Tahoe."

"I really liked that, when you did that," he says, pulling me a little closer to him.

"I liked it too. I remember wishing I could curl up in there and hide from the world," I say.

"You can," he whispers. It's the sexiest thing I have ever heard.

I smile and slip another button free. I can see his tight stomach muscles now, still tan and still adorned with that trail of hair. I close my eyes to regain myself a little. Corey has started to let his fingers wander. Everywhere he's touching me I feel like he is on my bare skin. I wish he was. I am regretting my jeans and sweater.

I pull the last button free and spread his shirt wide, then bend slightly to kiss along his collarbone. He twists his head slightly to allow me access to his neck, and I see his goosebumps erupt along his chest. I still affect him. Nothing feels better than that. Nothing.

"God, I've missed your hands on me," Corey says quietly. I feel like it's more to himself than to me.

I lean in and kiss him softly on his lips and he moans. The feelings that are coursing through me are so powerful tears form in my eyes. "I missed you so much. I thought I lost you," I admit.

"I should have gone with you," he says in between kisses and I pull back.

"What?"

"I realized as soon as I saw the taillights that I could have offered to go with you," Corey says.

"Well, shit. I'm glad I didn't think of that! I would have been so mad," I say, but I let a smile spread across my face.

"I was furious with myself, enough for both of us," he says.

"Good. I won't be mad then. I am tired of being angry," I say, feeling lighter than I have in months.

He pulls me closer, wrapping his arm around my waist, nuzzling my neck and peppering me with kisses.

"I am so fucking glad to hear you say that. My lips missed you, my cock missed you, hell baby, all of me missed you." His kisses are becoming more frantic. He pulls my face toward him and presses those full luscious lips on mine. I loved his beard, a lot, but kissing him without it? Bodacious. Awesome. Pure ecstasy.

He is tugging at my sweater so I lean back and pull it off, then drop it on the floor next to us. He moans and grabs both my breasts in his hands. "Fuck, you're so hot, Steph." He leans forward and grazes my nipple with his teeth, causing me to hiss in a sharp breath. I have missed his hands, his mouth, him, so much that all my desire to be in charge fades. I let him take the lead, needing and wanting to let go. I arch back, making it easier for him, and he takes it, releasing my bra with one flick of his fingers. He tugs on the straps and yanks the whole thing free, then moves to my jeans.

"Stand up and take those fucking things off. I need to be inside you right now," he growls out and I obey. I strip out of my jeans and underwear like a fireman changing to go to a three-alarm fire, and let me tell you, I am blazing. The way he looks at me while he slides his jeans down, like he can't wait to be in me, is intoxicating. He yanks his shirt the rest of the way off and steps out of his jeans.

He takes me by the hand and leads me down the hall to what I assume is his bedroom, but before he gets to the door he stops and turns to me and presses me against the wall in the hallway. He bends his knees so his face and mine are closer and he kisses me deeply. I put my hands around his neck and he quickly lifts me and pins me to the wall, my legs wrapping around him. I feel one hand leave my back and slide between us. He grabs his cock and runs it through my very wet folds, cussing out when he does.

"Fuck, you feel so good," he says in my ear and then slides into me in one thrust. "Is this all for me? You are so wet, so fucking perfect."

I gasp but he swallows it with his mouth, kissing me like I am his everything. He doesn't move his hips, just stays like that, deep inside me pinning me to the wall. He pulls back from our kiss and breathes hard, his forehead pressed to mine. "Son of bitch, fuck." His eyes squint shut and I watch as sweat forms on his brow.

I try and move and he grabs my hips holding me in place.

"Do not fucking move," he says, then adds, "Give me a second. I forgot how tight you are, my God, you're strangling me." He presses his forehead to mine, his breaths ragged.

I lean in and kiss him softly and he pulls us back from the wall and carries me the rest of the way to his room. Laying me gently on the bed before he pulls out of me and starts kissing down my chest and I know what he's trying to do. I won't have it.

"No, Corey please, I want you. Get back inside me now," I say, spreading my legs under him.

He stops his journey south, his hands splayed on my stomach, and looks up at me with those moss green eyes, "I don't know how long I'll last. I wanted to make sure you're taken care of."

"Just fuck me, Corey, and let me worry about that," I say, and a delighted smile crosses his face. He grabs his cock and brings it back to where I want it most, slowly pushing in this time. The slow drag creates a delightful sensation in my core. He does it again and again, slow steady strokes that aren't enough.

"Harder Corey, don't hold back, please, I have missed you so much. Just give it to me." I'm squirming under him.

He flips us over so I am on top and I reposition myself so he can suck on my nipple while he slams into me. It is absolutely the best feeling and when I start to feel him lose his rhythm and get a little frantic it makes me move faster as he hits that perfect spot, over and over until I am screaming out his name. He pumps into me and holds me firmly over him as he fills me, I watch as his stomach contracts, him curling up with each delightful spasm. My release hits me then, as I feel him shuddering. It's like a freight train, throwing me into a bliss I had forgotten. Everything trembles and I stare down at him in amazement.

God, I have missed him so much.

I collapse onto Corey's chest, enjoying my own aftershocks as he gently rubs up and down my back. He is breathing hard and our bodies are wet with sweat.

"I've missed you so much, Stephanie," he whispers in my ear. He rolls us so I am pinned under him, our bodies still connected.

"I missed you too, Corey. It was all just too much, getting in that car and leaving you, then finding out my mom was sick. When I lost her, I felt like I had lost so much more than just my mom," I say into his neck. He is still inside me and he starts to move again slightly. Rocking in and out. I don't think he's gone soft, but if he has I can't tell and now it seems he's ready for round two. Lucky me.

"What do you mean?" he asks. He brushes his fingertips across my face, moving my hair that had fallen into my eyes.

"Well, this sounds awful but, I lost her, and I didn't know how to find you. I thought that if I had at least a way to contact you, I wouldn't be all alone in the world." I am nervous admitting this, I don't want to pressure him, make him feel like he has to be with me because I have no family, like he is my only hope at happiness.

"I had a plan. I wasn't just going to give up, Steph," he says, the whole time moving slowly inside me and I can feel him growing even harder.

"A plan?" I breathe out, arching into him. God, he feels so fucking good.

"I had a list of florists in the San Diego area I was going to call." He stops moving and leans down to kiss me softly, moaning a little. "I was going to leave a note for you on the trail too in case you came back there to finish your hike," he says and that has me laugh.

"I was going to do the same thing!" I say wrapping my legs around him and pulling him into me.

"I couldn't let you go, I know we said it was just a trail thing, that we would part ways." He kisses me again and I feel my heart expand, threatening to burst out of my chest. "But I fell hard for you Stephanie, I need you to know that. I would have spent the last month we had together trying to convince you to move to Beaver Valley to be with me. I just never had the chance," he says, thrusting into me hard. We both stop talking as the act of love our bodies are playing out takes over. It's slow and beautiful and like nothing I have ever felt before. I am surprised when I start to feel my orgasm building like a hot fire in my core. He is staring into my eyes and moving at a faster rate now and just as I fall, I feel him thrust in hard and groan, emptying once again into me.

I stare into his beautiful face and tell him "I love you" before I can think about it too much and chicken out.

He presses his lips to mine and I feel him finally relax into me. "Fuck, Stephanie, I love you so much. I am so glad you're here."

TWENTY-FOUR
COREY

October 10th, 1987

I DON'T REALIZE we have fallen asleep until I am jerked awake by a truck's backup bell. I glance at the clock on my nightstand and see it's four in the afternoon. We weren't out for long. Stephanie shifts beside me and I pull her in closer.

We are both naked on top of my bedding, since I was too over-whelmed with lust to pull back the comforter. Just thinking about her moving beneath me, I feel myself growing hard again. I smile and kiss along the back of her neck pleased when she reaches back for me.

We both hear the sound of cracking wood and metal crunching. We freeze.

"What was that?" she whispers.

The backup bell has stopped and I hear yelling. Holy hell, what now?

"I have a bad feeling John wasn't done after the little Vegas show he had in his front yard," I tell her, and I slide off the bed to grab some shorts from my drawer. I pull out a T-shirt and toss it to her, then wait for her to walk back out to the living room. She tugs on her jeans and I slip my button-up shirt back on. We nod, like we are going into battle and we step out to the front porch and look towards Stephanie's new home.

The truck I heard backing up has buried its rear bumper into the side of her house. The driver is waving his arms and yelling at John who has a huge smile on his face.

"I told you to tell me when to stop! I can't see shit out those mirrors! Why didn't you tell me to stop?" the driver yells, and John cackles.

The driver runs his hand through his hair, assessing the damage to both his truck and the house.

"My poor house," Stephanie whispers beside me.

"I am sure it can be fixed. We will fix this," I say with a laugh, my astonishment at how far John has taken this, coming out as now uncontrollable laughter.

Stephanie starts to laugh too, thankfully, and we watch as Millie's car comes into view over the hill. Behind her is the sheriff and I see John's eyes go wide. He pats the delivery driver on the shoulder, literally jumps in the air and clicks his heels together, then scampers off towards the woods behind our houses.

I kind of want to yell, "Go you crazy fucker, go!" But before I can, Stephanie yells out, "Run John! Run! Good luck, you crazy bastard!"

See? She's perfect for me.

We laugh together and go back inside, not wanting to see the aftermath of the best day of John's life. Well, my life too. Was I dreaming or did Yoda tell me she loves me? I spin her when we get back inside the house, and hold her face in my hands to kiss her.

"I love you," I say very close to her lips, and I'm relieved when she says immediately, "I love you too."

"I need to make a phone call," I say, kissing her between each word.

"Okay, now?" she asks breathlessly.

"Yes," I grab the cordless and hit redial but pull her into me. I rest my chin on her head, keeping her under my arm.

"Dr. Miles, please. This is Corey," I say into the phone.

"Yes, I'll hold." I feel Steph trying to squirm away, but I hold her tighter.

"Hello?" Barb says.

"Dr. Miles, I have someone who I would like you to speak with." I hold the phone down and look at the confused woman in my arms.

"Hello?" Barb says again.

Stephanie says, "Hello? I'm sorry I am not sure what I am supposed to say. Corey just handed me the phone."

"Stephanie? It's Barb!" Barbara says loudly and Stephanie smiles wildly.

"Oh! Hi Barbara! How are you? Oh my gosh, it's so good to hear your voice!" she says, and my smile grows even bigger.

"Well, Grace and I are about to be a lot happier if we can hear you and Corey patched things up. That woman asks every day if I have heard from you," Barbara says, loud enough to make Corey smile.

"That is so sweet. Yes, we patched things up. He told me he loves me!" she says as she squeezes me a little tighter.

"Holy hell, put him on the phone this minute! I told him to take it slow. Jesus, that boy," she starts, and Stephanie cuts her off.

"No, it's okay, I said it first." She laughs.

"I can hear you, Barb. You speak loud enough for the neighbors to hear you," I say, and Barb chuckles.

"Hey listen kids, I have one more patient here to see, then I need to get up to Napa for a fundraiser at the winery. Grace is going to be so fucking happy. I'll call you soon!" Barbara clicks off without a goodbye and I toss the phone over to the couch.

"Barb is a doctor?" Steph asks and I nod.

"She's a fucking kickass orthopedic surgeon. She has a lot of weekend shifts at the hospital because of all the time she took off to do the trail with Grace." I say

"Did they get married?" Steph asks.

"You know, they never said! They were so worried about me and what a sad sack I had turned into when you left. I'm sure they did." I say and feel like a terrible friend for never asking that.

"What does Grace do? Does she own a winery or something?" Stephanie asks.

"No, she is the head chef at one in Napa. She and Barb are so cool. We got pretty close that last month on the trail. They went on after helping me find this place."

"I saw them!" she says.

"You did?" I ask, totally stunned.

"My first day in town, I saw the sign for the trail head and these two women stepping onto the path. It took a moment for my brain to register that it was them, but when I was sure, I wanted to yell for the driver to stop so I could chase them. I froze. I couldn't speak."

"Wow, well if you had, they would have told you where I was," I say.

She groans, "Don't tell me that. That makes me sad."

"Let's not worry about any of that. All that matters is this," I say and kiss her lips.

"Agreed," she says, sighing into me.

"Steph, I want to ask you something. You can say no, I really hope you don't though. I think it's a good idea and—"

"What, Corey?"

"Stay here with me, don't go back to the hotel," I say, then I kiss her quick in case it's my last time.

"Are you serious?" she asks.

"Dead. I can't let you sleep away from my bed even one more night. You belong here, with me, in my arms." I kiss her again, before she can answer.

"Corey, wait." She pushes me back a little and I brace myself for all the reasons why this is a bad idea.

"Can you drive me to get my stuff?" she asks.

My whole face lights up in a smile.

Thank God.

TWENTY-FIVE
STEPHANIE

November 10th, 1987

MY HOUSE IS ALMOST FINISHED. I am so grateful to Corey. He has been beyond wonderful helping me deal with the contractors and pest control. John's final act of defiance was filling each room with hidden piles of cat food. He made sure it wasn't obvious, but guess who knows how to find piles of cat food? Feral cats, sure, but not in the quantities you would think. Nope. A collective of raccoons took up residence in my home. That is what a bunch of them is called, if you're wondering. The gym teacher, Mr. Wallace, told me that, and he also gave me tips on how to fight them with my bare hands. I was polite but told him I decided to let the professionals handle it. He seemed disappointed and also slightly obsessed with the local wildlife and ways to engage them in hand-to-hand combat.

John had left the back windows open and propped open the cellar door and within a few days the house was like that children's book *The King, the Mice, and the Cheese*, but with raccoons and a few other brave forest animals. If it wasn't for Corey I wouldn't have been able to handle it. He made me laugh at every turn and helped me with the important stuff like picking out a new color for the exterior. John's children have been amazing and have paid every invoice I presented to them without even blinking.

He is apparently happy at his new apartment and has made friends with the woman who lives next door to him. I pray for her nightly.

"Stephanie dear, did you want to invite anyone for Thanksgiving?" Dorothy asks, snapping me out of my thoughts.

"Um, no that's okay," I say, forcing a smile. My first holiday without my mom and Ivy is fast approaching.

"Grace and Barbara are coming, and Dee Dee and Linda, of course. We have a big house, honey, are you sure?" she tries again. I know what she wants me to say, but I can't.

"Mom, let it go," Corey says, stepping out from the hall.

"Corey, you know what I always say, 'family and friends are forever, just like fungus.'" Dorothy throws her hands in the air in frustration.

I snort and Corey nudges me. "Yes, Mom, you do always say that."

"Dorothy, I haven't spoken to Ivy since I yelled at her, and I don't talk to Brian often. Thanksgiving seems like too big of a deal. Maybe we can start smaller?" I ask. I am not opposed to making amends, I just don't know how.

"Fine. Invite your father over this weekend for a small lunch, then when that goes well, we can invite him and the rest of your family for Thanksgiving!"

Corey leans in and whispers, "Sorry." I smile weakly up at him. It's not like I don't want to see these people. I have had lunch with Brian once since Corey and I patched things up, but it was just so uncomfortable.

With Ivy, where do I even begin? I must have hurt her so badly because she hasn't called me back. I left a message at both her house and at the shop with Corey's phone number. Every day that has gone by is like another mile between us. I screwed up so bad.

I don't know if Corey told his mom that I did try and apologize to Ivy. Dorothy is so sweet but also a little scary. I can see how she was able to wrangle twenty five-year-olds onto the carpet for story time. I can barely get my students to push their desks into a circle without fights breaking out.

"Tell you what Dorothy, I will call Brian and see if he is busy this weekend. But please let me decide if I want to invite him to Thanksgiving. That is such a big step," I say. I have learned to be firm but kind or she will just steamroll me.

She peers at me over her glasses, but the corners of her mouth turn up. "Alright dear. Now tell me the latest on your house!"

After we fill her and Henry in on all the latest developments on my house, Corey explains that we have to get going. There is a storm coming and he doesn't like to make the drive down to Beaver Valley in the rain.

"Let me know as soon as you talk to your father, Stephanie," Dorothy yells from the door.

"Just smile and wave," Corey says into my ear before he plants a kiss to my cheek. I turn and wave with the biggest smile I am capable of.

He opens the door for me and I slide into his car. I close my eyes and breathe deeply as he shuts my door. I still can't believe my life. All at once wonderful and awful. Sometimes I feel like I am betraying my mom by not trying harder to reconnect with Ivy, but then I remember how they both lied to me my whole life. Like I wouldn't understand, like I wouldn't have felt like the luckiest kid in the world to have two moms.

"You okay?" Corey asks. He hasn't started the car yet, just turned to me with his hand on my arm.

"Yeah, just still trying to wrap my head around why my mom and Ivy couldn't trust me," I say. Corey rubs his hand down my arm and links his hand with mine.

"I think Ivy should tell you that. I don't know why she hasn't called. I know it's hurting you and I hate that so much."

"Thanks, I appreciate you and your family. Everyone has been so wonderful and kind and patient." I squeeze his hand.

"One day you'll meet my brother and see we are not all perfect," he says with a wink.

"I am sure he's just as great," I say with a laugh.

'He's not," Corey says but there is laughter in his voice.

We drive back out to Beaver Valley, listening to music and not really talking. We are about a mile from his house when the first rain starts to fall. Big fat drops that sound like hail pelt the roof and I smile.

"Do you remember the night in the tent? When the rain and thunder shook us?" I ask.

"I do. I think about that night a lot. It was when I realized I was falling for you. Hey, now that we're talking about that, why were you so weird that night?" he asks just as a crack of lightning rips through the sky in front of us. The rain comes down even harder and he slows the car and turns the wipers to full speed.

I think back to that night, not knowing what he's talking about, but then I remember the thin braid I had at the bottom of my sleeping bag. I laugh and start to speak, but the memories of crawling across the ground at night to cut that damn thing off wash over me and I break into a fit of uncontrollable laughter. Tears streaming down my face, shoulders shaking, I wipe my eyes and try to breathe.

"What's so funny?" he asks, laughing along with me as he pulls into his driveway. The rain is coming down so hard I almost can't hear him. He pushes the remote for the garage just as the lightning flashes again. The whole street plunges into darkness as the power goes out.

"We are going to have to make a run for it from here," Corey shouts. He points to the garage door, which is still shut. I nod and we both push our doors open and dash for the back door. Corey unlocks the door and we tumble inside, completely soaked. I shake and start to pull my coat off, but he steps closer and pushes me against the wall.

"Not so fast. I want to know what had you laughing like a hyena back there," he says, wedging his knee between my legs and caging me in with his arms.

I look up into his beautiful face dripping with rainwater and start to giggle again. God, I hope he doesn't get mad. Sadly, the thought of that makes me start laughing again.

He puts his mouth over mine, stealing my breath with a slow sensuous kiss. His hands move up the front of my body as he pushes the wet coat off my shoulders. I think he is going to help me slide it all the way off but he stops when my arms are pinned to my sides, then he stops kissing me.

"Spill it, Hartford. What is so funny?" He squints at me and even though it's dark in here I can make out his face.

"You can't get mad," I manage to say between giggles.

"Let me decide that," he says, leaning in for another heart-melting kiss.

I breathe in to steady myself and say, "I didn't want you to discover what was in the bottom of my sleeping bag."

He pulls back, like that was not at all what he expected me to say. He cocks his head and repeats what I said. "You didn't want me to look in the bottom of your sleeping bag? What the hell, Yoda? Did you save all your toenail clippings in there or something?" He still has my arms pinned and his big thick thigh pressed between my legs. We have both discovered how much he likes to take charge like this and what it does to me. I turn to jelly, instantly.

I swallow hard and blink up at him, fighting off another round of laughter. "Gross, no. I had um, something that belonged to you down there," I say, then I wait. He will figure it out. He's smart.

I see the realization cross his eyes, then his face falls. He steps back, letting me go. "Oh, is that where you kept it?" he says in an angrier tone than I expected.

"Corey, I—" I say but he spins away from my grasp and walks off, leaving me in the dark kitchen. I fumble for the junk drawer and pull out a flashlight, then follow him down the hall. I hear the shower turn on and wet clothes hit the floor.

Shit. He's mad.

I reach for the bathroom door and turn the knob expecting it to be locked. When I inch the door open, I see there is a candle on the sink casting the room in a soft glow.

"Corey? Can I come in?" I ask, stepping tentatively into the small room. Once inside I see two more candles flickering away. I look down to his clothes on the floor and see the shower curtain move a little. I drop my jacket then quickly pull off my sweatshirt and jeans. I peel my underwear off and unsnap my bra dropping it with the rest of the wet clothes. I pull the curtain back just enough to slip inside then stand behind him watching as he dunks his head under the water stream. I gently put my hands on his hips expecting him to push me away, but he doesn't. I step closer and slide my hands around him up to his chest. I feel him take in a deep breath and he blows it out slowly. His head is dipped, still under the shower and he is moving it from side to side.

I don't speak, I just step closer into his back and wrap my arms around him letting one hand drift up while the other dances lower. I still expect him to tell me to go, or step away, but he doesn't. I slide my hand down past his cock to his thigh, then back up barely grazing his length with my thumb. I feel it pulse and jump so I do it again and again slowly while I step even closer. I press into his back enjoying feeling his breathing change as I press my chest to his firm muscles.

I move my hand from his chest down to his other thigh and stroke gently up, circling but not touching what I know is a very hard, thick cock. I lick my lips and close my eyes, praying for patience.

"I knew it was you," he says quietly.

"You did?" I ask as he leans back a little more and spreads his legs, allowing me easier access to touch him.

"Yeah, right away. I thought maybe you had forgotten about it," he says, dropping his head into the shower stream again.

My hands still, not sure what to do now, but then I feel his hand on mine guiding me to his very hard erection. I smile against his back and move both hands around him, one gripping the base of his cock while the other gently rubs the crown, smearing the precum around. He moans softly and curses under his breath but doesn't move to touch me. His arms hang limp at his sides and there is something about this position that I love. I press my cheek against his back and start to work my hand with a little more purpose. I feel him shift and he grabs the bar of soap and places it near the hand I am moving up and down. I stop and take the soap from him letting the bar travel up and around his shaft. I see why he wanted this as my hand is moving easier now, sliding up and down. I drop the bar and use both hands to stroke him and he puts his head back and moans again. This time he puts his hand on the wall and the other hand starts to help me. His head dips forward and I feel his hips start to move so I tighten my grip and hang on as he fucks my hands.

"Jesus, fuck, yes!" he shouts out and I feel him contract and still and I wish I could see around him. I have never watched a man come before but hearing that and feeling it in my hand as he came undone, I know I want to see it now. Soon.

MY LEGS ARE SHAKING as she continues to pump my cock. I have never had a hand job like that before and it's taking me a minute to calm down. Her hand slows and I feel myself go limp. I spin and gather her in my arms then bend to kiss her. I move my lips over her and love how she melts into me.

She pulls away a little and looks up at me. She is breathing hard and I don't know if it's from her confession or if she is turned on. "Are you mad at me?" she asks in a voice so quiet I almost can't hear her above the shower.

I stare into those beautiful big blue eyes and slowly nod my head yes, fighting a smile when she gasps.

"I still have it, I can give it back and you can bury it with your beard or whatever your original weird plan was. I am so sorry," Stephanie sputters out, grabbing for me, pulling me closer. I am about to let her continue when I feel her release a shuddering sob. Well, shit. Now I've gone too far.

"Hey, hey, no, Yoda, listen to me, it's okay," I say patting her back and that just makes her sob harder. I push her back and drop to my knees in front of her, wrapping myself around her and pressing my lips to her stomach.

"Stephanie, I am not mad. I was teasing you, please stop crying. Please." I pepper her with kisses all over now until she stops her sobs. When I hear her take a deep breath and sniffle a little I look up at her and smile. "I shouldn't have done that. I thought you'd get all cheeky with me and we'd have a laugh. I knew all along it was you. I am not mad."

"Okay, well like I said, I have it and I can give it to you. I was going to pin it to the student message board with that note because I figured your sisters would recognize it," she says with a sad little laugh. She is dragging her fingers through my hair, paying close attention to the back where it's now cut short. It feels heavenly. I close my eyes and moan a little at her touch hoping it encourages her to keep going, but instead she surprises me by lifting her leg and resting it over my shoulder.

"Oh. Hello there," I say, then lean forward and give her beautiful pussy a kiss. "I have missed you." I plant another kiss, softer this time and let my tongue dance out along her slit. She jerks her hips and sucks in a breath. "It seems as though you have missed me too, no?" I say, attempting a French accent. This earns me a giggle so I continue. "This is very nice of you to show up here in my shower, I do love a good beaver and you are perfection."

"Stop it!" she says with a laugh and smacks me on the arm but also thrusts a little more in my face. I wrap my hands around her ass and pull her in close so I can get to work. I lap and suck and swirl my tongue, while moving my hand slowly up her thigh letting the anticipation build.

"Fuck yes, Corey, please don't stop," she says bucking against my face. I slide in one finger, then two, curling them into her to find that spot. She gasps and I know I have hit my mark. I move my fingers, pumping into her while I suck her clit, then lap and lick until she is a shuddering mess, screaming my name. I love that she was so on edge that it didn't take long for her to fall. I ease up with my fingers and slowly kiss and lick her as she rides out her orgasm, then I lower her leg. I start slowly kissing my way back up as she hangs onto my shoulders for support.

"You okay?" I ask. I am still on my knees and I am hit by the urge to ask her to be my forever right now. She looks so beautiful staring down at me, fresh off her pleasure, but I have no ring and I want to do this right. I knew the minute she crawled out of the cupboard on that first day I saw her again, but I suspect she isn't ready for marriage. She has so much to sort out with Ivy and her father. I take a deep breath and stand, planting a gentle kiss on her lips.

"I am more than okay, I'm perfect. You are amazing, Corey." She wraps her arms around me and hugs me tightly.

"Let's get out of the shower before the hot water runs out and we turn to cold little prunes," I say. I reach back and shut off the water then pull the towel off the rack to dry her off first, then myself.

We walk to the bedroom and she goes to her purse that she left on the floor by her side of the bed. She rummages around and pulls out something then spins and hands it to me.

"What's this?" I ask reaching for the thin brown strip. I jump when it touches my fingers because it's so slippery.

"Your rattail. I told you I kept it," she says. Her shoulders relax and she smiles brightly.

"This is not my rattail! This is a sad little thing. My tail was majestic." I try and hand it back to her and she moves away.

"You think I cut off more than just yours and I have it confused?" She laughs then says, "Nope, that's what I stared at for weeks on end. That sad little scrap. Why is it so soft?" she asks with a shudder.

I hold it up and inspect it. Huh. I guess I never really got a good look at it since it hung down the back of my neck. It just felt bigger when I touched it, I guess. This really is a sad little scrap. I wince and toss it on the bed, then shudder myself. "My sisters taught me to use conditioner and how to braid it. Fuck I really thought it was bigger, no wonder you hacked it off." I say. I glance at it again coiled on the bed like an anemic gopher snake. It's like a really long earthworm that never found food. I shake my arms out like I just walked through a spider web.

"Fuck, I don't want to bury that with my kickass beard. Maybe I'll just flush it down the toilet," I say and step closer to it. I bend at the waist and peer at it lying on her bed. I straighten up and look at her. She has her arms crossed over her chest like she is protecting herself from something.

"Now that I see it, I should be thanking you. That is really embarrassing. I thought they left more hair when they cut all my rocker hair off. Here," I say, and cross the room quickly, grabbing a picture of me and my twin during our band days. "See? I had really long, thick hair. I told them to leave me enough for a rattail, assuming they knew what that meant."

Stephanie nods as she looks at the picture. I can see her shoulders start to shake, but she's not making any noise. She's just silently vibrating. I narrow my eyes at her and pull the picture back from her grasp because I don't want her tears of laughter to mark up one of the best photos I have of me and Codey.

She's trying to breathe in through her nose now, but since she is still laughing, she makes a squeaking noise which of course makes her laugh harder. Tears are streaming down her face and I put the picture on the shelf and stare at her in awe. She is so fucking perfect. Even as she laughs at me, I am struck by how beautiful she is. Her eyes, shimmering with tears, look like Lake Tahoe on a bright sunny day. Her hair dances around her face like rays of sunshine bouncing off the grass as it fights its way through the pines. Her skin is still slightly tanned even though we are well into November. Jesus, maybe that is her natural color? She takes a deep breath and puts her hands on her hips like she's trying to recover from running the mile. It hits me like a punch to the chin when I realize how I want to propose to her. It's perfect. It's the only way, I can hardly contain my excitement and I step forward and pull her into me so she can't see my face. I am sure that written across my cheeks are the words, "Will you marry me?"

"I love you, Yoda," I whisper in her ear. She lets out a little gasp and leans into me, wrapping her arms around my body. I rest my chin on the top of her head, but I have to lean over a bit to do that.

"I love you, Mr. R," she says with a sigh and squeezes me a little tighter.

TWENTY-SEVEN
STEPHANIE

THE WEEKS between Thanksgiving and Christmas are some of the best times to be a teacher, in my opinion. We just had a week off, and while Thanksgiving was wonderful and filled with more family than I have ever known, it was also sad.

My first one without my mom or Ivy. I feel like they both died instead of just my mom. Ivy still won't return my calls. I have tried and when Brian and his wife and my brothers joined us for Thanksgiving at Corey's parents' house, I felt her absence even more. I called her again and left yet another message on her answering machine.

Thankfully it wasn't my first time meeting Brian's wife and his sons, my brothers, but after spending only half an hour with them the first time I realized it would have been fine to meet them on Thanksgiving. They are super cool and were so excited to meet me. I look so much like my brothers, it's a good thing I didn't run into them on the street. Besides being taller than me we could all be mistaken for triplets. It's probably because Brian's wife, Cindy, looks similar to my mom. I guess she is my stepmom now? All of this is so strange, but their big boisterous ways made it impossible to feel awkward for more than a second. The boys fought over who could sit next to me at dinner. Corey was a gentleman and offered to sit across from me so the boys could be on either side. It's weird how my dad and Corey's parents are all teachers. Cindy works at the high school as the attendance clerk, so they all had so much to talk about, there wasn't a single quiet moment.

I am at my desk early Monday morning on our first day back, excited about the lesson I have planned when there is a knock at my door. I glance up from my lesson plan expecting Corey or Gloria to peek around the corner, but it's Allison. I set my pen down and fold my hands on the desk, taking a deep breath before I say, "Hello, Allison! Did you have a nice break?"

"I did, but I was hoping to talk to you before we start today. Do you have a minute?" she asks, sliding into the desk right in front of mine.

"I always have time for my students. What can I do for you?" I ask. I wish I didn't already know what she was going to say.

"Thanks. So I can't be partners with Jeremy. I just can't. My mom and dad found out that you paired him with me and they're really mad, so I need you to switch me out," she says, like she has the authority to ask for such a thing.

I sigh and lean forward ready to explain yet again that I don't make changes to groups unless there is an extreme circumstance, but before I can start my speech I hear a man clear his throat. I look up to find a gentleman who looks to be in his late forties. He's wearing an expensive-looking suit, and nice shoes. He has a sharp angled face and his hair is parted down the middle and plastered down on the sides. His large wire-framed glasses make his eyes look larger than they are. Allison sees him and jumps up, clapping her hands like a little girl.

"Daddy! You made it! I was just telling Miss Hartford that I needed to be switched out." She bats her eyes at him and I am tempted to roll mine. Instead I stand and smooth out my dress, extending my hand to him. I met her mother at back-to-school night and was not impressed with her either.

He glances at my hand like I am holding out a rotten salmon. I see a subtle shake of his head and he plasters on the same fake smile I see on his daughter's face every day.

"Hello. I just stopped by to make sure my daughter's needs are met without incident," he says in a clipped tone. Like maybe I am the hired help and he found a stain on his good shirt or something.

"Well, I am glad you're here. I was just about to explain yet again to your lovely daughter why I don't change partners without a very good reason. This project that they started on before the break—" I start but he holds up his hand and cuts me off.

"We have good cause. This is not going to be an issue for you," he snaps. I square my shoulders and level my gaze to him for a beat, then step out from behind my desk.

"Allison, why don't you wait outside so I can speak with your father?" I say in the most professional tone I can muster.

"Daddy?" she asks, like she needs his permission. He nods and flicks his hand, dismissing her. She scurries off to the door but stops when she gets there to glance back at me and give me a little smile, like a "you are in so much trouble" kind of a smile.

I lean against the front of my desk and fight the urge to cross my arms in front of my chest. Instead I strike a very relaxed pose, one I have seen my mother and Ivy take many times throughout my life when they dealt with brides who were demanding or angry.

"Mr. Young, I'm not sure if Allison has explained how our project works, but it would be unfair to move partners at this late date. We have two more weeks in this unit. When they come back after Christmas break there will be new groups and a new project," I say in a calm, even tone.

"Well, if you had listened to Allison in the beginning of the semester then you wouldn't be having this problem." He raises an eyebrow at me in a challenge.

"I drew names from a fishbowl to choose partners. I told the students I would be doing that, and that once chosen there would be no switching. We are so close to the end. It would be unfair to Jeremy and the other students to change now," I say, then cock my head at him. "Why is this so important to you?" I ask.

I watch him straighten his shoulders and then his tie. He glances around my classroom like the reason is written on the wall somewhere. He puts his hands in his pockets and smiles at me in what can only be described as a condescending way.

"Ms. Hartford, I understand you are new to our little town, so there is no way for you to know, or really grasp the situation here," he says. He has tilted his head to the left like he is speaking to a child.

"Situation?" I ask, then quickly add, "I have seen the way Jeremy works and he is respectful and thorough. He is actually one of the top scoring students in my class. I don't think I understand what the situation is, if you have a problem with him."

He sighs and shakes his head at me and although I'm bristling, I remain relaxed and calm, leaning against my desk like we're discussing the weather. I give him a patient smile instead and feel like I won that round.

"Well, his family is rather unorthodox and to be honest it is a huge problem with my values, and my wife's. We want to be clear that while we are sure he is a fine young man, we cannot condone what happens under his roof. We don't want our little Allison to be exposed to that, you understand?" he says, like maybe they murder puppies in their basement or something.

"I am afraid I have no idea what you're talking about," I say. I think of back-to-school night, trying to remember a one-eyed troll sitting in Jeremy's seat. There was just a man, I assumed it was his father. He wore a suit and we spoke about how Jeremy was doing in class. Nothing stood out as depraved behavior.

"Listen, it's not just me and my wife. The church is very clear on this matter. None of this is appropriate and quite frankly I am surprised the school hasn't done something," he says.

"And what would you have them do?" I ask, not sure what he is talking about.

"Well, pair Jeremy with students who have similar situations so that he isn't causing undue stress, of course," he says.

"I see," I say, even though I don't. Thankfully the bell rings and students start to filter in my class taking their seats. Mr. Young straightens up and looks around for either his daughter or Jeremy, I can't be sure which.

"I am afraid you'll need to leave now; I need to start my day. I am sure you could discuss your concerns with our principal if you are still worried about the situation." I really wish I understood the problem he has with my student, although it would not change the outcome. I will not budge on this matter.

Allison walks in laughing with her friends and sees her father still at my desk. I turn and walk toward the blackboard, like I have done every morning since the first day. I write the date and then one sentence about what was happening on this date in 1492.

I turn around and am grateful that Mr. Young has left. I glance at Jeremy's seat and let out a relieved breath when I see it empty. He had braces put on over Thanksgiving break and his father had sent word that he might be late or absent our first day back. I am glad he wasn't here to run into Allison's father.

I get through that class and the three others I have before lunch, pushing aside the strange encounter as best as I can. When the lunch bell rings, I grab my sack lunch from my desk and make my way to Gloria's classroom. She stopped eating in the staff room about two weeks into our school year because the English teacher's wandering eye freaked her out too much. I knock on the door frame.

"Come in!" Gloria yells, and I step through, about to launch into a discussion about the weird conversation I had this morning. Thankfully I waited.

"Thanks again, Mrs. Hernandez. I appreciate it," Jeremy says, then spins and smiles when he sees me. God, he is adorable even with his puffy lips and new braces. "Hi, Miss Hartford, sorry I missed class today. I had to go see the orthodontist because a wire had come loose." He points to his mouth like I might be confused about what he was talking about.

"No problem, we didn't work on the project today, it was just review of what we have done so far. Allison was able to explain where you guys were at fairly well," I say kindly.

"Oh good. I hope she didn't leave out the part about the scurvy," he says. "That's probably the best part."

"No, I think she mentioned that." I laugh.

"Well, I better go eat my yogurt. I hope my teeth don't hurt for too much longer. I miss food." He gives us a happy wave and walks out. Gloria slides back into her chair and pulls her lunch out, plopping it on her desk.

"Is it wrong that I want to eat turkey still? I can't seem to get enough. We had a ton of leftovers and I am sad to say this is the last sandwich." She holds it up like it's a prize.

"No." I laugh. "I love turkey sandwiches and all the other leftovers too." I glance back at the door to make sure we are alone. "Hey, did Allison's dad come talk to you today?" I ask. I scoot a desk over so I don't have to talk loudly.

"No, wait, Allison Young? Why would her father come talk to me?" Gloria asks. She takes a bite of her sandwich and rolls her eyes in delight. "Fuck, that is good."

"He came to see me, upset that his daughter is paired with Jeremy. I explained that we only have two more weeks and they are not going to switch. Do you have any idea why he would make such a request?" I ask. I take a bite of my ham sandwich, wishing it was turkey.

"OH SURE, people don't like Jeremy's family," she says with a shrug. She takes a huge bite of her sandwich.

"Yeah, he made a comment like that, but didn't elaborate. I met Jeremy's father at back-to-school night and I didn't see a problem. I don't get it, Gloria, what am I missing?" I ask. I can't eat, so I set my sandwich back down in my bag and push it away. I have to wait while she finishes chewing. I watch her as she eats what must be the best turkey sandwich known to man.

She holds her finger up imploring me to wait and eventually swallows and asks, "Which father did you meet?"

"Huh? I don't follow. I met Mr. Kristoph," I say with a furrow to my brow.

"Yes, I am sure you did. Which one though? Was he tall and lean with dashing good looks like Clark Kent, black glasses and all? Or was he a big beefy football player with dark skin so delicious you could spend your whole life and never learn how to have such a wonderful complexion?" she says with a sigh. She places her elbows on her desk and puts her chin in her hands then bats her long eyelashes at me.

"Um, the Clark Kent one, I guess. His dad is gay?" I ask, finally putting the pieces together.

"Yeah, they have been together for years. Great guys. I knew you had the Clark Kent one, because Mr. Beefy came to my room that night." She wiggles her eyebrows at me then adds, "He knows I have a crush on him, and likes to tease me." She laughs.

"Does your husband know this too?" I ask, leaning forward with interest.

"Yes, actually, Kyle and my husband played ball together in college. They kept in touch and we get together quite often. We might be the reason they moved back to Oregon. The Kristophs are a great family. You met Rich. He is an artist, Kyle is retired from the NFL and they live here in Beaver Valley." She finishes and picks up the last bite of her sandwich.

I am grateful for the information, but I have to make sure I understand what Mr. Young's problem is. I ask, "So Allison's father simply hates them because they're gay?"

"Well, sure. That's enough for some people. I think they were ignored for the most part when they moved here, but then when Jeremy came into their lives some of the town seemed to have a problem with them. I don't know why it changed, Kyle and Rich are such nice people." She sounds sad now, and I have to swallow to hide the rising bile in my own throat.

"They hired a surrogate and did the swirl thing, mixing the sperm because they didn't want to know who the father was." Gloria laughs out loud at that. "Like they wouldn't be able to tell once the baby was born, but it was a sweet thought. Their surrogate is Jeremy's biological mother and obviously Kyle ended up being the father. She lived with them for a while and still comes back to visit a lot. She is a part of Jeremy's life and always has been. It's a wonderful arrangement if you ask me." Gloria wads up the bag that held her lunch and tosses it in the trash can. "Goodbye my love. Until next year," she says wistfully.

I laugh at that and tell her, "You can make turkey all year long, you know?"

"No, it's not the same. Don't." She's holding up her hand like she knows I am going to argue. I want to. I want to talk about anything but the asshole father who couldn't stand for his kid to work with a boy who came from a family different from his own.

Somehow, I make it through the rest of my day and I wait in front of the school for Corey. I'm leaning against his car when he comes out with Garrett, our principal. They seem to be in a serious discussion, so I busy myself with examining my nails. A few people know we are together, but it's not like we made a formal announcement and I hope our relationship isn't going to cause a problem.

"Listen, I think if you move her to B group, her parents will just find a problem with one of those kids. The Youngs have always been this way, from what I hear. Talk to Gloria, she knows them better since she has lived here in the valley for over twenty years," Corey says. He smiles when he sees me and I love the way my stomach flips at that.

"Hey, if you need to talk I can wait in my classroom," I say, but Garrett holds up his hand.

"No, I actually followed Corey out because I knew you would be here. Could we maybe meet for dinner? The three of us?" he asks.

I glance at Corey, who is nodding yes, so I say, "Sure, that would be nice. Tonight?"

"Yeah, I have to run home and take care of a few things, so how about we meet at the pizza place at five?"

"Sounds good." I smile as best as I can. I am guessing that Mr. Young took my suggestion to speak with the principal to heart.

TWENTY-EIGHT
COREY

AS SOON AS we get into my car, Stephanie turns to me, and I catch how pale she looks.

"You okay?" I ask, my hand going to her leg immediately like touching her will allow me to know.

"Yeah, I am just rattled by the whole thing with Allison. Mr. Young came into my classroom before school, demanding I switch his daughter out from Jeremy's group. I had already explained this to Allison the first day. I thought the matter was settled. I don't switch groups, Corey. Ever. You get it, right?" she says in a rush of words.

"Yeah, you are doing the right thing there, if you change once they will ask all the time. I don't usually do group projects in math, but I will next semester when we get to the barter system. I should make sure to pair Allison with Jeremy," I say then add an evil laugh at the end for fun.

It doesn't make her laugh. Instead she grabs my hand and squeezes it. With her other hand I see her reach up and wipe away a tear. If we had a long commute, I would pull over right then. I drive the last block to my house and turn to face her once the car is in park.

"Steph, what's wrong?" I trace my thumb down her cheek following the line of tears.

"It's just not fair. He's a great kid, Corey, he's super smart and I have never, not even once seen him be mean to anyone. How can Mr. Young be so awful?" Her voice is cracking as the pain bubbles up to the surface.

"I don't know. I don't understand how people can be so closed-minded but they are. I mean, maybe I am different because I grew up in LA in a very liberal area. I knew there were gay kids at my school, and the charter school where I taught when I graduated from college had several same-sex couples. No one looked twice. I thought it was like that everywhere," I say with a shrug. I add, "Come on, let's go inside and we can talk more before dinner."

We make our way into the house and she drops her bag then bends and fishes her brown lunch sack out. I can see the stain the grape jelly left on the side of the bag and when she drops it in my trashcan I can hear a solid thud.

"Did you eat lunch?" I ask. I walk over and pull the bag out to open it and peer in. A very sad smashed sandwich and a bruised apple rest on the bottom of the bag.

"I couldn't. My stomach was too upset. Fuck, Corey, is this why my mom and Ivy didn't live together? Is it? People like Mr. Young?" Tears spill over her eyes and race down her face. "Bigots like him robbed my mother and Ivy of the life they wanted, the life they deserved?" She tosses her hands in the air and spins around like she's looking for something. She spots the phone book on the counter and grabs it, flipping it open and thumbing through the white pages. I step closer and see she is looking through the Y's.

"What are you doing there, Yoda?" I ask, moving slightly closer without wanting to crowd her.

"I am going to call Mr. Young and give him a piece of my mind. I am going to tell him that Jeremy and his two wonderful fathers deserve to be happy and that if he has a problem with that then he can just go straight to hell," she yells, and flips the pages faster tearing some in the process.

"York, Yost, ah-ha! Here we go, Young, there are only five. That can't take too long, I'll start with Albert and work my way to Mike. He's probably Mike, knowing my luck but hey, it's not like I have anything else to do." She grabs the phone and I dive to knock it out of her hand. It goes smashing to the floor then does a sad little bounce with the cord pulling it back up. The mouthpiece has come loose and it rolls across the linoleum, stopping only when it hits the fridge.

"Stop, Stephanie!" I snap as she goes to grab it. "You can't call all the Youngs and yell at them. You need to calm down, your anger isn't going to help anything," I say as I block her. I can hear the dial tone of the phone she's now angrily pointing at me.

"I need to tell him, Corey! I need to let him know what his ignorance and hatred are doing to Jeremy!" she yells. I step forward and gather her in my arms, pressing her into my chest.

"Jeremy doesn't know any of this. He is a happy kid. Let's just wait and see what Garrett has to say at dinner, okay? Please?" I say. I keep holding her tight against me until I feel her relax a little, then I loosen my grip. She darts away from me and grabs the mouthpiece and tries to screw it back over the bits and pieces that are hanging out. A green wire that probably was attached to something important is sticking up in the air. I grab her by the waist and start walking out of the kitchen, not surprised at all when I hear the phone pull away from the wall. She is freakishly strong for such a small person.

I toss her onto the couch and stare down at her. I am straddling her knees, pinning her in place so she can't get up. She tries anyway, so I put my hand on her forehead. It's a mean tactic since my arms are way longer than hers. She struggles for a bit then gives up, slumping against the couch. She twists her lips to hide the smile I see forming and she looks away. One deep breath after another, I see her relax for real.

"Are you okay?" I ask, letting my hand drop to her cheek. I stroke my thumb across her jaw then back up to her hairline, threading my fingers in and pulling her close. I kiss her lips softly and pull back to check on her.

"Yeah. I am now. That was not my best moment. I, um probably owe you a new phone." I follow her gaze to what once was my bright yellow wall-mounted phone. The cradle that held the handset is missing and the dial has snapped off. I see it on the floor next to the coffee table. Damn. I loved that phone.

"Yeah, that probably isn't going to go back together," I say. I sit next to her on the couch, then lift her onto my lap. She folds into me and nuzzles her face into my neck. We sit like that for a long time, neither of us speaking. I rub her back and tickle my fingers up and down her arm. I hate seeing her like this. I hate that there are people in the world that can be so awful. If only I could wrap her in a safe little bubble where nothing would ever hurt her again, but I know that isn't possible.

I nudge her a little when I see it's time to meet Garrett for dinner and she heaves a sigh and climbs out of my lap. I watch as she plods down the hallway to freshen up a little before we go. I hope to God Garrett has some ideas on how to handle all of this or I am going to have to start saving bail money for Stephanie.

We pull into the parking lot and I rush around to open her door, then hold her hand all the way inside. We are a united front, or that's what I hope she feels. I try to send that feeling down my arm and into my hand. I give her a little squeeze that I hope says, "I'm with you."

Garrett sees us and waves as soon as we walk in. I smile and relax a little when I see Jeremy's fathers at the table. We *are* a united front, not just me and Steph.

"Hello! Thanks for joining us, Stephanie, I hear you met Rich at back-to-school night. This is his partner, Kyle." Everyone is standing as Garrett makes his introductions. I had heard one of Jeremy's fathers was an NFL player and man, seeing him I am not surprised. The guy is built like a tank.

We all shake hands and share smiles and hellos, and Stephanie sits next to Garrett as I slide in across from them. Kyle and Rich have chairs on the end of the booth and I suspect Rich wouldn't fit even if he wanted to.

"I hear Mr. Young paid you a visit?" Rich asks. His voice is deep and commanding and I may have startled at the sound. I try to brush it off like I wasn't just a little bit afraid.

"Yes, he did, and I'm still so rattled. I may have tried to call and tell him off, but Corey stopped me," Stephanie says. I can hear the apprehension in her voice, the slight trembling that I am sure they don't notice.

"Now don't go getting yourself in trouble for us. We can fight our own battles, been doing it long enough now," Rich says. He puts his hand on her arm to comfort her and I am shocked at his size. It looks like a grizzly bear has wrapped its paw around her.

"But it's not fair or right and I—" Steph starts but this time Kyle cuts her off.

"Did you know that I was gay when I met you at back-to-school night?" he asks, and I see Stephanie's eyes go big.

"No, I mean I would never assume anything about anyone, but no," she says.

Kyle nods at his partner and laughs, "And if you met him at say, the grocery store, would you think, now there is a gay man?"

"No," Stephanie says with a smile.

"My point is, people come in all different forms, inside and out. We could spend a lot of energy trying to get people to understand something that is none of their damn business, or we can put that energy into being happy and raising our son. So far that decision has paid off. Jeremy has a good group of friends, a wide variety of interests and according to his history teacher, he's one of the top students in class." Kyle gives her a little wink. Stephanie's shoulders relax a little, but I know she isn't satisfied.

"Listen, when we moved here twenty years ago, this valley was just that, a big almost empty valley. There were a few houses, one store and a small post office. As it grew, we met some nice people and some who didn't seem to approve of our lifestyle. We decided to treat both exactly the same. When Jeremy came into our lives it brought out the divide more clearly." He pauses and reaches for Rich's hand. "We can't spend our time worrying about people like Mike Young."

Stephanie slams her hand on the table and yells, "I knew it!"

Everyone jumps and I laugh at the little firecracker of a woman. If I wasn't already in love with her, today would have made me fall for her. The ferocity of her love and loyalty to her students and their happiness is something else.

"I had a long talk with Mike this morning, Stephanie, and I want you to know that you are in control of your classroom and the choices you make within your lesson plans. I understand the rule about not switching groups, especially not this late in the semester. I don't want anyone to bend to pressure from students or parents, unless of course there is real danger. This is our first year and it's important to set high standards and consistent expectations. I want you to know that you have me and the administration behind you," Garrett says. He is speaking to Stephanie, but my chest warms at how lucky I am to be working here. This school, the theme teaching, and the way we're treated by the administration and the school district are like nothing I've experienced before.

"Thank you. I wasn't expecting this, to be honest. I thought I was going to have to beg you to let me keep things the same, let the kids finish the project," Stephanie says. She blows out a breath and runs her hands through her hair. "The thing that gets me is since that first day when Allison asked to be switched out, she has worked really well with Jeremy. I see them laughing and talking during the group time. It's not like she is miserable or anything. I don't know why her father came in today."

"I bet I do," Rich says with a glance at Kyle.

"Yeah, I probably shouldn't have invited her to game night." Kyle is shaking his head.

. . .

"WELL, you were just being you. Nice. You are always so damn nice," Rich says with a little smile dancing across his face.

"Jeremy and I were at the store getting things for Thanksgiving dinner and we saw her by herself in the produce section. Jeremy said most of her friends went out of town for the holiday to ski, but her parents had to work so they stayed behind. Jeremy felt bad for her so when he said hello, I told her about our tradition of playing board games the day after Thanksgiving. She looked interested and excited when I invited her." Kyle shrugs a little then continues, "I guess her parents didn't like that we invited her over."

"So, I assume she didn't show up at your place with Monopoly?" I ask.

"No, and it's really been a drop-in kind of thing with Jeremy's friends. Some come early and stay all day, some come for just one or two games. It's a no-pressure fun day, but clearly it made Mike angry," Kyle says.

"Thank you for standing up to him today, and I, well, we hope he doesn't make things difficult for you going forward," Rich says.

"I can handle it," Stephanie says.

"She can. Did you know she hiked the PCT from San Diego all the way to Truckee, California?" I say, pride evident in my voice.

"No shit? You did that? You can't be more than 5'2, what do you weigh, 110? 105?" Rich says, squinting at her.

"I will never tell!" Stephanie laughs.

"Her pack weighed almost as much as she does and she powered past me on most days like I was standing still," I explain, loving the chance to talk about how I met this amazing woman.

"You did the hike too?" Garrett asks.

"Yeah, that's how we met, then Steph had to leave the trail and I thought I was never going to see her again. Turns out we both had jobs here. Isn't that wild?" I ask, beaming at her.

"That is something else. What a great story," Garrett says. I glance at Steph, who has gone from smiling to fiddling with her hands. I guess there are parts of that trip and our coming back together that still bring her pain. I wish that wasn't the case.

TWENTY-NINE
STEPHANIE

AS WE SIT HERE DESCRIBING the way Corey and I met, I am hit by how much I blocked out when I was back home with my mom. My time on the trail was life-changing, and not just because of Corey. I grew so much when I was out there. I found out that I could do things on my own not just academic things, but hard physical things.

I glance at Corey and wonder what would have happened if we hadn't gotten together, or if I hadn't been pulled off the trail. I know I would have made it to Canada. I would have found a job somewhere, but thinking that, I just feel so empty. Like all that happened led me to what I have now. There are a few things I wish I had known, like I wish my mom and Ivy had been honest with me. I wish I knew how to mend the rift with Ivy. I wish that I could trust that part of my life would return. Corey thinks it will.

"So does Allison give Jeremy grief in class? Is she making this hard on him?" Kyle asks and pulls me from my thoughts. My mind shifts to my first period class. I see Allison laughing and leaning in to hear whatever Jeremy has to say. I see his face light up when she walks in the class. Huh.

"No, actually just the opposite. It seems to me that they're friends. Maybe that's why I was so thrown by her father showing up." I move my hands out of the way as the waitress sets the biggest pizza I have ever seen down on the table.

"More drinks?" she asks. Garrett asks her to bring two more pitchers of beer and a glass for me and Corey.

"So you aren't seeing a problem yourself?" Garrett asks.

"Not at all," I say. I lean back as the waitress passes out plates to everyone. I don't know if I can eat, my stomach still feels upset from all of this.

"That's the impression I got when we ran into her in the store that time. Jeremy seemed to think of her as a friend and it wasn't one-sided," Rich says.

"Maybe it is all coming from the parents then." Garrett sighs and continues, "He made it seem like Allison was miserable and he was doing this not just for his belief system or whatever, but for his daughter."

"Can you talk to her?" Corey asks.

"Sure, I will do that. I am trying to decide if I want to wait until just before our break, so that I don't inject drama into an already tense situation," Garrett says. I really like him. Brian was right, he's an incredible administrator. He is kind and thoughtful, never rushing to judgment or decisions.

The conversation turns to other things as we all eat and drink. I manage to get one whole piece of pizza down as well as a mug of beer, so by the end of the night I am beginning to feel a bit better.

***

WE HAD three weeks left in this semester when we returned from Thanksgiving, then we get another two weeks off for Christmas. I am looking forward to the break, even though I just had one. I bet if Mr. Young hadn't rattled my cage on my first day back I wouldn't be feeling this antsy. Corey has tried to get me to calm down and forget about it and I have to say his attempts have been successful for the most part. He really knows how to light me up with dirty talk and great sex.

"Ready to tackle the last week, Yoda?" Corey says in barely a whisper. He snuck up behind me in the bathroom and is currently sliding his hands under my sweater. I lean back into him and smile as his hands move up, cupping my breasts. He gives them a little squeeze then lets his thumbs graze across my already hard nipples. I reach back and find he is still in his boxers, and it's clear he thinks we have time for some fun before work. I am really going to miss these mornings together. My house is done and the last of the furniture I bought is being delivered today, so I really should move next door.

"We don't have time for that, Corey," I say as I palm his rock-hard cock. I don't really mean it, we never take too long and we can't seem to get enough of each other. He grabs my hand and spins me around to face him.

"Let's quit our jobs. We can just stay in bed all day and fuck." He wiggles his eyebrows at me. I laugh and push him out of the bathroom. He keeps his hands on my hips as he walks backwards toward the bed. He sits when his legs hit it, and I climb on him, straddling his lap. I grind against his hard length and smile as he gathers the skirt of my dress up around my hips.

"You are a naughty little history teacher, Miss Hartford. Where are your knickers?" Corey says in his worst British accent. He knows it makes me laugh and this time is no exception.

I gasp when he lifts me and pulls his erection out of his boxers and slides me down on his length. "Already so wet too, what kind of things do you think about when you are brushing your teeth?"

I close my eyes and lift up, then slam my hips down, causing him to curse out. I grab his face and pull his mouth to mine, kissing the life out of him as he pushes up into me. I want to respond with something cheeky so he will continue with his silly yet very sexy British accent, but we are both consumed with need and this position hits all the right spots. He grazes my clit with his thumb and that little brush is like the strike of a match. I gasp into his mouth as I feel the start of my orgasm. His kisses become more passionate, lips and tongues finding the same rhythm as my hips. I start to feel the slow tingle spread inside me and I grind down, letting the waves of pleasure rock my core.

As I come back down Corey grabs me and flips me onto my back, then slams into me again and again, covering my body with his. "One more, Steph, give me one more to get me there," he says huskily in my ear. Then he bites my neck right where I like it. I arch and let the sensation of him pounding into me take over and as I crest for the second time, he thrusts hard and stills as he empties into me.

"Jesus Christ. You are trying to do me in," he pants into my hair.

"Me? I was just minding my own business, brushing my teeth when Mr. Europe came in and got frisky." I laugh and he pulls up and wiggles his eyebrows at me.

"Are you saying you don't like my tea and biscuits?" He says sounding a little Australian now. I laugh and push him off me.

"You know I love them, but also, that is a weird term for your cock." I raise an eyebrow at him then push my dress down. I walk to the dresser to grab my tights and a pair of underwear.

He's propped up on his elbows watching me with a devilish smile on his face. Damn, I am so lucky. He is so handsome and smart and kind and, man, can he fuck.

"You should get dressed. You have to teach soon." I point at him and smile. I slide my underwear up then sit on the bed to put on my tights. Corey hasn't moved. He's just watching me with a slight smile on his beautiful face.

"What are you looking at, Mr. R?" I ask as I pull up the thick grey tights. It's cold and snowy now but I still love to wear dresses. Tights and boots and a nice cardigan, and I am usually fine.

"I was just wondering how many of my high school teachers went into class freshly fucked?" he says with a wink.

"Probably more than we imagined, actually come to think of it, it didn't occur to me that my teachers were having sex." I shudder thinking of Mr. Sweeney with anyone. The man was a lizard in a suit.

Corey finally gets up and goes to his closet to get dressed. Once he has his pants on and a shirt in hand he turns to me, cocking his head.

"Shit, today is the day, isn't it?" he asks, his shoulders slumping a little.

I sigh, unable to even act excited that my house is ready. "Yeah, the couch and my bedroom set are getting delivered today. Your mom offered to wait for the delivery."

"Of course she did. That woman is never not helpful," he says as he pulls his shirt on. He gets buttoned up and tucked in before he says anything else and when he does speak, it's not what I expect.

"We should go. Garrett doesn't like it when we slide in sideways at eight fifteen." He walks out and I wonder if he is mad at me. I mean it's not like I can help the fact that I have a place of my own. I was so proud of that fact and then crazy John and his desire to stay in his home pushed my move-in timeline back farther than I would have expected.

I sigh and make my way out to the kitchen expecting to find Corey making his lunch. Instead I see the garage open and the exhaust from his car as he warms it up. Damn, he is mad.

That day as the students file into my first class of the day, I pay closer attention to Allison and Jeremy. He comes in first and has a smile he's trying to hide, his eyes twinkling under his mop of curly brown hair. He's stopped slicking it back with gel and I for one am happy about the change.

Just before the final bell rings Allison darts in and takes her seat. I notice the flush to her cheeks and the slight bruising on her neck, the mark of a lover. Interesting.

I glance back at Jeremy and he is looking everywhere but at her. Holy crap. Jeremy, you sneaky little bugger.

THIRTY
COREY

I RUSHED us out of the house this morning because I needed to use the phone where Stephanie couldn't hear me. Since she murdered my kitchen phone, I only have the cordless and I felt like it would be weird to kick her out or go in my room and close the door.

Thankfully our principal is at meetings today in Bend and Miss Gee has a soft spot for me. My leg bounces as I wait for Barbara to pick up the other line.

"Hello?" she says, sounding rushed. She always sounds rushed though, so I don't take offense.

"Hi, you're still coming for Christmas, right?" I ask without hesitation.

"Hello Corey, yes, we're coming. We will be there Saturday just like we planned," she says with a chuckle.

"Can you come sooner?" I ask.

"No, we are lucky to get the week. Why? Is everything okay? Did Stephanie find out we're coming?" she asks.

I sigh heavily and tell her about Stephanie's house being ready and not wanting her to leave. That if I just had one more week I would be able to execute my plan to propose. Well, if the weather cooperates.

"Corey, you know I love you, but I can't get away any earlier. Plus we want to stay in Bend at the hotel so we can ski. As much as I want to walk through the snowy streets of Beaver Valley, I just can't. Grace can't either so don't think about hanging up with me and calling her." She chuckles knowing me so well. That was actually my next plan. I already had my little phone book open to her name. Damn it.

I get into my classroom before the first bell, feeling depressed and dejected. I don't want her to be five feet away from me let alone in a different house, but she is young and this is her first time having her own place. Her home that she was able to buy because of her mother. She needs to experience that. At least that"s what Barbara told me before we got off the phone. It's not the first time she has had to advocate for Stephanie's autonomy. I would strap that tiny blonde to my back like a bedroll if I could. I think about how I felt when I watched that car drive away and how it felt like my heart was in the trunk bouncing around like an old shoe.

I rub my hand down my face and try to make it through the day without going next door to ogle her. Fuck, I am stalking my own girlfriend.

At lunch I walk down the hall and head to Gloria's classroom because I know that's where Stephanie is. Yep, total stalker. When I rap on the door and peek my head in, I expect to see the two friends sitting and eating but what I see instead is two women looking through curtains and whispering ferociously at each other.

I clear my throat and Stephanie jumps in the air, spinning around, while Gloria holds the curtains together like they might fly apart and expose a naked man.

"Jesus, Corey, you scared me!" Steph says then turns back to the window and pries Gloria's hands from the curtain. "Let me see if they're still there!" she hisses, like whoever is on the other side of the glass could hear her.

"They left, damn it." Steph sighs and walks over to me to give me a quick little peck on the cheek.

"What, or rather who, are you two spying on?" I ask, pulling Stephanie onto my lap at a desk. She swats at me and stands up, getting her own seat right next to me. Still too far away, but since we are at work it will have to do.

"Jeremy and Allison!" Gloria says.

"Oh shit, is she giving him a hard time? Damn, we were just telling Jeremy's dads that everything is okay here at school," I say, and Stephanie shakes her head.

"No, she isn't being mean to him, just the opposite actually. I think they are dating!" Stephanie says while holding her hand to her chest. "It's like a modern-day Romeo and Juliet."

"You know that ended really badly, right?" I say with horror.

Gloria makes a shooing motion with her hand and looks all doe-eyed as well, "Don't you ruin this for us Corey, they are star-crossed lovers."

"They are minors and Allison's father is an asshole. Seriously, you think they're dating?" I ask. I am clearly the only adult in the room who sees this for the problem it is. I take out my sandwich and Coke, then use the brown paper bag as a plate. It still amazes me what I was able to survive on while hiking the PCT. I think when I got off the trail I gained ten pounds back in the first week. I am surprised I don't have stretch marks.

"So listen, I might be wrong, but this morning when first period was about to start, Jeremy came in looking well, rather dazed and shall we say, happy," Stephanie explains. "Then Allison came in looking equally flushed and she has a hickey on her neck, right here!" Stephanie points to her own neck like I don't know where boys put marks on girls.

"Could be a coincidence." I shrug and take a bite of my ham sandwich. I think I need to throw this ham out, it's a little sweaty. I wince as I swallow.

"Is that the ham from the fridge?" Stephanie asks as I fight to get the bite down. I grab my Coke and take a big swig letting the relief wash over me when it carries the bite away.

"Yeah, I'll toss it," I say, then start to take another bite but stop and shove it back in my bag.

"It tried to crawl away from me this morning. Here, I made two." She reaches in her bag and hands me a peanut butter and jelly sandwich. I smile and think about the day she made a sandwich on the trail and she had that bit of jelly on her cheek.

Gloria is watching me staring at Stephanie and I rein it in before I get kicked out. I clear my throat and ask, "Sorry. So you think Allison and Jeremy are an item?"

"Yeah, I do. When her dad came to see me she was acting like she agreed, or so I thought. What if the little smile she gave me was because she hoped I'd set her father straight?" Stephanie says.

"Interesting theory, and that makes sense, honestly. I have never seen them act like anything but friends," Gloria chimes in with her agreement.

"So what were you spying on through the window?" I ask.

Gloria stands and pulls her curtains open far enough for me to see she has a great view of the parking lot. All the kids that could leave campus for lunch must pass right in front of her window.

"Did you see them together?" I ask.

"Yeah, he got in her car and I think he leaned over and kissed her, but I can't be sure because you walked in and scared me!" Stephanie says.

This does make things more complicated, that's for sure. I mean not for me, but for the kids. We sit and visit through the rest of lunch and just as the bell rings I stand and turn in time to see Garrett running at a full sprint down the hall past Gloria's classroom. What the hell?

I step out in the hall and am narrowly run down by Miss Gee, who is also sprinting toward the office. Teachers are peeking out of classrooms and the kids that are back from lunch are starting to filter in. I can tell by their faces something is wrong.

"Stephanie, come on." I wave at her to follow me then head to the office after the principal. I see a group of girls hugging and crying and when I round the corner to the office I run smack into a police officer.

"Shit, what happened?" Stephanie asks. She is breathing hard like me, and we wait anxiously as Miss Gee's high-pitched voice comes across the loudspeaker.

"Attention Furie Beavers. Attention. Please make your way to your fifth-period class. We are aware of the situation and will be letting you all know the status of the injured students once we know. Again, please go to your fifth-period class." A squelch of static blasts across the speakers and we hear Miss Gee cuss like Minnie Mouse got stood up at the altar, before it goes silent. The students file away and Stephanie grabs my hand, pulling me along.

"Come on, Corey. We have to go, come on." She tugs me along and I follow, worried sick about what must have happened.

I sit at my desk and watch as all twenty of my students fill their seats. Okay so not one of mine. I pick up the phone and dial Steph's room.

"Miss Hartford's class," she says quietly.

"All accounted for?" I ask in a hushed tone. My students are staring at me and a few kids are getting out their books. This is the sophomore class, the ones that can't leave campus for lunch, so they are probably just as confused as I am.

"Yeah, I have everyone. Gotta go. I love you," she whispers before she hangs up.

"Sorry class, obviously something happened at lunch and I am sure once they have news they will share it with us. Why don't we all turn to page 50 and see if we can run through some of the basics before our midterm tomorrow?"

The promise of news hangs over the whole school for the rest of fifth period and sixth as well, but with kids passing in the hallway, the rumors have started. Car spun out, hit the ice, went down an embankment. No one knows who and about ten seniors are missing. Ten out of only fifty. Our senior class is the smallest because some of the

Beaver Valley families decided to stay in Bend to finish out their schooling.

My last period is freshmen and I pull out two decks of cards and make them play a game I invented with the charter school kids. It's fast-paced and cutthroat so I figure it will take everyone's mind off the waiting. About halfway through Pirate Booty, Miss Gee comes on the loudspeaker.

"Attention, Furie Beavers. All is well. The students who were in an accident at lunch are going to be okay. They have some injuries, but nothing life-threatening. We expect them to be back in the Beaver Den when we return from Christmas break. Go Beavers!" She clicks off this time without screeching or cuss words. My whole class heaves a sigh of relief then gets right back to the game. I step out into the hall just as Steph does and we give each other weak smiles. I am about to say something when I hear my classroom phone ring. I wave at her, then hurry to answer it.

"Mr. R's class," I say.

"Corey, it's Miss Gee. Can you get all of Allison and Jeremy's things together? They won't be back until after break."

"Of course, can you tell me anything?" I ask. my shoulders tensing as that request sinks in.

'I don't know any more than what I shared. They are at the hospital and their families are with them," Miss Gee says kindly.

"Thank you," I say, then I go to my file cabinet and pull out the final assignments for both Allison and Jeremy. They are both getting A's so I really could just tell them there is nothing to do, but I have a feeling they know there is still this assignment. I want to know more, but like the rest of the school, I'll have to wait.

When school is finally over there are groups of kids huddled together some crying, some somber and it seems the grownups aren't doing much better. Word has spread now that it was Allison's car that hit black ice, plunging her and Jeremy off the side of the road. Thankfully the snow was deep and stopped the forward movement of the car before it went down into the gully. At least that's what the kids have heard. I will feel better when I can get the actual story from adults.

Stephanie and I hang back, talking to some of the seniors, and finally make our way back to my house well after four o'clock. We are both silent until we get inside, I head straight for the fridge and grab two beers. I pop the tops and hand her one.

"Those poor kids." Steph says. She takes the bottle from my hand, letting her fingers linger a moment. She looks up at me and gives me a weak smile.

"Yeah," I reply. I take a big drink of my beer, then point out the obvious. "I bet Mr. Young knows that his daughter and Jeremy are together now."

"Yep. I wish I could have been there to see that. I bet Mike wouldn't be brave enough to spout off to Rich. That guy is like a brick wall." Stephanie giggles, then tips her beer back and chugs the whole thing. She sets it down on the table and burps loudly.

I tip mine back and do the same then try and top her belch but come up short.

"We should win 'most attractive couple' this year," Steph says with a smile.

"I agree," I say, standing to get more beer. Too bad it's not Friday. I hand Steph another beer, then walk into the living room hoping she will follow.

THIRTY-ONE
STEPHANIE

THE WEEK before Christmas break is generally the longest week in the history of time. But when two of the most popular kids have an accident and that's all anyone wants to talk about, it makes it even longer.

It wasn't even the accident that was the topic of conversation, it was the fact that they were together. Apparently they had a real enemies-to-lovers thing happen over this semester. Only a few of their closest friends knew they were dating. Although when I think back to the first day of school when Allison asked to be moved from his group, I think she always wanted to be more than friends. She must have known how her parents felt about Jeremy's family, so she tried to keep her distance. The heart wants what the heart wants.

After school on Friday, Corey and I have plans to go to their houses with cards and gifts from the staff and students. Seeing how everyone has rallied behind them makes me love this little community even more.

I finish up with my last period of the day and am piling the cards into a box when there's a knock at my door.

"Hi, Stephanie? Do you have a minute?" I hear my father ask from the doorway. I spin around and smile at him. It just happens now when I see him, I don't have to try or force it, my lips just turn up and I feel actual joy in my heart. I don't know how he could have won me over so quickly, but he did. Not just him, his wife and my half-brothers are all just so wonderful, it feels like I've always known them.

"Yes, of course! I was just getting things together for Allison and Jeremy. Corey and I are going to their houses now," I explain.

"Right, that's very nice of you. Garrett told me about the accident. Those kids were really lucky to just have minor injuries." He comes in and leans against the desk while I pack up.

"What did you need?" I ask.

"I just wanted to make sure you're okay with us all getting together for Christmas. I feel like Corey's mom kind of pushed you into the whole family thing at Thanksgiving, and I don't want you to feel any pressure. It's okay if we go slower," he says. I notice how vulnerable he sounds and it makes my heart hurt a little. I don't want him to feel that way. It wasn't his fault I didn't know him growing up. I mean I was going to try and find him, so I want this. I had that little epiphany at the huge Thanksgiving gathering. The feeling of family and love pouring out of the house that day helped reset my broken heart.

"Brian, I want to celebrate with you and Cindy and the boys. You are my family and I missed out on twenty-two years of Christmases with you," I say, then wonder if maybe his wife wishes this hadn't happened. "If you or Cindy don't want to though, I understand and we can—"

"No Stephanie, we want this. More than anything. I just wanted to check in with you to be sure. I know how kindergarten teachers can be about organizing and pushing everyone to be friends," he says with a chuckle.

"Corey's mom is the queen of those things!" I say with a laugh.

"Okay, well, I look forward to spending some time with you then. I hope it's okay that I got you a few gifts. Nothing major, just wanted to get my daughter something," he says. The last word comes out a little strangled. In all the times that we have been together I have not hugged him yet, nor has he tried to touch me. There is something about him standing here, checking in with me that pushes me into his arms. I dive into his huge bear-sized chest and wrap my arms around him, startling him. He smells just like a dad should, like Old Spice and flannel. When his arms wrap around me, I feel a sob rise up in my chest and I don't fight it. I let it bubble up and out unapologetically.

Brian stiffens a bit like he is unsure what to do with a crying daughter but then his father instincts kick in and he smooths my hair and rubs my back while saying things like *it's okay* and *hey now*. Eventually I pull back and look up at him, tears still spilling over my eyes.

"Thank you for being so welcoming to me. I know that finding out about me must have been earth-shattering, and you could have been a real jerk if you wanted. I am so glad you weren't," I say.

This makes him laugh and pull me back into his chest. "Listen, your mom—Rose—was an amazing woman. I am sure you know that, but the young woman I met all those years ago still holds a piece of my heart. She captivated me, and I see her in you. I see me too, and I gotta tell you, that is a powerful drug. I hope someday you can understand that kind of love. I know I missed out on a lot, but we can't worry about what was, we just have to enjoy what is."

"Everything okay?" I hear Corey ask from the doorway.

I sniff and straighten up then wipe my eyes. "Yeah, we are all good. My dad just stopped by for a visit."

Brian snaps his gaze to me and at first I don't even realize why. Then I do. "I mean Brian. Unless," I pause and wait. It feels like I just asked for something so valuable without any warning.

"I would love you to call me Dad, Stephanie, if you want," he says, and his eyes look a little damp.

"Yeah, I think I would like that a lot," I reply with that easy smile he draws from me.

"You two need to stop or I will be a mess!" Corey says in a silly high-pitched voice while fanning his face. It breaks the tension and we all laugh.

"I'll let you two go check on the kids. I have a meeting with Garrett about the spring budget and sports. Sounds like there were enough kids interested in playing baseball, so we might have a team of fighting Beavers!" Brian says.

After he leaves and Corey and I load everything into his car, we make our way to Jeremy's house first. Climbing the steps to his impressive home, I wonder how we will be treated once we get to Allison's house. The gossip among the children ranged from the parents having a fist fight at the hospital, to them all going skiing together for Christmas. The truth is probably somewhere in the middle. I am anxious to find out, but mostly I just want to know the kids are okay.

"Miss Hartford, Mr. Richie! Thanks for coming by. Jeremy was just asking when you were coming. I am afraid he's been quite bored here." Kyle holds the door open wide and ushers us in. I look around and try to seem unaffected by the beautiful home sprawling out before me. It looks like something out of a magazine. There are high ceilings and exposed wood beams that look like beavers maybe helped cut them down. There is a table in the middle of the foyer with a gorgeous flower arrangement that immediately makes me think of my mom. It has poinsettias and white carnations and pine cones. I lean forward and see a pomegranate tucked in like a hidden jewel. I suddenly realize that Corey and Kyle are no longer with me, so I follow the sound of their voices down into a sunken living room. Jeremy is on the biggest couch I have ever seen, surrounded by pillows and blankets. His right ankle is propped up and his bruised toes stick out of a cast. From the looks of it every senior has already been by to sign it. He has a splint on his right wrist as well, but he's smiling and laughing at what Corey said.

"There you are, I was just about to come look for you," Kyle says with a warm smile.

"Oh, sorry. I was looking at your beautiful flower arrangement in the foyer. My mom was a florist, and she would have loved that piece," I say softly.

"It is lovely, isn't it? I am sorry for your loss, I know how hard it can be to lose a parent," Kyle says. He then adds, "If you hadn't spoken of her in the past tense I would have asked for her number. I got lucky with that piece, but the florist here in Beaver Valley thinks a bunch of roses stuck in some foam is art. That one is from a shop in Bend," he explains.

I laugh and think about the arrangements that came to the house after she passed. None of them would have met her standards, or Ivy's for that matter, but I try not to think about that. It still hurts that she won't respond to my calls or letters. I know I yelled at her, but she has to know I was just hurting. I don't get why she cut me out of her life completely.

"Miss Hartford?" Jeremy calls from the couch.

"Yes?" I step closer to him and slide my arm around Corey, not even thinking about what that might look like. Jeremy smiles and raises an eyebrow.

"I WAS GOING to ask how we can present our final project, but now I have a different question." He laughs and points to where Corey and I are linked.

I start to pull away, but Corey stops me. "Miss Hartford and I are dating. We have known each other since summer," Corey says, and I can't help but smile up at him.

"Okay, well, that's awesome!" Jeremy says.

"What is awesome?" Rich asks as he steps down into the living room with a tray full of snacks. He sets it next to his son and smiles up at us.

"Mr. Richie and Miss Hartford are dating!" he says, beaming at us, like he knows the best kept secret at Beaver Valley High School. Which I guess since his secret is out, Corey and I are up.

"Wonderful!" Rich exclaims.

"Jeremy, you and Allison can present when we come back from break. We aren't moving on to the next unit on day one, we have your presentation and unfortunately two other groups that were unable to present this week," I explain.

"Oh, did they crash in their secret girlfriend's car too?" Jeremy asks with a wink.

"No, sadly, they got the stomach flu. I think your excuse is way more interesting. I bet you two could present on that and you'd have everyone's undivided attention!" I joke. Everyone laughs and smiles and I can't help but wonder again if it will be like this when we visit Allison. I decide I can't wait to find out so I ask, "Is Allison okay? We haven't seen her yet."

"Yeah, she is going to come over tomorrow for a little bit while her parents go finish their Christmas shopping," Jeremy says like it's no big deal.

"So everything is good with her parents?" Corey asks before I can.

"Well, good is probably a stretch, but she has two broken wrists and a nasty bump on her head, so they don't want to leave her alone and her parents figured out pretty quickly that my dads are fucking awesome."

"Language, son," Kyle booms from the kitchen. I hadn't realized he snuck out.

"Sorry dad" Jeremy yells, then snickers. "He acts like he's not the one who taught me all the cuss words in the English language and a few in Spanish."

Rich laughs and says, "Yeah, when Jeremy's birth mom first met us, I was afraid she would walk right back out to her car because in the first ten minutes Kyle had gone through just about every colorful word he knew. He was a little nervous."

"Penny is great, I can't imagine her doing that," Jeremy says.

"Well yeah, we know that now. At the time we did not," Rich laughs again. He watches as Kyle comes back in the room. It is clear they have a wonderful relationship. I can see the love in his eyes as Kyle comes to sit next to him, draping his arm around his shoulders.

"You two want a drink or something to eat?" Kyle asks.

"No, we can't stay. We still have to go visit Allison then start getting our house ready for Christmas," Corey says. I smile to myself at that. I know he was hoping I'd just stay at his house, but on Sunday night when I could go to my own home, I did. I won't admit it to him just yet, but I hate it. I miss his place, I want to be there with him, but we haven't had time apart since John destroyed my house. He deserves some space and I guess I do too. I mean it's not like we are really apart, since we lasted one night and Corey was in my bed. But for now, we have two homes and that is okay.

We drive over to Allison's talking about nothing too important and I notice for the first time that every time I try and get specific details about Christmas, Corey changes the subject. I am sure he's planning something and I don't want to ruin his fun, so I pretend not to notice.

Mike Young opens the door looking like he's aged fifty years since I saw him last. He's wearing a pair of jeans and a sweatshirt today instead of his fancy suit, but it's more than just the clothes. He looks like hell.

"Hi, Mr. Young. Miss Gee said she called you to let you know we'd be stopping by with some of Allison's things?" I say as kindly as I can.

"Yes of course, come in." He steps aside and holds the door open. Allison's home is a lovely ranch style home that shows the love of a big family. Right as we walk in I see the pencil marks on the casing around the kitchen archway. Allison, it appears, is one of six children. I had no idea.

"She is back this way in the den where we can keep an eye on her. The doctor said her concussion wasn't too serious, but she doesn't remember the crash at all and that worries me and her mother." I notice him wiping his hands on his jeans nervously as he leads us to the den.

"I can understand that, thank you for letting us stop by," Corey says. He's using his formal teacher voice, not the relaxed tone he had at Jeremy's.

We follow Mike down the hall and into a dark wooden-paneled room. Stephanie is in a recliner with a knitted blanket over her lap and both her hands are resting on a pillow on her lap. Two casts that are covered in hearts and signatures and well wishes are the first things I see. I look up and school my expression. She has a huge bruise on her forehead that still looks puffy and painful and some bruising under her left eye.

"Hi Allison," I say quietly. She doesn't turn her head but we hear a cheerful hello so we step in front of her.

"Hi Miss Hartford, hi Mr. Richie! Thanks for coming by. Sorry, my neck is still pretty sore," she explains.

"You don't need to apologize, we understand," Corey says. He sets the box of cards and gifts her classmates sent on her coffee table. "Hopefully your mom or dad can help you look at those later."

"No, that job has been given to my sister Amanda. She would kill me if I let Mom do it. She should be home soon. She and my mom and the other kids went to get something from Bend," Allison says, then a big yawn escapes her. "The pain meds make me really sleepy. My older brother is here somewhere, did he let you in?"

"No, it was your father," I say and she winces a little.

"Was he nice?" she whispers.

"Yes honey, he was. We just went by Jeremy's house with his things and he said you are going there tomorrow? That's good right?" I ask.

"Yeah, my brother Adam has to pick up his girlfriend at the airport and Mom won't trust the little kids to watch me so they agreed to let me go there. I can't wait. I am so tired of staring at these walls. I really need a change of scenery."

"I bet. We won't keep you, I'm glad you're doing okay," I say, and Corey steps up behind me, placing his hand on my back.

"I'm glad too, this last week wasn't the same without you to answer all the questions. It has me realizing that my other students need to step up their game a little bit more," Corey says.

Stephanie blushes at that. Her father has come in without me noticing and is standing silently by the wall just out of Allison's view.

Stephanie asks Corey something about the math final, so I take the opportunity to walk over to Mr. Young. "Are you okay?" I ask quietly.

He nods, then says in a low voice, "I can't believe how lucky they were. I don't know what I would have done if—" he stops and shakes his head.

I reach out and squeeze his arm a little, not sure how to comfort him more. I'm surprised by the change in attitude and his defeated demeanor.

"If it had been the other way around, if Jeremy had been driving, I wouldn't have been as gracious. I am not happy that they went behind my back, but I seem to be the only one that has a problem with this." He glances over at his daughter and I can see the turmoil in his face.

"Mr. Young, I have met Jeremy's parents a few times and I don't think they would ever cause your daughter any harm," I say. I can hear Corey and Allison still talking about his class, so I continue. "He's a good kid, and if it makes you feel any better, I know Allison tried to stay away from him like you had asked. I think we don't always have control over who we like, or love, for that matter."

"That's what Allie said. Her mother came around as soon as she met Jeremy's fathers. Joy was practically inviting them over for Christmas dinner right there in the ER the day of the crash. I was pretty angry, still am to be honest, but when I saw their son—" he pauses and rubs his hand down his face. "When I demanded to know what he was doing in my daughter's car, he didn't even flinch. He just calmly explained what happened, how Allison didn't see the patch of ice and how the car spun and rolled. He actually laughed as he described how it bounced back onto its wheels like it wasn't traumatic or scary. He never once let go of Allison's arm. He kept her awake and talking until the ambulance got there." Mike pauses and takes a deep breath to steady himself, then continues, "As he is telling me this, I am glaring at him like it was his fault somehow, but then I look down and see his ankle sticking out at a ninety-degree angle. He never once complained about his own pain. He just worried about my girl. I can't even wrap my head around how he had that kind of strength."

"Oh, Mr. Young, I am so sorry all this happened. But what a gift you have been given to see your daughter loved by someone." I reach out and pat his arm in the most awkward way possible. Do I hug him? No, that seems wrong, so I just keep patting his arm until he steps away.

"I am not condoning their lifestyle, but I will admit they have raised a fine young man. I am able to admit that." He is wiggling like he wants me to let him go, so I step back.

"Sorry, I get kind of emotional about these things," I say when I realize his discomfort. Just then an entire football team bursts through the front door. Well, that's what it sounds like at least. Two girls that look about twelve and ten respectively rush past us waving a cassette from Blockbuster Video.

"We got it! We got it!" They both yell and rush to their sister.

"You better not be lying to me!" Allison says and I hear one of the girls laugh.

"No, this time we really did get it!" the younger one says.

"What movie?" Corey asks. I leave Mr. Young and walk over to see what the excitement was all about.

"*Top Gun*! It's been checked out every time, even when we put our name on the wait list, we couldn't seem to get it! I'm going to go make popcorn. Jenny, you get the pillows and we meet back here in five minutes!"

"I guess that is our cue to head out. I am glad to see you're doing okay, Allison," I say and she smiles up at me.

"I really am. Don't tell my sisters I saw the movie with Jeremy already," she says with a wink.

I make a motion like I am zipping my lips and we say our goodbyes.

THIRTY-TWO
COREY

I CAN'T GET over the change in Mr. Young, although when Stephanie told me what he said, I guess it makes sense.

I have to get through the rest of today, then convince Steph to come with me to Bend tomorrow for dinner. Grace and Barbara are due in around four and my parents are picking them up at the airport. They will get settled at the hotel then come to the house for dinner and to surprise Stephanie. Linda and Dee Dee are done for the semester so they are already there with a friend of theirs who couldn't make it home for Christmas. I wish Codey was coming, but Mom said last time she spoke to him, it wasn't looking like he'd make it.

I have my plan to propose on Christmas Eve, so I try and focus on that instead of worrying about who will or won't be there to witness the most important moment of my life.

I picked up the ring earlier this week and I almost couldn't breathe when the jeweler showed it to me. I chose a rose gold band that has delicate ivy etched around the sides, a nod to both her moms. The center stone was my grandmother's and is bigger than I could have afforded on my teacher's salary. I left it at my parents' house because I was afraid Stephanie would stumble across it.

I pull into my driveway and hit the remote on the garage door. It works like one out of every five times since the power failure we had, but I know nothing about that kind of thing, so I just pray every time I push the button. This time it works.

Stephanie has been pretty quiet after telling me about Mr. Young and his revelation that his daughter was dating a wonderful kid. I know she also had a moment with her dad earlier, so this has been quite a day. I follow her into the house and grab her waist to spin her toward me.

"Can you stay for a bit, or are you going to your place?" I step closer, crowding her.

"I can stay, I don't want to be alone right now. My brain is just spinning."

"Right round baby?" I ask squeezing her hips with my hands.

"Yeah," she laughs, and it melts my heart.

"Why don't you kick off your boots and go sit in the living room. I have an idea," I say bending to kiss her gently.

Her eyes twinkle a little and she cocks her head at me. "What do you have in mind there, Mr. R?"

"You'll see." I turn her and gently push her toward the living room as I turn and walk down the hall to my room. It takes me a minute to find what I was looking for, then to change. I glance in the mirror before I pick up my ukulele. God I can't believe she let me kiss her while wearing this. I tug on the Speedo and my left testicle falls out. Jesus. I tuck it back in and pray I can walk down the hall without losing the other one.

I start strumming so she hears that before she sees me, then I break into the song I wrote at the hotel. "My Tail" really shouldn't be sung or remembered by anyone, but I can't let it live in my head alone. Plus, I added some verses and it's even worse than it was before. She deserves to hear it.

"Lost on the trail, my tail," I sing low and serious. *"My tail, the trail, yeah my tail. Trail is like tail but with an r, and the r is gone, yeah the r is gone."*

When I finish that first verse I am standing in front of her with my hiking boots and my too-small red Speedo.

"I knew it was you that snipped me, I knew it was you that clipped me, Oh my tail, lost on the trail, my tail."

Stephanie is covering her mouth with her hand and her eyes are dancing with joy. I continue with a few more verses about how hair brought us together and she doubles over in a fit of laughter.

"You don't know what you did that night on the trail, when you stole my tail. You stole my heart as well." I croon like Frank fucking Sinatra and she claps and whistles while tears are streaming down her face. She is laughing again, one of those deep belly laughs that make no sound. I set my ukulele on the coffee table and stand in front of her hands on my hips as if I'm mad.

"You laugh at my song? My love song to you, and my tail?" I say with feigned indignation.

She looks up at me and my cock jumps at the sight of her so close. She is still smiling but now it's different, it's the same look she gave me when I crowded her in the laundromat. "Stand up," I say, and she shakes her head. I follow her gaze as she rakes down my chest and my stomach. She reaches out and trails her finger along the line of hair that leads to the waistband of this horrible red Speedo.

That is all it takes, that glance, the slightest touch and I am hard as stone. I thought I would come out here, make her laugh, then I'd change and make us some dinner. It's clear by the way she is looking at me, she has something different in mind.

I look down and see the head of my cock is well past the waistband now. She grabs my hips and pulls me forward, wedging her knees between my legs. Her hands move around to my ass and she squeezes and guides me to her waiting mouth. I hiss as she licks the tip of my cock, then peppers kisses along my stomach. She is still holding me in place like I might try and tell her no. I look down at her and move her hair over her shoulder so I can watch her beautiful mouth tease me.

She traces along the head and just below where it's pinned to my stomach by the Speedo. I wish she would take them off so I could feel all her mouth on me, but she seems happy torturing me like this. She scoots forward on the couch and sucks just the tip of my cock into her mouth. It's the most erotic thing I have ever felt, and I wonder briefly if this is why people get into bondage. I am trapped by this damn tiny bathing suit, and I love it.

"Let's get these off before you lose a ball," she whispers against my skin.

I make quick work of the swimsuit and the boots and try to pull her up but she refuses. She resumes her hold on my hips and slowly brings me into her mouth as far as she can. My couch is the perfect height for this and I wonder why we haven't done this before. I rest my hands on the back of her head encouraging her, but not pulling her in like I want. It's taking all my control not to just unleash and fuck her mouth with wild abandon. She looks up at me just as I hit the back of her throat and I watch her swallow once before my eyes roll back into my head.

"Fuck Steph, I'm going to come. You need to stop," I rasp out but she holds firm and works faster sucking and slurping on my cock like it's the best thing she's ever had. I feel the tingle hit my balls and my stomach starts to tighten, "Baby, I am going to come, last warning," I grunt out then it slams into me and I feel the first spurt shoot in her mouth then she pulls off and I shudder as I unload again and again on her face and open mouth. It's the sexiest thing I have ever seen.

She looks up at me and licks her lips clean with a smile. I growl and grab her, tossing her over my shoulder. I march into my bedroom and toss her on the bed, then yank her tights and underwear off as soon as I can. I shove the skirt of her dress up and dive into her sweet pussy, lapping and sucking. "Jesus, you are so wet for me," I mumble against her and I hear her moan. My cock stirs to life like it didn't just give its all a few moments ago. This girl is going to be the death of me.

I slide one finger into her wet silky center and moan against her clit. I add another and curl it up feeling for that sweet spot that sends her over the edge so quickly. I pull my mouth off long enough to tell her how perfect she is, then dive back in. It's not long before her hips are bucking and she is chanting my name over and over.

As soon as I feel her relax a little I am on her and in her. One quick thrust and I am seated to the hilt earning a moan and nails down my back.

"God, Corey. You feel so good. Fuck me please, hard," she pants as I push into her again. I draw back slowly and thrust forward hard, moving her up the mattress with each push. I can't get enough of her, and I need to be deeper. I hook her knees with my arms and pin her legs back so I have more room, then I let my hips take over. I thrust in and up until she screams out my name again and I feel the clenching as she gives into another orgasm. I feel like a feral beast as I drop her legs and spin her to her stomach then pull her hips up and sink in again from behind. She drops her head to the mattress and pushes her beautiful ass back into me, moaning long and slow.

I drop my chest over her back and put my mouth next to her ear. "Hold on baby, I'm going to get a little rough," I growl. Then position myself behind her, grabbing her small hips in my hands. I pound in over and over, wanting it to last forever. The tightness and heat that surrounds my cock is like the most addictive drug known to man. I am losing my mind and my rhythm as I feel everything in me tighten. I shudder as I come inside her, feeling like I just gave my soul to her.

I collapse on her and slide out as I do. It's only then that I realize she's still wearing her dress. "Fuck, sorry Stephanie. I didn't even give you a chance to take off your dress." I roll off her and she turns so she can face me.

"That was the hottest sex we've ever had, don't apologize for anything. I loved that you had to have me so fast that you couldn't wait," she says.

"I couldn't. You undo me, Steph, I love you so much," I say as I trace my fingers over her cheek.

She leans in and presses her lips to mine, softly then again with more pressure. "I am so lucky to have you, Corey. I love you too."

I think we could have stayed that way all night if it wasn't for my stomach rumbling.

"Why don't you get dressed and I'll start something for dinner," Stephanie says as she pats my cheek. I kiss her and nod.

"Yeah, that's a good idea." I roll off the bed and grab a pair of 501's from my drawer and pull a black T-shirt on. "Good to know that the Speedo still gets you hot."

Steph laughs and shakes her head. "Sure, yeah that Speedo is like my kryptonite."

"Good to know!" I say.

We walk back out to the living room and I bend to fish the bathing suit from under the couch, then take it back to my room. I toss it in the hamper and set my boots in the closet when I hear a scream from the front of the house.

"How?! You just went that way, how are you here?" Steph says and I hear a deep chuckle that can belong to only one person. I sprint down the hall and throw myself at my brother, tackling him to the ground.

"How the hell did you get here?!" I yell at him. We are laughing and hugging and punching each other and rolling around like we're twelve years old again.

"Get the fuck off me!" Codey says, pushing at me. I stand up and start laughing all over again. Codey is wearing a black T-shirt and a pair of faded 501's, just like me. Some things never change.

"Nice outfit," I say, shoving his shoulder. I watch as he looks at me then down at himself.

"Fuck, I thought being apart for so long that would have been cured," he says as he sucker-punches me in the gut. I make an oof sound then swing at him, only grazing his arm before he hops away.

"Aren't you going to introduce me?" Codey asks, nodding toward Stephanie. She's holding a wooden spoon in one hand and an oven mitt in the other like she's heading into the battle of Betty Crocker.

"Codey, this is Stephanie. She's the one I told you about, the one I met on the PCT, Stephanie, this is my brother Codey." I put my arm over his shoulder and smile. I thought this moment was never going to happen and my heart is about to burst with joy that it's happening now.

"Oh shit, wow. You guys really do look alike. I'm sorry I screamed at you. That's not how I wanted to meet you." Steph sets the spoon and mitt on the counter and holds out her hand to him.

He grabs her and pulls her into a bear hug. "You've met the rest of the family, you really think I am just going to be okay with a handshake?" He laughs. It's weird to see Codey hugging her. She looks so tiny next to him. Is that what we look like together? I mean I know it is, but wow, it's weird to see.

"Why are you so short?" Codey says as he pushes her back to stare at her.

"I guess I forgot to grow," Steph says with a shrug. I see a forced smile and since I know she doesn't like people commenting on her height or how young she looks, I jump in.

"Do Mom and Dad know you're here?" I ask, reaching for Steph's hand and pulling her to me.

"No, I wanted to surprise them," he says, but something is off and it's not my twin instincts that are firing. Steph notices it too, she squeezes my hand and says, "Why don't you guys go catch up and I'll start some pasta."

I walk to the fridge and grab some beers then motion for Codey to follow me. I pause when he doesn't, and I catch his sigh before he straightens and plasters on a smile.

"So this is such a great surprise, Mom is going to wet her pants. Can we please play a trick on her, you know like we did when we were kids? I'll come in first and you'll—" I start, but he cuts me off.

"Janet left me," Codey says. He takes a swig of his beer and leans back onto the couch.

"Oh fuck, dude, I am so sorry. What happened?" I ask. I put my beer on the coffee table untouched.

"You know, same old story. She met another guy that plays bass and he had a recording studio and connections and he wasn't a pushover like me." He pinches his eyes shut and lets out a ragged sigh.

"I used the last bit of money I had to my name to buy a ticket home." He groans. "Fuck, I am such a wanker."

I laugh without meaning to, then say, "That's true, but it's still fucked up that she did that to you. You can stay here. No question about it. I have a spare room."

"What about Thumbelina in there?" He nods toward the kitchen where I can hear Steph making dinner.

"What about her? She lives right next door, and I mean, we spend most nights together, but she can be at her house if you need me," I say, because he is my brother, but my stomach turns at the thought.

"Yeah, that'd be great. I really don't want to be around a hot as fuck blonde chick right now. Fucking blondes, actually fucking women. They all suck," Codey says and unfortunately Stephanie walks in right at that moment.

"I was going to see if you want a salad or something with the pasta, but it seems like you two want to be alone. I'll just get my boots on and you can finish up in there. The water is almost boiling so just add the pasta. I have the hamburger meat browning and it should be ready to add to the red sauce in about five minutes." She bends and swipes her purse off the ground and then walks to the back door and stuffs her feet into her boots.

"Stephanie, wait!" I call and run to catch her.

"It's fine, Corey, he needs you. I'm okay. I'll just go home and work on the mountain of gifts I need to wrap," she says. She is trying to smile, but her eyes don't match her lips.

"I'm sorry, I'll call you later?" I ask and dip down to kiss her. Her lips are stiff against mine and I'm not having it. I grab her and pull her into me, kissing her until she yields. Her lips part to let me in and I take what I want until we are both breathing hard.

"Okay," she says pushing me away. "I get it. I love you, Corey."

"I love you too, Stephanie. More than you know," I say then kiss her again like she is leaving for Beirut instead of next door.

I walk back in and find Codey drinking my beer, his bottle is pushed to the edge of the table. "Hey, I am going to finish up so we can eat, come in here and we can talk."

"Nah, I'll just sit here and drink, it's cool," he says tipping back the beer in his hand.

Great, so Steph left so he can sulk by himself while I finish cooking? I fight the urge to kick his ass for being such a prick, but as I walk back into the kitchen it hits me. This is us. This is how we always are. I'm the grunt, the shadow, the second in line. If Codey is in a bad mood, the whole family knows it. I acted like his personal court jester our whole lives and never noticed it until right this minute.

I finish with the dinner prep and set a bowl aside for Stephanie. I will run it over to her in a minute. She worked hard on that and deserves to eat.

"It's ready," I yell. Codey saunters in and heads right to the fridge for another beer.

"I'm going to run this over to Stephanie. You can start. I'll be back in a minute," I say over my shoulder. I don't wait for him to answer. I just shove my feet into my boots and walk out the back door and across the yard to her house. I walk through her back door and find her at the table eating a bowl of cereal. Fuck that.

"Here, I brought you some pasta. My brother is an asshole and I'm sorry," I blurt out.

She stops mid-bite and I see the smile in her eyes before it reaches her mouth. She jumps up and runs to me, wrapping her arms around my waist and burrowing into my chest.

I lean over and set the bowl down and pull her closer. I bend down and kiss her. "I love you," I say against her lips.

"I love you," she mumbles while kissing me.

"I have to go," I say as I bite and nibble along her neck.

"Yeah, you should. He needs you," she says as she arches into me.

I slide my hands up her chest and squeeze her perfect breasts through her dress earning a whimper.

"I'm coming over tonight. I can't sleep without you," I say. I sound like a lovesick teenager and I don't even care.

"I'll be waiting. Naked. I'll be naked Corey, come when you can," she says between kisses.

I finally manage to pull away and make it back to my place. Codey's bowl is already in the sink, unwashed of course. I scoop out some pasta and carry my bowl into the living room where I find him with another beer. "If I had known you were coming I would have gotten something stronger," I say.

"Yeah, well I wasn't in the mood to announce my failures. I thought I'd show up and we could hang out. To be honest, I forgot about that Stephanie chick," he says. It makes me angry, but I bite back my reply.

"Well, you're here now. Do you know what you want to do? I mean are you staying?" I sit and take off my boots and set them on the side of the couch.

"Fuck, I don't know. I am going to have to, since I don't have a penny to my name. I'm twenty-five years old and I have nothing but a broken heart and lint in my pocket. Why the hell didn't you warn me about her?" He says and I notice he's slurring his words a bit. Probably because he's had four beers in about an hour.

"Not my job, but actually now that you bring it up, asshole, I did warn you!" I stand and tower over him.

"No, you were just jealous because I found someone. You were like," he pauses and pitches his voice up then says, "'I don't want you to have a girlfriend Codey, it's supposed to be you and me, don't leave me.'" He finishes and rolls his eyes at me.

I have never wanted to punch him in the face more than I do at this moment. Instead I just breathe in through my nose and out through my mouth and picture how happy I was a few hours ago.

This is not how I pictured my reunion with my twin going.

THIRTY-THREE
STEPHANIE

I'M NOT sure what time it is when Corey finally crawls into bed with me, but like I promised I am naked. That is probably why I jump ten feet in the air when he presses his ice-cold body against mine.

"Jesus, were you rolling in the snow before you came in here?" I giggle as he presses into me from behind.

"Shhhh, go back to sleep. I'm Mr. Snow Miser. Nothing to worry about," he whispers in my ear. He is attempting a German accent this time.

"Okay first of all, way to ruin my favorite childhood cartoon. Second of all, I think your dick fell off," I say.

"Hey! It's really fucking cold. It may have retreated back inside seeking warmth," he says then tucks his freezing feet between my thighs.

I screech then laugh and try to push him off, but he is bigger and stronger. He rolls me so I am under him pinned to the bed. It shouldn't turn me on to have him holding me down like this, but it does. "Oh! Well, hello there," I say when I feel him stiffen against my stomach. I guess it turns him on too.

"Hello," I say again and kiss him. I don't really want this to turn into sex. He needs to talk to me and tell me what happened with his brother, but his lips are moving down my body and I can't think straight. When the heat of his mouth makes its way to my breast I swear I will ask all the questions and say all the sympathetic things as soon as we are done.

After a couple of orgasms for me and one for him he finally feels warm enough to snuggle without fear of frostbite. "Okay now, tell me what happened over there. Why were you a block of ice when you got here?" I ask.

Corey flops to his back and sighs. "I went for a walk after Codey fell asleep. I was so mad, I couldn't just come here. I needed to cool off," he says.

"Well, that was achieved. Corey, it's probably about ten degrees out there. Was it that bad?" I ask rolling to my side so I can see him.

"Yeah, I mean he and Janet broke up, I am sure you gathered that," he says, and I nod. "Well, that wasn't all. I just realized for the first time in my life that he treats me like shit. I have always just allowed it. Fuck. I wonder if everyone but me saw it. Like did my parents know I was a doormat where he was concerned? I feel like such a fucking idiot." He whispers the last part and I almost don't hear it.

"You aren't an idiot, Corey. You love your brother. I don't really know what to say here, hi! Only child, but I imagine this is pretty normal with siblings and maybe worse with twins. How long were you guys apart?" I ask.

"Over a year," he says with a yawn.

"Why don't we talk about this tomorrow?" I ask as I snuggle into his chest.

We both fall asleep and only wake up when we hear a pounding on my front door.

I slip out from under Corey and grab my robe then rush to the living room. I stand on my toes to look out the peep hole and see Codey on my front porch. I unlock the door and pull it open.

"Hey, come in! It's freezing out there," I say and step aside. I glance over at the clock on the wall and am surprised to see it's after ten.

"Is my shithead brother here?" he asks. His voice is gravelly like he just woke up and I tip my head up to look at him, shocked at his rudeness. They may look exactly the same, but that is where the similarities end. Corey would never treat someone so rudely.

"Corey is still sleeping. Can I help you with something?" I ask in my 'Miss Hartford isn't taking your shit' voice.

"He's out of milk and there are no eggs," he says.

"Yeah well, we spend time at both houses, so our groceries are a bit scattered. There is a restaurant a few streets over called The Honey Covered Beaver. They probably have eggs and milk." I snap out the last part and put my hands on my hips.

"You're not a morning person, are you?" Codey asks in a flat tone.

"I AM A FUCKING ray of sunshine in the morning, when I'm not confronted with rudeness when I roll out of bed," I say with a glare.

"Hey, what's going on?" Corey says from behind me.

"Codey is mad you're out of eggs and milk," I explain, not taking my eyes off the evil twin.

He holds his hands up in self-defense. "I was just hungry, didn't mean to poke the bear, or do you guys say poke the beaver around here?"

Corey walks up and wraps his arms around me from behind and I feel myself relax a little. He rests his chin on my head and says, "The Honey Covered Beaver is open. My keys are on the counter in the kitchen. I recommend the ham and cheese omelette."

Codey just blinks at him then looks down at me. He shrugs and turns to leave.

"Wait, we're going to Mom and Dad's at four today," Corey says and I turn and look up at him. This is the first I am hearing of this plan. I was going to finish my shopping today. Crap, I better get moving if I have to be done by four.

"Okay, I'll probably go with you," Codey says then walks out my front door letting it slam behind him. God, what a petulant child. I won't say anything bad about him to his brother, I won't. He saw it, he knows how his brother behaved. He doesn't need me to point it out.

"God what a prick," Corey says, then tugs me closer and kisses along my neck.

"So we have plans with your parents today?" I ask then hum my pleasure as his kisses become more deliberate. Something has gotten into him and I am not going to lie, I love it. He's so passionate lately.

"Yeah, we are going to the house for dinner but Mom wanted help with something so I told her we would be there early. That's okay right?" he says, nibbling on my ear. His hands have moved to the belt on my robe and I feel it come undone. Big warm hands start to roam over my body, stopping at my breasts, then between my legs.

"I better get ready then, I have a lot to do before we go," I say

"So do I," Corey whispers in my ear. Then he picks me up and carries me back to bed where we spend the next hour getting sweaty and satisfied.

At eleven thirty I am finally able to get dressed and head out to run my errands.

"Be here by three thirty so we can drive to Bend. If it starts to snow, come back sooner, okay?" Corey asks and I nod.

"I won't be that long. I just have a few more things to pick up. You have a big family and now that Codey is here, I should pick up something for him," I say, tucking my gloves into my pocket.

"He deserves a lump of coal, so see if they have any of those," he says, trying to make light of the situation, but I can tell he's hurting.

"Sounds like a plan." I kiss him quickly then duck away before he can grab me again. There is nothing I'd love more than spending all day in bed with him, but I really need to get some gifts.

I drive to the tiny little downtown area of Beaver Valley and park in front of my favorite store. They have so many cute and original gifts. The Beaver Den is crowded this morning with locals who waited like me for school to be out to do their shopping. I squeeze past a few customers to get to the back of the store where I know I'll find something for Dee Dee and Linda. I already got Corey's parents something, but the girls were harder to shop for. Now I need something for the asshole brother that dropped in like the grinch down our chimney last night.

I find a cute scarf with matching hat and gloves for Dee Dee and Linda gets a coffee mug that says, "Beavers are happiest when wet" that should bring quite a laugh. Linda has a great sense of humor and is more relaxed about life. I like both of his sisters, but Linda and I have gotten closer because she is so easy to talk to.

I continue to walk along the aisle looking at options for my dad. I'd be lying if I said I have never bought a gift for him. When I was about seven years old I went through a phase where I thought he would come live with us. I bought a gift for him that year, wrapped it and put it under the tree. On Christmas morning when I saw it was gone, Mom told me Santa took it with him so he could give it to my dad. I believed that with all my heart.

She did so many things over the years to protect me like that, never letting the world hurt me too much. I just can't help but wonder if my life would have been better with Brian as a part of it. I shake my head to clear that thought because like he said, we can't change the past, but we can build our future. I finally find a sweatshirt that says "My Dad is worth a Dam" and it has a picture of a big fat beaver with his arm around a little beaver. Behind them is a stream that has been blocked off with hearts instead of sticks. It's cheesy and silly and I love it. I continue through the store until I have something for everyone. After this I have to go to pick up Corey's gift. I had it engraved and they said it would be ready today.

The bell chimes above the door as I walk into "Time's a Wasting" and I am greeted with a smile and a wave by the owner.

"Hello! I'm glad you made it in! The engraving turned out so good. I think your boyfriend is going to love it!" He reaches under the counter and pulls out the box. I smile when he opens it and I see the watch I bought Corey. He is going to love it. It's a special Seiko watch that is water and impact resistant, perfect for hiking and outdoor sports. I think it's the same watch that Arnold Schwarzenegger wore in the movie *Predator*. At least that's what the shop owner told me, but I never saw the film.

He turns it over so I can see the engraving on the back and I smile. "It's perfect! Thank you so much for getting it done so quickly. I love it and I hope he does too."

"I am sure he will." He closes the box and puts it in a gift bag for me. Looks like I have just enough time to pick up a bottle of wine before I meet up with Corey.

When I pull up to my house, I can see Corey and Codey loading wrapped gifts into the trunk of his car and they seem happy. Corey or maybe Codey pushes the other out of the way to get to the trunk first and once the box is inside it turns into a shoving match, then a snowball fight. From this distance I am ashamed I can't tell which one is my boyfriend.

THIRTY-FOUR
COREY

AFTER STEPHANIE LEFT to finish her shopping I stomped back to my house ready to kick my brother's ass. I found him on the couch with his head in his hands sobbing. That took all the anger out of me in one breath. Just like always, I can't stay mad at him.

We spent the morning talking about Janet and what happened over the last year. I let him talk, unload his pain, and I began to see why we work. He needs me to be his sounding board, and I look up to him. I am not sure the dynamic that carried us through the first twenty-four years of life is sustainable now, but what can I do?

I haven't told Codey that I plan on proposing to Stephanie on Christmas Eve, or that our trail friends are coming to surprise her. I feel like he's a big old wet blanket over what was supposed to be the best week of my life. I never thought I'd feel that way about my brother.

When we are loading the car we get into one of our juvenile fights and things seem like they are more normal. What does that say about us? If we are punching each other and rolling around wrestling everything is fine? Jesus that's kind of fucked up. As I am hurling a snowball at Codey's head I hear Stephanie's garage door closing.

"Hey, truce! We have to get going soon. Do you want to shower or change or anything?" I ask my brother. I am panting and sweaty so if he isn't going to use the shower, I am.

"Nah, I'm good. You were always the sweaty one. I'll just change clothes," he says, tossing snow in my face.

"Right, okay. I'll be out in a bit. Stephanie will be coming over so maybe don't be a dick?" I say as I walk off to my back door. As soon as I pull the door open I can hear the phone ringing from my bedroom. I still haven't replaced the kitchen phone, so I jog to the back of the house catching the phone mid-ring.

"Hello?" I say quickly.

"Hi, I'm all done with my shopping! Can I wrap everything tomorrow or do you want me to bring it all today?" Steph asks.

"No, you don't have to rush. I just wanted to take my things over now. We can bring yours over on Christmas Eve," I say, then add "I am going to take a quick shower, if you come over that's Codey in the living room not me."

She laughs and says, "Okay, I promise not to kiss him."

"You better not. I am the more attractive twin anyway. I am sure you can tell that," I joke.

My heart beats faster when she says, "Corey, there is no comparison. You have my heart and my soul."

I reply the only way I can with the huge lump in my throat, "I love you."

"Love you too, see you soon," she says and the line goes dead.

I stand there holding the phone to my chest like I can prolong that warm feeling that just washed over me.

"You really love her, don't you?" Codey says from my doorway.

"Yeah, she's it for me," I say. I'm not sure why I don't tell him right then my plan to ask her to marry me, but I don't. Instead I just go take a shower. When I come out Steph and Codey are sitting on the couch attempting small talk and failing miserably.

"So what parts of Europe did you see?" Stephanie is asking as I step out.

"London, that's it. Just London." Codey is rubbing his hands down his black 501's. He's wearing a blue denim button-down and I start laughing my ass off.

"I'll go change," I say as I wave my hand down my body.

"Oh my God! Don't! That is so funny. Your mom will love it," Stephanie says as she rushes to me. "Does this happen a lot?" She asks as she wraps her arms around my waist. She is so fucking beautiful looking up at me like that. I swallow hard and nod then grab her face and kiss her.

"Hi beautiful," I whisper against her mouth and I can feel her smile.

"Hi there handsome," she says back, but then pulls away and spins to look at Codey. He's glaring at us but we both ignore his pissy attitude.

"Yeah Mom will love it, plus we can confuse her. How about I walk in with Steph on my arm and see if she notices?" Codey asks and I feel Stephanie stiffen.

"Nah, let's just walk in holding hands. That will be funny enough, just like that picture she wanted every year on our birthday," I say, knowing he won't be able to resist that.

"What did she want?" Steph asks and I am surprised Codey jumps in to tell her.

"Well, it started with a spontaneous thing on our first birthday. We were walking toward her, holding hands, and she snapped a picture. Then she made us do it again for our second birthday. Every year since then we have had to hold hands and smile for the camera. I mean it was fucking adorable when we were little, but shit got weird as we got older," Codey says, and I see a light in his eyes that had been missing.

"Sounds amazing! How come I haven't seen these pictures yet?" Steph asks.

"They don't have them framed lining the hallway?" Codey asks and I shake my head.

"No, this house doesn't have the long hall like the LA house. Plus we missed last year so the streak is dead," I say with a shrug. It bothered the fuck out of me to miss our tradition, but I bet Codey didn't even notice. We spoke on the phone that day, but not for very long because he had a gig to play with Janet. "We better get going," I say. I hope that I was able to cover my sudden anger. It seems like since I realized the truth of our relationship, I can't control how mad I am.

The drive to Bend is quick and I decide to leave the stuff in the trunk so we aren't accidentally out front when my parents pull up with Grace and Barbara.

"Looks like Mom and Dad aren't here," Codey says, pointing to the empty space in the driveway. Dee Dee and Linda's Bug is parked on the street so I know they are here.

"They probably had to run an errand or something," I say. My voice is high-pitched, and I am starting to sweat. It's three fifty, so we only have a few minutes before they get here. Fuck, I can't wait to see them. My mom is excited about having a professional chef to help with Christmas dinner and my dad has a list of questions about his bad knees for Barbara. I have an apology bottle of red wine for both of them.

We walk in and find Linda and Dee Dee at the big table in the dining room wrapping gifts and bickering like they do.

"If you wouldn't wait till the last minute every time, then you wouldn't be so stressed. I don't know why that hasn't gotten through that thick head of yours," Dee Dee says. Linda just flips her off then gasps when she sees us standing there. From then on the next ten minutes are spent hugging and laughing. Noogies and arm punches and one thrown spool of ribbon that knocks over a vase bring the sounds of siblings to the new house. We only stop when we hear the car pull up. I know my parents will come in the back door and after waiting a bit my trail friends will knock on the door. I can't wait to see the expression on Stephanie's face when she sees them.

"Shhhh, they're here. Let's get in position," Codey says as he grabs my hand. We both stand in the middle of the kitchen like a couple of fools. Stephanie and my sisters find a good place to watch as Mom and Dad come busting in the back door.

My mom screams and my dad shoves her out of the way to get to Codey first. Arms and elbows and kisses and hugs assault us both. There are a lot of questions too and some slaps to the back of the head for both of us for keeping a secret from Mom. With all the chaos I barely hear the doorbell.

My mom is a professional surpriser though and she casually asks Steph to get the door. As she walks out mom hushes us all and we tip toe behind her to watch the reunion. My mom leans over and whispers in my ear as Stephanie reaches the door. "You're going to be surprised by who is out there." She squeezes my arm and steps forward for a better view.

Stephanie reaches the door and opens it wide to Barbara and Grace on the porch. I can only see a little of her face but the smile is evident. Just as Steph is about to reach for a hug, the women step apart, revealing Ivy standing just behind them. Stephanie steps out onto the porch like she is unable to believe her eyes.

"Ivy? Is that really you?" Steph's voice cracks and I see Grace wipe a tear from her eye and step inside the house. She reaches back and grabs Barbara, pulling her in, then she quietly shuts the door leaving them alone.

"They are going to need a minute," Grace says to all of us. When her eyes land on my brother she steps forward and pulls him into a hug. Just as she gets her hands on him, Barbara, who spotted me first, pulls me in. I turn my head to watch the confusion as they both look at each other then up at us.

"Hi!" we say in unison. This is the best part about having an identical twin.

"Barb, Grace, I'd like to introduce you to my brother Codey. Codey, these wonderful creatures are Barbara and Grace. We met this summer on the PCT," I say proudly.

"Nice to meet you both. Corey told me a lot about you," he says.

That kind of surprises me. I mean I did, but I didn't think he was listening. "I can't wait to hear about your experience. Did you start in LA with Corey?"

My parents guide everyone in and start taking coats and hats while Stephanie is—I hope—repairing her relationship with Ivy on the front porch.

THIRTY-FIVE

STEPHANIE

I BLINK a few times as I hear the door click shut behind me. She's
here. I can't understand how, but she's here. Do I hug her? Do I just
wave? Why are there no words coming out of my mouth?

"You look good, honey," Ivy says quietly. She reaches her hand
out and that's all it takes. I throw myself into her arms and squeeze
her with all my might. She smells like home, like flowers and linen
that hung out in the sun to dry. My heart stutters in my chest when I
feel her start to rub my back. "I've missed you so much, baby girl," she
whispers.

I pull back and look into her tear-filled eyes. She's wearing a scarf
and a big coat that must be new, since it's never cold in San Diego. I
grab her hands and hold them so she can't disappear, then tell her,
"I've missed you too. I'm so glad you are here."

"Me too, Grace convinced me that I was being an ass." She
laughs and a little sob breaks free, but I am smiling at her with all the
love I have in my heart for this woman, and she continues. "I didn't
mean to shut you out honey. At first I was just mad that you were
mad at me when I wasn't the one who decided to keep my relationship with your mom a secret. I wanted to tell you, hell, I wanted to

live with you both. I hated that I had to pretend, and be in my own house missing all the moments with you. Did you know the first month of your life we did all live together?"

I shake my head and wonder what changed, why my mom pushed her away. "No, I didn't know that."

She takes a breath and pulls her hand free to wipe at her eyes. "Can we go inside and talk? My ass is going to freeze off."

"Oh! Yes, sorry. I have gotten used to the cold I guess, come in. You can meet Corey and his family." I reach back and open the door then pull her inside where it's warm. I can hear laughter and talking from the back of the house where the kitchen and den are, but the front formal living room is empty.

"Here, we can sit and talk a bit if you want, or we can join that." I motion to the sounds of laughter coming from behind me.

"We can talk here. I need you to know what happened," Ivy says. She takes her coat off and I smile upon seeing her usual wide-leg jeans and band T-shirt. This one is faded more than the rest because it's her favorite. Janice Joplin, the woman who played music through my childhood almost as much as Creedence Clearwater Revival.

I sit and she slowly lowers herself next to me, carefully, like I might scoot away from her. "Tell me what I did to upset you so much. I am so sorry I yelled at you," I say.

"No honey, that wasn't it. Oh, you poor girl. God, I really was an ass," she says, wiping her eyes. She takes a breath and says, "The day after we spoke on the phone I was at the shop going through the files and I found something. That is what I was upset about, not you, honey."

"God, what was it?" I ask, reaching for her hand.

"I found a file marked BT and I thought it was back taxes or something so I pulled it out and stacked it with the other tax documents to take to the attorney. Before I did though, I opened the file. It was about your father Brian. She had been keeping tabs on him. She had newspaper clippings and addresses scrawled across napkins and a phone number or two," Ivy explains.

"Oh wow, okay I bet that will come as a surprise to him," I say.

"Yeah, Rose was quite the stalker." Ivy tries to laugh but it falls flat. "I don't think any of that would have bothered me if that was all, but it wasn't. There was an article from last year about how Beaver Valley, Oregon was about to open a new high school. Brian Tuck was leading the team to oversee the construction. There was a paper clipped to that was a rough draft of an application to teach at the school. It was in your mom's handwriting, honey. You didn't apply for the job. She did."

"Oh my God. No wonder I didn't have any memory of it! I can't believe she did that," I say. I am not sure how to feel about all this, but my stomach is in knots.

"So she knew your dad was here, and she wanted you to be with him. All my years of love and commitment to you and her meant nothing, she just planned on—" Ivy covers her mouth to hide a sob that is escaping. She squeezes her eyes shut, forcing a few tears out, then continues. "She didn't tell me, she kept it from me and from you. I don't understand why she would do that. We had always said we would be honest with you about your father, but when you were about two, she said she didn't want to lose you, or share you. She said she didn't want him to know because he would want to take you away from us. After our friend Stephanie killed herself it seemed like Rose started to worry more about how people would treat us, how they would treat you."

My mind flashes to an image of Mr. Young sneering at me while he explains that his daughter shouldn't have to work with Jeremy. Then to him standing disheveled in his den staring at his wounded girl. He isn't going to ever accept Jeremy's family, even if he is willing to be cordial.

Ivy continues, pulling me from my thoughts. "I was so hurt because it felt like it was her plan all along to leave me out. I didn't have rights to you, I didn't give you my blood or my genes but baby, you were mine too." Ivy is crying now, and fuck, does it rip me apart. I grab her and pull her to me and I start to cry as well.

"I love you so much, Ivy. You've always meant more to me than just my mom's friend or business partner. I am so sorry you felt this way, I wish I had known," I say between sobs.

We hug and rock back and forth and try to mend both our hearts at once.

"Hey, can I interrupt for a minute?" I hear Corey's sweet voice and I pull back from Ivy and look at him. It hits me when I see the gentle way he is looking at me, the kindness in his voice. God, I love that man so much. He is it for me. He is my forever.

"Yes, hi, sorry we are done for now, right?" I ask Ivy and she nods and wipes her face.

"Hi, it's nice to see you again, Ivy," Corey says as he holds out his hand. She stands and pulls him into a hug.

"I'm so glad to see you. God, what a wild couple of months this has been. I knew Stephanie loved you, but getting to know you through Grace and Barbara's stories has been something else. I hope you live up to their love of you," Ivy says with a chuckle.

"How are you friends with them? I am so confused. Grace told me that she called you and helped arrange this, but acted like it was no big deal. There was so much other commotion I decided to just come ask you," Corey says.

"Well, not long after Steph and I talked on the phone I got a call from a very pushy woman named Barbara. She demanded that I make things right and apologize to Stephanie. I hung up on her," Ivy says. Corey and I both laugh at that.

"But about a week later a very sweet woman named Grace called claiming she had some questions about flower arrangements for a wedding. She was so kind and we ended up talking for over an hour about other things. I missed having Rose around and Grace quickly became my friend. We talked on the phone a couple of times a week."

"She's pretty sneaky," Corey says, wiggling his eyebrows.

"She is. She eventually told me that she was the one I met on the PCT trailhead and that the woman who called and yelled at me earlier was Barbara, her partner. To be honest, that whole day I met them was such a blur, I didn't remember their names or even what they looked like. I just knew two women told me you were on the trail and would be crossing the highway soon," Ivy says.

"That was an awful day," I say, then reach for Corey, pulling him to sit by us. Then I tuck myself under his arm.

"It was." Ivy stops and gives us a weak smile before continuing. "Grace was just so kind and she and Barbara were living the life I always wanted with your mom. It hurt a little to hear how happy they were, and how open they were with their relationship. Barbara's family welcomed Grace easily and they never hid their love. I have been working on forgiving Rose for her fears and for this whole send-Stephanie-to-Beaver-Valley thing, but I am not quite there yet. Grace and Barb think this trip will help with that."

"I think it will. I know I feel better seeing you," I say. I smile at her and she returns it.

"Do you want to come back? Maybe having you there will help break up the weirdness of my father trying to get a free medical exam from Barb," Corey says as he nods to the back room.

"Oh my God! He's not, is he?" I ask in horror.

"Yeah, when I left he was trying to lie down on the kitchen counter so she could examine his knee." Corey is shaking his head in dismay and it makes me laugh.

"Sure, let's go back," Ivy says with a light giggle. Just as we step toward the kitchen, the doorbell rings and Dee Dee and Linda race in, shoving each other to get to the door first.

"She's here! Get out of my way!" Linda yells, then Dee Dee is pushing her and yelling, "She's my friend, not yours, bitch get off me." They continue to shove and push each other while yelling. I can hear laughter on the other side of the door.

"Jesus, I am sorry you had to see that. Come on," Corey says, grabbing Ivy by the elbow and leading her away from the mayhem.

Corey wasn't kidding. Henry is lying on the kitchen island with his pant leg pulled up while Barbara is putting his knee through gentle range of motion tests. Dorothy has Grace trapped by the pantry asking questions about spices and shelf life of canned peaches.

Good Lord.

I glance over to the couch and see Codey sitting by himself, so I bring Ivy toward him. "Ivy this is Corey's brother Codey," I say. I am pleased that Codey stands to shake her hand. "Codey this is my mom's partner, Ivy. She's my mom too." I don't know if that makes sense to him, but I need a way to introduce her that won't minimize what she is to me.

"Hi, second mom. Nice to meet you!" Codey shakes her hand and smiles the same charming smile Corey has.

"Twins! How fun!" Ivy says and Dorothy hears that from her spot in the kitchen and yells, "Fun the first time, but the second time it wasn't cute anymore!"

"My sisters are fraternal twins. Mom had a rough couple of years. She's still traumatized," Codey says in a conspiratorial whisper, then he laughs. His laughter stops abruptly though, when Dee Dee and Linda walk in with their friend. I watch as his mouth falls open and his eyes go wide.

"Codey, Ivy, Stephanie this is our best friend Cami. She is staying the week with us here," Linda says. Each girl has their arm around the most beautiful redhead I have ever seen. Her hair is thick and braided with the braid draped over one shoulder. She has a light smattering of freckles across her nose and cheeks and her eyes are a brilliant green. When she smiles, I swear Codey's knees buckle.

"Hi! It's great to meet you. The girls talked about you nonstop at Thanksgiving," I tell her, hopefully giving Codey a chance to recover from what is clearly love at first sight.

"Come on, you have to meet everyone else," Dee Dee says and they tug their friend away before Codey gets a chance to speak.

I turn just in time to see him sink onto the couch like someone stole the bones in his legs. I chuckle and grab Ivy's hand. "Come on I think Codey needs a moment alone."

The next few hours are spent talking over each other, hugging, laughing and eating. So much eating. Corey went out to the car and brought in all the gifts from his car, adding to the already huge pile under the tree. Christmas music plays gently in the background and Barbara and Grace argue over if it was ten lords a-leaping or twelve. Every chance he gets Corey is holding my hand or hugging me from behind. I feel so lucky to be in the middle of this big crazy family. On Christmas Day we will be adding my dad and his wife and my brothers. I hope Ivy can handle the Tucks.

THIRTY-SIX
COREY

IT'S past midnight when I finally round up my brother and Stephanie.

Codey seemed intent on staying at Mom and Dad's once he met Cami but Dad made sure we took him with us. I think Cami would have been happier if he stayed, but Linda and Dee Dee acted mad that she was spending so much time talking to him. No fights on Christmas is always a good rule to follow. Ivy, Barb, and Grace are all staying at the hotel in town with plans to ski all day tomorrow.

I was able to pull Ivy aside and ask for her blessing. I already asked Brian, but it felt important to have Ivy's as well. I showed her the ring and then spent ten minutes hugging her to get her to stop crying.

Steph falls asleep on the drive back and Codey is staring out the window with a stupid grin on his face. I guess he isn't heartbroken over Janet anymore. As I drive, I let my mind wander to my plan for the millionth time. I need to tell Codey and see if he wants to be there. I forgot the girls were inviting their friend Cami, so I guess some random girl is going to see me profess my undying love. Oh well, if tonight is any indication, big crowds do not scare Stephanie. I look over at her and her face is turned toward mine. Her lips are parted as she sleeps and her breathing is deep. Man, she is really out.

When we get back to my house Codey helps me get her in by holding the doors open for me. I whisper goodnight to him and carry her to bed.

The next morning Codey is like a whole new person. He's up and showered and cooking breakfast when Steph and I come out around nine thirty.

"Smells wonderful!" Stephanie says. She's so cute in the morning, all sleepy and disheveled. Her hair is up in a ponytail and she has the hint of a hickey on her neck from me. I can't get enough of her, but she doesn't seem to mind.

"I have enough for everyone, I took your car this morning and got groceries so we finally have eggs and milk," Codey says.

"When the fuck did you learn to cook?" I ask pulling out a chair for Stephanie.

"Janet was busy a lot, so it was a forced learning situation. I can make breakfast and sandwiches now, don't look for any kind of dinner from me." He chuckles.

"Thanks for this. I am going to eat and run though. I have a ton of things to wrap and I need to run out and get Ivy something now that she is here," Steph says.

"That's fine, I'll keep Corey company." Codey nudges my shoulder and sets a plate full of bacon and eggs and slices of fruit. What the hell is happening. I swear there are little bluebirds circling his head.

As soon as Steph is done, she's out the door. Codey and I clean up and chat about last night. He is obviously obsessed with our sister's friend Cami and brings her up at least five times during our conversation.

When we finish in the kitchen, we walk to the living room and sit to talk more. "Hey, I have something I need to tell you."

"Sure! What's up brother?" Codey slaps me on the stomach with the back of his hand.

"I'm going to ask Stephanie to marry me on Christmas Eve. That is actually why Grace and Barbara are here. We are going to the PCT trailhead in Bend to take a picture of all of us with the sign, then I am going to get down on one knee and ask Steph to be my wife," I say nervously. Saying it out loud to my twin makes it so real.

"Fuck, really? Didn't you just meet her? You haven't even known her a year, dude." Codey sounds mad.

I don't want to defend my decision to him, but I say, "She is everything to me, Codey. I lost her once and I can't lose her again. I hope you can get to know her like I do and you'll understand." I hate the way my voice sounds. When I asked Brian, he hugged me and congratulated me. Ivy did the same. Why can't he be supportive? I have never done anything irresponsible or rash, he knows that.

"But still, you've known her for like six months. I would wait, man. I thought Janet was it at the six-month mark too. You haven't had a chance to see all the layers of crazy that might be lurking," Codey says.

I tip my head back and stare out the window just as her little car drives past. I know he's wrong. She doesn't have crazy layers hiding anywhere. "Well, you don't have to go with us. If you can't support me on this, then please just wait at Mom and Dad's while the rest of us go."

"Okay sure, I get it. Look, I won't stop you if this is what you really want, but man, I left you alone for like year and you glom onto the first person who is nice to you." Codey shakes his head like he's speaking to a child.

"I'm sorry you feel that way," I say, and stand to leave the room.

"Don't be such a baby, Corey, I'm not saying anything that isn't true. You need someone to be your security blanket. You always have," he says with a shrug.

I leave before I hit him, because that is all I want in the moment. I want to feel my fist connecting with his jaw. I want to hear the crack of bone as I beat the shit out of him. Before I reach the bathroom, I turn to him and say, "Be gone by the time I get out of the shower, and no, I am not fucking kidding."

I slam the door and turn the water on, then strip out of my clothes angrily. I shave while I wait for the water to heat up and try to get my breathing under control. I take my time, letting the hot water wash away some of my anger. It worked a little but when I cross the hall in just a towel, I can still see him on my couch. He's looking out the window so I hope he's waiting for a ride. I put on jeans and a Furie Beaver sweatshirt because I know for a fact he doesn't have one, and by the time I come back out he is gone.

Thank God.

I spend the day organizing shit in my house, then my garage. I checked at Stephanie's house no less than twenty times to see if she had come home. Finally at around four she called to let me know she had met up with Ivy and they spent the day together. Apparently Ivy was more of a bunny slope kind of gal while Barb and Grace were skiing triple diamond runs. While I'm glad she has mended that fence, I'm feeling out of sorts without her. So I decide to be honest and ask, "When do you think you'll be back? I'm missing you."

"Oh well, I was actually going to see if you would mind not getting together tonight? Ivy wants to see my place and I thought she and I could have a sleepover and really catch up, you know?" she says.

I hate myself for only a second before responding, "Of course. No, you should totally do that."

We hang up and I realize my brother was right. I need a security blanket. The sharp pain in the middle of my chest the minute she said I wouldn't be seeing her tonight made it real. What the hell is wrong with me? Did I just fill the twin-shaped hole in my heart with Stephanie? Is Codey right? Fuck. The second she left the trail I glommed onto Barbara and Grace. I am like one of those stickers that clings to your sock, and when you try and pull it out it seems to burrow deeper. That should have been my trail nickname. Burr.

I put the phone back on my nightstand, then face-plant into my bed. Shame and other awful emotions wash over me and pull me down so I feel like I'm stuck at the bottom of a murky pond. I turn my head and groan loudly as I thrust my arms out to reach both ends of my bed. I wish my bed could hug me right now. I wrap my fingers around the edges and squeeze, imagining a mattress hug in my mind. What have I done? I already asked her father and Ivy, my parents know I want to propose, and my sisters. Barb and Grace came all this way to be a part of it. Everyone knows of my plan, and not one of them had the balls to tell me I was wrong, or that it was too soon? No one said that I was a needy motherfucker and there was no way in hell she would say yes. I lie there until it is dark outside, unable to do anything but wallow in my own self-hatred. I have spent the time coming up with new trail names for myself, so that's been entertaining.

Barnacle. That is what I am. I let out another groan then lift my head off the mattress. Was that a knock?

Fuck, it was. Someone has the worst timing in the world. I just want to lie here and regret all my life choices alone with my new best friend. My mattress.

The knocking has turned into pounding now. Jesus, I'm coming.

"Coming!" I yell and slide off the bed, then stomp down the hall like the child barnacle I am.

"What?" I yell when I throw open the front door.

"It's colder than a witch's tit in a brass bra out here, Corey, what the hell took you so long to answer?" Grace yells as she pushes past me with Barbara right behind her. They are rubbing their hands on their clothes and jumping around to warm up.

"What are you doing here?" I grumble.

Barb holds up a bottle of red wine and wiggles her eyebrows before saying, "Heard Ivy and Steph were going to hang out tonight, so we took the chance you were free! We want to go over the details of your proposal on Christmas Eve."

"Yeah, if I don't hear the entire plan I'm going to worry that you'll say something lame. So spill it, wait, get glasses first then spill, not the wine, fuck, you know what I mean," Grace hiccups a little and covers her mouth with her hand.

Barb just laughs. "We had a bottle with dinner then paid for a cab out here. We might have to stay the night." She kicks off her shoes and heads to my kitchen without directions. Alright, I guess I am having wine with the girls.

Grace wraps her arms around me and rests her head on my shoulder. "Corey, I am so glad we met you. I love you and your family so much. I have to pee more than I have ever had to pee in my entire life. Please tell me you have indoor plumbing." Grace slurs a little too close to my ear.

"Jesus, Grace, of course." I push her off me and point to the hallway.

"Thanks!" She giggles then bounces off the walls on the way to the bathroom. I hear a crash and more laughing but decide against investigating.

"Find the glasses, Barb?" I ask and walk in to find her with her face on my counter, death grip on a mason jar in one hand and the unopened bottle of wine in the other. Her eyes are shut and her mouth is hanging open.

I am guessing when Barb said "a bottle of wine at dinner," she meant *each*. They *each* had a bottle. Holy crap, if I wasn't so depressed this would be hysterical.

"Barb? Hey Barbara?" I poke at her shoulder and get no response. She is bent over, ass in the air, face on the Formica and I have never wished for a camera more in my life. I chuckle and say loudly, "Dr. Miles!"

She jumps and whirls around nearly clocking me with the empty mason jar. "Huh? What? I set the leg an hour ago," she says, her eyes wide.

"I seriously hope you haven't been anywhere near a patient tonight." I laugh.

It takes her a minute to recover and reorient to my kitchen, but when she does a slow smile creeps across her face. She steps toward me and grabs my face with her already full hands. A wine bottle and a glass jar are pressed into my cheeks as she says, "Corey. I love you so much. I love your family too. I am so glad we can watch you and Yogi Bear." She pauses and squints like she knows that isn't right. Her forehead pinches and her eyebrows work, like file cabinets of her mind are opening and closing and someone is digging through files looking for the right name. I feel bad, so I help her out.

"Yoda," I say, and she slaps at me with the hand she is holding the wine bottle. Hard. It's really more of a punch and I rub my cheek and step back from her out of fear she will do it again.

"Yes! Yoda! I am so glad we get to watch Yoda and you get engaged. You're so fucking cute, and she is like a tiny little nugget. I could fit her in my pocket! Oh, I want to try that. Do you think she would let me?" she asks with eyes wide again.

"No Barb, here why don't you let me have that bottle. I'm going to put it on the counter for now and we will have some in a little while. Come sit." I pull the very expensive bottle of red wine from her grip and ease the mason jar free as well. Then I steer her back to the living room and nudge her to sit on the couch.

"Stay here. I have to find Grace," I say.

"Fucking love Grace! Is she here? Damn that woman can suck a clit, Corey. Do you know how to do that?" She's yelling but I shake my head and walk away quickly. I push open the bathroom and see two brown boots sticking up from my tub. The shower curtain has been pulled down and is covering a giggling mass that I can only assume is Grace.

"Holy hell, Grace! Are you okay?" I say, and rush to dig her out.

"Corey! Hey, when did you get here?" She asks then whisper shouts, "I really have to pee, can you help me get up or should I just let it go here?"

I let out an anguished sound that is a little more high-pitched than I would have wanted, "No! Don't do that! Hang on!" I grab her and pull her up then spin her and quite unceremoniously yank her dress up, her underwear down then shove her on the toilet. Never thought I'd be grateful for helping my drunk-ass sisters, but I feel strangely qualified for tonight.

"Oh thank God," Grace says. She closes her eyes as the damn breaks. She wasn't kidding when she said she had to go. Her long dress is covering everything but I still tell her I am going to wait outside so she can finish. I say a little prayer that she can take care of the rest of that by herself. I consider these women to be some of my best friends, but this is a very unexpected turn of events.

I wait in the hall until I hear a flush and then a giggle. The sink turns on and I think we are in the clear, but the water doesn't shut off when it should. I open the door to find Grace's face under the faucet, drinking. Well, drinking is what she probably wanted to do. What's actually happening is her cheek is getting wet while she moves her tongue around in search of the stream.

"I have cups in the kitchen, Grace, come on." I lean over and shut the water off then lead her out to the couch and plop her next to Barb. They hug and start to kiss like they haven't seen each other in a year. Jesus Christ.

"Girls! Hey!" I snap at them so they stop making out.

"Geez, who crapped in your cornflakes?" Barb says while resting her hand on Grace's breast. She gives it a little squeeze and smiles.

"I'm putting on some coffee first, then we can talk," I say. I am going to tell them it's off, I can't do it. I don't want to be a barnacle. I hurry back into the kitchen and start a pot of coffee, then eye the bottle of wine. I wonder if Grace brought this from her restaurant. I haven't seen this label before. Hoffman Winery Napa California 1974 is written in beautiful script across the label. There is a small stamp that looks like a foreign language, Hebrew maybe, on the bottom left corner.

When the pot is ready I pour the girls some coffee and me some wine. If I sober them up while I drink, we might meet somewhere in the middle.

AS THE SUN rises on the other side of my eyelids, I take stock of my situation. Someone's stockinged foot is pressed into my cheek, forcing my lips open. That is probably why my throat is so dry. I hear snoring on my other side and feel what I'm guessing is an ice-cold hand shoved behind me. I am on my couch, I am pretty sure. I'm sitting, and I have one hand in my pants and one hand on someone's knee. Is that a knee? I squeeze a little but stop when I am met with more of a fleshy feeling than I expected. Maybe that isn't a hand behind me? I could open my eyes and look, but my head hurts.

"Should we wake them?" a voice asks.

"Did they pass out playing Twister?" another wonders.

"Maybe, that doesn't look comfortable at all. Why is he touching himself?" The first voice asks. I jerk my hand free of my pants and pry my eyes open.

Ivy and Stephanie are in my living room staring at me. Me and who?

"Good morning!!" Ivy says with a very large grin. Stephanie is covering her smile with her hands, but I can see her eyes, so I know she's hiding a laugh too.

I turn my head to the left and see Barb draped across my lap with her hands shoved behind my back and Grace is in some ungodly position hanging half off the couch. It's her foot that is in my face. I push at it gently and hear a thud and a whimper. That foot was keeping her stable, apparently. Sorry, Grace.

"What time is it?" I ask, closing my eyes again.

"It's after ten. Want me to put some coffee on?" Steph asks. I nod.

I open my eyes to see Stephanie wrestling something out of Grace's arms. "Can I have the coffee pot, Grace?"

"Sure," she says. She lets it go, then rolls over trying to get up. "Why was I hugging the coffee pot, Corey? Where is my boot? Barb, wake up. You aren't wearing any pants."

"Jesus," I moan and cover my eyes.

"Where the fuck are my pants? Ouch, wait here." Barb flops off the couch and sticks her arm under the cushion, retrieving her jeans.

"No more wine for me. Ever," she grumbles as she walks down the hall trailing her jeans like Linus's blanket. When she reaches the bathroom she yells, "I found your boot, Grace! You aren't going to want it back." Then we hear the door shut.

"So...it looks like you all had a fun night. Around about three a.m. I thought I heard someone singing "Hotel California," but figured I was imagining things. Now I can see I was not," Stephanie says with a giggle. She leans over and gives me quick kiss before taking the empty coffee pot into the kitchen.

Ivy is staring at me with a huge smile on her face. Grace starts to crawl toward the bathroom but keeps getting tangled in her skirt, so she eventually stands and walks unevenly, as one does wearing only one boot, down the hall.

Ivy leans over and whispers, "I'm going to take her shopping today if you need time to get ready for tomorrow."

Tomorrow. Christmas Eve. Fuck. Why do I feel like Grace and Barb fixed the problem I was having with this? I need to have the same conversation while sober, so I say, "Sure, yeah that would be great. Thanks, Ivy." I rub my hands down my face and remember too late that one of my hands was recently wrapped around my dick.

Ivy sits next to me and turns her body, pulling one knee up and holding it with her hands. She is smiling still and I have no choice but to smile back. "She really loves you. She talks about you all the time. She told me about how you met again at the school and about Brian. I hear I get to meet him and his wife on Christmas."

"Yeah, they are coming to my parents' house, you sure you're okay with that?" I ask

"I will be. I want to be. I mean I guess in a way Brian and I have something in common. Rose thought of Stephanie as only hers, she didn't give either of us the choices she had." Ivy tips her head back and grumbles something under her breath that sounded like 'thorn in my side still'. "Rose and I have, well *had* I guess is the way I need to say it now, been together since we were fourteen. She was my best friend first then my first love. There was never anyone else for me, but for Rose, there was Brian then Stephanie. I have been a third wheel my whole adult life. Now that Rose is gone, I can't even be mad at her about it. What good would it do?" Ivy says.

"But you were mad at Steph?" I ask, because she sure made things hard the last few months.

"No, I was just feeling sorry for myself. Stephanie can explain it all to you later. I want to go in and help her make some breakfast for you and your friends before I steal her away all day." She stands and walks off into the kitchen where I can hear Stephanie moving around.

"Is Codey here?" Steph calls.

"No, he's at Mom and Dad's," I say. I have to deal with that today for sure. If I do ask Steph to marry me tomorrow, I don't want him to ruin it. I feel like I had some kind of a breakthrough last night but can't remember what the fuck it was. I see the wine bottle Barb brought lying on my carpet and can only assume I finished that bad boy all my myself. I get flashes of the conversation we had about true love and not listening to idiot brothers. I feel like there was a big argument about John Denver and his song "Rocky Mountain High."

I groan and rub my hands over my face again hoping to get some clarity, but feel something stuck to my cheek. I pull it loose and squint at it. That is a macaroni noodle. Jesus. No more wine for me again either. Maybe ever.

THIRTY-SEVEN
STEPHANIE

SOMETHING IS GOING on with Corey and his brother. Everyone was acting weird when Ivy and I showed up, I mean besides them being ridiculously hung over, possibly still drunk and tangled on the couch like a bunch of middle school girls.

I finally gave up trying to figure it out. After breakfast and then cleaning up the kitchen we made plans for tomorrow's Christmas Eve with Corey's parents. Ivy and I left for another day of finding our way back to each other. I spent plenty of time as a kid with just her. In college there were weekends where she would come hang out with me without my mom, and I never thought it odd or anything. But now that I know who she was to my mom, it feels different. It's like I am meeting her for the first time. And I know she feels it too. She shared things I never knew about my mom and told me about how they realized they were more than just friends. Sleepovers at my grandma's house or at Ivy's parents' house were never questioned. By the time they were in high school they were a couple. They met their friend Stephanie who thought she was also gay. Her parents were very conservative, to the extreme even for that time, so Stephanie was never able to stay over or even spend time with them on the weekends.

After Rose returned from her road trip pregnant with her baby, the three girls spent a lot of time together coming up with a plan. Ivy and Rose believed that once the baby was born, they would be able to get a three-bedroom apartment and all live together. Their friend Stephanie was excited about the plan and being able to help out with the baby and the flower shop. She had plans to go to college but wasn't sure what she wanted to study. The girls learned much later that about a week before Stephanie took her own life, her father had arranged a date for her. The guy was about ten years older than her and a member of their church. Ivy thought Stephanie's father knew she didn't like men and he hoped to force her into marriage so she wouldn't be an "embarrassment" to the family.

My heart breaks for her, that she felt she had no other options. I can't help but think of how Allison's father had acted about Jeremy's family. It's all so fucked up. I hope someday people are able to love who they want. I just don't see how it's anyone's business.

Now that we have had dinner after our long day of talking, Ivy and I settle into my couch with mugs of hot chocolate. I have the curtains pulled back so we can watch the snow fall. The fire is going and I realize that for the first time since losing my mom I don't have that empty feeling.

"Thank you for coming here, Ivy," I say. I reach for her hand and give it a squeeze.

"Thank you for letting me in. I was so afraid I had blown it. You are so lucky to have met Grace and Barbara. Those women are quite a force, and we owe this to them." She holds up our linked hands then pulls them to her and kisses my knuckles.

"I agree," I say.

"Tell me what you learned about yourself on the trail," Ivy says. It takes me by surprise because we have spent so much of our time together talking about the past.

I have to think for a while before answering that. My time on the trail before I met Corey was very different from after. I focus on the time before and say, "I learned that I like who I am. When you are all alone with nature, you hear parts of your mind that get silenced by normal life. I listened to the bits of me that I had shoved aside. I was terrified to go, did you know that?"

"What? No! You seemed so excited, your mom was so proud of how brave you were for going!" Ivy says.

"Yeah, I know. I remember the first time I talked to her about doing the hike. She acted like I said I had found a cure for cancer or something. The more we talked about it the more excited she got. All the while I was going on interviews and getting turned down. I filled out so many applications it's no wonder I thought I applied to work here. I guess I felt like I was letting her down by not getting a job, and there was this thing, this impossible hike, that made her so happy." I shrug then finish with, "I guess what I learned is that I am just as strong as *she* thought I was."

"Well, that's an incredible gift, isn't it?" Ivy says softly.

We are silent again for a long time before she asks, "Do Brian and his wife know I am here?"

"Yes. I called him. He's nervous, but happy you're here," I say, wanting to be honest. I can tell her how nice he and his family are, but I imagine this is a meeting she never expected to have and there is no way I can make it easier.

"He gave us you, the best thing I could have asked for, you know?" she says, but pauses and swallows hard, turning her face away from me. "But he's the one person that could give my Rose something I couldn't. Over the years I've loved him, hated him, feared him. Now it's hard to wrap my head around the fact that I will actually meet him."

"I think this is a good thing. I imagine if Mom hadn't gotten sick, we would just all three be sitting here about to have a family reunion of the weirdest kind," I say.

Ivy laughs at that, thank God. She sighs and turns on the couch so she's facing me. "Maybe that was her plan all along? Maybe she thought we would all do this together. She had no way of knowing she was going to die, right? I mean I have been so mad at her, mad she didn't go to the doctor when her back started hurting, mad she didn't go when she lost weight. There were signs, Steph, and she ignored them, she ignored me. That's hard to get over all by itself, and now I have this crazy other thing to sort out, without her."

"I understand. I have been riding that roller coaster too. When I cleaned out our house, when I came here feeling so alone. I honestly don't know if I would have stayed if Corey wasn't here. Meeting Brian under the circumstances I did, it would have been too much," I say. Ivy laughs at that and pushes on my shoulder a little.

"Wait a minute! You pushed Corey away. You said earlier that you didn't speak with him for like a month after he made the introduction of the century!" Ivy is smiling like she knows the best gossip in all of Beaver Valley.

"Yeah, I did, but I knew he wasn't going anywhere. I guess I felt safe being a little bitch about the whole thing." I take the final drink of my hot chocolate and set the cup on the coffee table.

"Is this your first white Christmas, Ivy?" I ask.

"Yeah, it is. I have been skiing and seen snow of course. We would go once a year when I was little because my father liked to hang out in the ski lodge and drink whiskey. My brothers and I got bored just playing checkers, so we learned to ski. I wasn't good back then, and apparently it's not like riding a bike, because I wasn't good this trip either. More proof that Barb and Grace are saints. They went down the bunny hill with me more than once before they realized I wasn't catching on."

"They are pretty incredible," I say, then stifle a yawn.

"We should get some sleep. It sounds like we have quite an emotional day ahead of us tomorrow," Ivy says, then her eyes go wide and she says, "You know, with me meeting Brian. That will be a lot."

I ignore that weird comment and smile. "Yeah, I agree."

We walk down the hall hand in hand and I pull her in for a hug before letting her go into the guest room.

I climb into bed feeling more than just sleepy. I feel whole again.

THE NEXT MORNING I wake up to someone kissing all over my face. Soft sweet kisses. My eyes, my cheeks, my lips, then my neck and up to nibble gently on my ear.

"Corey, I've missed you," I say sleepily.

"How do you know it's Corey? Maybe I am a handsome stranger who snuck in your room to ravage you in your sleep," he says in a horrible French accent before continuing the kisses.

I hum out a noise that I hope he reads as appreciative and arch my body toward him. When I open my eyes, I burst out laughing.

"What the hell are you wearing?" I ask.

"What? This?" he says pointing to his hat.

"Yes. St. Corey? Saint Nick? Who are you?" I say with a laugh.

"I am Corey Claus of course. How could you not know that, Steph?" he asks in a complete deadpan. This man. He's too much.

"What did you bring me, Corey Claus?" I ask, not wanting to spoil his fun.

"That depends, have you been a good girl this year, or have you been naughty?" He asks, wiggling his eyebrows like a fool.

"I wish I knew my options so I could answer more appropriately —" I start but he silences me with his mouth. His lips are moving slowly over mine like he has all the time in the world. I want to ask what time it is, if we should get up and start getting ready but I have no will to move.

He slides his hands over my body, lacing first one hand with mine, then the other. He arches back and lifts my arms above my head, pinning me to the mattress while he rocks his hardened length into me. With nothing between us but soft fabric it feels amazing.

"Are you still in your pajamas?" I ask in between kisses.

"Yes, I couldn't wait to see you," he says like this is something I should just know and expect from him. I smile before his lips and tongue take control of my mouth again. He stops suddenly and stares down at me with a look I don't recognize.

"What? Do I have weird sheet creases all over my face or something?" I ask nervously.

"I love you. I love that I found you while I was looking for myself. I love that we fit together so perfectly and that you need me as much as I need you. I love how feisty you are, and how strong you are not just in body but in your soul. Your heart is my compass. Where you go, I will always follow, Stephanie Iverson." He pulls back, taking me with him so I am sitting up. I watch as he slides off the bed and gets on one knee, pulling a ring box from somewhere on the floor.

"I know we haven't been together that long, but I love you, Yoda. I will never not love you. I hope you feel the same way. I hope that you can see a future with me, not just here in Beaver Valley, but everywhere. I want to go places with you, every summer, every break, I want—"

I cut him off. "Does this proposal have an end or are you going to talk forever? I'd really like to answer you," I say with a smile and tears in my eyes. He hasn't even opened the ring box yet. I think he had much more to say, but I can't wait one more minute for him to know my answer.

"I can be done," he says with a shaky voice.

"I would be so lucky to be your wife. Yes, Corey. I will marry you," I say, then am immediately tackled to the bed. His lips and hands are everywhere. Ravenous does not describe this man. My T-shirt is off and thrown across the room as my sleep shorts are yanked off. His Santa hat is the only thing that remains on his body as he lowers himself to me, slowly kissing down my neck.

"Are you really leaving the hat on?" I say with a giggle because the little ball on the top is tickling me as he makes his way to my breasts. He cups them, sucking gently and nibbling at my hard nipples. He stops only long enough to say, "Yes."

He starts to move lower kissing my stomach, pausing just below my belly button to plant soft open-mouthed kisses. My breath hitches when I think about how someday he might be kissing my swollen belly that holds his child. It makes me want him more, driving me wild with desire. I tug at his hair and he looks up at me.

"Don't make me wait, I don't need you to do that. I just want you, Corey. Please," I beg, knowing he can't refuse me.

He moves quickly up and grabs his cock sliding it along my wet folds. I arch and moan wanting him to slide inside.

"You're always so perfect, so ready to take me," he says as he finally pushes in. We both moan in pleasure as he continues slowly, until he is fully seated. I expect him to move but he doesn't, he lowers himself so we are chest to chest and he kisses me again. I feel like I could come just like this, his thick length filling me up, his chest to mine and his lips worshiping me.

He starts to move slowly, dragging out and pushing back in, creating tingles that move from my feet up to my center. I feel so aware of everything about him, the way his lips feel soft but urgent. The way the muscles in his back are tightening with each thrust. His thick thighs pushing against mine keeping his movements slow and torturous. I never want it to end but I am desperate for my release. I feel like I am falling apart beneath him as I shake and squirm against his steady rhythm. My orgasm hits me without warning, and I gasp into Corey's mouth just as he thrusts harder. He must feel me let go because his movements get jerky and I know he is right there with me.

It's the most beautifully slow, sensual experience I have ever had. I know the difference now between making love and being fucked. I want them both, forever, with him.

"God that was incredible, I have never felt like this before," I say quietly in his ear. I am tracing circles over his back and down to his wonderful firm ass. I could stay here all day.

"It was, it's because I love you. I want to show you that every day," Corey says. I feel him soften and pull out of me, but he stays on me caging me with his body.

"I'm going to be in so much trouble," he says into my hair.

"Why? Are we late? What time is it?" I ask trying to push him off me, but he just starts laughing.

"What's so funny, Corey Claus?" Yes, he still has that damn hat on.

"I had a big thing planned today, the whole family was going to be there. Barb and Grace came out just to watch me propose," he says, then starts laughing again.

"What?! Oh my God, Corey! Why didn't you wait? They're going to kill you!" I shove at him but he just snuggles in more wrapping me in his arms.

"I realized when I woke up this morning that I couldn't wait. I thought I wanted this big thing, like I needed to make sure you knew how much I loved you," he says.

"I know that, I don't need a big show," I tell him, still trying to push him off me. Instead he just rolls us so I'm on top of him.

"Well, what if we do it for show like I planned? I won't tell you what I was going to do, that will still be a surprise," he says.

"Okay, that sounds fun, and since you never opened the ring box I will actually look surprised when you show it to me later," I say. I pat him on the chest and smile into his beautiful face.

"I didn't open the box? Seriously? You said yes without seeing the ring?" he asks as his eyes search my face.

"Of course, I don't need a ring, Corey. I just need you," I say, then bend forward and give him a quick kiss before jumping off.

"I am going to take a shower so we can get ready to go. I can't wait to see you propose again," I say.

"I can't wait for you to say yes again," Corey says, wiggling his eyebrows.

THIRTY-EIGHT
COREY

I CAN'T BELIEVE how much fun this is.

My spontaneous proposal this morning could have really ruined the day for everyone else, but since Stephanie is, in fact, perfect, she's letting me go ahead with the original plan and she will act surprised. That's what we decided before we went out for breakfast. I tucked the ring box into my jeans without showing her and I didn't let on how I will ask her later today.

Everyone else here knows the plan, but since she doesn't, I am having a really great time messing with her. My mom is big on traditions, so she has a special ornament for each person to hang on the tree on Christmas Eve. When it was my turn, I pretended to drop my ornament and as I was getting up, I lifted to only one knee in front of Stephanie, whose eyes went wide with excitement. Then I stood up and put my Snoopy ornament where it belongs. When no one was looking she smacked me on the arm and I just chuckled.

Then when we sat down for our formal meal, a lunchtime tradition, I stood to give a toast with Steph gazing lovingly up at me at each mention of her name. When I sat down without the proposal she pinched my leg hard under the table.

Then we opened stockings which are filled with junk food and candy and a few essentials like new #2 pencils. I pulled out a ring pop candy and couldn't resist winking at her. Then I acted like I was getting on one knee again, but just retied my shoe. I think she might actually say no when it finally comes time for the real thing. I need to stop laughing at her, but her frustration is so cute.

I am kind of glad for our little secret today, because the tension when we first got to my parents' house was through the roof. Brian and Cindy and the boys were already there. Brian came out to the porch and greeted us, then asked to speak to Ivy alone. I know how hard it was for Steph to walk in the house and leave Ivy out there. I leaned in and whispered in her ear that both Ivy and Brian had given me their blessing and today was going to be amazing. Just as I had finished telling her that, Cindy pulled her from me and hugged her for a straight five minutes. I had to squeeze past them and a floor lamp to make it into the living room.

By four, I had managed a few more fake-outs in between all the traditions my mom was trying to check off her list. I swear having all her children under one roof again has gone straight to her crazy little head. I have seen so many sweet moments between Ivy and Brian and his family. I don't know what he said to her on the porch, but when they came in it was clear the rest of the day would be fine. Barb and Grace seem to just fit so perfectly in our family, it's weird to think I just met them over the summer. Now that my father has stopped asking for orthopedic exams, he and Barb have moved on to discuss the triple diamond runs they have completed. Henry also had a lot of questions about the PCT that he never bothered to ask me, but I get it. Grace and Barb are fun to talk to.

Stephanie pulled me aside to give me her gift. I couldn't be happier if I tried. It's an awesome watch with the latitude and longitude of the Pine Cone Motel engraved on the back. She said she wanted me to always remember where we fell in love. For me, that would have been a few hundred miles south of there, but I'll never tell her that.

Codey is going to get murdered in his sleep for stealing Cami from Dee Dee and Linda, but he pulled me aside and said they wouldn't go when it was time. He realized that having a stranger there would be kind of weird so as he said, he's doing me a favor. Whatever. I know how he feels and I'm glad he's staying behind. I glance at my watch and feel my stomach tumble with nerves. Fuck, if I hadn't already asked her, there would be no way I could handle this stress.

"I think we should start *It's A Wonderful Life* now," I say to the room and everyone ignores me. I walk over to the TV and find the VHS tape of our family's favorite movie. Here we go.

"Corey, wait! Before it gets dark can we go to the PCT sign? I really want to get a picture. Barb and I fly out tomorrow and we keep putting this off," Grace says, tugging on my sleeve.

"Picture? Now? It's already getting dark, I want to watch the movie," I say, making my eyes wide and nodding to the TV. Stephanie catches it and smiles, thinking she has figured it out.

"My camera has a great flash. Come on, Son, we don't know when your friends are going to be here again. We can drive over really quick then come back and start the film," my dad says, and suddenly everyone is agreeing and pulling on boots and jackets.

I lean over and whisper in Steph's ear, "Sorry, unexpected detour."

She nods and shrugs like we might as well do this so we can get to the good stuff. With all the commotion and the twelve people that have to find a spot in a car, we are down the road before Linda notices Cami and Codey aren't with us. "I'm going to kill him," she says, and Dee Dee agrees. Steph just giggles and rests her head on my shoulder.

We all park by the trailhead and wait for my father to get his camera situated. Grace and Barbara are rushing ahead to plan out where we can stand for our picture. She and Grace on one side and me and Stephanie on the other side. My dad agrees and everyone else starts talking about hikes and how long they think they could go before quitting. When we are in our positions my dad uses his louder than humanly normal whistle to get everyone quiet.

"Okay, that looks great, Steph, can you scoot in a little bit? You're too far away from the sign. See how Grace is? Do that," Henry says, and I watch as she diverts her attention to Grace while I get on one knee. When she turns back to face my dad, I have the ring box out in front of her. Her gasp is real and everyone chuckles but gets quiet quickly.

"Steph, I couldn't think of a better place to ask you to be my lifelong hiking partner. Will you go on adventures with me always? Will you marry me?" I ask, and pop open the box just as her hands fly to her face. My dad starts snapping pictures, the flash blinding everyone but me.

"Yes! Oh my God, of course I'll marry you!" Stephanie squeals, and it feels just as good to hear the second time. I stand and her shaky hand reaches for the ring. I help her slide it on. Everyone breaks into applause and starts hugging the person closest to them. It's perfect in its own way, but I am so glad I had my own private moment with her this morning.

We take a few pictures by the sign and then pile back in the cars to go back. This time my sisters choose to ride in the other car and Barb and Grace are with us. My parents are in the front talking about their engagement and Grace spins to face me where Steph and I are crammed in the third-row seat of the Suburban.

"That was not how we practiced, Corey. It was still good, but you were supposed to ask her to finish the hike with you!" She laughs and Steph turns to me.

"Finish the hike?" she asks.

"Yeah, I did forget that part. I got nervous. Do you want to finish it this summer? Go from here to Canada like you wanted? We could spend some time like you and your mom were going to, I mean if you want," I say nervously. I did chicken out of that part of the speech. I didn't know if it would bring her pain to be in Canada without her mom.

"I would love that, Corey. Can we really?" she asks.

"Yeah. I can't think of a better way to spend the summer. Grace, do you and Barb want to meet us in Canada? Celebrate your anniversary?" I ask.

"Nah, we're going to Hawaii for our anniversary. I want a toes-in-the-sand vacation. Go to Margaritaville and look for a lost shaker of salt. Maybe get a tattoo like Jimmy did, a Mexican booty!" Grace says.

"What the fuck are you talking about? It's not a Mexican booty, you ninny, it's a Mexican beauty!" Barb yells.

"No! He's talking about a nice round bottom. I heard it in an interview with him. It's widely misheard," Grace says with all the confidence in the world.

Barb loses it and starts singing the song the correct way and I wonder if I'm the only one who catches the twinkle in Grace's eye as a small smile crosses her face.

THIRTY-NINE

EPILOGUE

Dear Barb and Grace,

So far the trail has been as beautiful as you said.
We are taking our time getting to Canada so we might not
be at the checkpoint when we originally planned. Don't
worry if we don't call.

In an interesting turn of events Stephanie's backpack
took a tumble off a cliff. Cliff might be too strong of a
term, but everything spilled out and it was a bitch to
collect it all and climb back up. We were able to find
everything, or so we thought until the next day when
Steph went to take her birth control. You know I can't
keep my hands off her so we might have some exciting
news by the time we get to Canada!

I hope you are both doing well and that you get
that question answered about Jimmy Buffett's tattoo.
Ivy has settled in nicely in Beaver Valley and is busy

as ever. She has not started dating anyone yet so if that friend of yours is interested, I suggest you plan a trip.

I better go, Steph just found my little red Speedo and she has that look. You know the one. Damn, I am one lucky bastard. Not just because of her, but because I met you two. I can't thank you enough for your friendship. You saved me from myself more than once and I owe you my happiness.

From the PCT with love,

Corey and Stephanie Richie

ABOUT THE AUTHOR

Pamela Dean lives in Northern California with her husband and their very spoiled golden retriever. During her lifetime she has held many interesting jobs that are currently making their way into her fictional worlds.

If you enjoyed this book check out her other books, available on Kindle and Kindle Unlimited as well as in print from various places.

And I Love Her Still

Box One of Two

You can keep up with the latest releases by following her on Facebook.

She can be reached via email at PamelaDeanWrites@gmail.com

www.ingramcontent.com/pod-product-compliance
Lightning Source LLC
Chambersburg PA
CBHW071404300726
48976CB00006B/1982